C.B. HAIGHT

FORGOTTEN ENEMY

A POWERS OF INFLUENCE Novel

FORGOTTEN ENEMY

'A POWERS OF INFLUENCE NOVEL

BOOK 1

 © 2012 Added Touch Publication

Printed in the U.S.A.

Second Edition Printing 2016

ISBN-13: 978-0615726496 (Added Touch Publications)

ISBN-10: 0615726496

Cover Design by: ExpertSubjects

To my sisters: the sisters of my blood, and the sisters of my heart, thanks for loving me unconditionally. May you always have the love you deserve.

"Our greatest fear is not that we are inadequate, but that we are powerful beyond measure. It is our light, not our darkness, that frightens us. We ask ourselves, Who am I to be brilliant, gorgeous, handsome, talented and fabulous? Actually, who are you not to be? You are a child of God."

– Nelson Mandela-

"Sometimes it is only through the eyes of someone who knows us well, that we can see the whole picture within our imagination and the future possibilities before us."

-C.B. Haight-

PRELUDE

VIRGINIA 1732

They were coming for her. Lyndell was sure now. Even with all the power she had within her, she could not stop them.

Her boys, her precious sons, whimpered in the corner as she prepared the few staples they would need to make the trip.

She had but one choice left to her, she must split them apart. The only way to save her infant sons was to give them to her most trusted friends.

She thought about her dreams of watching them grow into men as handsome as their father. She knew her little ones would grow to be tall and strong. She dreamed they would have soft, raven-black hair. Hair so shiny it would give off a blue hue in the silver light of the moon. When they grew up, their charming smiles would melt some maiden's heart. She pictured them having a slightly crooked tilt on the right side just like their father.

Lyndell had hoped and prayed their father would have been able to return and see them. She imagined him looking into their soft, tawny eyes that shone more gold than brown. Eyes just like his own.

For months, she planned for their births. She built their beds, knitted their blankets, and sewed their clothing. She never questioned that they were boys, or that they would be twins; she just knew it to be so.

The dreams began in the middle of her pregnancy. Frightening, horrific images of blood, fire, and pain terrorized her. Each night she awoke, frantically screaming as cold sweat clung to her ivory skin, her heart racing with panic.

In her dreams, they came to slay the babes:

"We will purge you of the demon spawn. We are saving you from the devil's hand," they would cry.

Originally, Lyndell thought the nightmares were random images born of fear. Fear of the heritage that had created the lives within her, fear that the villagers would find out her unborn children's true heritage. However, as the dreams continued, Lyndell understood they were a warning sign for her to prepare for what could come to pass. The thought of the violent slaughter of her infants was too impossible for her to believe.

Would they really callously murder her babies to serve what they considered the greater good? How could killing infants serve any greater purpose?

Inevitably though, with the horrid nightmares prodding her, she made the arrangements. She hoped her nightmares were just her nerves. She hoped her knowledge of their heritage was simply playing tricks on her fragile state of being. But, before long, the knowing overwhelmed her. She knew her plans were no longer just in case. She knew no matter what the cost, she must keep them safe.

When her sons came screaming from her womb, their fragile bodies entering this difficult and perilous world, Lyndell could delude herself no more. It was no accident her sons came forth on the night of the full moon. As the first pangs of labor assaulted her, she knew the truth of all she'd seen.

The dreams were warnings! She was aware of the gift of sight she'd inherited from her grandmother. The gift had been passed to her as it had to the generations of women before her.

She was also conscious of the responsibility that came with such a gift. She felt the mingled sense of relief and grief that this wisdom brought her.

When the plump, elderly midwife glimpsed the bright red mark on of both the newborn babies' left shoulder blades and their unnatural golden eyes, panic and fear consumed her. She crossed herself with wide eyes, and in that moment, the midwife set into motion the cataclysm that would turn Lyndell's nightmares into a reality. Without even bothering to help clean the infant's or tend to their mother, the woman ran from the cabin screaming.

"Demons!" she cried, "Satan born! God, save us!"

Lyndell's infant sons, tiny and perfect to her, were marked.

Each had a perfectly shaped crescent mark on their bodies. The mark of the moon was imprinted upon their tender skin, the mark of their father. She could not keep the babies with her in this place.

Thankfully, as planned, one of her closest friends had been with her. Merilynn stayed behind in those critical and desperate moments to help with the infants. It was she who put their carefully laid plans into motion, promising to return for Lyndell and the boys the next night.

Merilynn and Rowena had long been her dearest friends. They swore to each take a child and escape this foul place. Neither of Lyndell's friends were aware of the horrific fate that awaited her. She had withheld that from them carefully.

In these moments, when she should have been basking in the new life she brought forth into the world, she was instead preparing to give those new little lives away forever. Still weak and tired from the long and strenuous birth, Lyndell packed all she had prepared for her offspring. She moved as quickly about the one-room shack as her battered body would allow. As she did so, she silently prayed to whomever would listen to keep her precious son's safe; to keep them alive.

During her desperate and silent pleading, a feeling of warmth and hope washed over her. A tingling feeling tickled her senses, soothing her fears and worries. It offered comfort; removing all doubt from her heavy heart. Reminding herself that this was the only way, she regained strength and confidence in her choice and moved toward her sons' cradle.

Somehow her sons were important. She knew this as surely as she knew she needed air to breathe. She had known it instinctively the moment she felt those first little nudges pushing against her swollen, growing belly months earlier. She'd seen them grown and strong in her dreams. Now, as she watched them fuss and wriggle in the cradle before her, she had no doubts about the significance of their birth. Nor did she doubt the names she laid upon them then. She knew she could at least give each son a part of their heritage in their names.

Looking down at her first born she named him Jarrett, after her father William Jarrett. He had been a kind and gentle man, but clever and strong. She turned to the second of her sons and named him Cade, after her only love, the father of the tiny lives before her, Samuel Cade.

Oh, how she wished their father would have come. They could have left as a family, instead of being ripped apart by reckless, unforgiving fear. Samuel could have kept them safe. She imagined him teaching the boys the knowledge of their inheritance. She wished he could have held them in his strong arms at least once.

Unfortunately, it was not to be. Samuel believed that no love was strong enough to keep them safely together. If the villagers found out, it would surely mean death. People believed they knew him for what he was, and judged him for it. They didn't understand. They didn't know of his love, his compassion. They could never understand how he would do anything to protect her. *No, they did not understand him at all*, she thought.

She remembered back to that last night, as they lay in bed, and how she had begged him to take her away from this place. She was desperate to be with him, even if it meant living with others like him. He would not waver though. He knew that if his kind found out about her, the end would be the same. To be together would mean death. It was ironic that both of their worlds held the same amount of intolerance for each other; yet each one had no idea how much they resembled each other through their indifference.

A tiny cry from the cradle pulled her away from her thoughts. She scooped up the younger of her two sons, and his fretful fussing stopped as she brought him close. She knew that she would never regret any of it. She was given the most precious of gifts; her sons. His sons.

She hadn't the courage to tell him then. She knew it would hurt him too deeply to leave her knowing of the coming babies. He suffered so much when he left her. Lyndell could not cause him any more pain. If he learned that he had endangered her life in spite of all his precautions, it would only haunt him.

In truth, both of them would willingly give their lives to save the other. Now she would give her life to save their sons, and he would never know what happened here. She could spare him that, at least. She could only hope that her dearest and truest friends could cope with the changes they would be forced to endure…

A soft tap at the wooden door announced Merilynn's arrival. She hurried to the door, admitting her friend, and embracing her quickly.

"Are you ready, little sister?" Merilynn inquired urgently.

"Truly there is no way to be ready, but this is something I must do. They will come soon. They will come with their twisted version of faith and truth," Lyndell replied, pain lacing every word.

"We will meet at the creek to handle the parting. Come, we must hurry. Rowena already awaits."

Lyndell sunk into the old wooden rocker her father had lovingly carved for her mother so many years ago. She ran her free hand over the arm of polished wood, softened with age, and looked down at the tiny perfect face in her arms. She was aware what was to happen next, but found it difficult to get past the grief tearing at her heart.

"I will not come with you," she choked out past the lump in her throat. "I cannot be seen traveling with you. I must stay behind to keep them away." Tears began to well in her green eyes, causing them to shimmer in the dim candlelight. "They would follow us if they found me gone, hunting us down to brutally massacre us. I have seen it. I must remain here if you are to have any hope of saving my sons. I will tell them that the babes died in the night. I have already marked the graves."

Bending down and grabbing Lyndell's hands, Merilynn cried out, "You cannot! They will kill you!"

Already aware of her fate, Lyndell looked into her friend's soft brown eyes, and pleaded desperately, "You must keep them safe! Keep them hidden. Do not let their mark be known.

"Swear to me, Merilynn! Please tell me you will keep them safe. Protect my sons."

Shocked by this turn of events, but understanding there was no time for argument, Merilynn could only reply in a choked voice, "I swear it!" The moisture built in her eyes as well, and she turned her back to Lyndell in an effort to be strong for the sister of her heart. She walked over to the cradle and scooped up the younger infant, then said vehemently, "I will give all that I have, all that I am to protect them. We will love and cherish them. We will make sure they are told of you."

She knelt before Lyndell, the infants between them. Both women looked down at their little faces. Merilynn grabbed Lyndell's hand, and as the tears escaped her eyes, she promised, "I swear this to you, sister of my heart. On my life, I swear it!"

Lyndell nodded, nuzzled Cade's neck for a moment and kissed his soft downy hair. Then she leaned over and did the same to

Jarrett. The tears from her green eyes fell onto their soft pink skin as she did. The time before she had to let them go was short, and though she didn't fully understand everything, she knew she could not prevent what was to be in this time; she could only hope to alter things, and possibly avoid what she knew would come later.

After tenderly feeding each child from her breast, Lyndell wrapped them carefully in the soft, knitted blankets she had lovingly made for each one. After helping load them into the little wagon that would take them to the creek, Lyndell grabbed Merilynn's hands and slipped a small piece of parchment and a bulging envelope to her saying, "This is all that I have to give them to remember me."

Merilynn squeezed Lyndell's hand in response, taking the items from her.

Lyndell kissed each son for the last time, whispering a simple blessing of protection over them. The spell stole away the last of her strength, but that didn't matter anymore. She gave them all she could. She had poured all the love she had into them with a few simple words.

When she finished, she looked back to one of the two extraordinary women she was entrusting with her sons' lives. Merilynn tucked the bit of folded parchment into her dress and nodded solemnly. There was nothing more to say. Time was running out.

Lyndell could not look back as she heard the cluck of Merilynn's tongue urging the horses and wagon along to the north. It departed with the most precious cargo it had ever carried. Instead of watching them grow smaller with distance, she turned to look to the east.

I have done all I can do to save them, she thought as her silent tears fell softly down her face to settle on the damp earth at her feet.

The night turned grey, and as the lightening sky created soft morning shadows, Lyndell saw the torches in the distance. Squaring her shoulders, she stood proud and ready to meet her fate.

CHAPTER I

Colorado, present day

Exiting the suit shop, Cade tossed the bag carrying his old clothes over his shoulder. He smiled at the *chirp chirp* as he pressed the button on the keyfob he was holding in the palm of his hand. He pushed another button, and the ignition to the Jag turned over and hummed soothingly. Dropping his bag in the passenger seat, he traced the smooth, shiny metal with his fingertips as he moved around to the driver's side.

Reaching for the door, he glanced over the top of the car. Directly across the road, he saw her. A strange shock coursed through him. Her profile was remarkable. He paused in his movements to simply stare at this beautiful woman. She looked as if she were waiting for someone, or something.

The icy blue silk dress she wore caressed her soft curves, accentuating her exquisite form. He couldn't help but notice that she had a slim, limber body that moved gracefully, with curves in all the right places. The fabric swayed from the movement of her hips, enticing him with each step she took. Even in her nervous pacing, her movements were graceful. As she moved back and forth from the door to the building behind her, she lifted her hand and then dropped it, as though she'd changed her mind. She appeared uncomfortable, glancing down the street searching for whatever it was she was waiting for. Her discomfort intrigued him. What could she possibly be so nervous about?

As she paced back and forth, he noticed the slit in her dress, showing a good portion of her long, smooth leg. Looking even more closely, he saw her shiny, multi-toned, golden-blonde hair glistening in the fading sunlight as it cascaded down the middle of her back.

He would have been content to spend the rest of the evening standing there, just watching her. Then, as if it were part of a planned conspiracy against him, the air stirred, lifting her hair slightly off to the side. The breeze picked it up, tickling it across her back. His evolved sense of smell singled out her scent easily, floating over to him on the same breeze that stirred her hair.

He inhaled her scent. The beast within pulled at him, wanting to draw in more of her sultry and womanly flavor. Cade bit back a groan. The soft citrus smell held a tantalizing honey undertone.

In that moment, as he was still reeling, she turned, fully facing him, and he knew why he had stayed. He knew what he had been waiting for.

Her face held him captive. He froze, and looked upon her beauty in its entirety. She had soft, full, unpainted lips and iridescent blue eyes that took his breath away. Her eyes could stop any mortal man in his tracks. A small, pert nose that was just the right shape for her was set between cheekbones that looked to be created by nothing less than a master sculptor.

Cade could barely draw breath. His chest felt tight. He believed right away that he should know her. She looked so familiar, and yet at the same time she wasn't. No, she looked perfect, he thought. Almost as if she had emerged from a dream; a dream he would be happy to stay in for a long time.

As he stood there, entranced by the woman, a long, sleek limo pulled up to the curb, and the driver exited from the vehicle tipping his hat toward her. She smiled at him. It was an elegant and radiant smile, but less than sincere; as if it was somewhat forced.

Even more curious now, he watched while she made her way to the car with a slight wariness as she drew closer to the vehicle. She acted as if she were going to a funeral. Maybe she was.

He had a sudden urge to rush over and save the mysterious woman from whatever it was she appeared to be avoiding. When the driver opened the back passenger door, her smile fell. She cautiously scanned from left to right as if she knew someone was watching. The driver motioned for her to enter the car once again. She smiled slightly at him and took a slow, deep breath, as if calming herself. She then slipped gracefully into the limo.

The driver pulled away smoothly. Suddenly, he felt the compelling spell that had kept him rooted to one spot break, releasing him from the trance he'd fallen into. He shook it off, wondering what had gotten into him.

He glanced at his watch. Crap! He was late. He pulled out onto the road, heading out of the city at breakneck speed. Being late gave him an excuse to do what he loved—drive fast.

After a twenty minute drive, he drove the Jag he was borrowing around to the back of Rederrick's massive estate, parking it carefully next to the '68 Camaro in the garage. *Rederrick loves his cars,* Cade reflected; noting that this one was new to the collection as he stepped out and locked the doors. Straightening his clothes, he passed by the black Yukon on his left and strolled into the party. He went in as any other member of the family—through the garage entrance.

Dressed in the Armani suit that Rederrick insisted he wear tonight, Cade felt uncomfortable, even foreign. He normally didn't wear expensive suits. Well, okay, he didn't normally wear suits at all, but he could admit that this one wasn't too bad. Sometimes you get what you pay for, and his little ensemble had cost a pretty penny.

He stepped into the room and quickly scanned the crowd. As his keen observation skills gave him a feel for the people in the room, he began to relax, moving away from the threshold. As he did, his eyes suddenly fixed—upon her.

It's the same woman! She gracefully entered through the front door as Rederrick helped her out of her dress coat. He patted her shoulder with a fatherly smile and headed off to greet the other guests arriving. Who is she? he wondered.

He stood there rooted to his spot…again. This was an unbelievable twist of fate. His old friend knew this woman, and he had brought her to this party. *Well this is interesting*, he thought. He watched her, seeing her mingle with the arriving guests. Once again, he found it hard to take his eyes off her. Something about her pulled at him. He felt he should know this woman.

Blinking hard, he pushed back against the feeling; he didn't have time for this now. Finding some self-control, he shrugged off the gripping enchantment once more. Easily moving through the sea of people, he went to find out why Rederrick had insisted he attend. Finding his old friend, he lost sight of the woman and tried to put her out of his head as well.

He spotted his friend soon enough, across the room speaking to someone from the mayor's office. He waited his turn to catch a moment with the man. After a minute or so, the representative from the mayor's office turned and left. Arms open to display his suit, he approached Rederrick with a large grin.

"You win. You got me here, and in a suit, mind you. Now, where is that surprise you promised?" he queried. He grabbed Rederrick's offered hand in a firm shake as he pulled him in for a manly, one-armed hug, slapping each other on the back as men often do. "I hope it's a new bike. My last one is a total loss due to your infallible GPS system."

Rederrick, at 55 years old, looked as good as a man of 40. His salt-and-pepper hair was perfectly groomed, and his sharp, steel-gray eyes could see right through a man and spoke of deep intelligence. He was six feet tall to Cade's six-three and of a lankier build. Still, his sharp, toned muscles kept him as quick as a snake when necessary.

Years ago, Rederrick organized a secret group called The Brotherhood to help Cade. They dealt with threats or problems of the supernatural variety. They funded it together. Most people within the group were volunteers that were financially successful or had extreme flexibility with their "day jobs."

Tonight, as was the case on most days, his friend was dressed for success. He supposed it came with being a lawyer. Personally, he never understood the need to dress in such fine clothing. Part of that came from the simple logic that he ruined his suits more often than he wore them.

Giving him a hard, serious stare that held no weight due to the small smile he was unable to conceal, Rederrick relented and guffawed at him. "Now as I recall, it wasn't the GPS that was the problem, but your impatience and that damnable shortcut through the woods you insisted on, that caused your bike's untimely demise. So, no," he said, a smirk playing on his handsome features, "you, my friend, will be replacing the bike on your own. Although, I am not sure if you can easily replace a ride as sweet as that last one."

He looked at his friend with a grin, "So what then, may I ask, is this prize you promised me if I got into this monkey suit and made nice with the rich and famous in town?"

"Well. . ." hedged Rederrick, "How about a chance to help out your fellow man? In this case, it just so happens, it's a fellow woman. A good deed is a prize in itself, don't you agree, boy?"

"*Boy*? Boy is it? Let me just remind you, old man, I knew your mother when she was just a baby in diapers."

Rederrick turned to him with a less than serious look, "Just a slip of the tongue, I assure you."

"Uh-huh." He glared down at him for a minute. Then smiling, he asked, "What about my promised time to recuperate from the last good deed for my *fellow* man?"

"You know I wouldn't ask unless I really needed you." Rederrick's face took on a very serious look.

Cade stared hard at his lifelong friend. He desperately needed some time off. He also knew he couldn't turn down a friend in need, especially this one, whom he had a hard time refusing anyway.

In his long lifetime, very few people had proven to be true friends. This man was one of those few, and he also knew Rederrick would not ask if there was someone else in The Brotherhood who could help right then.

Rederrick stared right back, knowing he needed time off more than anyone. Resigned, Cade huffed out a deep breath and with a quick nod accepted the new job.

"So what is the assignment?"

Rederrick calmly looked over the floor crowded with people, "She is looking this way now. Over there, the pretty blond in the blue dress."

Cade didn't need to look. Instinctively, he knew exactly who Rederrick was talking about. Only fate could be so twisted by showing him a woman so rare and beautiful, and then with one hard tug pull the rug out from under him. She was to be his next assignment.

"Watch her," he continued, "She's about as nervous as they come."

I have the watching part down, Cade thought. He was having a hard time not watching her. Yes, he noticed her nervousness, but it was the furthest thing from his mind when he had seen her initially. He mentally berated himself for not paying better attention.

Finally, he opened his eyes, cleared his head, and got down to business. Facts are what he need now. He looked over the crowd until he sighted her. Letting some of his frustration leak into his tone, he asked, "How can I help?"

Rederrick didn't seem to notice his agitated tone. "She has power, Cade, and a good bit of it. That's something I am sure of. She's not aware of it yet, or she pretends not to be," he paused.

"What I'm not sure of is if, or how, we can help her. She's been working for my office for five months now. She is sweet, kind, always does her work, and never complains, but," he clicked his tongue, "I don't really know how to explain it. There's just something off here."

"What do you mean, 'off'?"

"She's always looking over her shoulder, seems real nervous about touching people because she gets these weird looks when she does. She doesn't seem to have a clue as to my other job. You'd think if she was a witch she would have sensed something by now. I think, well, I think if I tell her, she would run like a bat out of hell." Rederrick looked over at his friend who just stared through the sea of people at the beautiful woman who stood across the room. "She's in trouble. I'm not sure how much, but you're the only one I trust to help her."

"The Faction again?" Cade questioned.

"Who knows, but with the power Cynda senses in her I wouldn't be surprised."

Cynda was Rederrick's wife. She was a pretty, green-eyed, auburn-haired woman with some specific skills. One of those skills included the ability to sense power, of the supernatural variety anyway, because she could see it in a person's aura.

"Just how much power are we talking about here?"

"Well, it was enough to scare Cynda until she noticed the girl wasn't using it at all. We've kept a very close eye on her though. That's how I know she is in trouble."

Rederrick looked back to his friend as he finished, "She checks every window and door twice. She's a pro at verifying if she's being followed, lost two of my men when we tried to keep close tabs on where she goes. She runs a hard five miles every day as if she is running from a demon directly at her heels."

He let out his breath to show Cade he was worried, "Her bio is in my files. I found out very little. She doesn't leave much in the way of tracks. I knew right away that her social security card was false, so I did some digging. She keeps to herself for the most part, and the longest residence she's had, as far as I can tell, is here. The only thing that gave me a trace on her was her name. I found out she keeps using one name. She may change the spelling or its placement, middle name or first. She changes her last name every time, but for the last two years she has kept one name with her. You want to know the weirdest part?"

"Huh?"

"People don't remember her, even from when she worked with them. As far as Cynda can tell, they haven't been enchanted to forget either. They just don't remember her. It's as if she never existed. The few who can recall the name she used around them can't recall her face, or anything about her. It's the damndest thing."

Cade took his eyes off the woman and looked at his friend curiously. He could not believe anyone could forget her face? Rederrick was right; it just didn't make sense. "What name is she using then?" he asked with curiosity.

"Collett." Rederrick answered quietly to prevent anyone around them from overhearing.

He rolled the name around in his head for a moment to see if it was familiar. After close to 300 years of life you get to know an impressive amount of people. He could not recall a Collett in his life history so he moved on. "So all you want me to do this time is babysit a beautiful woman and verify whether or not she is a threat, and/or being threatened. Sounds easy enough," he stated lightly.

Rederrick gave him a big smile, and not bothering to hide his sarcasm, he quipped, "Well, I was sure someone of your *experience* could manage one beautiful woman."

"Don't you worry one bit. I can handle her just fine," he returned with a grin.

Rederrick smiled again then quickly sobered, "Be careful, Cade. Something's not right here. I can feel it down to my toes, and Cynda feels it too." He waited a minute to let that sink in, and then finished by saying, "I would hate to see this blow up in our faces. Much like your bike, I know I couldn't replace you."

He patted his friend on the shoulder to reassure him. Then he walked away, wondering as always how he was so damn lucky to get himself talked into these things.

How had she been talked into this? Collett wondered. Rederrick had convinced her to come to the fall party he hosted every year for his clients and friends.

"Everyone in the office will be there," he assured her last Monday.

She just nodded and told him, "I'll see what I can do."

Then the little sneak had his wife, Cynda, pick her up from work early last Thursday to go dress shopping. When she insisted she couldn't afford a dress, Cynda had just bought the gown for her, insisting, "That's what friends are for."

Cynda had dragged her to what felt like every store in town, looking at dress after dress. After wearing her down physically, and laying on the guilt mentally, she had finally surrendered. She agreed to let Cynda buy the blue dress. Cynda had insisted that it brought out the color of her eyes. Then they shopped for all the perfect accessories. They finished their trip with a dinner at some restaurant, which she could not even remember the name of; the whole event was like a whirlwind to her.

On Friday, Rederrick had told her he would send his limo for her on Saturday evening, insisting that she needed a proper escort to the house. In his manipulations, Rederrick said it was to ensure she made it safely to the party and back. She knew it was just a way to ensure she didn't change her mind about attending. Now that she thought about it, she understood better what he was doing. She suspected it was more of the latter he was worried about when he added, "After all, Cynda tells me you found the perfect dress."

So here she was, still wondering how she had been so tactfully railroaded into attending a party with at least a hundred people surrounding her on all sides. This was something she would have never done before she moved here.

From the moment she had arrived at the party, Collett felt as though something was not quite right. She told herself she was just unbalanced by all the people. She usually avoided places with a crowd this size. It was nearly impossible for her to get a sense of everyone.

She felt as though she were being watched the entire time. She was sure the man with dark, black hair and golden eyes was staring intently at her and was aware of her every move. She believed he was the cause of her unease. He was dressed in some sort of expensive suit, tailored specifically for him. Undoubtedly, he was the most intimidating man attending tonight. Not just because he was tall, fit, and filled out his suit rather nicely; no, it was the way he moved, watched, and assessed his surroundings. He made her very uncomfortable, the way he took stock of her. Of everyone in attendance, his eyes kept coming back to her.

She had never seen him at the office, of that she was certain. She would have remembered a man like him. Not many people could forget a man like him.

He looked to be about thirty or so by her guess. His thick, pitch black hair fell straight and loose an inch or two above his broad shoulders. He was very tall with a strong, muscular build.

His perfectly sculpted chin sported a faded scar just under his jaw line, running along the bone about two inches. He was too dark and too dangerous for her taste.

He moved about the room with a looming presence. Whenever she felt him watching her, she would turn and he would be gone or looking away. His golden eyes should have felt warm. Instead they felt cool and appraising. She could feel his gaze directed at her now. No matter where she went in the room, he seemed to be close by. The intensity of him began to chip at her fragile nerves.

Just when she had enough of his attention, she started to approach the strange man. She intended to confront him. It was at that very moment that she felt ill. The overpowering feeling slammed into her, stopping her in her tracks as if someone put up a barrier in front of her.

CHAPTER 2

The familiar, cold feeling snaked and slithered through her. The kind of tingling chills that crawled over her skin and clung to her spine, sending shivers through her entire body. Collett felt the evil and malevolence all around her. It rushed through her so strongly, so quickly, she found it difficult to keep her knees from buckling.

They had come for her again. She thought, *Not here, not now. This couldn't be happening now.*

Instinctively, she tried to seek out the source, but as always, it was difficult to find; unless she could get closer. Too many people were crowded around for her to narrow down exactly where the feeling was coming from. *Who am I kidding?* Collett thought. She knew she didn't want to get that close to it anyway. She didn't need to meet the person with such wickedness coursing through their soul. She knew what they came for. Her!

Who they were mattered little.

The grand room suddenly felt small and as airtight as a bank vault. Blood drained from her face. A cold sweat broke out across her forehead, rapidly cooling her flushed skin even more.

C.B. Haight

Immediately her survival instincts took over. *Out, I have to get out!*

She quickly turned on her heels and went for the nearest discreet exit. Rederrick was always so kind to her, and she cared for his wife as well. She would not keep this foul taint here, and endanger them or their home.

She went through the kitchen, passing caterers she had personally hired weeks prior and left them hard at work. She fled through the French doors at the back of the kitchen, grabbing a set of keys she spotted on the side counter as she passed. She prayed she could find the vehicle to match for a quick getaway.

Hoping her hasty exit was obvious enough to lead the evil away from the house, she didn't even look to see if anyone was following her. She didn't know what she'd do once she had diverted it away, but she'd rather die than have any harm befall the people of this home. She cared for them too much. In her rush out the back door she wondered how she could've let this happen, *Why did I let them get so close?*

Ignoring the cold, bitter air whipping her exposed skin, she hurried around back toward where the catering and wait staff had parked their cars. She pressed the grey button on the little black remote and saw the lights on a small red Cavalier blink.

She rushed over to the car, quickly pulling open the door to climb inside. She scanned her surroundings, and following her current run of bad luck, she realized the other cars around this one blocked her from the road. Her only way out would be to go through the field to her left.

Just as she inserted the keys she heard it. A low, deep, guttural growl. Not bothering to turn around to see what was hunting her, she twisted the key, sparking the engine to life, jammed the car into reverse, and backed out of the parking area.

Spinning the wheel and throwing the car into drive, she revved the engine and maneuvered the car around the other cars by weaving through the field, spitting dirt and rocks out from underneath the tires. She made her way out through the back field bordering the property, aiming to get to the road as quickly as possible.

The little two-door car bumped and jarred over the ground as she drove as fast as she dared over the rough, uneven terrain. She sped over a bump larger than the others, and heard a sharp crack emanating from the undercarriage. Ignoring it, she drove on, hoping to find a small advantage somewhere before the car gave out.

No such luck. She saw the road. In her frantic hurry she hit the gas, pushing the pedal hard all the way to the floor. She jerked the wheel solidly to the left, not accounting for the recent early wintry weather.

The car spun out of control on a thin sheet of ice no normal person would have seen. She shrieked as it slipped over the embankment, flipping and rolling downward. Metal crunched and glass shattered as the car made its short descent, landing on the passenger side with a hard and painful crunch.

In her rush, she'd neglected to buckle her safety belt. As the car had spun off the embankment, she slammed her head into the driver's door window with a loud, painful crack to her skull. She was thrown out of her seat when it rolled and smacked her hip against the passenger door armrest. When the harrowing, bone-jarring movement finally stopped, she slowly lifted her bleeding head from the passenger side.

She shook her head to get her bearings, causing pain to lance through her skull. She groaned slightly. Her body protested her every movement. She did not have time to assess her injuries though; fear and survival dictated it was time to move. Gritting her teeth through the pain of movement, Collett clambered to the driver's side, unrolled the window, and worked her way out of the side-turned vehicle.

Kicking her feet, she abandoned her shoes as she climbed free, knowing she could not run at full speed over the frozen, uneven ground with the heels that Cynda had helped her choose to match her gown.

Hearing another ominous growl, she bolted. Whatever was making that sound was much too close. She was not sure where she would run. She just knew she had to run hard. She was assaulted by trees and tangled bushes as she blindly attempted to escape the evil pursuing her.

The thick, black darkness made it impossible to see very far ahead. She ran over a small hill and suddenly slipped, half sliding, half falling the short distance down the other side. She scraped up her bare feet as she slid. Seeing a tree with a large, thick base near the bottom of the hill, she ran toward it seeking any amount of cover she could find to collect her wits.

I'm going to die! This one thought kept racing through her panicking mind, as she crouched down near the cold, damp earth behind a large tree. *This time I'm not going to find a way out,* she thought as desperate anxiety began to claim her senses.

She kept low, aiming for protection from the tree and the tiny hill. After a short while, her leg muscles began protesting the prolonged crouching position and began to quiver. She tried to keep her breathing as still and quiet as possible, however, this was not an easy feat considering she had just run a mile or more over frosty, rutted ground through whipping trees and pointy bushes.

Instead of smooth, quiet breathing, something she longed for at the moment, her breaths came out in shaky, shuddering pants. Not that it really mattered, her short breaths puffed out a mist into the chilly air, which she believed was the equivalent of waving a red flag in front of a bull.

The light, eerie fog snaked across the ground like creeping fingers trying to grab hold and keep her in one spot until the monster could find her. She shivered more out of fear than cold. Now that she had a few moments to take stock of herself, she realized if the beast did not kill her, the early winter cold might.

Collett's once beautiful silk gown was torn and tattered from the frantic run through the woods. Taking a quick look at her aching feet, she assessed her cuts and realized, thankfully, that the cold evening air numbed them. She didn't feel too much pain from the minor pricks and scrapes they suffered.

Her body was another matter. She ached as a result of the travesty with the ridiculous red car. *Why couldn't I have grabbed the keys to someone's SUV instead of that stupid little pop can of a car?* she thought to herself.

She reached up with her slender fingers to probe carefully at her throbbing skull. She felt wet stickiness and realized she was bleeding. Hoping she didn't have a serious injury, she refocused her concentration on finding her stalker.

She could not see the growling monster lurking in the darkness. She had the impression it was toying with her because she could sense it close by. She felt it watching her. A cold sensation of evil still radiated from it like a sonar beacon, confirming it must be near. The smell of musky-wet fur, man, and chilly winter enveloped her nostrils, engaging her in the frustrating notion that she must be losing her mind. Though, considering her situation, losing her mind would be preferable to the reality of what was happening at this given moment.

She silently argued with herself, should I move? Or should I remain hidden under the meager cover the tree offered?

Undecided, she didn't move. Terror kept her rooted in place. She took the opportunity to slow her breathing and regain what little strength remained in her already bruised and worn body. She resolved to listen and wait. She hoped she had outrun whatever it was that was pursuing her; knowing instinctively it still lurked near her in the shadows. Breathing in and out slower and deeper now, she continued to focus; squinting as she forced herself to think clearly. Closing her eyes tightly, both to ease the ache in her head and to concentrate on separating the sounds around her, she listened intently for a sign of her stalker.

The night felt too still, too quiet. It was if nature felt the same fear and terror that filled her slender frame. Even the wind in the trees seemed to keep silent, as if attempting to hide from the evil presence lurking about. The apprehending silence thundered in her ears, smacking her thoughts around in her head. One noise, one creaking branch, is all she hoped for to give a hint at a direction for her to escape. Her pursuer was not that gracious, however.

She couldn't comprehend the repetition of these events. How could this pursuer, this evil keep finding her? Frustration and fear clawed at her sanity. She'd been a fool to think she could be normal. How could she be so dense as to think she could actually enjoy a party? To laugh, to let go and socialize like she fit in was a fallacy she'd been dangerously absurd to believe.

That small and precious moment of normalcy was shattered the moment she felt it again. That hair-raising, frigid sensation she recognized right before something was about to go terribly wrong. She knew then, she had stayed too long.

She should have left months ago. She silently berated herself for her stupidity. She'd stayed because for the first time in two years she'd felt a bond, a friendship with others. She'd found people who seemed to care about her. She wanted so badly to stay, to have a place to call home.

She'd spent the past two years running. This very thing she was hiding from had been pursuing her wherever she ran. It always seemed to track her down. She'd spent all this time moving, running, and hiding from something she had never met. At least, she thought they had never met. Even so, since moving here, it was months since she'd sensed the darkness close by. She had begun to believe she'd finally outrun it. She'd been looking forward to a new life. Now she felt her imminent death was the price she would pay for wanting to fit in. There was something too different about her. She didn't understand it all; but she sensed it. She would never fit in. One difference was her affectation; it had somehow kept her hidden and safe— until now.

Maybe it was for the best, she thought. Maybe it was time to face this demon. She was ignorant to their interest in her. She didn't understand why they spent so much time searching her out. A feeling of resignation washed over her. Maybe if they got her this time, maybe if she was dead, no one else would be hurt in these pursuits. This time Collett felt she'd outrun her own luck. She felt an overwhelming sense that she could no longer cheat death. She wasn't sure she had it within her to try anymore.

The short, abrupt sound of a twig breaking woke her from her thoughts. Quickly, she snapped her eyes open, scanning the darkness for her pursuer. Her heart raced; she could hear it thundering in her ears. Despite this noise, however, she heard an ominous, raspy breathing close by. It sounded like some sort of animal. In and out it huffed; erasing any rational thought from her mind.

She rubbed her temples with the pads of her fingertips, attempting to clear her head. Peering into the darkness, she carefully looked around. Squinting hard and jutting out her chin, she saw it. The only thing that gave its position away was the glowing golden orbs glistening in the moonlight. They were locked intently on her. It was so close. One quick leap was all it would take to be right on top of her.

There, between the trees, stood a massive, very fierce looking wolf. It didn't approach her, yet. It just stood there in the black, quiet night ominously staring at her. Two deadly eyes locked on her.

The creature's dark, black fur blended perfectly into opaque shadows of the night. She couldn't tell where the silhouette of the beast began and where it ended. His, well she assumed his, eyes glowed like amber gems in the moonlight, piercing through her as they held her captive within their gaze.

As the animal stood there looking at her, she tried harder to make out its features through the darkness. It was magnificent and terrifying at the same time. It stalked forward just a few steps. It moved carefully, with the strength and confidence of a beast that had its prey right where it wanted.

Panic began to set in once more. Her breaths came more quickly; quiet pants escaped her lips. Her body shivered in anticipation and fear. She tried to pull herself up onto her shaking and wobbly legs, but they felt boneless. As her thoughts raced, she tried to prepare herself to meet her death. She was sure she was staring right at it.

Unexpectedly, the wolf stopped moving as she rose. She surmised it was taking its time for the kill; savoring the moment. Right as this thought coursed through her, the wolf let loose with a low, rumbling growl; a growl that she suspected it used to prove how many razor-sharp teeth it could eat her with.

Its broad body was wider than any wolf she had ever seen before. Now that was a strange thought… Even in her panicky state, she considered it more thoroughly. To her knowledge, she had never seen a wolf. Yet she felt strongly as though she had. She was certain there was no way she had seen one like this. Had she?

This was the end. The end of the recurring nightmare that had been her life these last two years, and she refused to face it cowering on the ground. Bolstered by her own thoughts, she stood, feeling just a little more firm as the courage rose within her. She would not die a coward!

Collett placed her hand upon the tree behind her, the same tree that had offered her a meager place to hide. This time, however, instead of hiding beneath it, she used it for support. She reached deep within herself for every bit of courage she could muster.

"Why… Why me? What do you want?" she pleaded; the words coming out at barely above a whisper, as if this wolf could somehow answer her. Just as she attempted to voice her frustrated confusion aloud, three things seemed to happen simultaneously: First, a strong arm grabbed her from behind. With punishing strength, it wrapped around her throat, jerking her back and holding her fast. The arm was applying enough pressure to make her breath wheeze in and out, as she now strained for air. Second, the large wolf lunged forward, forcing her wobbly legs to give out on her. Had it not been for the arm wrapping around her throat, she would have been in a heap on the ground. And finally, every last drop of the courage she had managed to collect drained right out of her body as if the shockwave of this final terror obliterated the dam holding and collecting her bravery for her.

With sudden revelation, she realized that tonight there was more than one thing after her, more than one monster who wanted her dead. Disheartened, she knew all her running, all her hiding had been futile. She closed her eyes in complete defeat and despair.

Chills crawled over her body as a cold breath tickled her neck. A male tenor voice gleefully asked, "Can you feel it? Can you feel her power? Can you, mutt? Smell." The man pulled in a deep sniff of her, burying his face in her neck as he did. "Smell her sweet aroma. She's afraid. Can you sense that too? Fear always makes it sweeter." She felt a tickle as he lifted a lock of her hair, dangling it in-between his fingers.

Curious, she opened her eyes and looked directly at the wolf, wondering why this man was talking to it.

"Have you come to savor this sweet treasure?" the monster holding her inquired of the wolf. "Oh, it would be so wasted on you. You only know how to kill, but this must be enjoyed."

The wolf took one-step forward, and the man's cruel voice admonished, "Ah, ah, ah. You know the rules. First come, first served." Pausing, he rubbed his ice-cold cheek against Collett's neck. She shuddered and whimpered. Her shaky knees unlocked, cutting off her minimal air supply momentarily until she was able to support herself again.

As if to himself this time, he pressed his lips against her ear and said softly, "I don't think I'll return this one. No, she is too sweet. Her scent burns through me like fire." He breathed in deeply again, "Yes… I'll be keeping this one. I think I'll enjoy her and forget the bounty." Pressing his lips to her ear he whispered, "You seem to be bounty enough for me."

Her captor's voice sounded cold. It was laced with a lewd malice and appalling innuendo. The arm that was in contact with her skin felt frigid. His touch on her skin seemed to transfer all the evil pouring off of him and fill her in a horribly intimate way. The sickening taint of him crawled through her, consuming her completely.

The intrusive contact with him was agonizing for her. She felt as though, somehow, he perverted and sullied her very soul. Goosebumps flared across her skin like tiny prickling pins. She felt dirty and disgusting from his tainted touch. Even her very bones felt the icy death and despair hanging around this thing in a heavy cloud.

She could only watch as the speaker's words riled up the black wolf in front of her even more. The wolf growled and snarled at them, his fur standing on end. His tense body vibrated with anticipation. He was alert, edgy, and ready to act. The monster before her was just waiting for the perfect opportunity, all while the monster behind her eluded her gaze.

Her body was pinned so tight against her captor that she could not even crane her head around to see the wicked man's face. She sensed her inability to see him left her in a better position, for she knew instinctively she did not want to see in his eyes. She could only imagine how terrifying and cruel they were.

The pressure on her neck was so tight, the grip so strong, she knew that the tiniest amount of added pressure could cut off all of her remaining oxygen. Her captor was in complete control of her life and he'd promised to drag hers out in agonizing fashion.

Once more, he spoke to the wolf in front of her with his sickly inhuman rasp, "Can you mongrels smell the sweet scent of a life-force pumping through the body? Even better, can you hear it? I can feel the thump, thump, thump as the fear takes over speeding up the heart before death. I can hear it as it slowly comes to a stop when the last drop of blood is drained." His excitement seemed to grow with each word. Then he asked, "Do you even bother with such things before you make a kill? I will tell you, it is fascinating and exhilarating at the same time."

She felt his free hand stroke her cheek. She shuddered as if cockroaches were crawling across her skin. His skin was icy cold like his soul. The prolonged contact with such a dark force was starting to sicken her physically. As if her body rebelled against the very nature of the evil within him. As nausea rose in her, she tasted the gagging bile at the back of her throat. Her head spun. It was a fierce struggle to hold back this overwhelming reaction. Not in all of her memory could she recall such an intense reaction. Well, then again, she couldn't remember feeling anything so evil or foul. She struggled to stay balanced.

As she fought against the nausea and bile, fought against the overwhelming dizziness, she stared straight into the eyes of the threat directly in front of her. Oddly, his presence seemed to ground her. The wolf before her was so close.

His once amber-gold eyes now looked back to her glowing a horrifying red. They looked as if they were on fire, like the burning glow of over-heated metal.

He let a growling howl escape his canine lips. Then suddenly, to her horror, his body started to contort and change in front of her very eyes. He became more than just a large wolf. With sudden clarity she understood why her captor kept talking to him.

With a sickening crack, the wolf's hind legs shifted and grew to support his large upper body as he twisted to stand on two legs instead of four. His front legs changed into thick powerful arms. His paws became huge, monster-like hands with five razor-sharp claws as deadly as any blade. His chest seemed to grow broader than any man's with cut, rippling muscles forming across his stomach as his ribs expanded and reformed. The wolf was now a rage-filled monster before her, and huge in comparison to her own meager five-foot-five height.

She wasn't sure if her mind played tricks on her, but it seemed that even his teeth grew sharper, longer. This powerful, amazing change seemed to take forever, and yet it happened in barely an instant.

She could feel the rage rolling off of him as the monstrous beast stood there staring down at her captor. He was emitting a wave of anger so strong and powerful she felt as though he would tear them both into little pieces without any difficulty.

The deep breath she now managed to choke down acutely reminded her of her other problem as it managed to slip painfully past her constricted airway. She blinked her eyes trying to force her body to wake up and escape this worsening nightmare.

"She's mine!" The huge animal that now towered before her rasped through his large, deadly muzzle. The sound of his guttural voice caused Collett to involuntarily shiver once more.

The werewolf stated it with such a calm confidence that she had to wonder what he had planned for her himself. She wondered which of these two monsters could inflict the most pain before they killed her. As she blinked her eyes against the horrifying wolfish thing in front of her, hoping the nightmare would go away or disappear, she heard the wolf continue to growl, "You have two choices, demon. Let her go and I might not hunt you down and tear you to shreds. Or, I'll make you let go by ripping you to shreds now. The choice is yours. You had better hurry though, I'm NOT very patient." His words were clear enough though his voice held a growling, raspy undertone that didn't sound quite human and grated against Collett's eardrums.

The large man-wolf didn't move his body. He tilted his head to the side as if he had simply asked what two plus two equals from a kindergartener and was patiently waiting for the easy reply. He held his thick, muscled arms out wide. She assumed it was meant as a non-threatening gesture, but it failed to put her at ease.

The frustration of the situation started to build within her. She couldn't figure out why so many creatures wanted to hunt her. What couldn't she remember about herself that made everyone, everything, want her dead?

As her frustration escalated, so did her anger. She felt it rising within her. However, she was sure it wasn't only her anger she felt. The werewolf's violent anger gave her a focus. She would rather feel his rage than her captor's tainted soul of death. She focused on the werewolf as best she could. She found it difficult and confusing. Furthermore, it was odd that seeing a living, breathing werewolf standing almost seven feet tall in front of her didn't seem out of the ordinary. *Why can't I remember*, she thought.

The cold, quiet voice of her subjugator let out an unnatural hiss that brushed over the skin of her neck and sent shivers cascading down her spine, effectively breaking her fragile concentration. He answered the werewolf, saying coolly, "You cannot best me, mutt! I have her, and you do not. I hold every advantage. Now be gone! I might leave you a scrap or two... after I've had my fun, that is." Her captor wrapped his hand roughly in her hair and yanked her head to the side with his other hand. Then he ran his slimy, cold, and abnormally long tongue from the base of her neck to behind her ear.

Her body shuddered at the polluted contact. Collett closed her eyes as she felt the rebellion she had lost moments before, rise. She was not ready to die after all. She was not willing to die. Not without a fight!

As the epiphany struck her, she heard the wolfish creature let out another fierce snarl. She opened her eyes and met his burning gaze straight ahead.

The energy all around her from the rage-filled contention was thick and tangible. She felt her adrenaline building.

Not even thinking her next action through, she twisted her body to get the perfect angle. Though this meant cutting off the little bit of air she had left, she realized it was her only chance at escape.

She then did something she was sure was born from the fear and pure adrenaline coursing through her body. Had she taken the time to think about it, she would never have been able to do it. She gathered her fists together, pulled her left arm forward as best she could, and slammed her elbow home, right into her captor's gut.

She failed to notice the bright, bluish light that sparked between them. Vibrations of pain moved up her arm. She felt as though she had slammed her elbow into a brick wall.

The pain proved to have been worth it. Her maneuvering achieved its purpose. Her captor jumped back from the blow, temporarily loosening his deadly grip on her. As that happened, the wolf, if you could call it that, sensed his opportunity. He lunged forward, tackling the monster behind her. The impact knocked her free. She fell to the ground with a heavy thud, worsening her already tender injuries.

She took a quick look at her pursuers violently engaged in a lethal grappling battle and didn't waste another second. She fled the scene, running as fast as her injured limbs could carry her. She began heading in the only direction she could think of, back toward Rederrick's home. As she ran, she prayed silently that she'd made the right decision.

CHAPTER 3

Cade lunged forward violently and grabbed at the bulky, gray-skinned demon. Wanting to gain the upper hand so he could finish this quickly, he grabbed hold of the smelly bastard by the arm, wrenching him around and smashing him into the thick tree behind them. The otherworldly beast hit the tree with a loud crack, hissing vehemently. He couldn't be sure if it came from pain or anger; you could never tell with such creatures. This time, he was hoping it came from pain.

Collett was jarred loose in the melee and hit the ground with a solid thump! As this happened, Cade made the rookie mistake of turning around, focusing his attention on the woman's escape.

The demon decided it wanted more than a little piece of him. Rushing at him with its unnatural speed, the demon moved around and jumped on his back. The nasty creature dug his filthy claws deep into his ribs to gain purchase as he plunged his elongated, serrated teeth into Cade's shoulder. He snarled past the sharp sting of the bite and reached behind himself to rip the monster free of his hold.

He managed to see her up and running out of the corner of his eye. *Good girl,* he thought to himself.

The battling monster made a reckless mistake. He let go, leaping away to pursue the woman. This gave Cade all he needed to finish this.

The anger of the animal within him rose to an uncontrollable level. His eyes glowed blood-red as he jumped toward the massive demon. Overtaking it, he grabbed hold of the demon's left leg with his own powerful, sharp canine maw, effectively stopping the creature's pursuit of Collett.

Once he got a solid grip, he pulled back hard, tearing through the putrid flesh, making his way to the bone, and he heard the horrible, inhuman screech emanating from the thing as he did so. The sound of it vibrated painfully in his ears, while satisfaction ran through his blood.

The demon dug its claws into the hard, frozen earth to keep from being pulled back any farther, hissing and thrashing. Cade clamped down harder with the great strength of his jaws, and felt the crack of the bone as he broke through it with unrelenting force. The ugly monster let out another unearthly wail as his calf gave under the vicious pressure, snapping in half.

The man within him knew he needed to get more information. He knew he could possibly get something out of this thing in front of him.

The animal in him didn't care. He couldn't see past the raging red haze consuming him. The burning sting in his back skewed his judgment as blood, trickled from his wounds. His actions became less logical as he recalled the image of this demon holding the fragile woman and touching her perfect skin as he prepared to sample her as his next meal.

He bent down over the now cowering demon, baring his sharp, long teeth stained with fresh black ichor. The demon blood covered his chin as well. A furious growl vibrated deep in his animal throat. Time seemed to slow down. He leaned in and inhaled deeply, taking a moment to savor the smell of the fear; for fear held such a powerful scent. The demon was right about that. It was empowering to animals and demons alike, and Cade was both. Fear confirmed dominance; it confirmed superiority. It poured off this creature in aromatic waves, smelling as sweet to him as a bakery would smell to a starving man. It reaffirmed his superiority over this night demon, affirming the death that stood before his opponent.

With lightning speed, he lunged one last time, clamping down on the exposed neck before him. He twisted and shook violently, tasting the salty tang of blood in his mouth. He jerked back then, fully tearing out the throat with a gruesome pull. As he viciously ripped through the creature's neck and spine, it blew apart into a mist of dust and settled back to the ground. The only evidence left now of the monster's existence was the powdery ash on the ground beneath him and the black fluid left on Cade's lips.

At least demons clean up after themselves, he reflected. He stood, straightening to his full, monstrous height. His breath was huffing in and out heavily. His broad, man-like rib cage kept expanding and contracting with the effort it took to slow his breathing. He panted out several more breaths before finding a small measure of calm.

Then he cursed himself for letting his temper take control of him. He generally had a good handle on his brutal and vicious side. He brushed off the self-recrimination and considered his lack of control valid considering it was a summoned demon after all.

Though now he would have to figure out what the hell was going on here without a nasty little informant to squeeze for some solid info. He needed to fill in some blanks. By the look of things, he needed to do it soon.

So, he thought, *the question is, what am I going to do now?*

Considering the sequence of events that he'd just experienced, he decided that right then he had two choices left to him. He could let Collett make her way back to Rederrick's house, or he could catch up to her and confront her. At this very moment, he wasn't sure if he wanted to catch her. The image of the fear in her eyes at the sight of him bothered him more than it should have. She was terrified of what he was, and he was too unsettled to deal with her reaction to him. For the time being, anyway.

Well, he thought, *at least I know how much she knows of the supernatural. She seemed to know very little, or nothing at all.* Otherwise, she would have stayed in the house where it was safe. If she knew it was a demon after her she wouldn't have run out of the safety of the house into the pitch black night where she was easy prey for the creatures of the night that can see in the dark.

He shook his head as he thought, *Demon Education 101: Don't run out of the safety of the house into the dark night where you're an easy target.*

This wasn't really the way he'd thought he was going to spend his night. After he'd spoken with Rederrick earlier, he decided to assess the woman a little himself and watched carefully throughout the night in order to get an idea of what this woman was about.

She had wandered around that night talking to several people Cade knew, and others he didn't. She blended smoothly into each conversation, laughing at all the right times, looking serious when needed. She knew precisely how to be seen and not noticed at the same time. She blended so easily, too easily, he'd thought. Cade recognized immediately it was a ruse. To be fair, years of experience gave him an advantage with such things.

She seemed hyper-aware of her surroundings. He saw her covertly check every exit. She discreetly avoided touching several people. He noticed when she did happen to touch people in what seemed like an unavoidable accident, her brow pinched slightly as if she were concentrating on something. Anyone watching would have to be concentrating hard on her to notice it. This was because she would carefully correct herself as she did it, moving gracefully into her next interaction. A normal person was not that practiced. She put up a good act; he could give her that.

He kept himself alert and focused to gain as much intel as possible. That meant surreptitiously eavesdropping a bit here and there. He listened to the conversations she had, almost all of them superficial.

The few that happened to turn toward a personal road, she politely evaded. She then would excuse herself and move on. He found she would often keep quietly to herself and move out of the way of those passing by. She seemed to watch everybody and nobody at the same time. From the looks of it, she obviously understood behaviors and mannerisms impeccably well.

Several times she behaved as if she knew someone was watching her, glancing quickly in Cade's direction. As a result, he decided to let her notice him watching her. He wanted to gauge her reaction to it.

Upon noticing his intense gaze, she looked annoyed right away, turned on her heel and moved to the other side of the room. He decided Rederrick was wrong in his original assessment of her. She wasn't nervous, she was cautious, very cautious; controlled even. She kept deliberate control of her environment.

When she'd had enough of his following her, she headed across the room directly towards him. He remembered looking forward to the exchange. He tilted his head just a bit, and aimed his full, eager smile at her. As if suddenly distracted, she stopped halfway through her march.

Her annoyed expression vanished as she stared at him. Her soft, feminine features took on a pinched, painful look and she stumbled back a half-step. With frightened eyes, she quickly scanned the crowd as if looking for someone or something. The color drained from her face as she turned around and fled the room.

Right away, Cade pursued her. He was interrupted by a voluptuous redhead he didn't know. She stood right in front of him, trying to introduce herself. Normally, he would have appreciated the attention, and the woman. Not tonight though. He excused himself as politely as possible, which wasn't very polite at all. He pushed past the woman with a rough, "Excuse me."

As he finally arrived outside, he saw her frantically opening the door of a small, red car. He looked around and sniffed the air to find a reason for her sudden flight from the house, catching the rotten stench left only by summoned leeches. The smell of a demon flitted about him. It was here, close by. He growled low in his throat and watched as she jumped into the car, backed out, and drove at a very reckless speed through the field.

He didn't bother to strip his clothes, ruining yet another suit. His body shifted and twisted. His spine bent over, accommodating his new form; the shape of a massive black wolf. His was a shape of nightmares, for children and men alike. This form enabled him to keep up with the car she *borrowed.*

Not that she made it very far before she crashed the little red car over an embankment. By the time he reached the wreck, she was already clamoring out. He waited to show himself, hoping to spot the demon before it got to her. He easily kept pace with her frantic run, through bushes and trees, keeping to the shadows so she wouldn't catch sight of him.

When she finally stopped and crouched behind the tree, he smelled her fear and despair. The urge to help her assaulted him then. Originally, he'd tried to approach her calmly. Then he had smelled the wretched scent of the demon again. He searched his surroundings, but even with his sensitive vision, he still didn't see it. As Collett stood bravely, he spotted it. The demon was hidden carefully in the tree above her.

The growling and snarling that erupted from him as a result of spotting the demon frightened her. He realized she saw him as the enemy, leaving him in the difficult position of trying to protect her while she thought he was the one pursuing her.

Now, as he approached Rederrick's home reflecting on the night's events, he shook his head and raised one brow. *Well, I'll just adapt,* he told himself. Considering his next move, he reached around to check the wound on his back. His inspection confirmed his wound hadn't torn open too badly; it should heal quickly. It was sore and bleeding, but by the time he changed back to a man it should be mostly closed.

He knew he could still turn this in his favor. The bulk of the guests should have cleared out by now. This meant he could sneak in through the upstairs balcony, get some clothes, and come out with no one the wiser.

He concentrated and shifted his form back to that of an oversized wolf. There was no need to scare any more people tonight by staying in the half-man, half-wolf form of legends and myths.

He took off at a full run toward the house, sprinting to the wrecked car to examine the damage. The car looked to be a total loss. Seeing it up close, he found himself surprised that she walked away from it at all, let alone running as she did. She was a lucky little thing…no doubt about it. He would have Rederrick call out a tow truck and deal with the heap of twisted metal.

Moving on, he continued back toward the house, slowing as he caught her scent. The sweet citrus smell drifted around him, making it easy to follow her trail. Concern gripped him as he noticed her perfumed scent intertwined with the smell of her blood. He hoped she wasn't hurt too badly.

He held back a moment, seeking out her exact location. He quickly spotted her about fifty or so yards from the house. He watched her, ensuring she'd made it back without any further incident. She had run hard, not even bothering to peek over her shoulder. *Smart girl*, he thought. He knew that nothing could slow a person down more than turning to make sure nothing was behind them. *Not that she could have possibly outrun me; whether she'd looked or not,* he mused.

As she reached the house, she hesitated. She looked unsure, as if she'd changed her mind about going in.

He loped quickly in her direction in an attempt to follow her more closely. If she bolted, he wanted to be close. Just as he closed in on her, he thought better of it. Instead, an idea came to him and he let out one long, eerie howl. Just as he'd predicted, she remembered why she'd headed this way in the first place. As the howl echoed past the trees through the quiet, still night, she straightened her spine, looked hard over her shoulder and started for the same door she'd snuck out a few hours before. Cade huffed out one last breath, and inhaled the scent of her relief. He knew Rederrick would keep her safe now that she was inside.

He ran over to his ruined suit to retrieve his cellphone and wallet. Once he had them locked gently in his jaw, he leapt up to the second-floor balcony. Dropping the items in his mouth, he commanded his body to change. As his body contorted, his bones cracked. His legs shifted and bent back to the angles that more closely resembled a human form. As his spine straightened out, he went from a large wolf to that of a man. As the final step in his transformation, his fur flattened out and seemed to melt as it reshaped itself into human skin.

He stood up, his muscular body naked and aching a bit from the multiple changes. He opened the French doors and went into the room Rederrick and Cynda kept for him. He approached the massive closet, sorting through the spare clothes kept here for this very reason.

Since there were no Armani suits available, he settled on a pair of grey slacks and a black, button-up shirt. Damn! He'd forgotten his dress shoes outside. He went through the dresser until he found a pair of socks. Sitting, he slipped them over his feet and then stood up from the chair.

He took a deep, temper-calming breath as he approached the bedroom door and opened it. *It's time for Act Two,* he told himself. *Try not to scare the pretty lady this time.*

Then, he headed down the stairs like any old friend who stayed here at the estate. He was simply one of the family.

CHAPTER 4

Collett stumbled past the threshold of the kitchen door, startling the kitchen wait staff, who were hard at work cleaning up from the night's event. They all stopped what they were doing and stared at her with shocked and horrified expressions as they observed her horribly disheveled condition. Reacting quickly, she attempted a cover story to explain her bruises and ragged appearance.

"Help me!" she rasped, her throat still tender from the earlier assault. "I was attacked. Please," she coughed, "Please! Get Cynda!" Adding panic to her voice was quite simple, considering this was how she was presently feeling.

A plump, gray-haired woman with softly aged skin and a concerned look in her eyes quickly bustled over to help her to a kitchen chair. Right away, she knew the older woman had a gentle, motherly nature to her. She enveloped Collett's shoulder with her arm and patted her with a soft hand. The helpful woman's touch soothed her. Collett felt the warmth and kindness in this woman wash over her like a warm blanket. Noticing the creases in the woman's face, Collett guessed she was in her late sixties.

As Collett eased gently into her chair, she leaned on the woman for support. She did this both to play the part of a victim properly and because she realized she actually needed it at that very moment. The woman sat her down near a small, shiny wooden breakfast table nestled near the large bay window.

The kind woman seemed to be in charge. She determined this as she watched the plump woman turn and snap, "Well now, why are ya just standin' there? Kari, go and fetch Mrs. Williams, hurry up now. As for the rest of you, there are chores that need doin'. Go on, get yourselves back to work."

Every one of them moved quickly back to work at the sound of her voice. She liked this kind woman right away. She stroked Collett's hair and said in a quiet voice, "Don't worry a bit, dear. I'll make you a cup of herbal tea, and we'll get this all straightened out."

The younger woman, who had rushed to fetch Cynda per the older woman's direction, came running in with a warm quilt. After she laid the quilt around Collett's shoulders, she stood staring with curious, wide eyes. The older woman noticed her fixed gaze and shooed her away.

Collett felt a bit of guilt worrying them all so much. However, she had little choice at that moment. Just what else could she tell them? *I'm sorry to bother you, but I think I might have been attacked by some sort of demon and a werewolf out in the woods?* She almost laughed out loud at the absurdity of this thought.

Just then, Cynda came bursting into the room like an agitated mama bear coming to rescue her cub. Right behind her was the big papa bear with a mean and fierce scowl spread across his handsome features. They both rushed over to her side immediately.

Cynda knelt down in front of her, looking at her with sparkling green eyes. As Collett looked at her, she wondered if Cynda's eyes sparkled more than even the greenest emeralds. As Cynda noticed her bruises and tattered dress, her normally captivating eyes filled with concern, and worse, the sparkle dimmed as she began to ask questions.

The kind, older woman who'd helped her set a cup of tea next to her on the table. Rederrick paced by the chair with his anger at a palpable level. A weight settled on her chest. This very reaction was one of the reasons she'd stayed so long in Colorado. This kindness, these wonderful people; they truly cared for her as a friend. They cared if she lived or died, cared if she was sad or happy. She cared for them in return. Friends were something she so desperately wanted, but felt she couldn't really have.

Tonight seemed to prove that. She knew she would have to leave. She cared if they lived or died as well, and if she stayed it could very well be the latter of the two.

"What is this all about? You were attacked here, on my property?" Rederrick's heavy voice boomed. "Where did this happen? Tell me, where is the S.O.B.? I'll teach him to think twice about threatening my guests, on my property; on any property for that matter." His jaw clenched tight. His face and neck turned red from the blood rushing to his head. She knew against any man he would surely be formidable, but her attacker wasn't just any man.

She tracked his movements with her eyes as he spoke. His angry words bit into her conscience, but she could never tell him what actually happened. She knew he would charge out there, werewolf or not, and try to help. That was something she couldn't live with.

Cynda calmly stood and looked at her husband with loving, patient eyes. She took hold of his arms firmly, forcing him to look at her.

"Dear, I think it best if you could hurry our last few guests along while I help Collett. I'll determine how bad her injuries are," she said with a reassuring tone.

Rubbing her hands up and down his arms, she gave him a pointed look that said without speaking, 'It is time for you to go. I'll get to the bottom of this.' He stared at his wife with a frustrated look for a moment. As he met her gaze, he relaxed and gently kissed her forehead.

"I'll come back shortly and we'll sort this out. Can I get you anything Collett?"

"No. I'll be fine, thank you," she said meekly.

As he started toward the kitchen doorway Cynda stopped him with a quick comment, "Oh honey, make sure you check with Cade to confirm his plans for the night."

He got the message loud and clear. What she meant was, check with Cade and see what he knows about all of this. Cynda always thought ahead.

Obediently, he left the kitchen. As he said his goodbyes to the remaining stragglers, he scanned the room for Cade; all the while thinking about what could have happened.

It seemed Cade could always find trouble quickly. However, this time it was Rederrick who had dumped the trouble right in Cade's lap.

After her husband left, Cynda turned her attention to Collett. As she looked her over she realized whatever had happened tonight had shaken the poor girl up. Her aura vibrated with fear and vulnerability.

"Now, let's see what we've got here," Cynda said. She examined Collett for any major injuries. She saw a nasty cut above her left temple, but upon looking at it closely she determined it would close up alright on its own. It wouldn't need stitches, but it might scar. Her bare feet were cut and scraped and left blood here and there on the floor, but again, nothing serious. The heavy bruising at her throat concerned Cynda most; this, and the possibility of internal injuries.

"Well," she said in a smooth tone, "maybe we should get you to a hospital."

"NO!" The response jumped from Collett's lips too quickly. "I mean, I'll be fine; just a bump or two. The car took most of the damage."

Cynda looked up, "Car? What car are you talking about? You didn't bring a car." Collett silently cursed her stupidity.

"Well, it's a bit complicated," she said hesitantly. Her voice sounded unsure and gravelly due to her bruised throat. "Um…he, the man, ah, forced me into a red car from out back. He made me drive it, which I did, until it skidded on the ice and ran over the embankment."

She decided to keep her story as close to the truth as she could. That way, the lies wouldn't tangle her up too much, and omitting the major details that would frighten normal people to death would keep them safe.

Her thought process paused momentarily as she reflected on why she just put herself in the abnormal people category. Though, she didn't have time to ponder on it much.

Cynda urged her to continue, "Go on, sweetie. Tell us what happened. We'll worry about the car later."

"Um, well, it gets kind of foggy after that. It all happened so fast." Tears welled in Collett's eyes as she recalled in her mind how close she'd come to dying tonight. She closed her eyes tight—both to stem the flow and to gain some perspective on the images jumbled in her head. Her tears flowed freely, running down her cheeks until Cynda gently placed a tissue in her hand. "He felt and sounded so cold. I never got a look at him. He stayed behind me the entire time," she said truthfully. "I ran away from him after the car fell down the embankment; a little over a mile from here. I didn't stay to see if he was alright."

She left it at that. Omitting the rest was easy because she knew it would be the only way to protect them from getting involved in her never-ending nightmare. Collett knew Rederrick's nature. He was a protector, and he would try to save her. Cynda would befriend her and care for her while he did.

That is, if they believed the truth in the first place and didn't have her committed. *It doesn't matter,* she admonished herself. She knew she could never tell them. She would give them just enough to believe her story; enough to make sense of her appearance and the wrecked car. Then she would disappear from their lives as soon as she could.

I'm going to have to start all over, she thought to herself. *Where will I go this time? How long will I have to run?*

Suddenly, she felt all the leftover adrenaline drain out of her. She felt very tired. She needed to think and configure her next move. Her foggy brain just wouldn't compute as she wanted it to though.

"I have to go. I need to get home," she insisted. As she started to rise, Cynda gently pushed her right back down to the chair.

"I don't think so, young lady. You will stay right here. What you need is a doctor and a bed. By the looks of that bump on your head you could very well have a concussion. Besides, we'll have to inform the police so they can track down this criminal."

The word police cleared some of the cobwebs from her mind. "No!" she protested too quickly, again. She calmed her voice, "Cynda, please, I just can't deal with the police tonight. I'm tired and hurting I want...I need to get to my apartment and get some rest. I'll go and file a report with the police tomorrow. Please, just get the limo driver to take me home? I'll be fine, I promise," she pleaded.

Cynda, having raised three children, two of which were girls, knew the tricks they could play with their soft eyes. She knew the tricks inlaid in the *Please... do me this one little favor*, voice. She also knew how to sway them the direction she wanted them to go. So, being a smart woman, she replied with a slight hesitation, as if she were suddenly coming up with a new idea.

"I'll make you a deal. You can stay here tonight. That way, I can keep an eye on you for my peace of mind. Then we'll see about the police tomorrow. I won't hear of anything else."

Cynda continued on right past the protest that started to form on Collett's lips, "Now then, let's see about getting you a room and a change of clothes. Jenny?" The plump woman, whom she had taken a liking to, came forward again. "Why don't you see about getting Collett a bath and a few first aid supplies in my bathroom? I'll get her a room ready and gather some clean clothes." She finished by turning away from them and heading out of the room up the kitchen stairs.

Confused, Collett wondered, *All right... what just happened here?* She felt slightly shell-shocked. *Have I just been coaxed into staying here tonight?* The slight tug at her arm to help her out of her chair confirmed it. Once more, she'd been manipulated by Cynda Williams. The worst of it was, she couldn't for the life of her figure out why it didn't bother her.

She looked up at Jenny with weariness pressing down on her and relented. She convinced herself one more night wouldn't matter. She would get some sleep and sort out her next step in the morning. She let Jenny lead her up the stairs and down a long hallway to a large master bedroom that was Cynda and Rederrick's.

The middle of the room held a huge, four-poster, king-sized bed with intricate designs carved into each post. She passed by a dresser that held several family pictures in varying silver frames. Glancing at one or two and seeing laughing, smiling faces in each, she felt a sad longing. They walked by a small sitting area in front of a beautiful marble fireplace. The room felt warm and welcoming. She envied the memories this room must hold. Her apartment held no family pictures, no pretty artwork or antique furniture. There was nothing warm about it. She lived with pure function and cost in mind. It was a lonely way to live.

They entered through a door set off to the left from the sitting area. As they walked into a huge master bathroom, Collett noticed it held an oversized, jetted tub, big enough for two. There was a separate walk-in shower with travertine tile and several showerheads. She couldn't help but think this might be worth the overnight stay. She almost whimpered at the sight of the tub. A sudden eagerness to wash away the dirt, blood, and evil taint she still felt on her skin overwhelmed her.

Jenny bent over awkwardly and started the water in the big bathtub. After adding something to the water, she retrieved a couple of towels from the linen closet.

"All right now Miss. I'll leave you to it. If you need anything you just buzz that intercom, there in the bedroom. There's a room right down the hall a bit and to the left; near the stairs. That's where Mrs. Williams will be havin' you stay. We'll be leavin' you some nightclothes out on the bed in there."

Turning, she pulled out some bandages as well as a dark-blue jar then said, "Here is some ointment for your scrapes." Setting it all down on the granite counter, Jenny softly rubbed her hand over Collett's back like a mother would to soothe a crying infant. "It'll be alright with a fresh bath, a soft bed, and a good night's sleep to clear your head a bit. You'll see." With a smile, she left the room quietly closing the door behind her.

She tenderly stripped away what was left of her two hundred fifty dollar gown. She felt a small sense of loss as she laid it carefully on the bathroom counter. She ran her fingers over the cool silk. The gown was the first gift she'd received in two years. The only gift she could remember anyone giving to her. She wiped at the small tear that had escaped and made its way down her dirt covered cheek, which only smeared the dirt and blood more.

It is ruined, she thought. She realized there was no hope to save it. It felt like such a profound loss to her. She knew it was silly to feel so sentimental over a dress at this point in time, but there was much more to it than that.

Her life was in tatters too. The ruined gown reflected this perfectly. For a while she'd begun to think the running may have come to an end. For just a short time, she began to hope it was over and thought maybe she could have a real life.

She gave into the sobs then, letting go of all her fear and frustration from the last two years for the first time. It came out in streaming tears and quiet hiccups. Her shoulders shook as she sobbed, and she sniffled as her nose began to run. After a long while, totally drained of every last tear, she slowly released a few deep, shuddering breaths to calm herself down.

It's over, she told herself again. She had to move on now. Take it one step at a time until she got it together, and there was no time like the present to start. She roughly threw the gown in the small trash can, violently pushing it down to the bottom; effectively pushing and throwing away the last of her dreams with it.

Resolved, she stepped up to the welcoming bathtub, inhaling the soft scent of lavender Jenny had added. The subtle, floral fragrance calmed her nerves a little more.

Easing herself down into the steaming hot water and feeling her muscles relax one by one, she felt a slight sting as the water made contact with her cuts and scrapes. It only took a few seconds for her sense of pleasure to kick in. The warmth of the water enveloped her. It washed aside almost all the aches and stings of the night. For now, it washed away the tears, sniffles, and despair. She eased into the water, lying back against the cool porcelain. She set her head upon the bath pillow. Her tired brain convinced her to close her red, swollen eyes for just a moment and enjoy the warmth surrounding her.

After the last guest left, Rederrick went in search of Cade. Swinging around the corner to head upstairs, he nearly ran over him, as he was bounding down the wide staircase a little too quickly in search of Rederrick. Quick reflexes on both their parts kept them from colliding. Moving back down a step, he eyed Cade and his change of clothing.

"It looks like you and I need to have a little pow-wow." Rederrick's voice turned to a forceful whisper as he asked, "You want to tell me just what the hell happened tonight?"

"I will, but not here. I don't want her to hear," he whispered, grabbing Rederrick's arm and urging him toward the den.

They walked across the wooden floors and past the large, handcrafted mahogany desk. They passed two comfortable, stylish, brown leather chairs flanking the desk front. The chair behind the desk was also brown leather, an expensive, Italian, suede-back on casters. Two bookshelves that matched the intricate desk sat against the wall to the left side. The shelves were packed full of a variety of law books.

Instead of stopping at the chairs to settle in, they approached the farthest wall. A collection of pictures, ranging in different shapes and sizes, hung in an organized pattern that covered the wall. Rederrick moved aside a picture of himself holding up a large fish. He pressed his thumb to the small panel behind the picture. An audible click sounded as the wall gave the slightest bit. He pushed the hidden door, and they both entered the "Extra Room," as Rederrick called it. Cade, quickly pulling the vaulted door shut behind them, followed Rederrick.

Rederrick spared no expense in this hidden security room. All the latest technology was in here. He'd even added a few things that were not available to the general public.

The room sported a masculine, industrial look. This was a stark contrast to the traditional warmth displayed in the rest of the home. Rederrick sat down in one of four comfortable, chrome and black, office chairs surrounding a glass and steel conference table set in the middle of the large room.

The floor was a stamped concrete, holding the original gray tone with a brushed pattern. Security footage played out on a few of the screens mounted on the wall to his right with a long table underneath to hold the controls for the cameras and alarms. It also provided more workspace, as was evident by the documents lying atop it.

To his left sat a bank of four computers and some other gadgets Cade didn't understand how to use. He often teased Rederrick, saying this room was mission control. Rederrick had always been fascinated by almost any electronic gadget. His son, James, shared his love of electronics and had personally engineered a good portion of the things in this room. The twenty-two-year-old genius was currently working out at Fort Carson doing only heaven-knows-what for Uncle Sam.

Cade walked around the table, not ready to sit. He was still too unsettled. "How is James these days?" he asked as he passed by some sort of scanner the size of a cell phone linked to one of the laptops.

"He's fine. Now, let's cut the crap, shall we? Why don't you tell me just what we're dealing with here? Then we'll figure out what to do next."

"I was working up to it, but fine. You want to know what happened tonight? I'll tell you, but I am positive you aren't going to like it." Cade's temper was right on the surface still. The encounter had left him feeling edgy.

He paced about the room feeling his anger coming back again. Events such as the one tonight always stirred him up. However, for some unexplained reason, tonight's events felt worse somehow.

Rederrick waited. Cade knew Rederrick would give him time to sort out his thoughts. He struggled to pull back his anger. He worked to rein it in and to gain perspective on the events from earlier. He knew Rederrick was impatient to hear what happened. He was also sure Rederrick knew he couldn't push him to outline it yet. Cade's temper could be a fragile thing sometimes— it was the nature of the beast.

"It was a demon; a nasty-smelling one too. Although I am pretty sure I have never, in all my years, found one that didn't stink to high hell. The gray-skinned leech that came after her said something about a bounty," he finally ground out, running his fingers through his hair in frustration.

Turning, he looked over at Rederrick. Taking a deep breath, he plopped down in the chair across from Rederrick. Then he meticulously reported the night's events.

Rederrick sat quietly and listened, absorbing the information stoically. He waited until Cade had finished. Then, leaning back on his chair, he laced his fingers together and laid them on top of his head.

"Well now, I am not sure I was expecting this. I was thinking more along the lines of an abusive husband. . . something simple. I guess I sensed differently, though. Like I said before, something here is not right."

"My money's on the Faction. Who else would put a bounty on a woman with a powerful aura like hers? It follows their usual M.O. You have no idea what she can do?" Cade asked as he stood, feeling restless once more.

"Nope, not a clue," answered Rederrick. He sat forward again, turning his chair to look at his gadgets, "Let's look at the security footage to see if we can catch a glimpse of this demon and get a name for him. Maybe we can make a connection."

"Alright, let's get to it then," he replied impatiently. The men headed over to the side of the room with the large flat screens for briefings and some smaller ones for the security cameras' feedback and went to work.

That is how Cynda found them in the Extra Room an hour later. Cade stood behind Rederrick, who was busily tapping at the keys. Cade leaned in toward the computer to get a better look at whatever Rederrick was zooming in on.

She stood there for a moment, watching two of the most important men in her life. She loved them both. Cade was so much like a brother to her. It seemed he'd unfailingly and forever been there for her and Rederrick. She smiled, Rederrick was everything that made her whole.

These wonderful men always wanted to do the right thing, no matter the cost. It worried her sometimes that they took on so much. This time, though, she knew Collett needed them. Her instincts told her it was very important. This could change lives. She somehow knew this.

Much like when Cade showed up for her all those years ago, changing her life. Cynda knew he would step up again for someone like Collett, regardless of the price to be paid. She could only hope that price wouldn't be too high.

In her heart, Cynda sometimes wondered if the day would come, in her lifetime, when someone would step up for him, regardless of the cost.

She pushed back her emotions and spoke lightly, "What do we have here? Two handsome, strong men putting their brains to good use? Will wonders ever cease?" She went over and placed a light kiss on Rederrick's cheek, "What are we staring at?"

He responded with a quiet, frustrated, "Nothing," then pulled her down into his lap, wrapping his arms around her in a warm embrace.

Cade stepped back to give them some room to hold each other. He watched as his friend closed his eyes to savor the feel of his wife, the woman he loved dearly. He seemed to garner strength from her very presence. He waited patiently for the moment to pass, keeping to himself.

After a few moments, the two of them filled her in on all they had discussed, retracing things in hope that they may think of something they might have missed. She waited and listened; much the same as Rederrick did before. When they finished, she compared it with what Collett had told her.

"She tells a completely different story. The way she tells it makes it sound as if it was just a random criminal out for some fun."

She paused, and Cade could tell she was thinking it over, "So you think she knew it was coming for her?" Cynda inquired of him.

He folded his muscled arms over his chest. Tucking his hands under his armpits he said, "That's what I think. The look she had on her face at the party told me she sensed it. Maybe she is a witch, unaware of her power? She definitely knows more than she is telling."

"I don't know. She could be. I'm not sure what she's capable of. Her aura is so strong and powerful. Why would they try to kill her though? Generally, they would try to harness the kind of power she has. If she is unaware of her capabilities, she could be more easily swayed, I would think."

"If she is unaware," Rederrick stated. They all took a moment to weigh his statement.

"No. I don't think she knows. As far as she was concerned, she was going to die. I saw it in her eyes. She was ready to die," Cade explained.

"If she knew she wielded some magical power, why not use it?" Cynda added.

"When she did fight back it was physically, and she fought hard," Cade continued. His brows pinched together as he thought about it, "In fact, I saw her slam her elbow back and hit the demon hard. She didn't even notice the light that she made with the contact.

"Whatever she did, hurt him. He cried out, and there was this strange burn on his stomach. Oblivious to it, she just grabbed her arm and ran. If she is aware of her power, whatever it may be, she could have probably hurt him worse than that. For that matter, she could have possibly hurt me as well. Werewolf blood aside magic stings, so whatever she is we better figure it out."

He let his comments sit for a minute. As he started to continue, Rederrick beat him to it, asking the very same question that was plaguing Cade, "Do we tell her and help her find her power? Or do we wait and find out what they want?"

Cynda answered, "I think we have to gauge how she'll deal with this little twist. She seems unready to me. This kind of information is life-changing. We have to be careful it isn't just thrown at her. Ultimately, I think we have to tell her.

"I think we should ease this on her by seeing how she reacts to the possibilities first." Her eyes lit up, "Maybe I'll take her out tomorrow for fun, and we'll stop by Selena's store."

Rederrick grinned, once again following his wife's thoughts, "Well now sweetheart, I think that is a fine idea. Cade?"

"I'm not sure I follow you. You want to involve Selena?" He asked skeptically.

"The only thing you need to follow is them," Rederrick stated. "Make sure you keep them both safe from any other witless bounty hunters dumb enough to come after them tomorrow. Cynda, plan the route you'll take. Cade and I will arrange for some precautions. You can go around lunch time."

"I appreciate all the protection, but I would like you to remember I am perfectly capable of taking care of myself," Cynda said standing up and giving Rederrick a stern stare.

"While I am fully aware of your abilities, I'll feel better knowing you have a bit of backup. You may be a great witch, but you're still my wife. It will give me peace of mind," he shot back. Softening his voice he said, "Just backup, that's all."

"Fine, I will have the list of stores I'll be taking her to in the morning. That is, after we talk her into it," Cynda said slyly. "Now, it has been a long day and is now past the witching hour. I'm going to try to get a bit of sleep. Cade, I put Collett in the room across from yours. I figured you'll hear trouble quicker than the rest of us."

"Well then, since we have nothing on the cameras, and we have a plan for our next step, I'll head up to bed myself," Cade explained. He gave Cynda a quick hug, clapped Rederrick on the shoulder and headed out of the room. Even though frustration still ran through him, he felt better having a plan.

"Do you think he can help her?" Cynda asked quietly, staring at the vacant doorway with worry weighing on her.

Rederrick rose, wrapping his arms around her from behind. He softly kissed her neck. "I hope so. Things have a way of working themselves out. Who are we to question the powers at work? I firmly believe timing is everything. I think Collett coming to us now, and Cade being there tonight, proves that. We're meant to help her, just as Cade helped us all those years ago, he'll help her. He doesn't know how to lose."

He turned and set the perimeter alarms. Grabbing her hand he said, "Now, let's make a few plans and then get some sleep. We have a big day ahead of us."

CHAPTER 5

While Rederrick, Cynda, and Cade had their discussion, Collett drifted in and out of sleep in the soothing bath, soaking in the hot water until it chilled significantly. She still felt the evil taint clinging to her body, and when she closed her eyes she could see gold, glowing eyes staring back at her.

Finally, she forced herself to shake off the frightening images and pushed herself out of the bathtub. She stepped out onto the bathmat and wrapped a large, blue body towel around her as she went over to the vanity mirror to do damage control.

The reflection staring back didn't bother or surprise her. The grayish discoloration under her eyes looked like light bruises. A gash below her temple looked clean and scabbed over. The scrapes and cuts on her feet all looked superficial now that they were clean. There was a very large, ugly bruise on her right hip bone that ached. The elbow she'd smacked into her assailants hard flesh still stung. All in all, she wasn't doing too bad for almost dying.

Finished with her assessment, she lifted the ointment and opened it. It must be a homemade herbal cream, she thought as she examined it. It was labeled plainly with feminine handwriting:

healing ointment. She took a curious sniff. It smelled of ash and honey. She rubbed it carefully over her injuries. She put a small bandage on her temple to keep it from opening. When finished, she methodically put it all away in the cabinet.

She opened the door, heading quickly through the master bedroom toward the expansive hallway. She felt the air chill her damp and exposed skin as she made her way toward the bedroom she'd been assigned.

She made it halfway down the hall when she saw him. He stood at the top of the stairs looking right at her; staring was a more accurate term, actually. She stopped, returning his gaze for a moment, stunned to see that he was still here. She was under the impression that all the guests had left. Then, she noticed he had changed out of the suit he'd been wearing earlier.

Will my luck never change? She thought. He must be Cade. She remembered Cynda saying something about Cade's plans or something along those lines. Well, she could avoid him for one night. She headed toward her room, but he stopped her.

Moving forward a step, he cleared his throat, "Sorry, I didn't mean to stare."

He didn't look the least bit apologetic. He also didn't take his eyes off her. She could have sworn he even took a deep breath through his nose, as if he was trying to smell her.

"No problem," she mumbled. Then, once again attempting to evade him, she nervously took another step toward the safety of her room.

Not ready for her to leave yet, Cade spoke again, this time moving even closer to her, "You must be Collett. I heard you had a bit of a scare tonight. Are you alright?" His voice was full of genuine concern.

He saw the bandaged cut on her head and wondered how bad it really was. He regretted that he hadn't been able to prevent the injury in the first place.

"I'm fine, just a bit tired. Goodnight," she said quickly, trying to escape his intense gaze. She almost made it to the door this time.

"I'm Cade, by the way. I'm an old friend of Rederrick's."

He noticed her shoulders slump, as if she really didn't want to talk to him. However, her manners wouldn't allow her to be rude. She turned around and put a smile on her face, "It's nice to meet you, Cade. I'm just going to stay for tonight, so we probably won't see too much of each other. Now, I am sorry, but if you don't mind, I'm very tired, so I'm going to wish you a good night."

"Oh, of course. I'm sorry. I just wanted to let you know I'm across the hall if you need anything." He hesitated, "Are you sure you're alright? From what I heard you had quite a night." He stepped just a bit closer and boldly put his hand on her bare shoulder.

She expected the sudden onslaught of his emotions. Nothing came. It was strange. She couldn't get one good, solid emotion from him. She couldn't sense any evil, but she didn't feel any major impressions of any kind. It was something to ponder later. She was too tired to dwell on it now.

"You have no idea," she mumbled under her breath as she eased away from his touch, backing through the bedroom doorway to escape.

Of course he heard every word. He couldn't completely conceal his smile. He replied easily, "Okay. If you change your mind, let me know. My door is that one there." He pointed to the door straight across the hall as he spoke.

"Well, thank you, but I'm sure I'll be fine," she said in a clipped tone, concluding the conversation by escaping into the bedroom and closing the door. Locking it, she leaned against her barrier in relief. She felt strange around him, off center. She could still feel the intensity of his gaze.

She quickly brushed aside her discomfort, moving her gaze across the dimly lit room. It was painted a soft blue tone with dark blue and cream accents.

The furniture was made up of several beautiful antiques put lovingly together. They all held the same dark walnut tone, to keep the mix subtle and elegant. A small lamp with a frosted glass shade glowed. It sat on a homemade doily atop the bedside table. The small lamp gave the room a soft evening glow that was perfect for curling in bed with a good book.

She spotted the queen-sized bed in the room's center. It's fluffy, cream-colored down comforter held little navy flowers stitched in a balanced pattern. She just wanted to crawl into it, snuggle underneath the warm comfort of the blankets, and hide away from the world. She wished she could sleep for a whole day. As it was, she didn't even bother to get into the night clothes sitting on the charming little bench at the end of the bed. Instead, she crawled underneath the plush comforter and between the cool sheets. Forgetting she only wore a towel, she fell asleep right away.

She could see the golden, glowing eyes intently staring right at her, as if they could see deep into her soul. She watched them as they filled with anger, hate. They turned from the beautiful amber gold to an eerie, bloody red. They smoldered like the embers of a glowing fire, burning right through her.

The dream changed, and shifted. She could suddenly feel the burn of the fire on her skin. It became so hot, sweat clung to her. She stood, confused, in the middle of the inferno. I know this place, *she thought.*

Then she heard it... the sound of a child. He was crying, coughing and sputtering angrily. She ran to help him, running down an endless hallway. Her skin burned, and she could smell the acrid smoke as it stung her eyes.

"Is this real?" she asked herself aloud. Next thing she knew she was at the door of a room. Collett kicked at the door hard. Once, twice, forcing it to give way. Suddenly, she heard a woman's

pained scream coming from the other direction. She turned, listening for the woman. Instead, she heard a coughing fit come from the room in front of her. Confused, she whipped her head back, looking through the doorway she'd created. It led into a small room.

There he was–a young, frightened boy with dark, shaggy hair and large eyes. The woman's screaming was now forgotten. She focused on this young boy before her. He was coughing so hard she was certain he was getting no oxygen.

She pulled him up, dragging him along. She had to get him away from the smoke and fire. She turned, attempting to exit the way she had come. With absolute horror, she found the door had disappeared. No matter where she looked, she could not find her way out. The window that should have been there was missing too.

"You can't save him," she heard the deep, familiar voice echo through her mind. It laughed with a malice-filled chuckle.

This is all so wrong, *she thought.* No. This is wrong, *she insisted to herself. She knew this was not how it happened. She did save him.* I saved him, I got him out!

The nightmare consumed her. The boy didn't cry. He didn't beg her to save his life. His body jerked with his deep, wracking coughs. In between coughs, he spoke. She couldn't make out his words. It was as if every time he spoke someone hit the mute button and his young eyes turned angry.

She turned away from him, knowing they must get out. He wasn't supposed to die! She had to save him. She knew this was important. He didn't cry and plead. He just tried to pull away defiantly; and kept trying to talk to her through his coughs. Anger filled his eyes. She didn't know what to do. There was no way out! They were trapped. The smoke poured in from all directions.

She swung him up into her arms and turned, looking, searching, hoping for a way out. Her charge felt incredibly frail as she held him.

The acrid smoke infused her lungs, and she started having wracking fits of coughing. In between her coughs, she noticed he wasn't coughing anymore. He suddenly went limp in her arms. His body's weight was now heavy in her arms. "Nooo!" she wailed. This is not how it happened. He was not meant to die! She kicked at the wall hard. Kicking and kicking over and over again. The young boy's limp body strained the muscles in her arms.

She felt so weak and powerless. Wait, *she thought,* how could I be powerless? *She could not let him die. She would not let him die. She kicked the wall again as hard as she could, digging deep within herself to find the necessary strength. "I saved him!" she screamed as tears ran down her cheeks. "I saved him!" she repeated.*

She knew it was too late. The child in her arms no longer drew breath.

She heard a loud knock on the wall, then a shout for her name. Everything became cloudy. The child in her arms disappeared, and she screamed out her defiance again, "This was not how it happened!" She fell to her knees crying as the dream began to fade away.

She wanted so badly to cling to what was happening here. This wasn't real. She knew that now. Still, she wanted more than anything to put it right. This isn't the way it happened. Collett heard the heavy thump again as the clarity of her nightmare began to fade. "You can't save them," she heard again. She knew that voice! Why did hearing that voice make her so angry?

A loud bang on the bedroom door made her jolt upright in her bed and pulled her violently from her dream.

"Collett!" she heard a deep voice boom. "If you don't answer me in the next five seconds, I'm ripping this door down!" With a pounding heart, she struggled hard to hold onto the fast-fading dream. She tried to clear her head enough to answer whoever was on the other side of the door. Her mind was too fuzzy. She was panting and sweaty; her skin still felt warm from the flames that had licked at her skin so realistically. She still felt the moisture that gathered in her eyes keenly and the horrid grief in her heart for failing the little boy. . . even if he wasn't real.

All the fog and emotion prevented her from regaining her focus in time. True to his word, she heard a thump and then the sound of wood splitting as the door ¯ broke free of its frame. It sent bits of wood from the trim scattering across the floor. She barely had enough time to grab the sheet to pull it up over her chest as Cade stormed in.

He stood in her doorway, taking up almost the entire space of the door frame with his half-naked body. His eyes scanned the room quickly then stopped as they landed on her. He was wearing faded jeans that were still unbuttoned and a layer of shaving cream on most of his face. It looked as though he recently got out of the shower. He had a white hand towel slung over his shoulder that stood out in contrast to his tanned skin. His jet-black hair hung damp, finger-combed away from his eyes. She sat there shocked for a moment. She was surprised, not only by his sudden entrance, but at his appearance and the intensity of his gaze upon her.

Cade had been too worried they might have another bounty hunter in the house to think. When she yelled something like, "Let me save him!" he stopped thinking entirely about barging in on her, and started thinking about what he was going to get to kill this morning. Then, giving her one last clipped warning, he had broken through the flimsy lock that held him at bay.

There he found her, sitting upright in the large bed, clinging to the sheet that covered her. "Just what do you think you are doing?" she shrieked at him.

As he processed her appearance, Cade quickly realized that she was covered by nothing more than one thin, navy-blue, cotton sheet. Her hair was mussed from sleep. Her soft, ivory skin looked flushed and pink. Clear blue eyes stared back toward him, wide with shock. Collett sat there looking so beautiful; and so angry. It was hard for him to think.

She looked at him expectantly, waiting for an answer to her question. He noticed her cheeks were tinged pink and couldn't help wondering if it was from embarrassment or anger? Either way, he liked it. He couldn't even remember what she had asked him. Hell, he was having a hard time thinking, period. "Um, I. . . I um," he stammered.

"Well?"

He finally gathered his wits together and answered simply, "I heard you screaming."

"Do you always break down doors when you hear a little scream? Maybe I just saw a spider or something," she replied curtly.

Enjoying this more than a little now, he gave her a cocky smile. He leaned against the ruined door frame, stating soberly, "Then I guess I would have killed it for you. And the answer to your other question is, when I feel it's necessary."

"And you really felt this was necessary," she said, gesturing to the broken door.

"It seems I did, doesn't it?"

The man actually had the nerve to smile! How maddening, thought Collett, giving him a hard glare in return. More than a little miffed, she spat back, "Well it wasn't!" Aggressively tugging the tangled top sheet free, she wrapped it around herself fully, swung her legs over the side of the bed and hopped down.

"Now, if you'll excuse me. I need to shower," she snapped. Then she stomped across the cool wood floor and past the dresser against the wall, heading into the adjoining bathroom.

She had just turned around to close the door when she almost collided with a hard, male chest. She jumped back surprised, a little squeak escaping her lips.

There he was, standing right in the door's path. Her surprise was so complete that she reached out and grabbed hold of the door handle to keep from falling down.

She was stunned by his movement. He moved so silently, so quickly. *How was it,* she wondered. She didn't even notice his impossible approach? His movement was so fast he was now standing less than a foot from her.

He stared down at her with those deep, hypnotizing eyes. He had cleaned off any remaining shaving cream, leaving a dark stubble shadow behind. Collett tried hard to stare right back. She tried to be firm. She tried to stand her ground. She failed.

She was lost in those golden orbs of his. If her feet had been on fire at that very moment, she wouldn't have been able to look away. His eyes were different from what she had originally thought, they weren't cool. They were warm. In the morning light, his tawny eyes reminded her of liquid honey.

Then he spoke and broke the spell, "You know you're wrong. It was necessary," he said quietly as he took another step toward her. "If I hadn't broken down the door, I wouldn't have had the pleasure of seeing you so angry. You can trust me when I tell you, it was well worth it."

She felt crowded by his presence. He was so close she could smell the soap from his recent shower. He smelled fresh and crisp, like winter mixed with man. It was a powerful aroma, a familiar scent. It clawed at her memory, trying to grab hold, but she couldn't think straight with him this close.

Cade could see that he was making her nervous, but for some unknown reason he couldn't resist pushing a little more. He took another step toward her and watched her beautiful blue eyes widen even more.

Trying to get more room, she moved to step back, but her hand on the door handle stopped her. For some reason, she could not let go of her grip. It felt as though it was a life raft churning in a stormy sea about to swallow her.

"I think you should leave now," she whispered weakly.

He stared at her, moving his appraising eyes over her body, thinking about what lay underneath the thin wrapping she held up in her clenched fist. "What is it about you?" he asked more to himself than to her.

He stared into the depths of those perfect blue eyes wondering what was going on in his head. He had never felt so confused and out of control. Not since the first ten years after the change had it been this hard for him to gain control of himself.

Collett thought about pushing him back, but realized she would have to drop the sheet covering her to do so. Instead, as forcefully as possible, she restated her comment, attempting a commanding tone this time, "It's time for you to leave." Straightening her spine to gain a bit of height and gathering her courage, she let go of the door handle and took a good step backward.

He shook his errant thoughts from his mind, and he moved back; keeping his smoldering eyes locked with her's as he did.

As soon as he gave her the room she badly craved, Collett rewarded him by slamming the door smartly in his face. He grinned as he heard the snick of the door locking, and decided he had pushed them both enough for one day.

Behind the safety of the bathroom door, she slumped against it for a moment in relief. Finally dropping the sheet, she stomped over and yanked the shower on. Still seething, she climbed in without checking the temperature. The water scalded her skin. She adjusted the flow until she had it right. Grabbing the shower gel left here for guests, she started scrubbing her body. She was just finishing her legs when she realized her hip wasn't aching anymore. In fact, it didn't hurt at all.

Twisting around to get a good look, she was stunned. It wasn't there; nothing, no mark, no ugly purple bruising, nothing! Not sure what to think, she exited the shower and went to the large mirror above the vanity.

She quickly scanned the rest of her body, shocked to find the scrapes on her feet missing also. Frantic, she yanked the bandage from her head. She found the deep gash on her temple was now a small red welt, much like that of a small cut almost healed. There was no nasty scabbing anywhere or greenish-yellow discoloration.

She wondered how it could be possible. Panic began to set in. How could she explain this?

Standing there in front of the mirror, dripping wet and cold, Collett tried to think back to any other time she had been hurt. Searching her scattered thoughts, she reached for something; anything. A scrape, a bruise, a headache. . .

A headache, she suddenly remembered she had a headache once, and it had been a painful, excruciating headache. How could she have repressed that memory? Her head had throbbed as if a hammer tried to split her skull in two with every painful thump of her heart. She recalled feeling that horrible and unbearable pain upon waking on a coastline with no memory, no past. She hurt then, alright. Hadn't her skull felt as though it had been cleaved in half?

Thinking it over further, she could not remember any other wounds on her body that day. Nor could she recall having physical pain of any kind since that time. Until last night…

That just couldn't be, could it? She reassured herself, knowing it was impossible. Two years. Two years without pain; without so much as a bump on the head or a scraped knee?

The knock on the bathroom door startled her, causing her to smack her elbow against the shower door. Murmuring under her breath, she heard Cynda's soft voice.

"Collett, it's Cynda. Are you alright?"

"Um… yeah. I'm fine, just getting cleaned up some. I'll be down soon," she responded.

"I brought up some clothes for you. Cade mentioned you were up and about already. I guess I'll leave them out here on the bench. I hope they fit." Cynda waited for a moment before going on, "We'll have someone fix this door. Cade told us what happened. Are you sure you're alright?"

On the other side of the door, she looked in the mirror at her unmarred body and answered, "Yeah, a bit of a bad dream is all. I'm fine. I'm feeling a lot better. Really, it's amazing." *Just flipping amazing*, a discouraged Collett said again to herself.

Cynda hedged, "Alright we'll see you downstairs for breakfast. Jenny said it should be ready in half an hour or so. That is, if you feel up to it."

"Okay, I'll be down. I promise. I'm really hungry too. Don't worry." As she spoke through the door, she told herself again, *I'm fine, just fine.*

CHAPTER 6

Cynda sat at the small table in the kitchen feeling the warmth of the morning sun leaking in through the large bay window. They decided to have breakfast here today instead of in the oversized dining room. She and Rederrick generally ate their meals in the kitchen, unless they had guests.

To her, this room was the center of her home. Her children had grown up eating at this table every morning before school. They used to prattle on about their teachers and friends here each morning as they got ready for their day. She remembered giving them cookies, milk, and helping them through their daily frustrations as they grew. These days, she and Rederrick sat in this room often, simply enjoying each other's company.

For Cynda, a quiet Sunday morning breakfast here with her family was always welcome. This Sunday, though, she sat in one of her favorite rooms with her husband, Cade, and Collett, thinking about how very worried she was.

She looked across the table where Collett sat eating her second helping of Jenny's homemade blueberry waffles. *At least she has a healthy appetite,* Cynda mused, sipping her orange juice. She noticed a stark white bandage taped to Collett's temple. Collett had refused any medication for the pain both last night and this morning. However, she looked pretty good considering what she'd been through the previous evening.

Collett wore a light pink cashmere turtleneck and a pair of dark grey slacks, all of which came from Cynda's own wardrobe. Cynda gave her a turtleneck thinking she would want to cover any bruising left from last night's attack. Her hair was pulled back into a long ponytail with some bangs swept over to the left; a very flattering look for her. Cynda had also loaned her some shoes, knowing from their shopping trip last Thursday that they had the same size feet. With her color back, it all made her look angelic in the morning sunlight.

No matter how lovely her outer appearance though, Cynda knew things still weren't right. Collett was still incredibly shaken. She just wished Collett would tell them what was really going on.

She examined the indigo tint of insecurity, mixed with the red of anger, in Collett's colorful aura. The colors wavered back and forth, seeking dominance over each other. She had breaks, holes and spots of blackness as well. She could tell Collett was feeling very imbalanced. The usual bright glow she emitted was subdued this morning.

Cynda had been hoping for a better moment, but it looked as though there wasn't going to be one. Not seeing a way to ease into this, she just decided to dive right in, "Collett, I was thinking I could take you to the police station today to file a report."

Collett looked up abruptly with wide expressive eyes, "Well, I'm sure I can handle it. There is really no need for you to come with me."

"No, I insist. You were attacked here on my property. The least I can do is go with you and be supportive. Besides, they might need to talk to me, too. This way I'll save them a trip out here. You know how overworked the police are. I'm happy to help," Cynda ended with a sweet smile.

Tentatively, she replied, "I suppose that's true. But really, there's no need to trouble over it. I'm fine today. It was probably just some drunk." Then she looked to Rederrick for support.

She realized her luck had not improved when Rederrick replied, "No, I have to agree with Cynda. They will probably need to talk to one of us, might as well make it easier on our boys in blue. Anyway, then Cynda can take you out to lunch to make up for last night."

She began to feel trapped. She had to get back to her apartment and plan her next move. How could she get out of this now? Besides, she truly didn't want to file a police report on a false man. Okay, somewhat false—there was something out there. Plus, she couldn't have them taking pictures of wounds that didn't exist.

As she swallowed the last bite of her delicious waffle, she came up with an idea. Infusing her voice with a slightly weak tone, Collett said, "You know I am still a bit run down from last night. Maybe I would be better off skipping all this and going home for some sleep."

"Oh my, how inconsiderate of me," Cynda said. Then she looked to Rederrick slyly, "Maybe we should take her to the hospital after all. I couldn't live with myself if you had some lasting injury we couldn't see."

Crud, that backfired, she thought. "No, I'm fine, really. I just need some extra rest that's all. Truthfully, I'm not up to going to the police. I just couldn't deal with it all right now," she insisted and then rushed on, "Besides what would I tell them? I didn't even see the man, and my injuries came from my own bad driving."

Rederrick felt satisfied. This was going just the way they hoped. They could avoid any police involvement and make it Collett's idea. So, he hedged on with a placating tone, "We don't want to make you do anything you're uncomfortable with, Collett. I'm sure we can figure this all out."

"I think I just need a bit more rest. Then I'll be fine. I promise," she replied softly.

"Cynda?" Rederrick asked politely, "don't you need to run a few errands in town? Perhaps you could take her home along the way. That way, you won't need to bother making two trips."

"You know honey, you're right. That would work out great. Plus, then we can stop for lunch as you suggested. She can rest upstairs for an hour or so until I can go. Some of the stores I need to go to don't open until ten."

Feeling caught up again in Cynda's manipulations, Collett honestly couldn't see an alternative. She tried hard to think of one.

Again, in her soft, weak tone, she suggested, "Maybe I should just call a cab out here. Then you wouldn't have to go to any trouble, and I could get home to rest."

Cade had sat back quietly during the entire exchange, but now saw his chance. With a grin on his face and a sparkle in his eyes he said, "Now, that's unacceptable. If you're not feeling up to a little trip into town, then I would be happy to take you home. It would be my pleasure."

She gave him a sharp, annoyed look. He had done it again. Cade managed to frustrate her with a few short comments. It was as if he couldn't resist taunting her.

His pleasure, she thought. *Yeah, I bet. Not a chance.* She wasn't sure why she found him so unnerving, but she wasn't about to put herself in a car alone with him to find out. "You know, on second thought," she said sweetly, acting as if she was rethinking her previous offer, "I think you're right. Some fresh air and a girls' lunch might be just what I need." *My pleasure, ha!* she thought again.

He offered a smug grin, making her believe he knew she would react just as she had. His chair scraped across the tile floor as he stood, excusing himself with, "Some other time then." He nodded toward Rederrick, stepped away from the table, and replaced his chair carefully. "Cynda," he nodded as he left the room.

Rederrick also stood, "It's all settled then. As a lawyer, I'm sure I can take care of things with the owner of the car and you can get some rest for now. I'm glad we worked this out. Collett, I'll see you later. If you need tomorrow off, just give me a call." He kissed his wife sweetly on the forehead as he followed Cade out, not even giving Collett time for a response.

She had a bad feeling about this now. Looking over to Cynda's smiling face she wondered, *How do they keep doing this to me?*

Collett went up to the guest room to gather her things together. When she walked through the broken doorway, she noticed the soft color of the room with the bed already beautifully made.

She realized she didn't have any things. She walked over to the bed and lovingly ran her fingers over the smooth, polished wood of the ornate headboard. This room had so much feeling and warmth to it, just like the people in this house.

Her nostalgia started to depress her more, so she decided she would go down and wait outside to get some air. She opted to go down the main staircase into the receiving room so she could head out front to the gardens. As she got to the bottom of the stairs, Cade passed her as he headed into the den. He looked at her as he passed, giving her a quick smile that tilted up slightly a little higher on the right side into a smirk. He then offered a cocky wink.

She stared at him as he went by, holding her breath for just a moment, not wanting to have another verbal exchange right now. She wasn't sure why, but Cade made her edgy. He didn't stop this time, and she let out the air that was burning her lungs with a great huff of relief.

"Charmin' man, that one." The words came from Jenny. Her drawled statement startled Collett.

She looked toward the back of the room at the entrance to the expansive dining room they'd had dinner in the night before. Jenny stood there with a spray cleaner and rag in her hands. She wore long yellow dish gloves.

"I was thinking more along the lines of idiot," She replied.

Jenny smiled and made her way over, "Oh, I don't doubt that. He's a man, isn't he? He's bound to slip up now and again."

Collett let go of a little laugh; a real, honest laugh. "So, how long have you known the idiot?"

"Oh, Mr. Werren has been a part of this family for a real long time now," came Jenny's cryptic reply.

"Is he always so. . .strange and frustrating?" she asked, looking back toward the den.

"Oh yes, he is that. But he also happens to be one of the best men I have ever known. He can stir up a room like a nest of angry snakes, to be sure, and sometimes he can make a sane woman want to pull out her hair."

She knew the feeling.

"But I'll tell you this," she continued, "He can always settle the snakes, and he surely knows how to calm the woman." Her eyes turned sincere and thoughtful as she continued, "But most of all, Cade doesn't have a selfish bone in his body. Plus he looks pretty good too. Yep, he's a charmin' one alright." With that, Jenny made her way to the stairs and headed up, leaving Collett with her thoughts.

She felt a bit of guilt now for her original reaction to him. If everyone here loves him, then he couldn't be all that bad. Why did she feel so out of sorts around him? Why did she feel like she should stay far away from him? Shaking her head and letting it go, she made her way outside into the crisp morning air, to let go of all her troubled thoughts. Besides, she would probably never see him again.

It took them longer than expected to get organized for the trip into town. Cynda needed to confirm all her plans with Cade and

Rederrick. They went over it twice to make sure they all understood how to keep the women safe.

Cade dragged his feet on this, truthfully not wanting Collett out of his sight even for a minute, even though he still wondered why he felt that way. His sudden need to protect Collett was odd to him. Instinctively, he knew this was a bad idea. In his opinion, this left both women way too open. Reluctantly, he finally agreed that he would follow them as they journeyed into town.

Then he would discreetly keep an eye on them throughout their trip. All three of them agreed on signals if there was any trouble. They found safe spots that would be defendable. It was a great deal of work. Rederrick insisted on it, however, saying, "It pays to be prepared," and no one could disagree. They had all learned that lesson the hard way over time, and none were willing to forget it.

So now it was just after eleven o'clock, and Cynda sat in the car with a silent Collett heading down a two-lane road going forty miles an hour toward the city, rather than using the much quicker interstate. They had all agreed it was safer this way, more controllable. Fewer cars traveled this road, and they did it at much lower speeds.

Brad Paisley lent them background noise, his voice crooning through the radio. Looking out at the world with fierce concentration, Collett sat in the passenger seat of the black Yukon Rederrick had insisted they take. Cynda wondered what thoughts were going through her mind and how she could ease some of the weight pulling Collett down. She looked so defeated. Cynda knew she was losing hope. She had seen that look before. Heaven knows; she had worn that look before. Collett was retreating within.

Cynda decided she needed to break the silence, and distract Collett from her weighted thoughts. She decided to start small, "Did you get enough sleep? I mean with having that dream and all?"

"Um, yeah, I think I did. The bedroom you set me up in was very comfortable," she answered tentatively.

"My daughter, Tracy, loves antiques. She's the one who put that room together. She has a real skill for it. As far back as I can remember she has loved the history of things; and the feelings she gets from old furniture. She always says it is important to have a connection to the past."

"I'll bet she got that from you. Your whole house feels as though there is this warm, loving history behind it."

Cynda smiled at the observation. "Well, I've never thought of it that way. You see, to me, it has just been home. I think you're right, though. Now that you say it, I see it. It does hold a lot of warm, fond memories for me. I guess that's what defines home, really: a warm place full of fun and happy memories, trials, and triumphs."

Collett felt a deep, aching sadness within her. The emptiness felt like a hole, trying its best to suck her in. At the very same time, she felt happiness for Cynda. Despite her own sad loneliness, Collett felt grateful to have this rare moment with someone she saw as a friend. She wanted happiness for Cynda, for all of them. Yet another reason she would have to leave.

She wanted Cynda to know what she meant to her. Cynda had given her a gift better than money could ever buy. She and Rederrick were more than employers these past months; they became friends. She decided right then she would never get another chance to tell her, so she tried to put together some words in her head that wouldn't give too much away.

"Cynda, I may forget to tell you later so I thought I would tell you now. I really am grateful to Rederrick and you for all you have done."

Cynda noticed Collett's nervousness and tried to ease it, "Oh it was no big deal. Honestly, I would have never thought to turn you away last night. I felt somewhat responsible."

Collett hedged on, "I know you would have never turned me away, and I know you don't really blame yourself. You're just a good person. You're always willing to help. It is a part of your nature."

Letting out a heavy breath, Collett decided to be more direct, "Let me be clearer now. I am not just thanking you for last night. I am thanking you for every day. You have always been so kind and giving to me. To everybody you meet, really. I see how you love people. It's just a part of you. So I'll tell you again, thank you. Thank you for being who you are, and giving me a part of it."

Cynda felt the emotion in her throat choke her. She could not let this woman out of their lives. She was a part of them now. So she decided to push a little harder, "Collett are you alright, really? You just don't seem yourself."

Pulling away from the serious conversation, Collett forced a big smile on her face then answered, "Oh don't worry so much. I really am fine. I feel much better this morning. Thanks to your wonderful bathtub and some great ointment, I don't even ache much."

"I am glad to hear it. I just want you to know... Well, I'm here if you ever need to talk. I had three kids you know, and can make a good sounding board. Even better, a shoulder to lean on. I make a great shoulder."

This time her smile was sincere. "I believe you would make a good shoulder, truly I do." Her smile fell some as she finished the last part.

"Tell me then, what is troubling you? Maybe I can help. Please? Let me try." Cynda took a quick glance toward this woman she had come to care for, hoping she would confide in her.

A small tear started to make its way slowly down Collett's cheek. She quickly stopped it, swiping at it with the back of her hand. Bending and pretending to check her shoe–she muttered, "There is nothing you can do." Then she added barely above a whisper, "Nothing anyone can do." The words were said with such finality, such hopelessness.

The words struck Cynda hard right in her chest. Cynda's breastbone hurt from the grief she felt for Collett. They all suspected Collett would run, but now she knew it. If they couldn't find a way to help her, she might get herself killed.

Cynda snuck another quick look in her direction. She noticed her bandage had fallen away when Collett bent down to hide her tears. It took her just a minute to decipher what was wrong with the picture before her, only a moment for it to slam into her brain.

When the light clicked on in her mind she was so dumbstruck she lost all concentration on the road. The long, angry slash that marred her skin the night before was now only a small, pinkish scar of a healed-over wound. Her skin wasn't even puckered, and Cynda couldn't think past the sight of it.

"**Cynda!**" Collett shouted when she saw they were fast heading off the road.

Cynda hurried and gained a small measure of control by slamming hard on the brakes and tightening her grip on the wheel. She slammed down with enough force that both women were thrown forward with bruising force against their seat restraints, as the screeching brakes halted the vehicle's momentum.

Fortunately, this was not a well-used road, and there was no oncoming traffic speeding toward them. They now sat in the left lane, right in the path of any opposing traffic.

Collett looked over at Cynda with shock. Then she noticed in what direction Cynda's gaze was focused. Quickly, she reached up feeling her head. She became aware of the bandage hanging by one small piece of medical tape, exposing her secret to Cynda.

Frustrated by Cynda's reaction, she tore the last piece of tape away, pulling the bandage free.

As Collett kept her gaze straight ahead, trying to avoid Cynda's eyes, she noticed a moving vehicle further down the road. "Cynda maybe you should move the car. There is a truck headed our direction," she coolly pronounced.

Cynda became acutely aware in that moment. She realized she'd upset Collett with her sudden reaction to what she'd seen. She calmly let her foot off the brake, moving the SUV to the proper side of the road. She pulled the Yukon over to the shoulder, and as she did, the old orange truck passed by on the opposite side.

She knew Cade hid close by, near the river, watching. The trees offered him cover so Collett would not see him. He would be worrying about what was going on. What made her stop, but Cynda needed to clear this up with Collett right away. She trusted Cade not to move too soon. He had keen eyes; he could see she wasn't in danger… so she hoped.

Collett folded her hands and set them in her lap waiting for Cynda to speak. She couldn't explain it, because she didn't even understand herself.

Sitting there, she stared out in the distance gazing at an opening in between the large, ageless trees; not even realizing Cade was hidden among them. She felt some measure of calm by watching the quick rushing flow of the river. Collett saw there was an unpaved road that ran lower than, but parallel to, the same road that she and Cynda currently sat still and quiet on.

The sloped ground between the roads held the yellow-brown look of late fall and early winter. There were trees all over, sprouting up from each other's roots, living timelessly bound together. Every now and then, she spotted a break between the trees where picnic benches or tables sat. Families would stop there she thought. They would have lunch and simply enjoy the gifts of nature's beauty and family all at once.

Collett wished she could stay to see the new life that spring would bring to this place. The trees would provide shade to those gathering at the picnic areas. As evening fell, the shadows would inevitably lengthen. Then, as they had many times before, they would stretch to cover the unpaved road. The soft, blossom-perfumed breeze would blow, making the trees dance to a slow rhythm. She knew the cottonwood trees would drop so much cotton it would cover the earth like snow.

She knew these things. She could picture them. She could see the radiant colors that would come after the cold winter passed; smell the blossom's fragrance in the air.

And yet, she could not remember why someone wanted her dead. She couldn't remember how her body avoided serious injury when a two-door Cavalier rolled with her in it. She couldn't even remember her real name.

She risked a small, hesitant glance in Cynda's direction, not being able to handle the eerie silence any longer. She wasn't sure what to expect, but it wasn't what she saw. Cynda sat there, staring at her steering wheel, with a small smile and a thoughtful look, shaking her head slightly.

Feeling Collett's attention on her, Cynda turned to face her. She smiled, letting out a small laugh, "I'm not sure what I thought your secret was, but it wasn't this."

Collett was stunned, confused. Cynda didn't look horrified; only accepting. Collett wondered, if she would always be so accepting if she told her everything?

"Look Cynda, I don't. . ."

The words died in her throat as her body shivered and jerked; as feelings poured over her: anger and violent destruction, excitement-filled challenge. Collett could feel it closing in. They were coming back for her already.

CHAPTER 7

"Cynda, turn around and drive. Now! Move! We have to move!" Collett shouted.

Cynda didn't question her. In fact, she was already in the process of turning. From Cade's recounting of last night, she recognized the fearful pinched look Collett's face displayed and knew it was time to go.

Just then, they both heard a loud screech of tires, followed immediately by the horrific sound of breaking glass and crunching metal. They both knew that whatever caused the noise, at the source of it, would be the evil being that Collett sensed.

Cynda rapidly flipped the car into a sharp U-turn, tipping the car slightly, but she quickly regained control. When the car fully faced the opposite direction, she pushed down hard on the gas, gunning the engine. The tires squealed against the pavement in protest before finding purchase.

Once they were speeding forward Cynda yelled, "What is it? What do you feel? I need to know!"

Collett felt so confused she could barely think. Things were happening so fast. She snapped her head around to Cynda and stared at her with an unreadable expression.

Cynda knew there was no time to placate her or explain what she knew, or that she dealt with more than her share of supernatural forces. "Collett!" she snapped, "Tell me! I need to know. What is it?"

Collett stared at the woman, unsure of Cynda's out of character reactions. She answered quietly, "I don't know." Then finding her voice she stated louder, "I don't know! I feel it. I can't see it. I feel a cruel destructiveness. I can't explain more than that."

Cynda hissed out an oath. She knew it could really help their advantage if Collett knew what was after them. *Well, we'll just have to improvise*, thought Cynda as she picked up her cell phone while driving full speed toward home. Pressing the voice activation button, she waited for the prompt then said, "Rederrick," into it. The phone dialed then started ringing.

Before he answered, Cynda spotted the cloud of smoke up ahead and knew the road was probably blocked further along. Rederrick, never failing her, answered on the first ring, "Hey there, sweetie."

"No time! We're on the run. I'm giving the phone to Collett, so I can drive. Get the satellite images. We are on Well Spring Road heading north about 20 miles out." Cynda tossed the phone over to Collett.

Still shocked by this new side of her friend, she fumbled with it for a minute before finally setting it to her ear, "Um, hello Rederrick?"

"The road is blocked by a truck of some kind. Tell Cynda to cross over to River Road at the upcoming bridge!" the clipped reply came back from the other end.

Obeying, she shouted out his directions.

Cynda, trusting her husband and his eye in the sky, immediately swung the Yukon to the right, making the screeching turn without slowing. Then she made a left on the parallel, unpaved road following her husband's direction. Rocks and dirt spit out behind them as she floored the gas once more. As Cynda did this, she felt a frisson in the air around them and recognized the tingling of magic.

"MAGIC!" Cynda shouted, "It's magic!" At the same time she made this announcement, both women felt a hard jerk, and the SUV came to a whip-lashing stop. "Get out of the car!" Cynda ordered.

Stunned, she looked over at Cynda and noticed her mumbling. No, she realized, she was chanting something. It wasn't all clear. Collett was sure some of it wasn't even English. She thought she heard the words, "holding the key" and "let it be seen." Suddenly, a bright light burst forth right in front of them.

When the light cleared, Collett saw him. On the road in front of them, stood a man. She couldn't take her eyes from him. He was frightening to say the least. He was dressed in black jeans and a Goth t-shirt with a large skull in the center. Biker boots and a long dark overcoat, with silver latches aligning it, added to the look. Several different piercings mottled his face and earlobes. His hair was long and black with thick streaks of purple and blue mixed in. He looked so young to her, maybe early twenties at the most, and for some reason she felt a pang in her heart for him.

He stared straight at them, with one arm outstretched, palm straight up, and his fingers opened and tilting forward. Feeling transfixed by the sight before her, Collett could not tear her gaze from him, and he met her stare head on. Except, his eyes were completely devoid of light or color. Black, she thought. His eyes were a deep, soulless black. Then he tilted his lips in a sinister smile, and she felt a shiver run through her.

Fear clawed its way through her. As she sat frozen in her leather seat, she could hear Cynda chanting again. She could also see that the nameless man in front of them was moving his hands in a hypnotic pattern, and she found she couldn't think past it. As if she were like Alice, falling down the rabbit hole, she could only wonder what kind of world she just stepped into.

The odd-looking man suddenly jerked back as if some force pushed him. Tearing her eyes from him, she looked to Cynda, and saw her with her hands straight out, palms facing forward as if she had done the pushing. Questions raced through Collett.

Cynda tried hard to keep her focus. The sorcerer standing outside right before them was trying to throw the Yukon through one of the wider breaks in the tree line and into the icy cold river.

She felt the strength of the sorcerer against her own power. He was strong, too strong, and she was a little unpracticed at battle magic.

The tires made the grating, scooting sound of resistance against the gravel road as they moved at an unnatural angle, and the vehicle vibrated and rattled. She kept trying to focus and attack the sorcerer, to provide even more resistance as the Yukon was forced through the tree line, turning backwards as it went. Before long, a picnic table sat between them and the river, until they were dragged along it as well.

The ear-splitting sound of metal scrapping and bending broke Cynda's concentration. Anyone watching would have cringed and shuddered at the sound, but for the two women inside, there would be no time to think on it. A popping sound echoed as the window shattered. Glass cascaded over them, and the driver's side door bent in unnaturally, pushing against her legs. The car angled and turned as it finished scraping past the ruined table, facing Cynda's side parallel with the river.

Cynda couldn't even spare a glance for Collett. A powerful mental assault slammed against her consciousness. Her nose bled from the cognitive blow and the necessary magic she unleashed to defend against it. She knew that the attacker now held every advantage over her weakened mind, but she refused to relent.

"Get out Collett, Get out!" she ground out between clenched teeth as she concentrated. She heard the rushing water outside the vehicle and knew they were past the last barrier between them and the icy cold fingers of the mountain waters.

There was a thump above them, and the car bounced from the impact. Looking up through the tinted sunroof, they both saw a massive black werewolf in his hybrid form. At the sight of the beast, Cynda felt relief and Collett felt panic. Even though it had been dark the night before, Collett recognized him right away.

He leaped down to the ground effortlessly and reached forward with his huge, muscled arms, the long claws scratching at the metal on the passenger door.

"Oh no, Oh no! He came back!" Collett let the words out in a strangled, panicked cry. She locked the door, as if it would help her somehow, and looked to Cynda for help. All she found was Cynda in some sort of trance. Her eyes were a cloudy white, staring forward at nothing. Meanwhile, the Yukon now sat on the muddy riverbank too close to the edge. Before she could even look away, Cynda let out a cry of pain, and her eyes fluttered closed, losing the battle for consciousness.

The werewolf tore the passenger-side door off violently, and ear-splitting creaks and groaning sounded as the metal bent unnaturally, tearing free of its hinges. Glass from the tempered window cracked and split, then popped before spilling all around the ground.

Terror gripped her; and not only terror for herself, but for Cynda too. Her breathing panicked; she turned and stared at the enemy face-to-face. No more than a foot separated them. She realized his eyes weren't red this time but a glowing gold instead. Her thoughts flickered. She felt his eyes were familiar somehow. *Stop it!* she admonished herself. *Panic is making you crazy.*

Knowing her mind must be playing tricks on her, she reminded herself firmly, *He is only familiar because he almost killed you last night.* For the second time in less than 24 hours, Collett swore she gazed upon death itself.

The monster returned her stare, grabbed a hold of her seat belt, and tugged with unnatural strength to free her from it. He tore the heavily stitched safety belt completely free of the metal buckle, as if it were no more than a thread through a needle. He grabbed a hold of her and yanked her harshly from the vehicle that now sat on the precipice of the riverbank. The ease with which he managed to do this terrified her, but it also inspired her to fight harder to get away.

She refused to be an easy kill. She began fighting for all it was worth. She wriggled and struggled while kicking, biting, and clawing with a savagery she could not remember ever using. She felt her desperation rise as she saw out of the corner of her vision that the Yukon splashed into the water. It now sat in the frigid river making its way in the center of the deep river.

"Nooo!" she shrieked, renewing the fight with all the strength she had.

Cade growled. Collett was stronger than she looked. Her kicks and punches stung, and her struggling made getting her to safety more difficult than it should have been. He needed to get to Cynda, but he was also aware the sorcerer was now directing his attention their way. He couldn't fight three battles at once, and even though it pained him to leave Cynda for now, he felt there was little choice.

Promptly dropping Collett on her butt, rougher than necessary within the trees, he turned around to face what he figured was his biggest problem. He rushed at the sorcerer, taking the focus from the women, hoping his attack would give Cynda time to help herself.

He didn't know, though, that Cynda now lay unconscious in the Yukon.

Stunned, Collett watched as the black werewolf ran toward her other attacker as he had the night before. She didn't understand what was happening, and she couldn't fathom why the massive werewolf left her alive a second time to attack the dark man in the road.

Having no time to figure it out, and not willing to wish away her tiny fraction of good fortune, she dismissed the scene before her and moved on to more important things, Cynda.

Clambering to her feet, she rushed to the SUV wading into the frigid water. The freezing temperature shocked her system, chilling her to the bone, and the current pulled hard at her feet, almost tripping her as she waded frantically toward Cynda.

Planting herself firmly, and leaning in through the opening made from the missing passenger-side door, she reached for her friend.

Cynda looked much too still to Collett. She made no movement even though the rushing water now swirled around her shins. Her face seemed extremely pale, and a trickle of blood dripped from her nose, leaving a crimson trail over her pinkish blue lips. Her worry increased significantly. Reaching for the seat belt release, she tried to depress the button and free the safety belt. It didn't budge.

Desperation gripped her, and she shook Cynda vigorously, yelling her name in an attempt to wake her. Cynda rolled her head to the side and moaned. The small movement, accompanied by sound, gave her a sliver of relief. Her relief was short lived, however, when the river's current shifted the Yukon. It lurched forward, and Collet's grip failed her, throwing her into the frigid water as the vehicle moved further downstream.

Sputtering as she came out of the water, Collett screamed, venting her anger and frustration. In front of her very eyes, someone she cared for was in dire peril. Behind her, she heard the growling and shuffling movement as the fight to kill her escalated.

She should be freezing, but wasn't she realized. She felt heat rising in her body. She refused to be helpless and watch a friend; her only friend, die. *Not like this*, she thought, *not this violent, cold, meaningless death.*

Jumping forward, she reached out latching onto the Yukon frame looking for a strong solid grip. Fighting the current that pulled at her feet, she levered herself into the car. Grabbing Cynda by the arms, Collett shook her again screaming frantically, "Wake up! Please!"

Cynda moaned again, and her long slender fingers moved to her head then dropped. She failed to open her eyes, her body once again going limp. The water was swirling up to Cynda's lap now, soaking through her jeans.

Reaching down to the seat belt connection, Collett pulled with all the strength she had. The lock still wouldn't budge. She looked down at it hard, and then she cursed. "Open! Open!" she repeated at a high-pitched wail. Unwilling to give in, she pulled harder. Closing her eyes and giving it everything she could she tried one more time to loosen the belt. With a loud snapping click, the lock finally gave way. It came loose so abruptly, the momentum from the opposing force smacked her body back against the dash.

Without taking any time to question her fortune, she hastily but firmly wrapped her arms around Cynda and pulled her free over the console, into the passenger seat. Her skin felt so cold. She looked too pale.

She struggled with Cynda's limp body. Losing her adrenaline now, Collett's strength began to wane. She knew they had to get free of the Yukon before the river took it into the deeper center, or it tipped. Awkwardly maneuvering their bodies around, she maneuvered out of the ruined Yukon with Cynda in tow.

Then she saw him heading right at them. He made his way toward them at a powerful run, much faster than she expected. She didn't even have time to think up a plan of attack before he covered the distance between them. Even though she was sure any plan would most definitely fail, she would have liked to try, but his body practically leaped the entire distance in an instant. Then he stood right before them in his massive, terrifying glory.

His breathing hard and his fur soaked and dripping from the run through the river; he moved a step closer, though this time carefully. His open jaw showed sharp and threatening teeth, and his large imposing form towered over her. He stood there a moment and looked at her. It felt as if time stopped the moment his golden eyes met hers again, but it was only mere seconds. Then he broke contact with her and regarded Cynda awkwardly limp in her arms. She became aware that she didn't feel any malice or hate from him, but that did little to reassure Collett. She couldn't feel much of anything from him.

He reached out with long arms and deadly claws grabbing for Cynda. Unwilling to let her friend die in this monster's hands, she wrapped her arms around Cynda with bruising force. Leaning away from him as far as possible, she defiantly refused to give up her friend.

"Let go Collett. I can help," he growled weirdly. Surprised by his use of her name, but still scared, she gripped Cynda even tighter.

"You can't have her! If you want me fine, but you can't have her!" She cried desperately.

The words came out with a firm confidence she didn't feel. And, to her dismay, tears of desperation began sneaking out of her eyes, no matter how hard she tried to stem the flow. She stood there, waist-deep in the middle of the frigid, fast-paced river, struggling to keep her balance. Bravely staring down a monster that could rip off car doors and defeat unnatural men, she knew logically she couldn't stop him. Even knowing that, she refused to give Cynda up to him willingly.

He snarled fiercely. She jumped, shrinking back. Her body began to shiver and shake violently, both because her nerves were now at the end of her endurance, and the cold water seeped through her skin into her bones. Still she clung to Cynda bravely.

Cade pulled back. He didn't want to frighten her any further with his frustrated growling, and truthfully her stubborn bravery impressed him. They were running out of time though. Both women were bound to be close to hypothermia, not counting whatever internal damage Cynda must have suffered because of the sorcerer. He knew he couldn't check that, and wouldn't know how to help her even if he could, but he could help with getting both women out of the cold river to someone who could help. He wished he could've gotten there faster, and prayed he didn't make a fatal mistake in his choices. He would never forgive himself if Cynda didn't make it.

Trying to explain would take too long. Acting quickly, Cade knew there was only one way to convince Collett he would not hurt her, one way to get her to release her tight, protective grip on Cynda's limp form.

Cade commanded his body to change into that of a man.

Clinging to Cynda's limp form, Collett watched in astonished horror and yet fascinated amazement when the monster's body contorted and twisted right in front of her. Cracking and bending until…that monster became a man. Not just any man, a man she knew.

There, standing in the middle of the river's current, was Cade. His now furless, muscled chest heaved with his heavy breathing. He looked up and gazed at her with his worried golden eyes. So many thoughts jumped into her troubled mind at once.

Cade pushed them all back with soft, calm words, "I swear to you, I would never hurt her. I'm here to help. Now let go Collett. Please, let me help."

His eyes were so sincere.

The mystifying events occurring right in front of her made it difficult for her thoughts to assemble together for a reply. It was simply too much. Feeling far too tongue-tied to speak the words, she numbly nodded instead. Releasing her tight, desperate hold, she surrendered Cynda to Cade's care.

He scooped Cynda up with quick, efficient ease and turning, moved swiftly toward the riverbank. She hurried after him, unwilling to lose sight of her charge, and friend.

Charge? she thought. *That's a strange word.*

As they made their way up to the river's edge, Collett struggled to stay upright with every step through the pulling current. Even though she fought for every step as the water level decreased, it was impossible not to notice how lean and muscular Cade's entire body was. As she looked, she saw a strange crescent shaped mark on his suntanned skin, directly on the left shoulder blade.

Her eyes roamed some more, and then, in a moment of bashfulness, she began to comprehend that she was staring at his powerful and exposed body. She quickly turned her head away, but it was too little, too late. She lost her footing and fell into the frigid water face first. Before she could even pull her head out of the water Cade was there wrapping his strong arms around her and cradling her as he made his way to the bank a second time. He set her carefully down on the ground and asked, "Are you alright?" Before she could even answer, a low moan from Cynda rapidly drew their focus back to the urgent nature of the situation, reminding them what was important.

Moving to Cynda, he began checking her over, running his hands quickly, but carefully, over her body looking for wounds. "Her heart is beating strongly enough, but she's too cold," he said with slight fear lacing his voice.

"Go Cade! Take her to Rederrick! You have to get her out of here. Get her the help she needs. You have to go now," Collett insisted in a shaky but determined voice.

Torn between the needs of both women, Cade decided quickly he couldn't leave. He couldn't bring himself to leave her unprotected. It was more than obvious she was in serious danger.

Besides that, he knew if he left she would run. He could see it in her eyes. More than that though, he knew their attacker could not be far away.

He looked up at her with a pained expression, and his deep voice replied, "I can't leave you alone. Rederrick will come," he added hopefully.

Collett scooted over closer to Cynda and knelt beside her. She noticed that Cynda's body didn't even shake or shiver. She looked as if she slept. Her skin had a gray pallor, her lips a soft blue hue. She knew they needed to do something quickly.

She looked to Cade for answers, knowing she could not let Cynda die. Cade returned her gaze with so many emotions flowing in his eyes: fear, concern, anger. So many things came from that one set of beautiful golden eyes that she now knew were so captivating because they retained a wild, animalistic quality. She could see it there now, hidden in the depths of them. Collett could see the animal within.

"Cade please... Go," Collett pleaded softly.

With a sad but sure expression, Cade shook his head and began focusing his attention on helping Cynda.

Bending over Cynda's still and pale form, Collett focused all her attention and energy on Cynda's needs as well. On instinct, she reached up and placed her hands upon Cynda's soft pale cheeks. She closed her eyes, "Cynda you'll be fine. You hear me? Come back. It is not time for you. You have to be fine. Rederrick needs you. We need you. Your heart holds too much warmth to be cold." Her tone turned pleading as she continued, "Please! You have to find the courage to fight. Find the love you have for your family and don't let go. Please don't let go. Fight Cynda."

Cynda's cheeks felt as though they were warming, but it was probably just her desperate imagination.

As Cade rubbed his hands quickly up and down Cynda's arms trying to restore her warmth, he heard Collett's words and the love and desperation in her soft pleas. He felt an odd strength in them. He felt his own hope rise within. *Cynda is going to make it*, he thought. *She'll be fine.*

Collett quickly moved to remove Cynda's soaked clothing, and an idea struck her. One she was afraid to ask, but knew it could very well save Cynda.

"Cade, can you change when you want?"

He narrowed his eyes, his features showing a hurt expression, "This is hardly the time to be sating your curiosity."

She felt annoyed by his snotty tone, but ignored it, "I meant can you change, so you can warm Cynda with your fur coat you dolt."

"Oh. Well yeah, I can do that," he said sheepishly. Then he stood to change.

As Cade stood, Cynda moaned and fluttered open her eyes. She quickly shut them, Cade assumed, when the sun speared into her irises. The sharp light would be painful. He immediately dropped back to his knees upon hearing her soft whimper.

"Collett?" Cynda croaked out quietly.

"I'm here. It's okay. We're both here. Cade is going to get you warm. Right?" she said, directing the last of it to Cade.

He sprang up again. "One fur coat, coming up," he replied, feeling better. Then he made the change to an oversized wolf as quickly as his body could. Choosing this form, instead of a hybrid, to give Collett a small measure of comfort. He knew she must still be uncomfortable with all of it, and the wolf was slightly less intimidating.

Laying his body over Cynda's prone form at an angle and taking his weight to his hind legs so as not to hurt her further, Cade closed his eyes. The feeling of thankful relief rushed through his body. Cynda would be alright. It was truly amazing, a minor miracle. Even through his thick fur, he felt the slight rise of her body temperature. Lending himself as a heat blanket would help Cynda beat the hypothermia.

Cynda began mumbling, "I could hear you Collett. You were so warm. I could hear you in the dark."

Cade noticed Collett didn't seem to hear or understand Cynda's incoherent mumblings. She simply continued to offer her soft words of encouragement while stroking Cynda's wet hair. Collett was shivering, and yet she was unconcerned with her own well-being.

Cade's sensitive ears picked up on every word. He was unsure of what they could mean right now, but he would bet his life savings, which for his long life was substantial, that it did mean something. Cade filed it away for further thought later.

Collett brought Cade from his internal thoughts with her next words of comfort to Cynda, "Shush. It will all be fine. Cade will keep you warm, and I am sure Rederrick is on his way by now," she said, looking into Cade's eyes hopefully. He knew she needed his reassurance that help would come.

He nodded his head with one jerk, giving Collett his answer. He knew Rederrick had trackers on all his vehicles, not to mention Rederrick's access to satellite feedback. Before the SUV even entered the river, he had likely already left to come help.

He looked at her, seeing the tears in her eyes and the concern intertwined with guilt covering her features. He could see she blamed herself, and he understood they were going to have to be clever to convince her to let them help her.

His ears pricked, and he heard a car speeding down River Road heading south toward them. He listened carefully and tipped his head to hear it coming better. He understood after a moment that explanations and blame would have to come later, because Rederrick was only a mile away and driving like a madman to get to them. Right now, they would all focus on one thing: helping Cynda survive.

CHAPTER 8

Having survived a frantic Rederrick at the wheel of a speeding car, then enduring his moody snaps and short concise questions, Collett figured out there was nothing more intimidating than a devoted husband worried about his wife. Not even Cade as a werewolf made her as nervous as Rederrick had. Granted, most of her nervousness came from the guilt.

Cade stayed in his wolf shape, opting to stay with Cynda who lay across the back seat. Cynda had just begun shivering again before Rederrick showed up, which was a good sign. Cade continued to keep her warm with his higher body temperature and soft fur, leaving Collett to answer Rederrick's questions.

Now that Cynda was shivering, they knew she was coming out of it, not to mention she became somewhat coherent by this time as well. They returned to the house and called Cynda's healer. When she insisted Cynda needed a doctor, Rederrick told her their friend was the best of his kind. He instructed Cade to see to Collett's needs, as he carried his wife to their room.

That moment was the first time she realized her teeth were chattering from cold, or that she stood there in her soaked-through clothing. *I probably look like a drowned rat,* she thought.

Cade led her upstairs and, explaining he did not want to raid through Cynda's drawers, handed her some of his pajama bottoms and a t-shirt to change into then instructed her to get dry.

After a quick hot shower, she then donned the loose pants, which almost swallowed her whole. As it was, she had to roll them several times at the top just to keep from tripping over them. When she pulled on the t-shirt, she smelled the fresh clean scent of him. It was subtle, but powerful. The crisp smell of him invaded her senses. *The man definitely smelled good,* she admitted to herself, and she found it odd that his clothing and scent offered her a small measure of comfort.

Taking a fortifying breath, she walked barefoot down the hall to check on Cynda. She softly tapped on the door to the master bedroom.

Rederrick answered her knock with a worried expression. "She's doing much better now," he assured her. "She's stopped shivering and is resting peacefully. I'm sure she'll be fine."

Collett nodded solemnly.

"Go on. Get some warm tea in your body, and then we'll all have a talk later. We'll get this figured out I promise."

Understanding that he wanted to get back to his wife, she turned to move down the hall. She only made it a few steps when she heard Rederrick say her name. Spinning on her heel, she faced him once more answering, "Yes?"

"Thank you! Thank you for saving her," Rederrick said with emotion choking at him.

She didn't understand what he was talking about. If it hadn't been for her, Cynda would have never been in danger in the first place. *Maybe he doesn't understand that,* she realized. She stood there stunned, staring at Rederrick. She began to work up the words

to correct him. He shouldn't be thanking her, but before she could, he backed into his room closing the door quietly.

Moments later, upon Rederrick's advice, Collett sat in one of four barstools with a warm cup of herbal tea between her slender fingers, only sipping at it every now and again. Jenny had gotten her the tea and, noticing she was in no mood for conversation, left her alone with her thoughts. The solitude suited her.

As Collett waited for news about Cynda, she thought over what she should do now. She knew she obviously needed to leave. There could be no more pretending. They'd found her again. Staying even the one extra night had almost gotten Cynda killed. For that matter, if she counted the danger to Cade, she had almost gotten two people killed.

This is entirely my fault, she told herself. *If only I had left sooner.*

As she stared into the depth of her cup, wishing she knew the answers, Collett ignored the small, silent tears running down her face. The guilt and confusion began to consume her.

When Cade passed Jenny on the stairs, she told him where he could find Collett. He wanted to explain himself, wanted to tell her he was sorry for deceiving her. He mostly wanted to make sure she was unharmed. Really though, being honest with himself, he simply wanted to see her.

Upon entering the kitchen, he saw her in her fragile state sitting alone. Witnessing the silent tears she shed, he felt a tug on his heart. She looked so lost and sad.

He approached her loudly, so as not to scare her, but she remained lost within her own thoughts and didn't notice. Laying his hand on her shoulder, Cade gave her the only comfort he could think of, friendship.

She felt his hand on her shoulder and started at the contact. She knew without looking who it was. She recognized his scent. It was the same scent covering the shirt she wore. She realized that he must have showered as his clean, crisp, winter scent wafted around her. Right at this moment, his touch didn't make her nervous. Instead, it offered her comfort.

"Cynda will be fine. I suspect she'll have a new appreciation for the word 'cold' now," he said lightly, as if trying to reassure her, but his smart remark fell flat for both of them.

She looked to him with sad, blue eyes, "It was you last night, wasn't it?"

He huffed out a breath and sat on the stool next to her. Folding his hands together and laying them on the counter, he stated simply, "Yeah, it was me."

He prepared himself for her reaction. For some reason he couldn't fully understand, it would mean a great deal to him.

"Why? Why would you? I just don't understand; why?"

That one simple word she used, why, asked so many complicated questions. Some of them Cade wasn't even sure he knew the answer to. He decided to start from the beginning, as he knew it anyway.

"Well, um, Rederrick knew something was wrong with you. He could tell you were afraid of something. He helps people pretty often, so he notices these things. He knew you might be in trouble, so he called me."

Collett stopped him abruptly, "Called you? You're a werewolf on call to aid and protect the people? Is that it?"

Her cutting tone made his lips twitch. He knew she needed a way to vent her confused frustration, and her sarcastic words reminded him of a comic book, although the situation was far from comical.

"Something like that, I suppose." Looking directly at her skeptical expression, he continued, "We work as a group, a small organization that helps people like you."

A steely glint came into her eyes, then her expression changed to confusion. "People like me?" she questioned icily.

"Yeah, you know, people with, for lack of a better term, supernatural abilities. People pursued by The Faction or some other group because of their power."

"I am not sure I understand what you are talking about. I certainly can't twist my body into a werewolf scary enough to place on my top ten list of worst nightmares. I definitely can't chant spells like some sort of witch. Which, I am now positive, is exactly what Cynda was doing. And I know, unquestionably, that I can't make my eyes turn to a soulless black while I move a car into the river, like the man who came after me today," Collett assured him with exasperation. "So tell me what you mean when you say, people like me. As far as I know, I'm nothing like that."

He recognized her tone, and remembering Cynda's statement about her ability to deal with this, decided he would need to tread lightly. "Um, maybe I should get a basic understanding here of what you know. Or better, what is after you, before we continue."

"To answer your first question, I have no idea. I'm sure that answers the second one as well. Besides, I don't recall asking for your help. I don't really want any help, thanks just the same. I'm not willing to risk any more live; even yours," she replied with annoyance.

"Had I not helped you last night, and I'm pretty sure if I hadn't been there today as well, you would have found yourself cold and dead already. Is that what you really want?" he snapped, feeling angry and annoyed as well. Her stubborn, ungrateful attitude irritated him. He simply wanted to help. Why on earth would that bother her so much?

His words came out too harshly, even to his own ears, but he felt frustrated. Could she truthfully not see that now it wasn't only about her? How could she not understand they were all involved just by association? Narrowing his eyes, he said firmly, "You don't get to decide where or when I get involved!"

"You can't help me if you can't find me," she fired back, "And you can bet I won't be sticking around now." Closing her mouth into a tight narrow slit, she stood to leave.

As she passed him, she found herself stopped by a firm grip on her upper arm. With a sudden yank she was spun around to find herself facing a very angry, very determined Cade.

"Honey, I could find you anywhere you go. Don't try me!" he stated with a deep rumbly voice.

Their eyes held. Collett couldn't look away, and he grinned, but it felt cold. It didn't quite reach his eyes. *No,* she thought, *it was wild, like the wolf that he was.*

She was stunned silent, unsure how to respond, because Cade's voice held more than anger. It held a note of desire as well. His amber-gold eyes held her gaze. They reaffirmed the promise of each of his words. She didn't doubt his confident statement, not even for a heartbeat.

"Besides, if I can find you, so can they, but you already knew that. I'll bet this isn't the first time they've found you," he challenged. Her stunned silence, along with her frightened expression, gave him back a little of his control, so he reined in, trying his best to stay calm.

Letting go of her arm, Cade tried in a patient tone to make her understand, "Collett, don't you get it? By helping you, we are involved. They won't take a hit like we've dealt them and leave us alone. Things aren't that simple. They'll want blood, our blood! These people don't let things go. Otherwise, no one would fear them. They will not simply let these last two days pass! Instead, they'll come back harder and stronger, wiping away any hint of the resistance against them."

Her face lost all color, leaving her ivory skin looking like fragile porcelain.

"Oh. . . no," she muttered quietly. "This can't happen. What have I... what have I done? How could I be so stupid, so blind?" She seemed on the verge of panic. Her free hand flew up to cover her lips, effectively stemming the tide of guilt-filled words from escaping her mouth, but not her heart. "What have I done?" she mumbled again. Her knees bent slightly as if they would give out at any moment, and her fingers moved up to her head now as if she felt dizzy. It seemed as if she even forgot to breathe as the horrible revelation settled heavily in her mind.

He felt a twinge of guilt for putting these thoughts in her head right now. She didn't need him to make this worse. She looked so vulnerable and broken, and he just wanted to help, not make things worse. Even so, she needed to understand.

She stood there before him looking as if a slight breeze could easily blow her over. She was overwhelmed. He could see that. Then he realized she wasn't only overwhelmed, she looked horrified by the possibility that someone besides her could be hurt. She still didn't even consider that she could be dead right now.

Wrapping his arms around her in case her legs did give out, he ushered her back over to the seat she previously occupied. "Deep breaths. Stay with me," he coaxed. He promptly went over to the custom cabinets, and getting a glass down, he filled it with water. He took it to her, gently setting it between her slender fingers.

She just stared at it. Looking at the glass of clear water as if it would save her, or wishing it would give her answers. "What have I done?" she softly repeated.

"You haven't done anything. We involved ourselves. We chose to involve ourselves," Cade insisted in a firm voice meant to reassure her. Her panic subsiding, she did look up at him then.

"You're an idiot," she said concisely.

He glared at her, "Would you mind repeating that please? I'm not sure I heard you correctly." Truthfully, he preferred her anger to her despair, so he decided it wouldn't hurt to try to pick yet another fight. With her, it seemed an easy thing to do.

"You heard me. You're an idiot. You really think you can handle this. You have no idea the powerful evil that wants me. You said it yourself, they'll want blood. My blood! They don't care who they're killing in the process, as long as I die. You are right about one thing. You won't be the only one they kill, unless I get away from here. I have to go. Don't you see? I can't stay here."

"Give me a little credit now," he said with a smug grin, "I'm much tougher than I look."

She wasn't amused. She couldn't deal with inflicting more danger on them, on anybody. She couldn't live with the thought of anyone, or anything for that matter, spilling someone else's blood to get to her; even if one of those people annoyed her to no end.

Saying each word precisely, she tried spelling it out for him, "You really don't get it do you? I will not stand idly by while anyone, including you, dies to save me. I'm just not worth it! Don't you see? People love you. Count on you."

She sighed and continued with a softer voice, "The same goes for Rederrick and Cynda. There is no one counting on me; no one waiting for me. I cannot be the cause of that hope, that love, being destroyed. I can't rely on you, because it's too dangerous. I can't destroy what you have here. You should've never gotten involved. I'm sorry you did."

Nothing could have surprised him more. By the desperate conviction in her voice, he could see Collett truly didn't believe that she was worth it. She couldn't see that people here did care about her. Baffled, he sat there facing the most beautiful woman he ever laid eyes on, trying to understand why she placed no value on her own life.

She set the untouched water down and rose from her seat again. Then, with short terse words, she tried once again to leave the room, "I have to go."

This time she made it to the doorway before his calm, quiet words stopped her, "You're wrong. About any of us dying, I mean. We know what we're doing, and we know the risk we're taking. This is what we do; if not for you, then for someone else."

She heard the shift of the chair as he rose, so she didn't move. To her surprise he didn't come toward her this time. His heavy footsteps walked across the room, away from her. She turned around to face him. He stopped at the same door she had escaped through last night and said determinedly, "You're also way off about one other thing. You are worth it, every life is worth something." Cade's cool tone had a finality to it that left no further room for argument. She could only stand there as if roots had grown from her toes and plowed through the tile to keep her feet from moving forward.

He opened and closed the door quietly; his movement precisely controlled. The soft click of the door closing echoed through her brain, more so than if he had slammed it. She closed her eyes briefly, trying to gain perspective on the entire exchange. It would have been easier if he had stormed out or shouted at her, but his quiet words and careful movements cut straight into her already heavy heart. She knew he believed every word. Though, she couldn't understand why. *He's wrong,* she thought. *He just doesn't know it. He doesn't realize how risky this is.*

"He has to be wrong," she insisted out loud.

He is such a good person, and truly loved. His life meant far more than hers ever had. People counted on him, needed him. She didn't realize, or at least she wasn't willing to admit, that she might need him too.

CHAPTER 9

Cade decided a long walk would help him clear his head. He wanted to patrol the grounds around the estate again anyway. Two attacks so close together meant that they needed to stay vigilant. As he walked, he wondered about the size of the bounty placed on Collett.

He considered this last attack a sign that it must be a damn big payoff. Jeffery, the sorcerer who had shown up this afternoon, was only stimulated by big dollars, or sometimes a good challenge.

He had crossed paths with the nasty little mage before in the last ten years. Just like the previous encounters, Jeffery always had an escape plan; well, in his case, an escape spell. Whenever things got into close combat, the little runt took off. Three times now he'd engaged him, and twice now Jeffery had been smart enough to leave the minute Cade brought the battle too close.

He couldn't wait to wrap his long, clawed hands around the cocky mage's neck again. Only, this time if he did, he wouldn't let go. He would only need to get past Jeffery's shields, and keep him from popping out when he did. He decided he would need to talk to Cynda about it when she was up and about again.

Even though he had trained himself over the years to have a strong self-control, sometimes he found that control slipping. Now happened to be one of those times. It boiled on the surface stronger than he could remember in a long time. The encounters bothered him of course. Mostly though, he felt bothered by the fact that Collett needed help, but to his ultimate frustration, the confusing woman didn't want it.

And why, he thought, *because she thought herself unworthy of the risk?* "Unbelievable," he muttered.

Walking by a perfectly placed group of evergreens at the corner of the yard, he kept thinking about all that occurred the last two days. As he walked the estate grounds, the freshly fallen leaves crunched under his feet.

He checked the position of all the security cameras seeking out any blind spots. He made a mental note to make sure he talked to Rederrick about placement of two or three more cameras, and they'd need to recheck the perimeter alarms. Overall though, the angles covered would be very helpful to them. It was a great security system. Like almost everything else here, the security was top of the line. In their line of work, it had to be. Satisfied with what he saw her, he moved along the grounds.

Working through everything in his head as he patrolled, Cade realized the problem was that they were in the middle of too many unanswered questions. The questions seemed to be never-ending. Of course, the biggest problem, for him anyway, kept circling around in his head. *Why do I feel this inner pull for Collett?*

He decided to dissect the last question first. Considering he had a difficult time controlling himself around her, he felt a pressing need to rationalize his attraction to her. Collett was beautiful, and clearly smart. *She is a fighter too,* he thought with a wry smile, remembering how she kicked and punched at him by the river. There was a strange, but enchanting and mysterious allure that seemed to surround her. Most of all, that intoxicating scent of hers pulled at him in a way he never before experienced. That sweet citrus scent following her drove him out of his mind.

Shaking his head to shake away the memory of it, he broke down each factor one by one. First things first, he told himself, he would have to stop drawing in that sultry scent like a drug addict. That way, he could at least keep better focus.

That's all it is, Cade began telling himself. *It's simply basic attraction 101 stemming from pheromones. Yeah, that must be it.* He always admired beautiful, smart women. Then there was the mystery. *Well, who doesn't enjoy a mystery every 100 years or so?* he reasoned. Once he got to know her and her secrets, Collett probably wouldn't be so incredibly attractive to him. She would just be Collett; his next assignment. As for that enticing, sweet aroma of hers, he would have to work around it. He concluded he would need to make it a priority to get to know her, and all her secrets. Not only to save her life, but to save his sanity as well.

That thought brought him back to the first questions on his list. Who would want her dead?

He mulled it over as he made his way over to the south side of the house. A little stream ran through the property grounds. Staring at the water that sparkled and trickled downhill, making its way to the small pond three miles away, he considered what someone could gain from such a senseless death. In order for a bounty to be worth it there must be something to gain, but what could that be?

After a while, he realized his thoughts were going in circles. There were so many what ifs and maybes, to consider. What if she had something they wanted? Maybe she had turned traitor on them. However, no matter how long he thought about it, he just couldn't figure it out. None of it felt as though it fit.

Next, he wondered why Collett got so bent out of shape when he mentioned he knew she had power. Maybe she was trying to hide it. Maybe she was under the impression if she didn't use her abilities, they couldn't track her. He realized he would need to explain to her that wasn't truly the case, and considered for a moment what abilities she could be hiding.

He still felt strongly this was all Faction related. The bounty alone had Faction written all over it. The sum it would take to stir Jeffery out of his hole would be substantial, and not many groups had those kinds of resources. Unless, he thought, Jeffery was brought out by the challenge, but that would still mean a big bounty anyway. Anything that challenged Jeffery, or someone like him, meant bigger risk to any hunters. Therefore, bigger risk bigger rewards.

Whatever was going on felt big to Cade, and he secretly hoped that this time they'd find out who the leader of The Faction was.

By the time he made it around the entire estate and examined every possible security flaw, he decided through all his thinking, he'd only been able to answer two things for sure. First, he would have to keep picking at those questions one by one until he found out the answer to the one question that would save her life. *And second,* he thought, *I might have to learn how to hold my breath around Collett.*

He entered the kitchen about a half hour later feeling refreshed; both from his walk and from sorting things out in his head. He spotted Rederrick sitting at the table, his head cradled in his hands, and his eyes were firmly closed. Had Cade not seen the movement of Rederrick's fingers massaging his forehead, he would have believed him asleep.

"How is she?" he quietly asked. His momentary relief was replaced with guilt upon seeing Rederrick's worried features.

"Well, she's tired but good. She said I was hovering and shooed me away to find you," Rederrick answered, still keeping his eyes closed. He massaged his temples for a moment more, then opened his eyes and tilted his head to Cade as he continued, "Cynda says he slammed her with some sort of mental slap when she tried to stop him from throwing them into the river. She fought back as best she could. In the end though, he won out. She says she's never felt something like this before, and told me the force he used was barely controlled." He dropped his hands and leaned his back against his chair. "Just what exactly happened today, Cade?"

He walked over to the table, pulled up a chair next to Rederrick, and began to recount the events of their encounter, "She's right. It was barely controlled. It was Jeffery."

Those few words explained a great deal. They both knew Jeffery the sorcerer. He came into his power at an age much too young to understand it. Even worse, he was quite powerful; more so than most sorcerers, even without training. As a result, he had no discipline when it came to his craft. Cade tried to help him once, but The Faction got a hold of him first.

He continued recounting what happened, "When they made the neck breaking U-turn I started after them. I hit some sort of barrier. Felt as if I slammed face-first into a wall. I tried to make it through. I swear, Rederrick   I beat at it so hard. I knew enough hits would eventually take it down." Guilt now laced his words.

"Are you really so stupid that after all these years of knowing me, you truly believe I would blame you for this?" Rederrick asked. But looking at Cade, he found his answer, "No. You didn't think I would blame you, but you blame yourself. Don't you?"

"I was right there; so close. I couldn't get through. I beat at the barrier so hard knowing it would take concentration to keep it in place. I watched what happened, watched as they moved closer and closer to the river's edge." Cade hung his head as he spoke, closing his eyes and recalling the image; recalling his fear that he wouldn't get there in time.

He spoke carefully now, trying to clear all the details in his mind. "I'm pretty sure Cynda broke the barrier, and afterwards I saw our pal Jeffery, appear; which I am sure she also made happen. He never likes to show himself unless forced. I should have killed him the first time we met," he mumbled.

Rederrick looked at him sharply. Hearing the mumbled words, he calmly said, "When will you stop taking the weight of the world on your shoulders? You did the right thing, both ten years ago, and today. Ten years ago, as I recall, Jeffery was just a kid; barely a teenager. Yeah, so you could have killed him, but you would've never forgiven yourself. Jeffery's blood on your hands would've imprinted a dark stain on your soul, and immortality would be a whole lot harder with a guilty conscience. Giving the boy a chance to turn around, a chance to be something worthy and honorable, even if he was too stupid to take it, was simply the right thing to do."

Cade looked at Rederrick closely, then smiled slightly and said, "I guess being nearly three hundred years-old doesn't always mean you have all the answers."

Rederrick's features changed, his grin spread. Feeling somewhat better, he responded lightly, "Boy, you could live for an eternity, and I would still be smarter."

"Yeah? You just remember how smart you are when you're pushing a walker and eating applesauce, old man," Cade answered in kind.

The short, light bantering session brought both men out of their dark moods.

Getting back to business Cade said seriously, "This is big. I still don't really understand it all, but Jeffery's appearance tells me there is a lot of money on the table."

Rederrick didn't need any time to think about it. He felt the same way. "I know we all feel it. I think we're going to need some help on this one."

Cade thought about who could add an advantage to this and asked, "Is Rory available?"

"I have him undercover trying to get recruited by The Faction. We need to find the ringleader. I can check on his progress. I really think though, what we need here are able bodies to take on some shifts for security duty. We can't stay awake all the time. I'll check and see if Cody and Nate can get here. Of course, having Rory on the back burner is not a bad thought."

He decided to leave it in Rederrick's hands. He knew it wouldn't be long before someone tried to attack again. Therefore, they needed to get reinforcements soon, among other things.

"We have to find out why they want her dead," Cade declared, bringing up their next important topic. "Why is she such a threat to them?"

"She doesn't even know that herself," came the smooth musical tone of Collett's voice. Stunned, both men turned around and saw her standing nervously in the kitchen doorway.

CHAPTER 10

Cade quickly rose. His automatic reaction came from many years of ingrained protocol and good manners. Wrapped up in his conversation with Rederrick, he hadn't even heard Collett's approach.

He noticed right away how tired she looked. Her blue eyes spoke volumes. The last two days had taken their toll on her. She needed rest badly, and he also guessed she needed something to hope for.

Despite all of that, she was still stunning to him. Forgetting all about his earlier realization, Cade drew in the sweet smell of her. She still wore his shirt and baggy sweats. The clothes should have made her look shapeless and unattractive, but to him it was even more enticing to see her standing there, drowning in his clothes; his things covering her soft skin.

"Please come and join us," he said encouragingly, hoping that she would finally provide her insights on all this. He gestured to the chair he pulled out, inviting her to sit down.

She came into the room slowly, unsure of whether or not she was doing the right thing. She didn't know if she could tell them everything. She'd kept it all to herself for so long, keeping it as her problem, out of an unknown fear she could not explain. Lastly, she was uncertain of their ability to help her solve her problem, of anyone's ability, really.

She knew though, as much as it bothered her to admit it, Cade's earlier words were correct. The last two days inflicted this mess on them. By default now they were all a part of this. She also wondered if they might be able to give her information. Information she had been unable to obtain on her own. For the first time in two years, she started to believe she might be able to understand her life.

She sat down in the proffered chair then folded her hands gently, resting them in her lap. Her posture was stiff. She understood she needed to start talking, but in that moment she couldn't think of where to start. "What would you like to know?" she asked tentatively.

Cade was so glad she was suddenly willing to talk to them, he couldn't keep the relief from showing. His posture relaxed, and his eyes lightened. He intended to help whether she talked to them or not, but her cooperation would make it easier on all of them, including her.

"I want to hear everything," Rederrick said, but held up his hand to stop her from starting. "I do think though, Cynda should hear what you have to say as well. It's almost dinnertime, and none of us has eaten lunch. Let's gather together in the parlor in a half hour. I'll have Jenny bring us something to eat there. While she does, I'll go and get Cynda. Then you can tell us what you do know."

Rederrick stood and looked down to her. "And it looks like you are in need of some proper clothes. I'll have some brought to your room. That way, we can all be much more comfortable for this discussion. Now, come on then," he said, offering Collett his hand, "I'll escort you to you room so you can change." He was silently challenging her to take the offer and follow him. It was more than an offered hand though. Rederrick invited her to trust him, and it was an offer of help.

Cade knew this, and he waited. He wanted her to take the offer more than he even realized.

Several heartbeats passed before she accepted the support they were offering by lifting her hand carefully and taking Rederrick's large soft hand. Rederrick encircled her hand with his fingers. He tugged, pulling her from her chair. His next move was unexpected. Cade watched as Collett's expression turned to pure shock. She stood still and stiff when Rederrick pulled her into a warm, fatherly embrace.

"It's going to be okay. Trust in us to help you now." he assured her with a deep voice.

With those few short words, Cade saw the stiffness melt away. Closing her eyes softly, she wrapped her arms around him, returning his hug. There was a level of desperation in her gesture. It was as if in her heart something hard had just been chipped away.

Cade stood there watching as Collett's whole demeanor changed from a tense fear to a tentative trust. Trust was a fragile thing, and Cade knew it.

He knew he would do whatever it took to ensure her trust was not misplaced. Cade understood in that quiet moment he could not fail her.

Collett changed her clothes before appearing downstairs. After slipping on a cream camisole, dark maroon sweater, and black slacks, she felt less awkward and more herself.

They finished a delicious meal of roast chicken, sweet rolls, and steamed vegetables. Rederrick insisted they wait until after dinner to get down to business. Instead they enjoyed this time eating together in this beautiful room, as if there were no evil outside in the world.

The conversation was light. They talked of upcoming meetings at the office. Rederrick and Cade easily teased and bantered back and forth, calling each other "boy" and "old man." Collett knew their friendship was a long and lasting one from just watching them. She kept mostly quiet throughout the meal, only speaking when asked direct questions.

Even though the atmosphere seemed light, the tension remained. Everyone sat thinking about the events leading to this moment in the back of their minds, and each wondered what would come of their planned discussion.

After dinner was finished, she offered to clear the plates and dishes. She wasn't, however, fooling anybody. She needed the extra time to collect and organize her thoughts.

Upon her return, they all sought out comfortable spots to listen calmly, as she readied herself to tell her vague version of the events leading to her current problems.

She stood with her arms wrapped around herself in an apparent effort to protect herself from what was to come. Her gaze was drawn to the enchanting fire in front of her. She watched as flames danced and swayed. Occasionally, she would hear a pop, and a few little sparks would flitter up; making an escape through the chimney.

Behind her, Rederrick sat in the corner of the beautiful mauve sofa, his right arm extended across the back of the couch. He crossed his left, leg laying his ankle across his knee. He looked completely relaxed, as if he was waiting for an enchanting bedtime story instead of Collett's dark and confusing tale.

Cynda snuggled in close under his extended arm. She lay upright on her side, her knees tucked in, with her head resting on Rederrick's chest. Rederrick absently tangled his fingers in Cynda's soft auburn hair. With her color now returned, it gave her cheeks a warm glow. Her green eyes glittered softly in the firelight.

They look so perfect together, thought Collett. They melted into one another. Looking at Cynda now, Collett would have never guessed she had a brush with death merely a few short hours ago. It seemed to her that Rederrick's calm vestige gave Cynda the comfort and support that she needed to overcome the harrowing experience of earlier that day. The sight of them there, loving and supporting each other, brought raw emotion to Collett.

Cade stood behind the wing back chair closest to the fire, his hands clasped together, his forearms resting on the back of the chair, and his body leaned forward slightly, thus giving the impression he was at ease. Much like Collett, Cade's gaze was captivated by the beauty before him. It wasn't the fire that held his attention though. It was Collett.

As she stood there looking so alone, so vulnerable, he wanted to offer her comfort. He felt a protective need to go and shield her from her own personal agony. He knew however, right now, his efforts would be rebuffed.

Everyone was ready to hear Collett's story, except Collett, he noted. No one said a word though. Instead, they waited for her to start whenever she was ready. The silence should have put them on edge, but for some strange reason it offered comforting solace, a peaceful moment to reflect on all that has happened. So they all patiently waited.

More than ten minutes passed before she began, "The only thing I think I know about all this is my name. I don't even know my whole name. 'Collett' is the only thing I knew when I awoke on a storm battered coastline almost two full years ago.

"I remember the sound of the ocean waves rushing up the coast. The sun warmed my skin and pierced my throbbing headache."

She huffed out a relieved breath. With just that tiny little bit out she felt as though she started to take an offensive stance for the first time. Releasing that one small piece of a very large puzzle, and knowing it was there waiting for her to connect it with another, felt proactive.

"I'm not sure how it happened, but I awoke close to a private beach, wearing some sort of lightweight, silk, silvery gown. I had no shoes, no purse, no ID. Yet I knew my name. Strange isn't it, how you can forget your entire life, but remember your name?"

She stared off at nothing as her mind drifted back further into the horrible memory, "My head pounded so painfully. I remember it took me a long while of lying completely still before I could fully open my eyes. When I finally did manage to pry them open, and I slowly sat up, the motion made me nauseous because the pain was so intense. I distinctly remember the horrible pain now."

Reaching up, she moved to grip her shoulder as clear images came back to her. "The shoulder strap of my gown was torn. I remember because I had to reach up to hold it in place. Then I saw my hands.

"My hands were stained with dried blood. As I looked down at my hands I saw the dark, rusty-brown blotch covering my dress. The bloodstain seemed so odd to me at the time..." While she spoke, Collett narrowed her eyes and looked at her hands, focusing; as if she could still see the dark crimson stains.

Cade couldn't stand it anymore. He stood tall and walked over to her. Placing his hand tenderly on her shoulder, he whispered gently, "Go on, we're all here for you." He took it as a good sign she didn't recoil from his touch.

Collett could feel the warmth of Cade's touch just then, and she soaked it in so she could continue, "As I gained my bearing, I remember hearing the sea birds cawing around me. When I started looking for them, I saw the chaos, the pure destruction before me. I remember debris. It was everywhere. There was driftwood and seaweed all over, simply pulled out, unwanted by the ocean and left there lying on the beach.

"I even remember seeing dead jellyfish strewn across the sand; all kinds of sea life, for that matter. The stench of lifeless and rotting fish was pungent in comparison to the fresh salty air.

"I made my way across the littered beach for a while, and I clamored over the hot and dry sand dunes. I went looking for help; looking for answers. What I found instead was pure, unbiased destruction no matter where I looked." A small tear escaped one of Collett's crystal blue eyes, making a path down her cheek.

Feeling a small encouraging squeeze on her shoulder, she was once again reminded Cade was there. He was offering his support, and she needed that support more than she realized. It gave her strength.

Soaking it in once more, Collett decided to move on to the cause of the devastation she witnessed, "A small hurricane; that's what I was told later. How could something small cause so much pain? A simple whim of nature caused the violent destruction of so many homes and upheaved the sea. It took so much."

No matter how much she wanted to trust the people in this room, Collett could not tell them of the heavy guilt she felt upon seeing the turmoil before her. As if maybe, she was part of the cause.

She skipped past those thoughts and feelings and continued, "I guess the people who were there that day had survived the storm, or they were just coming back from evacuations. Their faces held so many emotions. I saw it. I saw their fear. Some were so angry. Most though, wore the sad, lost expression of confusion and loss. They came back wanting to try and recover something left of their horribly devastated lives.

"I couldn't help. I wanted to. I wanted to help so badly. I felt an urge to ease their burdens. It was so strange, yet difficult to resist. I saw them crying over broken homes; weeping for the loss of shattered dreams. My heart bled for them. The feelings were so intense that my throbbing head just ached more," she drew in her hands, fisting them to her stomach as if trying to push back all the pain.

Quietly listening to the way she told her tale, everyone present noted how she was more than simply remembering. She saw it in her mind clearly, as if living it all over again.

Cade wanted her to stop. He wanted to remove these awful images from her mind and take away the pain. He knew though, deep down, they needed to hear all of it. Any small piece of missing information could make it more difficult to put things together for her.

For unknown reasons, she looked directly up at Cade. Her eyes glistening from the tears she held back. She continued her tale, directing the next part to him, "You see, it wasn't until that moment I realized I could not remember. I saw their sadness, their pain, and their broken homes. Then I thought to myself, *what of my home?* The question stopped me. With a single thought I realized there was no home in the back of my mind. I couldn't remember my home. I wracked my brain. I couldn't remember anything. Nothing was there, no home, no family, nothing."

Cynda, who could barely stand the raw emotion on Collett's face, had been working on a theory. She felt she should share, "I think you're an empath," she blurted out.

Collett turned her head to face her, and noticed her sitting forward intently on the edge of the sofa; her hand still firmly locked with Rederrick's.

"You think I'm a what?" she asked.

Cynda smiled at her confusion, "An empath; empathic. You feel other people's emotions. Really strong empaths can even sense thoughts."

"It makes sense. That's how she senses the trouble before it occurs," Cade injected.

Collett turned her gaze back to him now, "Wait, how do you know that?"

"Honey, it's written all over your face. You take on this pinched, distasteful look as if there's a foul smell in the air," he answered. She looked around to Cynda again and saw her nod in agreement.

"Oh. I didn't realize. I mean, I guess I've never exactly seen a mirror when I feel their evil."

"Is that what you feel; evil?" Cynda questioned.

"I can feel a taint of evil or malice when it's close. I can feel other things, like Jenny's nurturing nature or Rederrick's need to protect. I have always felt it, though I have never really understood how. I usually run whenever I get a hint of any dark feelings. Mostly, I've avoided the evil following me by staying on the move," Collett explained as she looked down at the floor.

Because he was a lawyer, and a damn good one, Rederrick recognized her move as a guilty gesture. He asked, "What's bothering you Collett?"

Much like a scolded child, she could not look up. She quietly answered him, "If I had left here sooner, you would have never been affected by this. I fooled myself into thinking it was over. I brought this to you. Saying I'm sorry isn't much, but I really am sorry."

Rederrick stood. Letting go of Cynda's hand, he approached her. He said, "Collett." He waited until she looked up at him to speak again. When she did, he spoke soft words, "Now why is it you can't see the possibilities here? Maybe, just maybe, you were meant to find us. We can help you better than anyone else, and to me that is an encouraging thought. Maybe you stayed here with us, longer than your usual two or three-month stint, because somehow you knew the same thing."

"You felt a connection here- not to the place though. It was the people that held you here, wasn't it?" Cynda added quickly.

Rederrick heard his wife approach from behind. He stepped to the side to give her access to Collett. Cynda stood there for a moment looking at her. She wanted to hug her so badly, but knew all the affection was too much for her right now. "We can help you Collett, all you have to do is let us," Cynda said with emotion choking her throat. "Let us be here for you. Let us try."

As Cynda stood there, hoping Collett would accept their help, she saw the tears escape the tight hold Collett had kept on them; and heard her sniffle slightly. Rederrick offered her a white handkerchief. As she grabbed it with her right hand, she realized her left hand was currently held by Cade. She didn't even know when he had grabbed it, Collett just knew it felt good.

Praying she was doing the right thing Collett closed her eyes as she quietly spoke, "I don't know how to put a stop to all this, but for the very first time I feel like, with your help, I might be able to."

Cade gave her one of his charming smiles with the slight lift on the right side and said, "So, let's get started shall we?"

His height made it necessary for her to tilt her head in order to make eye contact with him. She stared up at his golden eyes for a moment then asked him, "I'm just curious, and I don't really want to sound ungrateful. Why is it you would want to help me? You don't even know me."

He tipped his head curiously, and his smile got even wider. His brow rose. "I told you before. This, honey, is what I do," he answered simply.

She continued to stare into Cade's strange golden gaze until Rederrick cleared his throat, "Ahem." When they both directed their attention in his direction he said, "Now then, let's get down to business. In order to work on your memory problem we need to get more specific. What beach did you wash up on?"

She nodded her head, "I later found out I was in Texas, near Matagorda. That's where I ended up anyway.

"There was this paramedic. He saw me standing there in the middle of all the chaos. He asked if I was okay. I guess I probably looked like I was horribly injured, being covered with blood and wearing a torn and ruined dress.

"I asked him right then where I was and what had happened. I felt panicked by this time. I was very afraid and felt extremely alone. The paramedic thought I needed medical attention, so he took me to the hospital, which was a total madhouse by this point. They checked me over and found no injuries. There were simply too many people for them to worry much over someone like me, who was not physically hurt. They told me I would remember. I was in shock or something like that, from the traumatic events."

A small sudden laugh escaped her then. Cade looked at Collett strangely wondering to himself if she might be having a psychotic break.

"What's so funny?" he asked.

She smiled and answered, "I was supposed to go back. 'Come back in a couple days if you're still having trouble,' the doctor told me. I guess I missed the appointment."

Cade still didn't understand her humor. By the looks on Rederrick and Cynda's faces they didn't either. "Are you alright?" he inquired.

"Yeah, I guess I am just a bit tired. I only found it somewhat ironic that I was supposed to see him in two days and now it's been two years." She let go of Cade's hand to move over and plop down on the chair Cade had stood behind earlier.

He felt a small sense of disappointment from the loss of contact, but he didn't show it on his face.

Rederrick jumped in at her response, "You mean you have not been to any doctor since that day?"

"Well, no. It's not exactly like I had the resources to pay for one. I have been scraping by on what little I earn from each odd job I get. Whatever I've had left, I put away for run money. Whatever is hunting me doesn't generally take long to find me. Going back to a doctor didn't matter to me. Besides, today I realized why I haven't really needed to see a doctor."

Cade spoke then, "What do you mean by that?"

She looked up at Cade from her chair and said, "Didn't you notice my head today Cade?" He looked at it carefully now, taking only a second to see the gash on her temple was healed.

"Huh. Why didn't I notice before? Was it like that all day?"

"All day," she confirmed.

"How could I have missed that?" He asked more of himself than anyone in the room.

Cynda answered him anyway, "Maybe because you heal so quickly yourself, you just didn't think about it."

"Yeah, maybe," he mumbled.

Deep down Cade wondered if it wasn't something more. He knew that his constantly off center feelings when he was around her kept him from being focused. He simply didn't have his senses in order. He knew he would have to step it up if he intended to keep Collett alive. *Hadn't she come into the kitchen earlier without me even hearing her footfalls,* he remembered. He couldn't go around missing details like this without consequences. If he didn't find a way to center himself, they would all be in big trouble.

Gazing upon her then, Cade noticed Collett's yawn and the tired, worn expression covering her pretty features. He recognized the signs of her total exhaustion. He looked to Rederrick to adjourn their little meeting; and without words conveyed that they had done enough for one night.

Understanding the message, and knowing Cynda was worn down as well, Rederrick agreed with a nod. "I think we should all try and get some sleep. Tomorrow we will work on strategy, and figure out what to do next. For now, it's late. Let's all sleep on it, shall we?"

Moving to Rederrick's side and hooking her arm with his, Cynda agreed, "I think that is a great idea. Tomorrow's another day. We'll talk over breakfast about some proactive plans." She quickly bid Cade and Collett a goodnight.

After they walked out of the room arm-in-arm, Collett stood slowly. She looked at Cade trying to find the words to thank him and apologize for her earlier behavior. In the end, she opted for a simple, "Thank you."

He walked to her until he stood nearly right in front her. She felt her heartbeat quicken. With a deep and quiet voice, he replied, "You are doing the right thing."

"I pray you're right. I couldn't live with more deaths because of me," she whispered without meeting his eyes. Then she turned her back to him and strode from the room, with her stocking covered feet barely making a sound.

More deaths? Cade thought to himself.

CHAPTER II

New York, NY

The throbbing, heavy-metal music pumped loudly from the speakers placed throughout the gothic club. It was so loud, you couldn't hear the person next to you unless they shouted near your ear. All was as it should be.

Men and women jumped up and down; moving and gyrating in frenzy with the quick rhythm pouring into the room. Vibrations echoed throughout the packed crowd letting the people feel the thumping sensation in their chest and stomach.

The painted graffiti glowed bright with the help of black lights placed strategically throughout the club. Strobe lights blinked wildly in tune with the pulsing, manic beat of music. People crowded the bar, pushing and shoving their way in, wanting to be served. The patrons shouted out their orders hoping to be heard correctly. Men hit on women way out of their league, and women continued to prowl for a handsome companion to offer them company for the night.

Nodding in satisfaction, he thought to himself, *Yes, all was just as it should be.*

He was lord of this domain. He sat in the back corner blending in with the painted black walls and darkness as he observed the frantic happenings of this place; his place. He blended into this room so well that no one chose to notice him. No one wanted to notice him.

As a part of the darkness surrounding him, his shadowed, feral appearance gave the impression to everyone around, *Stay away*. And that's the way he wanted it. If one was brave enough to move in to get a closer look, they may have mistaken him for a demon in human form. They would be wrong though, because many demons could attest that he was much worse than their kind from the abyss.

He wore his usual black silk suit, with the black button-up shirt open at the collar. His eyes seemed dark and merciless from a distance, and very few had ever been close enough to see their true color. It was a sure bet that those few had never forgotten the sight of them. Also, his semi-long, obsidian hair almost seemed an unnatural color, as if the glossy black color had been a curse from a god to ensure his place with the wicked creatures of the night. Everything about this man spoke of Danger. He was, "The Hunter."

Scanning the crowd carefully, he watched for potential problems. After seeing all he needed, The Hunter pushed up, easily rising to his full height, which was substantial, and made his way smoothly through the teeming crowd. People gave him a wide berth as he passed.

When he made it to the stairs leading to his office, he took them effortlessly two at a time. Before he even opened the door, The Hunter knew company waited. He recognized the smell of his visitor right away. The pungent odor was like that of a burnt fungus, overpowering any other smells around. It wasn't intolerable, just horribly obnoxious.

Opening the door, The Hunter gave the intruder a sharp glare. The scrawny half-man, half-demon stood, but his shape remained somewhat bent over as usual. Under the unwanted visitor's coat, The Hunter knew he had some thin, bat-like wings. The imp's skin held a sickly, grayish pallor, and the dark hair on his head appeared thin and greasy looking.

The Hunter tipped his head to the side annoyed. "What do you want, bootlicker?" he ground out and then moved past the imp to his desk.

"Hey now, you might hurt my feelings talking like that," the intruder, Finnawick by name, replied with a sinister smile.

"We both know you don't have any, so we know that won't be a problem," The Hunter stated factually. "You have one minute to tell me what it is you want then I'll remove you from my club."

The scrawny thing that looked like a man hissed, "Now, that's why I've always liked you. Fear is just not in your make-up. So many of your kind cower at His feet. They fear Him, as they should. You... no. You have never feared Him, have you?"

"You have to give a damn about something to be afraid, and I just don't give a damn. You're down to 30 seconds. You better start talking," the dark hunter finished by dropping his clipboard with the current liquor orders on the desk with a harsh slap.

Finnawick, the imp, was no fool. He knew how to play his cards. It remained the only reason he'd stayed alive so long, especially with this one. "We need you for your... expertise. The pay is better than He has ever offered."

Propping his hip on the desk and folding his arms over his chest, he pretended to consider the imp's words. Truthfully, he was uninterested. As he said before, he cared about little in this life.

"The job?" The Hunter asked anyway.

"It doesn't matter how it's done. Have fun with it," he encouraged, handing over a file with his long bony fingers.

Finnawick's wicked smile reminded him of a hyena waiting for his turn to tear into the meaty flesh of a stolen carcass. "He wants this one eliminated. The pay is 500," the imp hissed.

The Hunter gave him a cold, callous smile. It was the kind of calculating smile that would've sent chills through a normal man's soul, giving him the feeling that death was not far off.

"To people as old as He is, five hundred thousand isn't much. I have that much invested in this club, and I've got time to wait for the return. Besides, if you're here it means no one else could get it done. We both know how much you loathe working with me. So, I think one million should do it. We both know He can afford it. That is, if I feel inclined to take the offer."

Being no normal man, Finnawick looked at The Hunter with a droll stare as if he was bored. He knew that to do otherwise would reveal too much. In truth, he did fear the monster that stood a few feet in front of him, but he feared failing his master even more. He straightened his crooked spine and uttered, "For one million it will have to be done by the end of the month."

Flipping open the file, The Hunter looked at the picture stapled on the inside of the cover. The face of the striking woman staring back at him felt slightly familiar. He studied it for a while longer than he needed. So long in fact, that he knew Finnawick considered the long silence as a sign that he would take the job.

However, unwilling to give away any of his own thoughts, he lifted his left eyebrow at the picture, "Pretty; not his usual query. She's not a demon. Why is it she makes Him so nervous?"

"He's never nervous, just very cautious. You of all people should recognize the difference." The imp was starting to get irritable, "Just do the job, and I'll put the money in your regular account."

He flipped the cover closed with little concern, "You're right. I do know the difference, and the fear in your voice tells me something's off here. So, the answer is NO." He straightened to his full height, and then moved around the smelly imp to the door leading downstairs.

"What do you mean, 'No'? You don't get to tell Him no! No one tells Him no!" he hissed, his pitch rising, anger and worry lacing his words. Finnawick did not want to be the one to tell his master he failed.

The Hunter actually laughed. Not a happy laugh, but a cold, mean chuckle rolled past his lips. Over time everything about him turned cold, and his cruel laugh was no different.

"I thought someone as old as you would know what that meant. Well maybe I should put it another way. Let's see, here is one you may understand: If you don't get out of my bar in the next ten seconds I will tear out your throat, dismantle your skinny, deformed body, and mail it to him in pieces. Then he'll get it. The real question is, do you?"

His expression turned dark and menacing, much like his feared reputation. He stepped up, getting right in the putrid- smelling imp's face. His deep voice vibrated, "I told you once before, I am not his lap dog that comes running whenever called. I am done. Out. If I change my mind, then I'll come to you; when I want. I decide which jobs I take and the ones I don't. Do not *ever* make that mistake again."

Turning his back on the nasty errand boy, The Hunter opened the door that led down to the club. The imp felt fear rise within him. He needed The Hunter involved on this. Even though Finnawick hated dealing with him, this one never failed. All the others he sent so far were unable to get the job done, and only managed to make it worse, making it necessary for Finnawick to escalate matters now.

Failing his master was not an option that one would want to live through, *if* you lived through it. Finnawick also knew his master would come calling soon, expecting the job done.

Suddenly, the fear slightly ebbed as the other information the imp found clicked in his brain. Information Finnawick knew The Hunter would not want shared.

The imp let out a cruel cackle.

The sound of it grated on The Hunter's angry nerves, and he stopped.

"He should have killed you the first time he met you," Finnawick said. "Although, I have to admit, keeping you alive continues to have benefits. This time will be no different. Your existence will again pay off. You and I both know once you're in, there is only one way out."

Finnawick kept speaking to The Hunter's back with his sickly, rasping voice, "You see, I make it my business to motivate people. You could say it's my job. It's why he has kept me around so long. I believe it is important to take pride in your work. You are no different than the rest of them my friend. You merely need, shall we say, proper motivation."

The Hunter turned around with a cold, deadly stare, a look befitting the rumors told of him. "Tell me, just what do you think would possibly motivate me away from tearing you to little bits right now, *friend*?"

The imp returned his stare measure for measure. Then he stammered with false confidence, "I know you won't, because you hate me too much. You would never attack me unless you were sure you could kill me. You know my master would not send me here unless I was protected." The Hunter saw the bluff for what it was, but wasn't willing to deal with the consequences of killing this inconvenience in front of him- for now.

"One day I will kill you, remember that bootlicker. You and I, we both know it is just a matter of time, and I, well I have *all* kinds of time," he promised.

The imp stared at the man before him. Finnawick knew The Hunter spoke honestly and wasn't willing to chance his death today. He also knew one good look in the file on his desk would ensure The Hunter's participation.

To make sure The Hunter viewed the contents of the file, he threw out some enticing information, "We already have Jeffery working this one. You remember Jeffery don't you? Nasty little magic user; a bit hard to control though. Oh, that's right, you two haven't met. Oh well, never mind. Anyway, last I heard he was somewhere in Colorado," he paused to let that sink in, "Remember Hunter, we don't care who dies in the process, just as long as she is handled. Hurry! You know the rules; first come, first served. Oh, and remember, life is all about the proper motivation. And trust me, right now, Jeffery has plenty of motivation."

Using his natural magic, he blinked from the room with one last hissing comment, "Is that fear I see in you, Hunter?"

The Hunter walked over to the file and opened it. He knew from the imp's words exactly what he was looking for. Scanning over the pages of info on the target, he looked for it. When he got to the second to last page, he saw what he knew would be there. There in black-and-white print he found his motivation spelled out for him in a single four-letter word. A word that might as well be the four-letter curse he was thinking in his mind.

Expressing the foul curse out loud, he dropped the file and stomped from the room, knowing with angry frustration that he was on his way to Colorado.

CHAPTER 12

Four days. It had been four days, and still nothing new came to Collett's memory. She sat in what Cynda referred to as the workout room, though it was far more than that. Frustration kept brewing in her these past days. She felt trapped both inside and out. She kept her hands propped palms up on her legs, with her ankles upon her knees in a classic meditation pose. She breathed in and out in a slow rhythm keeping her eyes closed, but relaxation eluded her.

One of the things they decided over the last few days was to be proactive. This in turn, meant finding a way to restore her memory. At the moment, she tried to do that with meditation. Then maybe, just maybe, she would remember something.

She repeated this process every day since Cynda showed her how to do it four days before. She came up here to this room, and every day she left without success. She was truly beginning to despise this room.

The room received a large amount of natural light. It leaked in through the three huge windows on the wall behind her. The light also trickled down from the large skylight above her, and Collett could see the bright light through her closed eyelids and feel it on her skin. Despite the sunlight, the room felt cool.

She could also smell the subdued aroma of the lavender candle she lit earlier as it infused her senses. Thinking about the candle, her thoughts drifted to the room itself. The cool, teal color of the walls gave the room a tranquil feeling. The workout room, the largest on the third floor, was devoted to training. A treadmill and an elliptical took up a corner of the room, and a flat screen on the opposite wall provided visual stimulation to those who wanted it. Several yoga DVDs lined the shelf below it. It seemed, at least to Collett, that it was one of the largest rooms in the house. Though, the reason behind its size was likely the specific purpose it served for training. She sat in the large space in between the machines and the TV on a soft mat for stretching and yoga.

The black matted sparring circle, taking up most of the room, impressed her the most. Free weights of all shapes and sizes ran along the wall behind it. At the back of the circle there was a weight bench holding a long bar with more than a few sizable, round weights on each side. A large mirror covered the wall behind the weights. She assumed the mirror made it easier to keep one's form in mind when lifting weights or sparring with an opponent. The other wall held several styles of poles and weapons used for sparring. Between the cardio area and the sparring/weight side of the room hung a large, black punching bag. Over the last few days, she'd often heard Cade working the bag in the evenings.

As she tried to relax, she could admit she felt thankful to be wearing her own clothes again. During breakfast, the day after revealing what she knew of her vague past, they all had decided it would be safer if she stayed at the estate for now. Wanting to make her comfortable, Cade went to her apartment and retrieved most of her clothes and shoes.

She felt better, more like herself with her own belongings. Even if the thought of Cade rifling through her underwear drawer was incredibly unsettling, she was very grateful for the gesture.

Now she sat in her own yoga pants and white tank top, trying without success to reach into her mind for small pieces of the large puzzle that was her life. As each day passed with no progress, she felt as though frustration would be her constant companion; not to mention the guilt she continued to feel for the extra workload her presence created for everyone here. Even Jenny, the family housekeeper, had more food to cook and one more place setting she had to clean. When she offered to help her, Jenny refused in her sweet southern manner, shooed Collett away, and told her that she liked to keep her hands busy. Collett felt like a burden, and she wasn't sure if this would work. Though, she wanted it to, badly.

Rederrick and Cynda were balancing time between their law firm and helping her. They all agreed that it was too dangerous to return to work at the firm for now. It was yet another way she was inconveniencing them, but she did not intend to endanger any more lives than necessary by appearing in a place full of office personnel.

Rederrick had promised her in a kind fatherly way, "When this is all over and we've beaten them, and Collett, we will beat them," he assured, "If you still want to stay here, I'll still have a job for you. There will be no more running for you; no more forced decisions. Only choices about what you want."

Then the next day, using his resources, Rederrick began to research the hurricane in the Gulf two years ago. He did find out the storm had appeared from practically nowhere. Generally, people got a few days' warning when a tropical storm turned to a hurricane while moving toward a coastline. This storm simply appeared hours before it hit the Texas area. Even stranger, it only affected a small area, and within 24 hours it was gone. Also, the storm was registered as a category two. With more warning, it could have given people more time to prepare properly, keeping the damage limited.

The storm. Collett began to try concentrating on the storm, breathing in and out slowly as Cynda had taught her. She focused, trying to pull forward something, anything. Thinking about wind and rain, she meditated for more than an hour. She strained her mind until she felt a dull throb in the back of her head, moving down her aching neck. Nothing. She couldn't remember anything, and frustration built within her.

Giving up for now, she opened her eyes and huffed out a breath with an upturned bottom lip, causing her bangs to flutter softly up. Today would be no different from any other day this week.

Tipping her head back and looking up at the skylight put in the middle of the tall ceiling, Collett again tried to calm herself. She remembered Cynda telling her days before, "Frustration will just make it harder."

Had it not been for Cynda's encouragement, Collett probably wouldn't have tried today; wouldn't have bothered to even come into this room. Cynda was right, though. Her frustration was beginning to affect her ability to relax at all.

Trying to think of the positives, she reminded herself that there was a significant lack of bad dreams lately, thus allowing her to feel better rested, thankfully. Although, she would like to be rid of the sight of a certain person's liquid gold eyes appearing occasionally in her sleep. Aggravated, she tried to steer her thoughts in another direction. She found herself thinking of Cade all too often these last few days. She wasn't sure just what to do about her newest annoying habit either.

She could smell his crisp scent even now. She inhaled the masculine smell, and figured out why she could smell him.

Crap! she thought, *It never fails, speak of the devil, and he will appear.* She lowered her gaze from the skylight toward the entrance of the room. There he stood, crowding the doorway with his tall, imposing body.

He wore a black pair of long basketball shorts, and that's it. His lack of a shirt against the cool color of the room highlighted the dark tan color of his skin. It was a natural color, received from spending long periods of time in the sun, and though she hated to admit it, she couldn't help but appreciate the whole picture of him. Who wouldn't?

He smiled at Collett, "Do you know what you need?"

"I am sure you're going to tell me," she answered sarcastically.

His smile spread even more. He loved the way her face pinched when she was irritated with him. He ignored her tone and said, "You need a good solid workout. There's nothing like taking out your frustrations by pushing your body's physical limits."

She glared at him, "Well, it just so happens I already worked out before my meditation session with some yoga."

He laughed aloud, "Ha! That, honey, is not a real workout. I was thinking more like three minutes on the heavy bag, or hey, I have an idea, how about a small sparring match; you against me. It will give me a chance to teach you some self-defense."

"I don't think so," she replied, slightly stunned by his proposition. "I wouldn't want to bruise your ego. Besides, I've taken a self-defense course."

"Oh yeah, one whole course? Well then, show me. What can you do?"

His sarcastic tone hit a nerve and made her angry again. Why was he able to get under her skin so quickly? As much as she would like to smack the crooked smile off his face, she knew she remained too intimidated by him to even try.

Instead, she declined as politely as she could, "I am sorry Cade, but I don't think it is a good idea right now. I'll leave you to your workout." She uncrossed her legs, standing gracefully.

He could tell the idea of sparring with him made her as nervous as a rabbit that had just spotted a wolf. An analogy that was not far off the mark, he thought to himself. Hell, just staying in the same room with him made her jumpy.

He couldn't help himself though. For the better part of a week, he gave Collett space and tried not to provoke her. He watched her become more and more frustrated as the days passed, and as her frustrations built, so did his. Although, for very different reasons. His frustration came from her constant need for space from him. Her cool attitude and avoidance drove him mad.

He came up here intent on a physically draining workout. He had hoped to block out his all too often thoughts of her, only to find her sitting there with her distracting scent filling the room. *What is a man to do?* he thought.

Seeing her in tight-fitting workout clothes that allowed her sexy belly button to peek out when she lifted her arms, he could no longer resist the challenge, or the urge, and wondered somewhere in the back of his mind why he bothered to do so in the first place.

She made her way to the doorway where he stood. He decided not to move. "Why," he started, then corrected with a quick mental shake of his head. "You're scared of me," he stated as a fact rather than a question.

Collett stopped then and looked up at him, "Excuse me?"

For some unknown reason, he felt a need to goad her, "That's it isn't it? I think you are afraid; afraid of me, afraid of anything that challenges you, for that matter. You won't even try. I don't think you could fight off a flea. Just how do you intend to fight off another demon? I wonder, are you going to keep running Collett, or are you going to stand and fight?" He knew the accusation sounded harsh, but he wanted an answer and wouldn't take it back.

She narrowed her eyes into slits, giving him an icy and mean glare, "Why you—mean, snotty, arrogant, egotistical, overbearing, monster! Just who do you think you are? You have no idea what I can or can't do!" The tone of her voice rose with every word, "How dare you come in here and accuse me of being afraid of you. YOU! You're nothing, you hear me! Nothing! Compared to what has followed me every day, you can't even begin to measure up to the malice that sticks to my heels. Now, you had better get out of my way."

He returned her glare, and with a soft, yet firm voice he challenged, "Make me."

His taunt pushed her over the edge. Her temper boiled over. Collett couldn't recall ever feeling this angry and frustrated at the same time. She wondered why he kept pushing her.

Losing control, she rushed toward him, closing the distance between them in a second. Stretching her arms out, she moved to push him with all the momentum she had collected.

He saw her coming, and using his quick reflexes, easily grabbed her right arm. He used her own movement against her and swung her around, hard. Her back was now to his front. Then effortlessly, despite her struggles, he grabbed her other hand, crossed her arms, and pulled her back forcefully. The maneuver effectively pinned her against his hard body; not that she was thinking about that, Collett told herself.

However, she wasn't ready to give up yet. She dropped her left leg, swinging it backward, almost hitting the intended target between his legs. He barely dodged the crippling blow. Her heart pounded and her thoughts raced. She knew she would have to outthink him as she was no match for his strength.

She tried the classic tactic of forcing a captor to deal with the dead weight of his victim by letting her body fall limp. On a normal man, the ploy might have worked, but Cade's superior strength still gave him the advantage. He easily lifted and supported her extra weight, not even slightly bothered.

He then leaned close to point out her mistake, "You know, this tactic won't work on anybody with supernatural strength. You're not even a minor burden to them." His breath tickled against her neck with every word.

Instinctively knowing this is what would happen, she sighed and, feigning frustration, said, "Maybe you're right." Then with shocking speed and foresight, she promptly and efficiently threw her head back.

Her head slammed with vicious impact right into his mouth and jaw. "But, that will hurt some," she huffed out in a satisfied breath. He stumbled back, dropping her on the mat because of the blow.

Caught off guard, Cade started to curse, but stopped when he saw her scramble from the floor, making her way to the door to escape. "Oh no you don't!" he said. He moved quickly, easily grabbing her arm as she passed.

She tried again to use his own move against him by whipping around and jumping on his back, forcing his arm at an awkward angle. He let go of his hold without regret, knowing he still held every advantage. Though, he did admit to himself that her quick thinking impressed him.

She began to lock her arms around his neck intending to choke the arrogance right out of him, when she felt him reach behind, grabbing her just under her arms. He bent forward and effectively lifted her, flipping her off his back and onto the mat with a thud.

She lay there huffing in and out for a moment, with Cade staring down at her. She noticed he wasn't even out of breath and felt somewhat humiliated by the emotional and physical outburst. At the very same time, she felt relief. It felt good; great, in fact. Even though she happened to be the one lying there prone on the floor, she felt so charged and excited, more alive than she had felt in a long time.

Tilting her head back she looked to Cade, who stood above her, waiting for her next move. His lip was cracked, but it no longer bled. Knowing she smacked him hard enough to draw blood gave her a slight satisfaction. *At least I got him with one good hit,* she thought. Smiling slightly, she burst out with laughter.

He watched her with an unsure and confused expression, which made her laugh even more. She rolled to her side in an effort to get up. He moved to assist her, pulling Collett up by the arm.

As she staggered to her feet with his help, she settled her laugh down somewhat to say, "You were right."

He tilted his head in that way she'd seen him do before when puzzled by a question or a problem. "I'm sorry, right about what?"

Giving him a full and sincere smile she explained, "I really needed that. I feel..." she paused, "better."

Cade stared at her captivating smile, unconsciously locking the sight away in his mind. *She is absolutely beautiful,* he thought.

Seeing her happy for the first time in days became nearly as invigorating for him as the workout ended up being for her. Pulling gently, he moved her right before him.

His intense scrutiny and the butterflies in her stomach kept her from offering any resistance. Completely sober now, she looked up at him with her perfect, clear, innocent eyes. Uncertainty and desire warred with each other and covered her features, replacing the smile.

Unable to hold back any longer, he put his hand behind her neck, leaned forward, and waited just a moment, a split second, to give her time to stop him. When she didn't resist, he moved the rest of the way.

Their lips met tentatively at first. He kissed her softly, and she tasted to him as sweet and delicious as she smelled. As he began to move his lips against hers, Collett felt her arms move up his chest to his shoulders, and she began kissing him back. She felt the heat between them rise, the power of the kiss rise, and wondered if their sizzling connection would surely cause them to combust. She heard a soft whimper and hardly realized it came from her.

Suddenly, the tempo of the kiss increased. Cade's control snapped. He fisted his hands in her hair, wanting, no, needing more. He pulled her in tighter, closer, feeling as though they couldn't get close enough. He wanted to touch, to taste. He felt her soft curves press against him through their clothing as he sipped on the sweet flavor of her mouth pressed against his.

The blood rushed out of his head. He knew he needed to stop, knew this was going too far, but in this moment with her spellbinding citrus scent assaulting his senses, the sweet flavor of her on his lips, he just couldn't bring himself to care.

She wasn't entirely sure what was happening. She felt needy, confused. She was enjoying this far too much, so much in fact, that it scared her on a very basic level but thrilled her on another. She moved her hands to his chest, pushing half-heartedly, thus displaying her own control was slipping.

Her head spun and her brain felt fuzzy. Nothing mattered except him. Cade nipped lightly at her bottom lip and kissed the sting away. She lost her battle of trying to stop him and wrapped her arms tighter around him instead.

They kissed each other with a fierce urgency and lost themselves in the desperate heat and fervor of it. With their lips touching and arms tangled and clinging to one another, they didn't notice the heavy footfalls coming down the hall.

CHAPTER 13

"Ahem."

As they heard Rederrick clear his throat awkwardly, they immediately released their grip on one another, snapping away from each other as if a rattlesnake had just been dropped in the space between them.

Collett turned around too embarrassed to face Rederrick at the moment. She felt the heat in her face. She knew it would be beet red right now.

Keeping his eyes on her, Cade kept his back to Rederrick as well. He wasn't sure how he felt about what happened; even more so, he felt unsettled by her reaction. "Is there something you needed, Rederrick?" he asked.

"When you have a minute, I just came back with Nate. He made it into town a little over an hour ago. He's downstairs. I thought we could go over some security plans together," Rederrick answered quickly.

"Yeah, sure," came Cade's terse reply.

"Well, um, I'll just meet you downstairs when you're ready." With that, Rederrick turned and left the room. Shaking his head as he moved to the stairway, he thought to himself, *I didn't see that one coming.*

Standing silently in the room with her back turned to Cade, Collett felt unsure how she should handle this. Several emotions ran through her system all at once. Her mind felt overloaded, and her body felt as if it was on fire from the needy feeling he stirred within her. It was frightening. Turning, she met his warm eyes.

He stood there silently, looking as confused and as flustered as she felt. She wanted to lash out at him to help her feel better about what happened, and if he'd have given her that cocky smile of his, she would have done exactly that.

The words died in her throat. He was as uncertain as she was. In fact, he looked a bit worse. She could see he felt torn about what had happened. For some reason, she knew couldn't handle, nor did she want to hear the words, "I'm sorry," uttered from him. She could see he was thinking about saying it, too.

Finally, after a minute or so, he ran his fingers through his hair, then dropped his hands to his sides as if not sure what to say. Without being aware of it, he chose wisely by saying softly, "I guess I better get downstairs."

She nodded, "Yeah, probably."

"Collett, I um…Well I'm not really sure what just happened. I'm also not honestly sure what I should say."

She tried for easygoing nonchalance, "Well don't worry about it. It just happened, no big deal."

Surprised, he could only stare and silence stretched once more.

"Um, you better get going. Rederrick is waiting for you."

"Yeah," he mumbled.

Even in his quiet voice, she could hear the anger in the single word. Her response must have bothered him. He took one step backwards and then turned abruptly, escaping from the room.

She stood there confused, alone, and feeling very vulnerable. She took a deep cleansing breath to center herself, but it didn't help. She moved across the room to the door.

She stepped off the end of the hallway rug feeling the cool wood floor underneath her uncovered feet. She reached the stairway and picked her way down each step, trailing her fingers down the smooth polished banister as she went. As she distractedly reached the second-floor hallway and walked down to her room, she was so lost in thought she failed to notice Cynda.

Cynda stood at the entrance of her own room only a short distance from the stairway. She watched the way Collett moved and wondered what had put the confused look on her face.

Making her way to Collett's room, she lightly tapped on the closed door. No answer. Worried she opened the door a small crack, "Collett? It's Cynda, can I come in?"

"Sure," she answered quietly.

Pushing the door open wider, Cynda took a good look at Collett. She sat on the little bench at the end of the bed staring at her hands. "What happened? Did you remember something?" Cynda questioned as she moved to sit down by Collett.

"No," was the mumbled reply.

She put her hand on Collett's shoulder. With concern apparent in her voice she asked again, "What happened? What's wrong?"

Collett lifted her head looking at her as if barely considering her presence, and then she blurted out, "Cade…Cade kissed me."

"What was that?" Cynda asked surprised.

Collett stood and paced to the window to look outside. She could see winter storm clouds now blocked the sun. The dark, angry-looking clouds slowly drifted overhead in the massive sky. Small white flakes floated down every now and then.

Cynda tried to remove the shock from her tone and talk to her as a friend, "Well how do you feel about it? I mean, Cade um, kissing you."

Without turning she replied, "I'm not sure. I mean really, it wasn't as if I pushed him away or stopped him. *I kissed him back* for heaven's sake, and I felt this…this tingling inside me," she paused, looking at the moving clouds again. "What if there's someone waiting for me; someone who loves me, someone I can't remember?"

Cynda knew how to answer this. She knew exactly how to help Collett with this problem at least. She asked simply, "Do you feel an empty feeling in your heart, as if you're missing a part of it? Like there is a void there?"

Collett turned and looked to Cynda, then asked confused, "What do you mean? My whole life is missing."

Cynda smiled and patted the seat next to where she sat, "Come here, let me explain." When Collett eased herself down into the seat, Cynda continued, "You see when you love someone, truly love, they become a part of you. You would sacrifice everything you have to stay whole. Love like that lasts forever. It doesn't end when this life does. It goes on into the next.

"I truly believe that if our roles were reversed, and I had no memory, I would know a part of me was missing. I would go to the ends of this earth and beyond to find it. Nothing! Nothing would stop me from knowing that piece of my life, that piece of myself, was missing. I know Rederrick would feel the same. He would give his life up for me. He almost did once long ago. It's not something you could just forget, or something you would ever forget!"

Collett's shoulders slumped forward, "I think you're right. I never even wondered before today. I have always felt like," she paused, "I'm alone in this."

"Was alone," Cynda corrected firmly. "You are no longer on your own. You have all of us now. If this thing with Cade makes you uncomfortable, I'll talk to him. He would never want to hurt you or make this harder on you."

"It's not that. I do feel something for Cade. It scares me. I feel so confused. I'm scared to face any more right now. I'm scared to find out the truth about myself in general. I feel like I am constantly standing at the edge of a cliff, and it would only take a small breeze to push me over."

Cynda knew the answers would come. She also understood that waiting was the worst part. It felt nerve wracking, and it made people edgy, so she spoke carefully trying to comfort Collett's frayed nerves by reaffirming her previous statement.

Choosing more fitting words, Cynda said softly, "When you're facing a long fall it's nice to know there are people there waiting at the bottom to catch you. That being said... If you're not ready to jump, step away from the cliff." Cynda stood then saying, "Fear can be a good thing. It keeps us safe. It keeps us from running out in front of speeding cars, but you can't let it control your life. Without fear, there is no courage; and without courage, there is no valor."

She let silence fill the room, allowing Collett to think about what she said. The words came from Cade. He had once told her the very same thing, many years ago.

"How do I know when I will be ready?" Collett whispered.

Cynda moved around to the bed, fingering a fringe on a throw pillow as she passed. Then her eyes took a faraway look as she said, "Only you will know. No one can tell you when to be ready to face the truth. I think-when you are ready, everything will come back to you. I think the best thing for you right now is taking things one step at a time until that day comes."

Collett looked at the kind woman standing there trying to help her through all the conflicting emotions she felt. Cynda's soft, auburn hair looked darker in the lamplight. Her sparkling eyes held sincerity and compassion. She made Collett realize she felt ready to change one thing for sure. Collett knew she was ready to quit running. She wanted to make her life here. She desperately wanted to make these caring, compassionate people, who shared their home and their love with her, a part of her life for good, because being alone after this would be an empty life indeed.

"Cynda?" Collett stood and walked to her.

"Hum?"

"Thank you," she said sincerely.

Cynda couldn't stand it any longer. She wrapped her arms tightly around Collett, and, surprisingly, Collett returned the embrace. "You truly are important to us, and when you fall, or jump, whichever the case may be, we'll be there to catch you."

Collett nodded, unable to speak any more words. She knew Cynda would be there for her. Still frightened of what the future held for her, and confused about her past, she felt relief at knowing right now, in the present, she was okay.

Letting go and stepping back, Cynda wiped at the glistening tears forming in her eyes. "I think that is enough of that," she said with levity. "Now then, since it's best you stay in the house, I rented a couple of chick flicks and rounded up some chocolate-covered strawberries for a girl's night in. What do you say?"

Collett let a smile spread across her face, another real smile. She seemed to be doing that more and more lately. Hooking her arm through Cynda's, she said, "What are we waiting for? Lead the way."

"Want to talk about it?" Rederrick asked after they finished their plans, and Nate had left the security room to get some sleep. Throughout the meeting, Cade remained distracted, distant. Not that Rederrick had blamed him after what he had seen upstairs. He understood the way a woman could twist you up inside.

He looked at Rederrick with an innocent expression, "Talk about what?"

Rederrick just gave Cade a bland stare, silently saying, 'Nice try, but I'm not buying your line of crap.'

Cade still tried to evade, "Really there is nothing to talk about. It just happened. It won't happen again. End of story."

"Nothing is ever that simple, Cade."

Cade gave Rederrick a slanted look, "No, old man, not generally. This time it is. It's just all the stress of this impossible situation. I was weak for a moment. I won't let it happen again."

Rederrick nodded and lifted his hands in surrender, "Fine. You don't want to talk about it, I get it. But you know, it just goes to show you-"

"Goes to show me what?" Cade asked in an exasperated breath.

"That you never know when fate will smile on you. Or smack you in the face. Depending how you look at it, of course." His friend stated simply as he stood from his chair and began heading to the door.

Cade stopped him with a strong grip on his arm, "What's that supposed to mean?" he asked with a fierce expression on his face. Without knowing it, Cade answered one thing for Rederrick. This meant something, and Cade friend was bothered by it.

"You're not a stupid man, Cade. You know exactly what I mean." With an arched brow, Rederrick looked pointedly at the hand holding his arm.

Cade let go. Stepping back, he ran his fingers through his hair. Rederrick spelled it out for him and he didn't like it. By some sick twist of fate, Collett became important, more important than any woman in his life. *How could this be happening?* he asked himself.

Rederrick stood, watching his friend come to terms with the truth. He already knew the same thing Cade was just figuring out. After seeing them locked in each other's arms, he realized he should have seen it coming. It explained Cade's odd behavior during the past week. He was irritable and edgy. Beyond that, Cade spent a lot of time and effort avoiding Collett. Well, until today, he mused.

Finally, Cade confessed, "From the first moment I saw her, I knew something was different. Why would this be happening now? Only once have I felt strongly about a woman, and what happened with her nearly killed me. I can't go through that again. I can't.

Besides, she's afraid of me, of what I am. Hell, she doesn't even like me."

"She didn't look very scared to me. Seems to me, she likes you fine," Rederrick implied with a grin, but when Cade didn't smile he sobered. "Sometimes we can't avoid fate. You know that better than anyone. I'll leave you with one question though. Knowing what you do now, would you trade the pain of the woman you lost for the good memories of your time together?"

Cade had no reply, and Rederrick left the room leaving him with his thoughts.

He stood there in the empty room alone. He watched the many screens playing security footage; seeing Cynda and Collett in the media room together. He saw Collett smile at something Cynda said. Her beautiful, radiant smile pulled at his chest. He wanted to get to know this woman; wanted to have memories of her.

In his earlier years, Cade had been married; not realizing the cost he would pay for it. He knew of the beast within him. He had even learned to control it by then. Though, he never would have guessed then that he was immortal.

He met Mary during the French Indian war. Full of himself back then, he joined the militia against the French. He learned so much in those turbulent years. He saw so much; witnessed the true nature of man, both the ugly and the beautiful.

He had seen heroes risk all to save one comrade, and watched the horrible way men changed their beliefs, twisting the term honor, all in the name of vengeance and justice. War was a very ugly thing. In all that ugliness, he found one beautiful thing: Mary.

Cade had courted her appropriately, falling in love with her slowly, or what he thought was love anyway. Eventually, they were properly married. He could still see her smiling face as Mary walked toward him that day. They made vows and promises, and when the priest said the words, "...until death do you part," he truly had no idea exactly what that would mean.

Around the age of thirty, his body stopped aging. He watched, as Mary grew older. As she aged, she grew sad and bitter too. He had never been able to give her a child. He suspected it was because of the beast within him. Though, much later, as he met others of his kind, he learned differently.

He saw the sadness in Mary every day though, and he blamed himself. It tore at him to watch her love turn to hate. She hated what he was, what he couldn't give her. Her hate was too much to bear, and ultimately she had ended her own life one day while he was away.

He never again wanted to be the cause of that kind of pain, but it wasn't like Collett didn't already know about him. He knew more now too.

After hours of thought, Cade resolved that he couldn't walk away from this uninjured either way. He had feelings for Collett, and he wanted to know her. He was going to make the most of the little time they could have. He was just going to have to spend some time convincing her of that.

CHAPTER 14

As the night's darkening shadows crept in, Jeffery felt his recurring agitation creep in as well. For three long days, he kept watch on this house, waiting for his chance. For three days, the target hadn't set one foot outside.

The branch Jeffery sat on high in the tree was hard, rough, and his joints were cramping from sitting here so long. On top of that, the dark heavy clouds rolling in and the cold, biting wind indicated snow. The clouds rolled in across the sky around three o'clock, making the night's darkness come that much quicker.

Other people came and went from the house in routine patterns. At this point, he was thinking of using the fat, old housekeeper as leverage. He had to do something. Boredom was fast taking over. He had never been very patient. He also did not intend to tangle with that stupid witch again.

"It is time for you to go," Jeffery heard from a deep, growling voice below.

He jumped, almost falling from his tenuous perch. Looking left and right he sought out the source. He thought he saw movement near the pine trees, but then it was gone. He felt as if his mind was playing tricks on him. Whoever it was, they couldn't be talking to him. There was no way anyone could see him past the spell he'd cast.

The deep voice spoke again, "I know you're not deaf, Jeffery. This is my kill."

He looked around once again for the speaker. *There,* he thought, squinting his eyes at the darkened landscape. The stranger leaned against a pine tree. You could barely see the shadow blending with the dark base of the tree. He decided not to release the spell keeping him hidden, just in case the speaker wasn't positive on his location. For that same reason, he chose not to speak.

The mystery speaker's voice quickly ruined that illusion for him by saying calmly, "Did you know, Jeffery, you reek? You smell like a foul mix of onion, from the burger you had an hour ago, hair dye, and the horrid stench of BO. I'm slightly curious though, when you popped out for a bite to eat, why not get some fresh clothes?"

How had this man known when he blinked in and out? Jeffery worried. The fact that this man knew of his movements stunned him. As if on cue to his own thoughts, the speaker answered for him.

"As I said, you stink. Oh, and you're about as quiet as a jackhammer pounding into the payment. Now, how about I give you one more chance to zap your skinny ass out of here before I come up there and throw you off that tree branch to see if you can fly."

Jeffery decided to speak up, asking defiantly, "What makes you think you can?"

Before he could even take his next breath, the shadow moved to the bottom of the tree he occupied and jumped the impossible distance to crouch on the branch nearest him. As it happened, that very branch put the stranger above him.

Tilting his head down, the man spoke again, "What makes you think I can't?" This time his voice sent chills through Jeffery's very soul.

He peered through the darkness, straining his eyes to get a good look at the man who had put a lump of fear in his throat. He couldn't see much. Jeffery was sure that was done on purpose. The shadowy man wore all black. Even his thick hair was like polished ebony that had a glint despite the dark night. It whipped about in the wind, concealing the stranger's face. Hidden by the tree's shadow and his own hair, anything identifiable on his face was kept a mystery. Dark Oakley's completed the dangerous look by hiding the mysterious man's eyes from scrutiny.

Why would someone wear sunglasses in the dead of night? How could anyone see in this blackness with sunglasses on? Really, who the hell did he think he was, Blade? Jeffery wondered to himself.

For a long moment, the only sound around them was the winter wind rustling the tree branches and stirring leaves on the cold earth. Jeffery carefully considered his next move. He liked a good challenge, but something about this stranger's attitude sent up red flags of caution in his head.

On any other assignment, he would have just moved aside. This man was too confident not to be deadly and had found him way too easily. Jeffery still held his invisibility spell in place, yet this dark stranger stared right at him. He didn't have a death wish. However, on this night, there was more at stake than only his life. His previous failure of not capturing the woman came at a price. A price he prayed would never be cashed in.

With bravado he didn't feel, Jeffery croaked out, "Look man, you can have the kill and the money. I just need the body."

"Tell me, how am I to get paid if you have my finished work?" the dark man asked sounding almost amused.

His fear and worry for his mother prodded him to compromise. He tried again, "How about we work together?"

The dark man didn't flinch. Nor did he speak. He just stayed there, looking in Jeffery's direction. In that silent moment, Jeffery was profoundly grateful he could not see the dark man's eyes. He knew without a doubt, looking into them would be the same as looking into a soulless abyss. What he could see of this man was almost enough to make him want to jump willingly from his perch.

Even without the words, he knew the answer. This man would not play well with others, ever!

His decision made, he would have to be very careful with this idea. He would have to convince this dark man before him that he was valuable.

He pleaded his case, trying not to sound too desperate, "Look, I can help you, and you obviously know me. You must know what I can do, right? We can do this together. You can have my share of the money; just let me come with you to turn in the kill. I'll do whatever you want. I'll follow your lead. I need to be a part of this kill."

The Man moved so quickly Jeffery didn't even have time to blink before he found himself lifted up to eye level with the stranger, his feet dangling above the branch he had previously sat on.

The stranger ground out, "Time's up, little boy."

Knowing the statement may prove true in a matter of seconds, Jeffery quickly made the gestures necessary to blink from the man's deadly grip. Leaving the tree to the dark stranger, he transported himself back to the small diner he'd eaten in earlier.

Now what am I going to do? And who the hell was that dark man? he wondered to himself. He needed to think of something else. He needed a new strategy. With shaking fingers, he picked up his cell phone and dialed. He needed information even more.

The phone rang three times before he heard a familiar voice, "Hello Jeffery. Do you have good news for me?"

"Not yet, but soon."

"I see. Well no matter; I think your mother is beginning to like it here."

"Look, I'll get it done. Don't hurt her."

"I'm sure you will; now that you have the proper motivation…"

Jeffery ground his teeth in frustration and anger. "Who else did you send?"

"Oh, you met your competition then? Don't worry, he's not so bad." Finnawick the imp broke into a hideous cackle. "First man to bring me her body gets their reward."

The line went dead. He had to figure out a way to get to the woman first. His mother's life depended on it.

Back in the tree, sitting on the very same thick, heavy branch Jeffery once occupied, The Hunter watched the house carefully looking for his way in. Unlike Jeffery, he knew the people here were not stupid. They would not let the target out for anything. It would leave her too open, too vulnerable. To get to her, The Hunter would have to go in.

He felt comfortable enough in the tree Jeffery picked, and it offered a great view of the house. Not relaxing his senses, he relaxed his tense body. Folding his arms, and leaning back, he waited. Waited, even when the first flakes fell, and kept waiting while the brown earth was eventually covered with a soft, white blanket.

His dark shape didn't even twitch. He melded into the blackness of the starless night. This was his time, the time of The Hunter.

He knew the best way to beat an opponent was to understand them, and know what makes them tick. So he waited, watched, and learned. With his keen vision, and a massive amount of patience, The Hunter always got what he wanted.

Then, sure enough, the next morning he saw it. He saw his way in. It would take a few adjustments, but now he knew this would be much easier than he thought.

Jumping from his high lookout spot with fluid ease, The Hunter sprinted off to make the necessary arrangements, putting his devious plans into motion.

The morning after her talk with Cynda, Collett stood in the kitchen by the large window behind the table. With a glass of orange juice in her hand, she looked out the window at the soft, white flakes. She watched them drifting and dancing their way down to lie gently on the already white blanketed ground.

Her long talk with Cynda, and the time spent watching movies with her last night laughing and joking, provided her with a much needed morale boost. She would not give up so easily. As for the situation with Cade, she promised herself to take that one step at a time.

She stood here to watch the snow. She was trying to picture a time in her life when she saw it before, a time when she felt the cold seep through her clothes. Collett knew she saw it before, knew what it felt like.

She thought about the cold, wet feeling as you packed it in your fingers and the fresh taste of the flakes on your tongue when you were lucky enough to catch them falling from the sky. She pictured the way it glistened when the sun peeked through the clouds after a storm. She knew it would reflect light so bright you would have to squint to tolerate the blinding glare. While thinking these things over in her head she thought about things you do in the snow: snowmen, snowball fights, snow angels.

She smiled. Juliet had loved to lie in the snow moving her arms and legs to make an angel…*wait, Juliet*? Her sister. Her sister Juliet. *I have a sister*! Collett remembered. Splotchy images flashed through her mind; pictures of Juliet in the cold winter, giggling while she made the perfect angel. She could remember, "Juliet!" she cried out.

Her orange juice slipped from her fingers to fall to the floor. She barely noticed as the glass shattered when it struck the tile, splattering the remaining juice.

On the stairway, Cade heard her shout and then a sound of breaking glass. He rushed down the stairs into the kitchen. When he came into the room, his panic ebbed slightly. He saw her there standing in the middle of broken glass and juice. It had splattered all over her jeans around the ankles.

He asked quickly, "What is it? What's wrong? Are you ok?" He went over to her intending to help with the broken glass. He didn't get that far. She met him halfway, throwing herself in his arms with excitement, almost knocking him over.

She didn't even think about what she was doing as she launched into his arms. He caught her, accepting the hug even though he remained confused. It was the first time she willingly came to him.

He wrapped his arms around her, enjoying the feel of her. After Cade's surprise passed, he risked pulling her back. There she stood before him with an excited smile stretching across her pretty face. Seeing the light and happiness in her eyes nearly undid him. Finally, he croaked out, "What's going on?"

"I remember her! I remember Juliet," she rambled excitedly.

Because she was practically jumping out of her own skin from the excitement, it took him a second to decipher what she said.

Still trying to sort this out, but loving how thrilled she looked, he prodded happily, "Who is Juliet?"

"She was my sister! I remembered my sister." She blurted out quickly, as she jumped forward and hugged him again. "I was looking out at the snow, and then it just popped in my head. I was watching her play in the snow. She was laughing while she made an angel. My sister, my sweet Juliet. She was like an angel."

He stayed silent, letting her work through her vague memories. He rubbed his hand up and down her back.

Thinking hard and crinkling the bridge of her nose, she replayed the image, "It was so cold. I remember the cold now. I was there with her. Juliet had long, dark hair. It used to be so tangled. She had little freckles across her nose and cheeks. They were like angel kisses. Her eyes were like melted chocolate, and glittered when she was happy. I remember her that day. I remember her laugh. She had such a pretty laugh."

His happy feeling turned grim. He didn't think Collett noticed she was using the past tense when she spoke of Juliet. He noticed, and he was sure he knew what it meant but was unwilling to say it. Knowing he needed to keep the memory fresh he asked, "What else do you remember? The place, do you know where you were? Were there people there?"

She didn't hear him. Her face pulled tight, "Why can I only remember her face as a little girl? I can only remember that day, that one moment. I can see her face now. I can see the freckles, and her cold, pink cheeks. Her dress was too small for her, and it was tattered. Her fingers were red from the cold. We didn't have any gloves."

She stopped then, realizing something wasn't right here. Her head started pounding, the pain originating right behind her eyes. Using her fingers to knead at her temples, she kept trying to push the memory through, forcing the confusing image to the front of her mind. "Her dress, there was something wrong with Juliet's dress," she whispered. "Why can't I remember more? I need to know more!" she voiced defiantly.

Instead of clearing, the memory started fading away. The pain of her throbbing skull was making what was once a clear image start to blur. *Maybe I'm wrong,* she thought. *Maybe it was something else I remembered.*

Cade noticed the change in her right away. She wore all her emotions on her beautifully expressive face. He wrapped his arms around her and said, "Don't get discouraged. It will come. Remembering someone like a sister is a big thing. Give it time. I have faith you'll figure it out."

Collett looked out the window as he held her and said, "I want to remember her, Cade. I want my life back."

"I know. We'll get there. It's going to take time. They say Rome wasn't built in a day. Remember what you can; the rest will come."

He pulled back, put his hands on her shoulders, and looked into her sad eyes. "Come on then, let's get some aspirin for your headache," he suggested. "Then I'll take you to your room. After a short nap, you'll feel much better."

"How did you know… never mind." Her look turned pleading, "I have to find out if she is real, Cade. I need to know if I really did remember. I need to find her."

"We'll figure it out together," he promised. "Whatever happens, whatever you remember; we will figure this out. I swear it to you. You were beginning to believe, don't let go of that. You have taken a very big step, whether you believe it or not. Now we know you can remember. Come on then, once you lie down you'll feel better. Give yourself a break."

She nodded numbly and let him escort her to her room. She prayed he was right, and she could remember. She wanted so desperately to remember. She was extremely tired of not knowing. When she first remembered Juliet, she was ecstatic. Now the image seemed wrong to her. Something was very off about Juliet's clothes and the building behind her. It was more than that. She felt pain in her chest when she thought of her sister. She felt like she was going crazy.

As they walked up the stairs, Collett wondered if she was beginning to make things up subconsciously out of a desperate need to know. Either way, she reasoned, it didn't feel right.

Cade called the office to fill Rederrick and Cynda in on this morning's event. After hanging up, Cynda left Rederrick to handle things. She wanted to be there to help Collett coax free her memory further. When she arrived, she went looking for Cade.

Finding him in the den, she moved to him with purpose, "Where is she?"

He looked up from where he sat in the dark-brown, leather chair. Her entrance tore him from his deep focus on the laptop screen sitting on top of the desk. Over the past hour, he'd been going over missing person reports from the last two years. He had a friend forward them to him a couple of days ago. It was horrifying to him how many people had gone missing in such a short time.

He managed to narrow the list some by looking for females between the ages of 23 to 28 years old. He was sure Collett couldn't be any older than 26, but he thought it best to be as thorough as possible. Even considering those, the size of the list still made him sad.

Stretching his stiff neck Cade answered, "She's upstairs napping." As she turned to leave, he stopped her saying cautiously, "Cynda there is something you should know."

Turning around, Cynda furrowed her eyebrows wondering what he left out on the phone, "What?"

"I think her sister is dead," he bluntly stated.

"Why would you think that?"

He stood from the chair he occupied, walked around to the front of the desk, and stopped next to her to explain his theory, "Collett didn't realize it at the time, but she talked of this Juliet in the past tense, several times. Plus she got really upset and frustrated when she couldn't picture an older, adult version of her sister. She took on a sad, lost look."

She leaned against the desk next to him, thinking about what he was telling her. Doubt clouded her voice, "You could be wrong, maybe it was just because it was a past memory."

With some anger in his tone, he shot back, "Then where are they? Tell me, why haven't they been looking for her? I have been through so many reports it makes me sick, yet I have not found one that matches her. Not one."

She offered him a sympathetic expression, "You of all people know, that just because you have relatives; doesn't mean you have family."

Cade brought his hand up to the back of his neck rubbing away the tight stiffness. Her remark hit home. Still, he felt strongly from the way Collett reacted, her sister had most likely passed on. He didn't like the idea any more than Cynda.

Huffing out a heavy breath he continued, "It's just a guess, and I think, if I'm right, we should let her come to terms with it on her own. When she does, I think it will be a hard blow."

Dipping her head and looking at her hands, Cynda agreed with him, "It will be like losing her all over again. This is not a good way to start recovering her memories."

"I don't like this anymore than you," he admitted solemnly. "If you take the optimistic path though, she did remember something. According to Collett, it's the first memory she's had in two years. No matter what happens, it's a start. Now we need to figure out how we help her keep remembering, even if it does become painful."

Straightening her frame, Cynda patted him on the arm. With an encouraging smile on her face, she said, "We just need to be there for her, Cade. We just simply be there. Now, if you'll excuse me… I think I'll go upstairs and do exactly that." With that declaration she sauntered off.

Knowing she was right, he turned and headed back to the reports he had been going through earlier. Hoping for a little luck, he searched through each case carefully, searching for a link; something, anything similar to Collett's story. An hour later he gave up on the files and moved to the bio Rederrick had compiled on her. After all, when you can't remember something, it was always a good idea to retrace your steps.

CHAPTER 15

Cynda didn't bother knocking. She didn't want to wake Collett if she was sleeping. She opened the door slightly to peek in and saw Collett was awake. Her eyes were staring straight up at the ceiling. She was lying on her back, with her hands folded and placed on her stomach. She looked to be deep in thought, so Cynda moved to close the door.

Seeing the movement out of the corner of her eye Collett stopped her, "It's alright… you can come in."

Startled some by her smooth voice, Cynda came in the room and quietly closed the door behind her. "I thought you'd be sleeping," she said.

"I'm not really tired. My head hurts a bit, so I was just resting." She sat up and brought her legs over the edge of the bed.

"Cade called," Cynda declared.

Collett smiled, "I know. I figured he would."

Not sure what she should say, Cynda sat on the side of the bed next to Collett, just waiting silently with her until she was ready to discuss what happened.

"I'm not sure that what I saw was real, not anymore. How could it be real?" Collett asked, thinking aloud.

Cynda put her arm around her and squeezed her shoulder slightly. Trying to offer reassurance she asked, "Did it feel real?"

With emotion in her voice, she answered, "Yes. It felt very real. I felt so much at once...excitement, love, and happiness. They all came from one small flash."

"Why then, is it hard to believe it?" Cynda questioned.

She tried explaining her impressions, "I saw her, Juliet, I mean. She was so young." She couldn't help smiling as she recalled the flashed memory, "She had a cute little pixie face. Freckles brushed across her nose and cheeks, and she had pretty little heart-shaped lips. She was smiling, and she looked so happy."

Standing, Collett paced, "That is all I see. This happy little girl, giggling as she moved her arms up and down in the snow making the image of an angel."

Cynda believed it was real. It sounded too vivid to be imagined. She also noticed the same thing Cade had before, the sad sound in Collett's voice and the use of the past tense. Damn, he was probably right, she thought to herself. "That sounds like a beautiful moment. It is a wonderful first memory."

Nodding in agreement, Collett went on, "I thought so, too. I was so happy and excited. Then there was this unexpected, sad feeling in me. It was so strong. I tried to focus more on the quick flash. I started to notice other things, too. It had to be made up. It couldn't be real. It was her clothes. There was something wrong with them. I sat here for a long time trying to reason through it. None of it makes sense," she stated, starting to bite at her thumbnail.

"Collett what didn't make sense? What was wrong with- Juliet, was it? What was wrong with her clothes?"

"They were old. Not just old, they were really old." At Cynda's puzzled expression, she sighed again and then spat it out, "She wore a tattered frock or something. Some sort of dress, a very old dress. She didn't have on a modern coat or gloves, just a dingy brown cape, like a cloak, and a sort of bonnet. It was all she wore to keep the cold away. Her hands were red from the cold. Her little button nose to. Now tell me, how could that be real? It just can't be. I must be remembering a story I read or a movie I saw. It's just not possible"

"Do you believe that it's true?" Cynda asked seriously.

Throwing up her hands in exasperation Collett replied, "I don't know what to believe anymore. I do know I am not old enough to have a sister who wore those kinds of clothes. At the very same time, I feel strongly that I saw my sister. Even her name, I know her name, Juliet! I can remember her face, her sweet pixie like face. She felt so real. In my heart, it was real," her voice cracked. "Yet when I concentrate harder, trying to see more, my head feels like it is going to split in two." She took a heavy breath before continuing, "I feel so lost. How can it feel so right and be so wrong? Be so clear, yet so foggy at the same time? I'm not really sure of anything anymore."

Cynda sat still and quiet, thinking over this new information, considering the possibilities, and truth be told, there were many. She had a quick thought of Selena again. She was not sure what to tell Collett. She had a few ideas but was sure this was not the time. She wanted to talk to Cade first and find out what Selena could see. She also wanted to do a little research of her own.

Therefore, Cynda decided to keep her advice vague, "Don't focus so much on the clothing… that will come later. Just focus on Juliet. Think about the feelings and impressions you get from seeing her face. I really think you'll figure it all out. This is a great start. Cade's right. This shows us you can remember."

Collett's shoulders drooped as she walked back to the soft bed, sat down, and conceded reluctantly, "Maybe you're right. Perhaps I'll be able to explain it later when I remember more."

With an encouraging note in her voice, Cynda agreed, "You will. I do think we could try something new. I have a friend who I think you should meet. Her name is Selena."

"Why? You think she can help?" Collett asked skeptically.

"Actually, I do. She has the gift of reading people. Sometimes she can get a sense of the past and future. Would you be willing to give it a try?" Cynda asked hopefully.

Deciding it couldn't hurt, she agreed, "Alright, I'll give it a try. I guess right now anything is better than nothing."

"Okay. I'll go give her a call. I'll try to get her out here tomorrow. I think it would be best if we can all be there with you. Tomorrow is Saturday, so it will be much easier for all of us." Standing, Cynda went to the door.

As she reached for the brass handle, Collett asked, "How is it, you can always make me feel better?"

Turning with a bright smile on her perfect lips, Cynda explained, "Because once, long ago, I gave up hoping. Then someone very special helped me find it again. It's hope, in ourselves and in others, that keeps us going. Having a strong belief that it can, and will, get better, and having faith that it is all worth it, can make it all okay. Without that, there would be no point in fighting."

Collett thought for a minute, "Who?"

"Who, what?" Cynda questioned, slightly confused.

"Who taught you how to find it? Hope, I mean."

"Oh, I think that's a story for another day. I'll see you at dinner." And with that, Cynda left her new friend to her thoughts.

Later that night, Collett sat down to a wonderful dinner of Jenny's homemade beef stew and bread sticks. Almost everyone was there. Cynda sat next to Rederrick, and Cade sat on his other side, putting her right between Cade and Cynda. Jenny had refused to join them saying she had other things to tend to, and Nate kept an eye on the security screens Rederrick had shown her a couple of days ago.

As she swallowed another healthy bite, she enjoyed the warm feeling from the stew, inside and out. It felt like the perfect meal to go with the cold, snowy day. She felt much better now, especially surrounded by her new friends.

Maybe it was crazy, but ever since Cynda told her the theory on her empathic abilities, she felt more attuned to the feelings surrounding her. On the other hand, maybe it was simply that now she had people who cared about her, and she felt it inside herself. Either way, it was a wonderful thing.

When Rederrick finished filling Cynda in on the rest of his day at the office, he turned his attention to her. "Cynda tells me Selena is coming by tomorrow," he offered kindly.

She nodded, "That's what she tells me, too."

Cade smiled, "Don't worry. You'll like her. Selena has a very gentle nature. She might be able to help."

"Have you ever had her help?" she asked.

He looked directly into her blue eyes, "Yes, once, about seven years ago. I asked for her help. Unfortunately, she couldn't tell me anything I didn't already know."

"What about you, Rederrick; has Selena ever helped you?" She asked as she reluctantly tore her gaze from Cade.

"No, not her, but her mother did. Her mother helped me find what I truly wanted about 30 years ago."

Considering his words she asked, "What was it you wanted?"

"Why me, of course," answered Cynda ruefully.

Then Rederrick took Cynda's hand and kissing it agreed, "That's the truth of it. She didn't steer me wrong."

"Does she tell you what to do then, what you need to do?" she inquired, curious now.

"No… it is more like she can tell you a destination and you can choose the road to get you there," Cade explained. "Depending on the road you take, the destination might be closed to you. It is somewhat cryptic and confusing at the time she sees you, but eventually it makes sense. Sometimes she can get a sense on past experiences as well, to provide insight."

"It's a stepping stone," Cynda supplied. "Everyone I know who has received advice or insight from her has learned something from it. Just a little guidance, that's all."

Thinking as she took another bite of stew, Collett considered what she would possibly learn tomorrow. She was a little afraid of what would happen after tomorrow. Who was she? What would they all think of her when they knew? And as she thought about it, her nervous stomach twisted itself into tight knots. She looked down at her warm, delicious stew and could not stomach another bite. The warmth of her mood dissipated.

Cade took her mind from her worried ponderings. "On a different topic," he said, "I think we should all be working on self-defense techniques. To be prepared if we're attacked, we need to know how to work as a team. Collett, for instance would be the most vulnerable in a fight. We know she would be their prime target. Therefore, I feel it necessary we each work with her in turns. Help her. She needs to be familiar with each of our skills, and we can help her work on hers. I've spoken with Nate, and he has agreed to spend some time with her on military tactics as well. Learning to use a gun will be first on that list."

"Agreed. I can set aside time tomorrow after Selena leaves," offered Rederrick. "I'll take her to the Extra Room to show her around, and we'll review exit strategies in case of an in-home breach."

Collett looked from one man to the next as they spoke, acting as if she wasn't even present. Then Cynda added happily, "That's a great idea. I'll take her upstairs and show her some of my works. Maybe we can see if she's able to use magic. I'll bet she can, with a little help and practice."

Her mood quickly began shifting to annoyance, "Um-" she began.

Cade cut her off as if he didn't hear her, "I'll take the physical training since it is my area of expertise. If she intends to hold off anything worth their salt, she's going to need to work hard at it. We don't have much time before they'll get tired of waiting for her to come out."

With a piercing glare and temper in her voice, she blurted out, "You all know I am in this room right? Don't you think I should get an opinion here?"

"Not if you want to stay alive. We're trying to do what is best for you," Cade replied. Across the table, Cynda gave Cade a warning glance. He didn't notice.

Collett stared right back at him, seething now. How dare he tell her what's best in that egotistical tone. "You know, I've managed to stay alive all this time without you planning my every move!" she retorted snidely.

"Really! How was it you did that again? Oh yeah, that's right… you ran. Besides that, if you count last Saturday and Sunday, you really haven't stayed alive all on your own," he stated sarcastically.

She felt somewhat humbled by his on-the-mark words, but she was unwilling to concede to his point-of-view so easily; as a matter of pride.

She groused, "Fine. I'll do it your way for now, but do not make the mistake of talking about me as if I wasn't here again. I may not remember who I am, but do not underestimate me. I'm just as strong and as resourceful as any of you." Finished ranting, she rose from her chair and left the room with an indignant attitude, heading upstairs with purpose.

Now how did that happen? Cade wondered as he ran his fingers through his hair in an aggravated gesture. He looked to Cynda and Rederrick for advice on how to handle this. Rederrick just stared back with a goofy, knowing grin, and Cynda's womanly features pinched with a worried expression.

"Dammit!" Cade barked. Throwing his napkin on the table, he abruptly rose from his chair to follow her.

When he got to the top of the stairs, he heard her moving to the workout room. He stopped for a moment, trying to decide what he would say to her. Then he heard the sound of Collett violently punching or kicking the heavy bag. He leaped up the stairs quickly.

When he got to the doorway of the workout room, he stopped and watched as she furiously threw herself at the heavy black bag, vigorously punching it over and over again. He waited and watched as her arms tired and her punches lost their strength. She gave her invisible enemy one last violent kick, then suddenly lost all her fight. Leaning her forehead against the heavy bag, Collett began to sob.

Unsure what he should do, he hesitated. She was unaware of his intruding presence, but he could see her shoulders shake. He could hear her muffled squeaks and hiccups. Finally, he made his decision. He couldn't bear to watch her like this.

He moved to her slowly. He carefully put his hand on her back, hoping she wouldn't turn around and deck him for the effort. He was relieved and surprised when, without needing any further encouragement, she turned into him and laid her head on his chest while he enveloped her with his arms.

He brought his hand to her hair, softly stroking her soft golden locks, repeatedly whispering reassuring words, "It will be alright. I'm sorry. Just let it out." He felt a horrible guilt for bringing her to this point, knowing he had pushed too hard.

She stayed there in his warm, comforting embrace for a long time. She cried and sniffled for so long she wasn't sure it would ever stop. After a time, her last tear fell down her face and the final hiccupping mumble passed. Feeling drained and tired, with puffy, red, swollen eyes; she lifted her eyes to meet his. His expression was so full of worry and guilt. It almost made her smile. She could tell he blamed himself for her temper-tantrum.

She sniffed, and then looked at his soaked t-shirt, "I ruined your shirt."

Looking down and giving her a half-hearted smile, Cade responded kindly, "I have more. Honestly, I have a lot more. I ruin them all too often myself."

She felt terrible now for her outburst. He was only trying to help her, and she kept fighting him the whole way. It was so hard for her to let go and put all her trust in other people. Surrendering your life to someone else's care was not an easy thing to do.

Untangling herself from him, she took one-step back, effectively giving her a safe distance from him. She liked the way it felt having him hold her all too much.

Well, I suppose I can eat crow as well as the next person, she told herself. Straightening up, she offered her apology, "I am sorry for earlier. It is very difficult for me to let go of all my control. I know you're trying…trying to help me. And I know I haven't really given you a reason to believe I'm grateful, but I am. I'll try harder to remember you're just trying to keep me safe and try to keep my emotional instability to a minimum."

He smiled, but half-heartedly. He came up here intending to apologize to her, believing this was mostly his fault. He knew they would need to come to an understanding so there were no further frustrations, but he couldn't let her take all the blame, either. He had acted like a jerk downstairs. He understood that this fierce protectiveness he felt for her made him tense and edgy.

"I could have handled things better- a lot better. I apologize. I should have talked to you regarding my thoughts and ideas. You're right; you are a strong, capable woman. I only want to make you stronger. I just want to keep you safe," he admitted.

He stopped for a moment, running his hand through his hair again in his common nervous way. Then he hedged on, "I think- no, I know you can do this. Beat this. I just want to help you do it; give you the best possible chance."

She saw the pained look in his soft, golden eyes. He was hurt. He believed he was the cause of her tears. From his wounded expression, she was now sure Cade was, just as Jenny stated several days previous, the most selfless man she knew. She considered each of his actions in a new light.

He was willing to take the blame for her outburst, and he was willing to teach her how to stay alive regardless of her poor attitude and snide comments. He was willing to risk his life to protect her, without so much as a second thought about it. She wondered then, *How many other people has he so selflessly helped?*

At that very moment, she knew, without a single doubt, she would trust this man with her life. He would do whatever it took to help her. She knew she would follow him blindly. She understood now that Cade would never do anything to hurt her. Trusting in someone so fully was something she was sure she had never done before.

This astounding revelation came with one more that was even more complex... she was beginning to have strong feelings for him.

Humbled, and full of conflicting feelings, it took her a moment to respond to him. "Cade, you have no reason to be sorry. I have been fighting you at every turn. When you," she paused, "You've been trying to help me. I can see that now. From now on, I'll try to listen to you; without rebuking your every effort." Then trying to reassure him, she said sheepishly and somewhat embarrassed, "It wasn't your fault I was upset." She hesitated once more, not wanting to admit her weakness. He stayed silent, giving her the time she needed. "I mean, that little breakdown was a long time in coming. I've been holding all of this in for two years now. It was bound to come out eventually."

He nodded, accepting the truce between them, "I'll try harder to consider your opinions then."

She smiled slightly, "Thank you. Not just for that, but for all your help. You are a good man. If only there were more men in the world like you. We would all be better off."

With her last words, she felt a sudden sadness wash over her, and as quick as it came, it was gone. It came from him, she knew that instantly. She saw his expression falter before he quickly recovered, covering it with a less than sincere smile.

"Yeah. Sure."

"Is everything alright?" she asked.

"Yeah. Fine," he said quickly, "Now that you're alright, I better go relieve Nate from patrol so he can get something to eat. I'll catch up with you later."

The wash of sadness she had felt was covered up so quickly she wasn't even sure it was real until she saw his quick frown. Even though he tried to reassure her that he was fine, he didn't smile. Deep in his golden eyes, she had seen the hurt.

She nodded, baffled by his quick reaction. She didn't believe he was fine. Not for one minute. As he turned and left the room, she stood there thinking. *Was it something I said?*

Curious, she headed downstairs to seek out Cynda. She decided after she made her apologies to her for the earlier outburst, she could ask some questions about Cade's odd behavior.

When she got to the bottom of the main staircase, she heard Rederrick on the phone in the den. Swallowing her pride, she decided to talk to him first. She moved to the open doorway and stood there patiently waiting for him to finish his call.

Rederrick saw her right away. Waving his hand, he gestured for her to come in. She walked quietly into the room and couldn't help listening to his end of the conversation.

He sat silent for a moment then said, "I'm glad to hear it kid. I'll let Cade know you'll be here on Sunday. Truthfully, I'm sure Nate will be relieved. He's been pulling some pretty long shifts." Silence, then, "No, you know you can stay here... Yeah that'll be fine... So we'll see you Sunday." He promptly hung up then looked to her.

She quickly apologized, "Sorry I hope I'm not bothering you."

He smiled, "Nonsense, now what can I do for you?"

"You can let me apologize for my little temper tantrum."

"Ha, temper tantrum? Obviously, you have never seen Cynda mad. She would give you a serious run for your money," he quipped.

"All the same, I am sorry," she repeated with a smile.

He looked at her with his steel-gray eyes and a deep, sincere grin, "Say no more about it. All is forgiven. Besides, it's good to see you have a good dose of fight in you. You're gonna need it."

Not wanting to speak of what was coming for her anymore tonight, she changed the subject, "Who's coming on Sunday?"

"Oh, Cody," he answered, "He'll be an extra hand on security for a while."

"Ah," she said.

Rederrick could tell there was more to her visit than small talk, "What's on your mind, Collett?"

"Well, I was just wondering. How long have you known Cade?" she hedged.

"I can't ever remember not knowing him. Why do you ask?"

She felt somewhat awkward, "I just was curious that's all...." She waited a couple heartbeats then blurted out the truth, "I just want to know how I upset him a little while ago."

His face turned serious. "How do you know that you did?" he questioned.

"I think I felt it," she carefully replied.

"Okay, why don't you sit down and tell me what happened," he encouraged, not even doubting her statement. He was completely accepting of her possible empathic abilities.

Sitting in one of the two chairs across from Rederrick, she recounted their conversation. She carefully neglected to tell him about her sobbing all over Cade's shirt. When she finished, Collett waited nervously for his opinion, hoping he could shed some light on the subject.

He scrutinized her with his hands folded together atop the desk, thinking over all she told him. He wasn't entirely sure he could explain. He was quiet for a moment, then told her, "I can't really answer this question."

Right away she could see Rederrick knew something. She could tell he held back, so she called him on it, "Can't; or won't?"

"Alright, a little of both. But I can tell you that it wasn't you that upset him," he said. The truth was he wanted to share more, but Rederrick knew it was not his place.

She huffed out an annoyed breath, "Fine. Just tell me what I can do to avoid it in the future."

"You know," he began sincerely, "Everybody has demons, even Cade. Nothing you can do or say will change that for him. One day he'll either face his demon or come to terms with it. Either way, I have faith he'll come through it."

Even more confused now, she stood, "Alright I get it. It's personal. I would like to say one more thing to you. The three of you here have taught me one very important thing over this last week. Nobody should have to face their demons alone, especially Cade. Without so much as blinking an eye to the risk, he is ready and willing to face my demons for me. So when the time comes, if I live through this, I will do the same. I'll face his demons with him."

As she left, Collett failed to notice the broad smile that had spread across Rederrick's face, highlighting the laugh lines at the corner of his mouth and the twinkle in his eyes. All he could think when she left was, *It's about time.* For years, for so many decades, Cade had always stood up for others, sacrificing anything he could to protect anyone he could. He selflessly fought against everyone else's enemies, and now, for the very first time since Rederrick had known him, someone else was willing to do the same for Cade.

"Yes, it's about damn time," he voiced aloud.

CHAPTER 16

As Cade showered the next morning, he thought to himself about what today might bring. Today, they might learn something about who Collett is. *What then?* he thought. After all, when this was over, what would she do? Would she stay here?

Not that it truly mattered if she did. He didn't live here, didn't live anywhere really. He always jumped around from place to place, going where he was most needed. He kept a place in the mountains, not far from here that few people knew of, but he was rarely there these days. He was always busy with Brotherhood business. The Faction's furious actions lately barely gave him time to rest at all.

He considered that maybe he should start thinking about finding a place he could stay for a while. Then he jolted back to reality. He remembered why he couldn't. Permanence was an impossibility when you lived forever. People tended to ask questions when their neighbor didn't age.

No, he would never have a normal life. He would just continue what he was doing, staying as long as he could before moving to his next project. Helping others gave him purpose. If he didn't have his work, he wouldn't have much at all.

He hated admitting it to himself, but he was getting tired of being alone. After you pass one hundred, the loneliness wears on you. After nearly three-hundred years, it only got worse. Maybe that's why he felt so strongly about her. He considered that thought more seriously. Perhaps, his need for a connection was driving him to this? No, he quickly admonished, his feelings for Collett didn't feel false, and he refused to justify them in such a way.

Quickly drying off, he entered his room to get dressed. He walked over to the large king-sized bed to retrieve the jeans he laid there earlier. As he did, he looked around. This room had a masculine atmosphere that suited him. Years ago, when Cynda and Rederrick had built this house, they had included this room for Cade. He stayed here as often as he could. Here, he felt the most at home.

All the furniture was a sleek, dark cherry wood. Because of his height, they had furnished it with a large, king-sized bed. A beautifully carved armoire sat in the right corner, and a matching six-drawer dresser was on the left wall facing the bed. The room had its own balcony on the other side of two French doors; the very same balcony he'd used the other night to sneak into the house. The colors were dark green tones mixed with light neutral tans.

Rederrick told him once how Cynda fussed over this room, insisting it should be like a second master suite. As a result of their efforts, this room held a special feeling for him. They had surprised him with it when the house was complete. Rederrick and Cynda reminded him that day that he would always be a part of their family. Even their three grown children, Tracy, James, and Ashley, still referred to him as Uncle Cade; much like Rederrick had done in his youth.

Thinking of all these things reminded him that, for now, he wasn't alone, and he hadn't been for a long time.

Shaking off his self-pity, Cade quickly dressed and headed downstairs to the den in search of his old friend. He wanted to touch base with him about plans for the day.

When he got to the den, Cade saw no sign of Rederrick. Knowing his friend was an early riser, and was probably hard at work in the Extra Room, he went over to the wall to gain entrance through the hidden door.

When he moved through the doorway, he was surprised to find not only Rederrick, but James as well. James, Rederrick's son, was a tall six-one. He was right in between Cade and Rederrick's heights. His build was much like Rederrick, with a slim and lanky body. His brown hair was kept short and precisely cut. He always had that clean-cut military look, even as a boy. The eyes, he got from Cynda. They were the same deep green as hers. He always had a soft spot for this kid, and seeing James now removed the last of his self-pity.

When James caught sight of him, he smiled excitedly, showing the dimple in his left cheek. Walking over to him, James said jokingly, "I told Dad to keep the riffraff outta here. Why doesn't anyone ever listen to me?"

Hooking his arm around James' neck, he gave his hair a good ruffle with his other hand. He knew it would annoy James. "If there's no riffraff allowed, how is it you made it through security?" he asked. After Cade released him, James tried to straighten his mussed hair. "Are you AWOL? Don't they still hang you for that?" he asked teasingly.

"Ha, ha, very funny. If you must know-"

"I must," he interrupted teasingly.

"I happen to be on liberty. I came up here to show Dad my new toy. I have to get back tonight."

Cade smiled, "I'm hurt, and here I thought you came to see me."

James looked at him seriously, "Now why would I go and do something like that?" Then his features broke into a grin.

"Yeah, it's good to see you too, kid." Cade smiled back as he spoke, "Maybe later I'll have time to go one round with you upstairs. We'll see if military life has done you any good."

James gave him a cocky look, "I won't have the time today. Besides, I wouldn't want to hurt you, Uncle Cade. You are getting up there."

He laughed, "We'll see."

"Well, on that note," Rederrick interrupted, "James you had better get your butt out there to see your mother before she has my hide for keeping you so long. Cade and I will be along shortly."

James smiled again at him, but responded to his father saying, "Yes sir," offering a mock salute. He moved around Cade, giving him a wide berth.

Cade quickly jumped at James as he passed by, purposely missing. He flinched, as Cade predicted he would. Laughing, Cade said sarcastically, "I guess you'll have to go easy on me, then. You're much too fast for me."

Laughing along with Cade on his way out, and always wanting the last word, James quickly replied, "Yeah, I guess I will. Don't blame yourself Uncle Cade; you are getting pretty old. Didn't you date Shakespeare's mama, or was it his grandma?" Smirking, he promptly closed the door before Cade could retaliate.

Cade laughed again and looked over at Rederrick, "That boy has a smart mouth."

Rederrick sat at the conference table using a magnifier to look over a tiny little black dot he held with a pair of tweezers. He didn't even look up but grunted, "He gets it from his mother. There's nothing like that on my side of the family."

"Oh no, nothing like it at all." Cade responded with sarcastic disbelief. Then bending down closer, he asked, "What did he bring you?"

"I'm not sure yet. He wants me to guess. We've been playing a game, Stump the Tech. So far, he's winning. I think it's some sort of a tracking device, but this looks like a camera here." Rederrick pinched his brows trying to focus.

Cade moved on, "Is Nate still in line to pick up Selena around one?"

Rederrick finally looked up, knowing they needed to work out the details of today. "As far as I know," he answered. "He did say he had something to do after though, so one of us will have to take her back to the store."

Last night they had both agreed Selena should have an escort just in case The Faction was getting itchy. Therefore, Rederrick assigned Nate. Nate was an Ex-marine who Rederrick himself had recruited to the Brotherhood, though they both had known him as a boy.

Nate had intimate knowledge about The Faction. His mother had been a witch. When she would not join The Faction, they had brutally killed her right in front of him. At the time, he had only been eleven. He never truly got over it. Cade made sure he was placed with a good home and checked up on him over the years. Rederrick kept tabs on him too and snatched him up after his contract with Uncle Sam expired. He was sharp and skilled in several martial arts. It was also handy that he was a lethal sniper.

Cade nodded, "Fine. Are you going to go over some things with Collett today?"

"If she is up to it after Selena leaves. I'll bring her in here and show her the setup. I also want to show her the other safe escape out of the house."

"Good idea," Cade agreed. Then he went on, "I'm starting to feel edgy. It has almost been a week. They should have tried something by now. Two attacks so close together, then nothing? It doesn't make sense."

Rederrick tried to be optimistic, "Maybe they found out we are involved now and let it go."

"When has that ever stopped them before?" he asked with a cynical stare.

"Good point," Rederrick granted. "You know though, we're still not positive it is The Faction."

He shook his head, "No, my gut tells me it is. I know we shouldn't jump to conclusions, but who else could it be? One of these days I would sure like to find the face behind them and get my hands on him."

"You and me both, boy, you and me both."

"When will Cody get here?" Cade asked.

Rederrick stood from his chair, stretching out his muscles as he said, "Should be here tomorrow sometime. He's driving in from Texas. I had him check on a few things down there for me."

"Anything new?" he asked as they walked to the door together.

"Not much. Although, I am pretty sure something besides nature caused the storm Collett told us about. I haven't told her though."

"Don't. Not until we know."

"If she is the cause, or part of it at least, we could be in big trouble here," Rederrick responded seriously.

Appalled, Cade insisted, "She would never hurt anybody. She's just not capable of it."

Rederrick nodded, "I agree, but I'm not talking about her. I was referring to whomever, make that, whatever was with her that day." At the door, Rederrick stopped before he opened it. "See, I have this theory. I wanted to wait to share it until I knew more. I don't think Collett was only hunted these last two years. I think it may have started before she lost her memory."

Cade thought about it for a second and agreed, "It's possible. It could account for the storm. Someone with elemental control could have been after her, but elemental control is rare." He scowled as he thought about it further. He thought about Collett fighting for her life against that kind of a power.

Rederrick watched his reaction to the new insight, and then he repeated, "Like I said: big trouble. We need more intel, and soon."

C.B. Haight

She felt nervous and jittery most of the day, but meeting James helped keep Collett's mind from her upcoming meeting. He was very outgoing and optimistic. His lighthearted personality was infectious. He was a handsome young man with a vibrant personality. Fun and energetic, James' green eyes sparkled whenever he was teasing someone. James had an easy, charming smile, with a small dimple on his left side. His grin added to his handsome features, and it put her at ease around him. She was sure it would be hard for anybody to not like him.

They all ate lunch together, minus Nate. He was currently on his way to retrieve Selena. Even Jenny sat to join them today. It felt so normal, sitting there talking, laughing, bantering back and forth. It was a rare moment of pure enjoyment.

During their meal, everyone talked and teased each other, telling embarrassing stories and wasting the time away until Selena's arrival. As they all sat around the table in the kitchen gabbing, she kept mostly quiet throughout the meal, simply watching the family interaction. James referred to Cade affectionately as "Uncle Cade," which she found endearing. She also noticed the way James teased Cade and how he responded in kind. They had an affectionate, brotherly relationship. In one story, James spoke of how Cade had once *scared him out of his skin*.

"Don't you remember that time you caught me over near the stream in the middle of the night?" He asked when Cade didn't recall right away.

Cade's face broke into a fond smile from the memory, "I do remember that. Let's see… you were around fifteen at the time. I saw you climb from your window, going down the trellis, and I followed you. It was pretty late to be out for a walk. Wasn't it around two in the morning?"

James' smile got even bigger when he said, "All I remember was, that night, I knew what it felt like to be hunted like a deer."

"That's because you were being hunted. You're just lucky I wasn't hungry," Cade quipped and then laughed, "I remember your scared little face when I came out of the bushes."

James tried to defend his honor saying, "In my defense, it's not like you had ever changed in front of us kids before. Let me tell you, being on the other side, watching the transformation is a scary place to be. I didn't even know it was you until you finished."

Cade laughed a full, hearty laugh, "I'll give you credit. You stood your ground. Your little friends down by the pond took off after a couple howls and a few rustling bushes."

"That was the first and the last time I ever tried to sneak out. Your impromptu visit that night put me on the straight and narrow," James admitted.

Cade laughed out loud along with him.

"Why is it I am just hearing about this now?" Cynda asked with a firm, motherly tone.

James tried to look serious and failed, "Well Mom, as old and as wise as Uncle Cade was, he decided it was best to keep it between us men. And I, being a smart young man, agreed."

Cynda looked at Cade and scoffed, "Old and wise my butt. He just wanted to keep you out of trouble.

"He's was always keepin' people out of trouble. Especially his favorites, and young James there was definitely one of his favorites," Jenny added with a grin as she got up and began clearing plates.

James snickered. He couldn't disagree with his mother. In fact, several other memories popped into his mind. And by the look on Cade's face, he was thinking of the very same memories.

Caught up in the fun and antics, Collett joined in, "Besides he can't be that much wiser. He is only about ten or so years older than you."

Everyone in the room stopped smiling and suddenly turned their attention to her. Cade's expression was resigned. *What did I say wrong this time?* she wondered.

James smiled, breaking the tension. Then he quipped sarcastically, "You know, I think you could be right, Collett. He really can't be that much wiser. I can't remember, Uncle Cade, how old are you again?"

Cade gave him a heavy glare, "Leave it alone James. She doesn't know."

She looked to him, "Know what?"

Seeing that Cade and Collett needed a moment, Cynda stood, "Rederrick, why don't you, James, and I help Jenny in the kitchen?" she insisted.

"Now?" James complained.

Cynda gave him a stern motherly look, "Now."

Baffled, Collett wondered what in the world is going. Everybody but Cade rose from their chairs, picked up a few plates, and left the room without a word.

He looked at her puzzled expression, wondering how was best to tell her.

Finally, he began, "Collett, I don't usually share what I am about to tell you. Normal people can't really understand, and they don't want to either."

A little worried she answered skeptically, "Alright."

He let out a calm breath. Because she was becoming important to him, Cade feared her reaction to the revelation of his immortality. She was barely getting used to the idea of his animal half. Whether he was ready to deal with it or not, Collett mattered. Therefore, so did her opinion. Trying to hedge his way through this, he asked tentatively, "Collett... how old do you think I am?"

Answering, she said, "I would guess you are about thirty, but I'm starting to get the impression that I'm wrong."

"I am much older than thirty. I was born in the year 1732," he took another steadying breath upon seeing her eyes widen with shock.

She was not expecting this. Trying for words she stammered, "Oh… Well, um, ok. Wow." She took a moment to think about it. A moment that felt far too long to Cade. He waited, tensed, trying to appear calm, though he didn't feel it. The lapsing silence was awkward and strained, until finally she said, "I guess that really does put you in the older and wiser category."

He was a little stunned himself. Her lighthearted comment reassured him. She was handling this amazingly well. He narrowed his eyes. She was dealing with his revelation better than even some of his closest friends had. "Are you ok?" he asked.

She answered honestly, "I won't lie, it is quite a shock. But considering the week I've had… I have to say it's not totally unbelievable. If you had told me last week, you might have gotten a different reaction. Now," she shrugged nonchalantly, "I have been attacked by a demon, saved by a werewolf, and watched a sorcerer pop out of nowhere and force a big SUV into a river. I have seen Cynda use and control magic, and I'm about to have a visit from some sort of *seer* to help me remember my past. So, all in all, your revelation is not so hard to believe."

Cade smiled, "I guess that's all true."

Seeing his relief, she smiled back, "I am curious about one thing, though."

"What's that?" he responded.

"At your age, can you even remember your birthday?" she quipped with an easy grin.

He let go of a hearty laugh, then grabbed her face and pulled her to him for a quick, surprising kiss. Pulling back, he grinned devilishly and said, "Don't you worry. I can remember all sorts of things."

She was just about to respond to his entendre when Cynda peeked in, "Everything okay?"

He stood, keeping his honey eyes locked with hers, "Yeah, everything's fine."

"Good. Go ahead and bring Collett into the parlor. Selena is here."

With that one comment, Collett felt her nerves develop legs and crawl all over her skin. She involuntarily shivered. He reached down, grabbed her hand, and said, "We'll finish this later." Then he pulled her from the chair.

With her feet on the ground and her hand in Cade's, Collett voiced her fear, "I'm a little scared."

He was surprised by her willingness to confide her vulnerability to him. "No matter what we find, I'm not going anywhere," he said meeting her worried gaze.

Feeling bolstered by his support, she said with a nervous sigh, "Let's get on with it then."

Not willing to let go of her hand, he pulled slightly, and together they went to meet Selena.

CHAPTER 17

When they entered the parlor hand in hand, Cynda and Rederrick noticed right away. They gave each other a pointed look.

Upon entering, Collett observed that sitting in one of the off-white chairs, was a slender woman. When she stood to greet them, Collett got her first look at the woman she assumed to be Selena.

She was a breathtaking brunette. Her straight, brown hair that reached her waist glistened. Selena wore a loose teal blouse, a lengthy denim skirt, and brown high-heeled boots. Her skin was a natural, dark tan. That, and her high cheekbones, hinted at her Native American heritage. She was absolutely stunning.

Cynda confirmed her assumption, "Collett, I would like you to meet Selena."

Selena smiled and tilted her head, "I'm pleased to meet you, Collett."

Collett squeezed Cade's hand reflexively, and then she said, "I am grateful you could come out here to see me so quickly."

"I was happy to do it. Cade, it is good to see you as well. Did you find what you were looking for?" Selena replied.

He shook his head. "Unfortunately, I was unable to travel down that road," he said cryptically.

Selena nodded with understanding.

Rederrick, who stood over by the fireplace with James, spoke soberly, "Collett, we are all here for you. We can begin whenever you're ready."

She looked around the room. Everyone was there: Cynda, Rederrick, James, Jenny, and even a stoic Nate, whom she had hardly seen since his arrival, stood in the corner with his deep-blue eyes staring at her.

For some reason she could not explain, at that very moment, Cade's presence was in truth the only one that mattered. With his hand holding hers, she felt grounded.

"Okay, let's get started. How do we do this?" she said with false courage.

Selena answered her with a soft, soothing tone, "We will try the easiest way first then go from there."

"What is the easiest way?" Collett asked apprehensively.

Selena smiled, "You come over here and take my hand."

"That doesn't seem so bad then," she replied with a relieved sigh.

"Not at all," she said with a laugh, "and I don't even bite." Selena raised her brow and smiled in Cade's direction. "Are you ready Collett?" she finished.

"As ready I can be," she replied and moved to Selena, reluctantly releasing Cade's hand.

Selena held out her small, soft hand, palm up, her slender fingers perfectly manicured. "Calm yourself Collett. There's no need to be afraid. I won't hurt you," she offered reassuringly.

Of course Collett knew that, but she felt excited and scared at the same time. She took a deep breath, looked around for reassurance, found Cade's warm, encouraging eyes, then placed her hand carefully in Selena's.

The quick, small spark between them jolted her. It almost made her let go. As it was, she startled slightly. Selena kept her grip tight and held her in place, closing her eyes. She felt strength and peace from Selena. Her battered nerves calmed as she let the tranquil feelings in. It was the most peaceful and relaxed Collett had felt in a long, long time.

After what only seemed to be a couple of minutes Selena loosened her firm grip and stumbled back a step. Collett opened her eyes and saw Cade's worried expression. He now stood right next to her, looking like he was ready to catch her in case she fell over.

"Are you alright?" he asked concerned.

Answering him with a nod, she looked over to Selena, who was now sitting in the chair, looking drawn and tired. Hesitant but eager, she asked, "Did you…. Did something happen? Did you see something to help me?"

Jenny handed Selena a cup of water. Before Selena could answer her, "Let's give her a moment to recover. Are you alright, Selena?" Cynda said.

Selena nodded and took a sip of her water.

"I don't know about the rest of you, but that was one of the most intense thirty minutes of my life," James said.

"What? It couldn't have been thirty minutes," Collett said surprised.

"Collett, why don't you sit down, too," Cade said calmly. Then he carefully led her to the couch and sat down with her.

"Thirty minutes?" she whispered, "How can that be? It seemed to happen so fast."

"I was surprised myself," Selena added. "Never before has it taken so much."

Collett looked to her, "You look tired, I'm sorry. I had no idea what this would do to you."

Selena waved away the apology, "As I said, it has never happened this way before. Trust me, it is very much alright. It was worth the experience."

Collett was still anxious to know what Selena saw, so she inquired politely, "Does this mean you saw something?"

Selena took on a pinched, sad look and with a controlled, precise movement she set her glass of water on the table. She looked at her with her deep brown eyes. Then, using a sympathetic gaze and an apologetic voice, Selena answered, "Collett, every journey has pitfalls. This is just one of yours. I really am very sorry, but I cannot help you."

"What! What do you mean you can't help her?" Cade countered. "You must have seen something in all that time. Felt something?"

Selena dismissed Cade's tone, and gave him a kind look when she answered, "I did. And I cannot help her because she does not need, or want, my help."

Softly Collett pleaded, "I don't understand. I do want your help. I do need your help. Please! I'm desperate to know who I am."

Selena looked back to her. Her expression sincere, she said vaguely, "Collett, you already know. You're hurting now, so you do not want to see it. Time is what you need. You will see the truth when you are meant to, and you won't need my help. In truth, it is we that need you. When you remember who you are, you will only want help from one, and it is not me."

Collett looked at Selena with a sad, broken expression. Cynda went to her and laid a hand on her shoulder to offer support. She directed her gaze to Selena, "Thank you Selena. Don't worry Collett, we'll help you though this."

Cade hated seeing her so disappointed. He wanted to fix this for her. Wanted to make Selena tell him what she saw, or even shake her until she told them something. Cade knew though, it wouldn't matter. Selena had given them all she would. She always stood firm in the information she gave. He knew that from personal experience.

He did ask, "So are you saying she will remember?" He wanted her to at least have some hope.

Selena answered him carefully, "I'm saying she can. When she will, is up to her." Standing she said, "I better get back to the shop. Collett, it was truly a pleasure to meet you. I hope one day you will come back and see me."

Rederrick straightened up from his spot near the fireplace and said, "I'll take you back."

Selena moved to leave, then looking back she asked, "Cade? I wonder if you could give me a minute before I leave."

Cade looked away from Collett, "Can it wait?"

"No, it can't," she said with a firm tone.

Giving her a quick nod, he murmured, "I'll be right back," to Collett. Then he stood to follow Selena out of the room. She walked into the foyer, turned suddenly, and held out her hand.

With a lifted brow, he looked down at her hand seeing the challenge for what it was. Defiantly, he asked, "Haven't we been down this road?"

Selena looked at him and said, "You know as well as I the ripples a small drop of water can make in the still pond. So, humor me." Resigned, he lifted his hand and placed it in Selena's soft, warm grasp. She closed her eyes for a moment.

"Sooner than you'll be ready for," she began, "You will come to an old broken bridge. You can burn it, and try to keep everyone away from the possible danger of crossing it, thus forgetting what great things you might see and feel on the other side. Or you can shore it up, taking your time to work your way carefully across it, fixing and strengthening the weak points. Then you will witness for yourself what treasures lay there waiting for you and all the people who will be able to cross after. This is a life-changing decision that will affect more than just you; more than just her.

"You will be presented with a true opportunity here, and every decision has consequences. It is entirely up to you whether they are positive or negative. When you are faced with this decision, weigh it carefully. Then, no matter what, don't turn back."

Selena opened her eyes and looked into his confused gaze. She gave him a brilliant smile and called Rederrick to inform him she was ready. While they waited, Selena put on the coat that hung over her arm, and Cade could only think about what she said.

When Rederrick entered the room, she threw out one more cryptic comment, "Cade, when the time comes, trust in her to know what is right. No matter what, no matter the cost, believe in her. She is not willing to cause anyone undue pain; especially you. Some things simply must be done with fierce courage and resolve."

Rederrick shared Cade's puzzled expression as he finished and turned away, exiting through the large front door.

"Now what in the hell am I supposed to do with that?" he asked Rederrick.

Rederrick shrugged his shoulders, "I'm not sure, but I'm glad someone got some advice today." Then he followed Selena out, shutting the door behind him.

He stood there by himself, repeating her words in his head, trying to make sense of them. He knew she must to be referring to Collett in part. The confusing part was the trust thing. He did trust her; didn't he?

Moreover, what was all that crap about the bridge? Why couldn't she just tell him something the straightforward way? "Here's the problem, and this is what you need to do." Why did it all have to be some vague puzzle? He hated puzzles.

"Cade?" Cynda's voice startled him.

He turned, "Yeah?"

She looked at him with a motherly expression, "Are you alright?"

His answer was short and clipped, "Yeah, fine. Why?"

She scrutinized his face and body language. Seeing his tight jaw and narrowed brow, Cynda knew he was bothered by something. "Could you come and sit with Collett? I'm going to talk with James before he goes."

"Yeah okay, I'm coming," he said, shaking off Selena's cryptic words.

He entered the room and walked over to the couch where Collett still sat. Her arms were folded, and she was slouched over. It looked as if she were trying to contain all of her frustrations and emotions, when they just wanted to come bursting out.

"I was so scared of what she would tell me today," she quietly said as she heard him enter the room. He sat next to her and put a hand on her back. He rubbed in soothing motions, not speaking, just letting her talk. "I didn't want to find out something bad about myself. I was afraid I would hear something I couldn't live with. I wasn't prepared to find out nothing. Why is this happening to me? Why can't I remember?" Collett pleaded. He wrapped his arm around her, letting her lean into him.

"Selena said you can remember. We just have to figure out how. Don't get discouraged and give up yet."

She sat up and gave him a cross look, "Is that what you think; that I would just give up? You think I haven't been trying?"

"That's not what I meant-"Cade started to answer

"Don't you get it? For the last two years of this horrible nightmare, I have been trying to figure it out! Trying to remember anything about who I am! I am desperate to understand why someone wants me dead. You have no idea what it's like not knowing who you are! Not remembering the people who may have been important to you!"

He stood, frustrated, and ran his hand through his hair roughly, "You're right. I don't understand it, but I'm trying to help here, Collett. I am not your enemy. We, the people here in this house, are not your enemies. So quit trying to attack us when you get frustrated.

"I understand you're scared, but you can't let your fear rule you. Do whatever it is you need to do to get over it, and move past it. Let me enlighten you a little on the subject of fear. We're all afraid of

C.B. Haight

something. It's how we act against our fear that makes us who we are.

"I've seen men who were afraid of dying march into battle strong and proud. Watched them pray to their God along the way that they would prevail. They were fighting for their beliefs, trying to make the world a better place.

"I have watched while sickness and death spread through towns. I've seen things as simple as colds kill children, all because selfish doctors, afraid to get sick, simply stepped away and watched people die.

"The actions we take against our fears and trials shape us in this life. That is what makes us strong and courageous."

Collett looked at him quizzically. Her face had visibly paled. "What did you say?" she whispered.

Cade, confused by the sudden change in her, asked, "What? What did I say?"

She mumbled softly, "Sickness. They were all so sick. Then she was sick. She was so horribly sick. Oh no!" Her hand covered her lips as the image became clearer. A single tear slipped free of her crystal blue eyes.

Cade quickly figured out what was happening and, cursing under his breath, went to her, "Collett, look, we don't have to talk about this right now." She looked at him with a pained expression and eased herself back onto the couch.

"Juliet coughed so hard she could barely breathe. Her skin burned with fever. When I touched her head I could feel the heat." Collett stared down at her hands. "It burned my skin. When she slept, I could hear the rattle in her tiny chest. Then one night, she took one last rattling breath and just...stopped. Stopped smiling; stopped breathing. She just stopped living. Just like that, she was gone. I held her frail body; felt the weight of it when she died." More tears escaped her eyes, running down her ivory cheeks.

Her tears tore through him. Wanting her pain to stop, he sat by her again and said firmly, "That's enough. Let's go and get some tea."

"NO! I need to remember!" Collett protested. It hurt so much. "Someone needs to remember! Don't you see?" she was pleading now. "It matters if I remember. She mattered! I'm supposed to remember her! I loved her; my sweet, innocent Juliet. I have to remember. Why can't I remember?" the last words came out in a pleading whisper.

He couldn't stand it anymore. "That's enough," he said as he wrapped her up in his arms and pulled her body to him, cradling her tightly in his embrace. Then he repeated softly, "That's enough. For now, it's enough. I'm sorry, Collett. I'm so sorry."

Collett pushed away from him enough to look into his eyes, "You knew," she accused.

"I suspected," he said carefully with a voice full of compassion.

Deflated, she leaned back into his warm, comforting embrace. This up-and-down emotional roller coaster was wearing her out. She sniffled, "You were right. I don't mean to attack you. It just seems you're always there whenever I lash out. I'm sorry."

"Does it help? To lash out I mean?"

"Sometimes," she answered honestly.

"Then I guess I'll have to keep being there," Cade replied as he pulled her closer.

CHAPTER 18

One week after Selena's visit, Collett was at an impasse with regard to remembering who she was. There were no more vague memories or terrible nightmares. Her mind fell into what she felt was a sleep state. She had a hard time focusing on anything. There was too much jumbled in her head, and she couldn't pull one thought forward at a time. When she did, her thoughts centered on Cade and their budding relationship.

Rederrick watched her, looking at her dazed expression as he called her name for the third time, "Collett?"

This time she heard him. Looking sideways, she saw his pinched and concerned features and realized that this was not the first time he had said her name, "Hum?"

"Are you alright?" he asked.

Trying to ease his mind, she answered absently, "Yeah, fine." Seeing his appraising eyes, she relented, "Sorry, I was just thinking."

He scrutinized her, "You know, we can do this another day."

She smiled at him and responded, "No, I need to get all of this down. Cade keeps reminding me we may not have a lot of time. On top of that, with the upcoming holiday and Cade's tight schedule for my training with him, it seems my time with you is limited."

Rederrick wondered to himself if Cade wasn't pushing too hard. He knew Cade was trying to keep her safe, but the phrase, *all work and no play*, jumped into his head. He decided he would go over the emergency numbers one more time, and then he would give her a break.

"Why don't we go over the phone list one more time?"

She stood from the chrome and black chair she occupied in the security room and walked over to the bank of screens playing out security footage. Rederrick was teaching her how to work some of the more basic equipment and briefing her on emergency protocols. Cade insisted she needed at least an hour a day going over the vast amount of information in this room.

Answering him, Collett recited the four numbers Rederrick had taught her for emergencies: his cell and Cade's cell, not that Cade showed any sign of leaving the house as long as she was in it. Then she rattled off Nate's number and finally Cody's, who had yet to arrive.

Cody called Rederrick again yesterday to tell him he would be delayed until this Tuesday. Apparently, an unexpected emergency had come up.

As she rattled off numbers, Rederrick thought about all that she had been through this last week. It had been exactly two weeks and two days after her run-in with the demon, and they were no further along in understanding any of this.

Cade and Rederrick had done a massive amount of research, looking for any small clue they could find, trying to make some sense of this. They were still coming up empty-handed. Making matters worse, the waiting was making everyone edgy. They expected her attackers to make a move by now.

Thanksgiving was only one week away. If they didn't find something soon, he worried it would cast a shadow over the festivities. All three of his children were making plans to come home for the long weekend.

As she finished her list, Rederrick heard wistfulness in her voice. He could tell she was starting to feel cooped up here in the house. She hadn't been outside for more than two weeks now. She didn't utter a single complaint about her self-imposed prison. She just took it stoically, complying with anything to make it easier on those around her.

When he didn't speak up after she finished, she twisted her neck, looking over her shoulder, and asked, "Was that right?"

"Yeah, it was right," he answered. "You won't have any problems remembering if you need them now."

She squinted her eyes and studied him. Realizing his thoughts were preoccupied as well, she tried a positive tone to reassure him, "Maybe we could go over it a few more times, just to be sure. I would hate to forget your number if Cade needed you. Or we could review the safe's codes in the garage," she suggested.

He gave her a fatherly smile and questioned, "Do you really believe you'll forget, or are you trying to reassure me that you won't?"

Collett sighed and walked back to her seat next to him. "No, I won't forget. I just don't want to let any of you down. I want you to be sure that I will be able to play my part."

He considered her words and her tone. She was worried for everyone but herself. She spent long hours each day working and studying. She didn't want to be anyone else's weakness. "Collett, why don't you ever consider your own feelings; or your own safety for that matter?"

"I do," she insisted.

"No you don't. You're always concerned about our safety; letting us down. The word 'I' rarely enters your vocabulary. When it does, it comes out as an, 'I'm sorry.'"

"That's the way it's supposed to be," she answered without thinking.

"Why?"

Again automatically answering, she said, "Because, it's part of my purpose."

Rederrick saw Cade enter the room quietly and said nothing about it. He didn't want to distract her from her current automatic responses. He asked curiously, "Purpose to do what?"

She looked at him, "My job, my calling."

As soon as the words escaped her mouth, her hand flew up, covering her lips in shock. Her blue eyes opened wider than Rederrick had ever seen them. She could only stare at him.

Cade, hearing the exchange, kept quiet. Like Rederrick, he didn't want to distract her from her thoughts.

"What calling?" Rederrick asked.

She stared at him with her surprised eyes, thinking carefully over the words she had thrown out so easily.

He tried again, "What purpose, Collett?"

"I don't really know…" she admitted softly. "I don't even know why I said that. How do I know I have a purpose, a job, but not understand what it is? What do you think that means?"

"I think it means, it's coming back to you slowly, as you're ready for it," Rederrick answered. "Don't think on it so much. Your answers were automatic before. Every time you try to force it, it gets harder for you." As he finished, he lifted his gaze and looked over her shoulder.

She quickly turned to see what he was looking at. Cade stood just inside the hidden doorway. His body was keeping the heavy, self-locking door open.

He nodded and stepped forward, "Rederrick is right. It's coming back to you now. Even though it's only a few pieces at a time, it is coming back." Then his eyes twinkled, and grinning, he teased, "Anyway, at least we know you have a job. I would hate to have to support you when all this is over."

His joke fell flat on her, though. In the back of her mind, she couldn't help thinking about how his tilted smile warmed her heart. She looked at him as sternly as possible, "This is not funny. There is no way I would let any of you support me anyway. I can do my share, earn my keep. Besides, what if I am letting someone down right now because I can't remember what my job or calling is?"

Cade tipped his head to the side considering her words, but it was Rederrick who asked, "What about letting you down?"

She turned, focusing her attention back to Rederrick, "I just don't want anyone to suffer because of me, especially anyone here."

Now standing right behind her, Cade replied, "And you think we're all suffering because you're here?"

"You're all working so hard to help me. It has to be tiresome. I can see all the things you're doing for my benefit. Nate hasn't even had a proper night's rest since he arrived. Jenny has to cook for two more people; make that soon to be three more. Rederrick spends any of his extra time away from his firm doing research and taking turns on security watch. Cynda is trying to help me tap into my magic side, which I can tell wears on her, and Cade, you have barely left my side since I arrived. I know you haven't even left the house unless you're checking the perimeter outside.

As he listened, Cade had a difficult time keeping a straight face. He could tell she needed to get this off her chest. He could see she was genuinely concerned for all of them.

She had such a serious, stern look on her face though, and for some reason, he found it incredibly attractive.

When she finished her tirade, he spun her chair to face him head on. Then he bent down, put his hands on the armrests, and leaned in so close she could do nothing but stare into his playful, tawny eyes.

"What if I promised you that your continued presence here was not causing me to suffer in any way? Having to stay by a beautiful woman's side is not my idea of hardship. Besides, when I'm standing next to you, it makes me look better," he said lightly, finishing his words with that charming, tilted smile.

She blushed at his reference to her beauty. Trying not to let his flattering comment or his smoldering eyes affect her, she moved her eyes to his teasing smile and couldn't help smiling herself. She dryly replied, "Well… I wasn't referring to just you, now was I?"

His grin spread even more at her prim tone, showing his perfect white teeth. Without pulling his intense gaze from her, he directed his next question to his friend taking on a sarcastic proper tone himself, "Rederrick? Is Collett's current occupancy in your home causing you to suffer in any way?"

Even though she could no longer see Rederrick's face, she could hear the amusement in his words as he answered, "Nope, no suffering here."

Cade angled his gaze to her again and said, "Okay then, there you go, no suffering. I'll tell you what, I'll ask Nate and Jenny for you, if you want. I can tell you though, feeding and fussing over people makes Jenny happy. You're not the first guest we've had here, and you wouldn't be the first to try to make her stop. It generally offends her when they do. You won't be the last to either.

"Now, our Nate is a team player, and if he wasn't here he would be assigned to some other job, so don't worry about him. You're welcome to ask Cynda yourself, since she is waiting for you upstairs right now. I will warn you…her Irish temper may come out if you do, and it's not a pretty sight. You should also know that playing with magic is her thing. It makes her extremely happy, so I doubt you would find protest there. But, by all means, feel free to ask."

Collett stood, forcing him to straighten up or risk having her head smack into his chin. She stood so close to him that he felt enveloped in her sweet scent. How she got that wonderfully enticing scent of hers to stay with her each day was amazing to him. It was like a drug pulling him in and always left him wanting more.

"Alright, I will." Then she pretended to rethink it, "Although… it's not as if any of you would actually tell me the truth. So, I guess if you're suffering, you'll just have to suck it up. Don't say I didn't try."

Cade gave her an encouraging, "Atta girl," as she finished.

Rederrick kept smiling as she headed for the doorway. He was glad to hear a light, fun tone from her. She seemed to come by it much easier this last week.

When Collett reached the door, she flipped her long, honey-blonde hair back and looked at both men over her shoulder with her radiant smile still in place, "Thanks for giving me a boost." Then she turned on her heels and left.

Cade loved having a tense, verbal exchange with that woman. He inhaled one more deep breath of her now fading scent and closed his eyes, savoring its flavor.

"You lied, you know," Rederrick stated with a grin.

"About what?"

"You are suffering, from being around her all the time," he replied.

Cade's smile grew and he huffed out a breath, "Yeah, I know, but what can I say? It's the best kind of torture, and as the lady so eloquently put it, I'll just have suck it up."

Rederrick laughed aloud. Still laughing, he got up to leave Cade to his watch.

Cade settled in for his shift to watch the perimeter with a huge smile on his face. He swung his legs up onto the table, crossing them at the ankles. He wondered, just how much torture could one man take? He was absolutely positive he was going to find out, and it didn't bother him one little bit.

Cynda sat at her worktable in one of the two rooms across the hall from the workout area. This was her space; her room to study the Craft. Candles in a wide variety of colors and sizes sat on several surfaces.

Cabinets and shelves lined every wall storing crystals, candles, bowls, herbs, and other various supplies. Books old and new took up the remaining shelf space. They had been passed down to her by aunts, great aunts, grandmothers and so on. One day, Cynda would pass these books on to her daughters, and they would do the same for theirs.

She was currently looking at one such book. It was an old leather-bound book, covering several empathic topics. She was researching empathic abilities when Collett strode into the room with a wide smile on her face.

She set down her book and said, "Don't you look chipper this afternoon."

Still smiling, Collett replied, "You know; I feel chipper too."

"Well, I am very glad to hear that. Today I want to try something new with you, and it will help to have positive energy."

Her smile fell apprehensively, "Try what, exactly?"

Cynda shook her head, "Now don't go losing your good mood already. We need that smile in place to create a positive space. So, whatever put you in that good mood, hold on to it."

As the source of her good mood, Collett's mind automatically flashed back to Cade. During the last week, she enjoyed more and more of their time spent together. He was moody, arrogant, and difficult, but he was also kind, generous, and supportive. Collett's feelings for him continued to grow. There was a constant buzzing tension between them as well.

Turning her attention back to Cynda, she watched her lay out three crystals in a row, setting each one on the floor. Collett carefully studied each crystal. She could identify two out of three. She said, "I know that purple one is Amethyst, and that clear one is Herkimer. I'm just not sure what the dark one is."

Cynda looked up at her surprised, "It's hematite, for grounding."

Collett thought about the other two, "People use Herkimer for dreams and memories, sometimes telepathy."

"That's right. Do you know what the Amethyst is for?"

The image of a beautiful young woman praying, clenching a small stone in her hand, popped into her mind. Collett carefully said, "Guidance... direction, maybe."

Cynda felt pleased. Collett had properly named the crystals' uses. She would have to explore that further another time. Right now, she wanted to help Collett learn her capabilities and boundaries.

Making a mental note to log her knowledge of the stones in her book, Cynda nodded, "Very good. Amethyst can also be used to bring wisdom, peace, and harmony. Some witches believe it can help contact your spiritual guides. Today we just need it for harmony and wisdom."

Collett was intrigued. Knowing the names and purpose of these crystals so easily made her wonder what else she might discover she knew.

Cynda moved away from the crystals and gestured for her to sit down before them. Collett sat and crossed her legs, tucking her feet underneath her knees. She looked up to Cynda, "What now?"

"Now we are going to see if you can channel your empathic abilities better." Cynda then grabbed the book she was looking at earlier and sat in front of Collett, folding her legs to the side and behind her. She laid the book on the floor in front of her and continued, "It says here in this book you can learn to control the feelings you receive. In some cases, you will be able to focus on them, reading the person's thoughts behind their emotions. Ready?"

Collett smiled, "As ready as I can be."

"Okay, first you need to understand that the crystals I laid down before you will help you through this. You can pick any one of them up if what you feel is too strong or too weak and you need to channel into them."

"Alright."

Cynda looked in her book again, "I also want to remind you, I am not empathic, so I will not be able to guide you as well as I'd like. I am, however, here for you. If it gets too intense, you can grab onto me. I will try to be your anchor, okay?"

Collett again gave a simple reply, "Okay. What next?" She felt almost eager to try something so new, so proactive.

Concentrating on her book, Cynda explained, "We need someone in the room with emotions to read, which would be me."

"You want me to read your emotions?"

"Well, yes."

Collett looked at her skeptically, "Are you sure? It sounds like an invasion of privacy."

She smiled reassuringly, "Not if I give you permission. Besides, if you're ever attacked again, are you really going to concern yourself with your attacker's privacy? We all have to start somewhere. You're lucky enough to start with me."

Collett sighed, "You have a point. All right then, if I have to start somewhere, I'm grateful it is you."

Like Rederrick, Cynda realized how different Collett was now. In just two short weeks, she had begun to hope and trust in those around her.

Moving on to the next step in the process, Cynda went on, "Okay. First, you have to clear your mind. Similar to meditation, you will need to calm all of your own emotions. Then, you have to focus upon the feelings of the person you're trying to read. If we can get that far successfully, we can try to move forward."

Collett nodded her head, closed her eyes, and breathed in and out, individually relaxing every part of her body. Clearing her mind of any doubts and fears, calming her excitement too, she pulled in, focusing on that clear, white space in her mind.

Once she found it, she focused on the energy in the room. There was positive energy swirling all around her. She could smell the burning waxy scent coming from the yellow candles Cynda lit.

When she was ready, Collett opened her blue eyes, directing her gaze and her mind toward Cynda. She focused on her facial expression, trying to feel for the thoughts that raced through her mind. After some time, she found it. It was a small feeling; slightly hard to grab onto.

"You're worried," she pronounced.

Cynda opened her eyes and locked her gaze with Collett's. Keeping a smooth, quiet tone she encouraged, "Yes, I'm worried. Now try to feel for the thoughts behind the emotion, try to tell me more."

She closed her eyes again. Picturing Cynda's clear, sea-green eyes in her mind, she focused harder, pulling the emotion forward. Suddenly, she felt the worry in her own heart, felt the insecurity increase. Foggy thoughts began to form, speaking carefully she said, "You're worried this won't work. You don't want to cause me any more disappointment."

"Very good. Now try to focus on any other feelings I might be having," Cynda instructed, keeping her voice low.

Collett tipped her head, slightly pinching her features, as she tried to find some more of Cynda's emotions and the reasons behind them. She was beginning to feel a slight drain on her physical strength. Dots of sweat broke out on her brow. Straining, she felt something else, so she focused on it, "You're concerned for Cade too. You don't...you don't want him to be alone, but... you're afraid he will be."

Cynda smiled and watched as Collett pulled these things from her. Truthfully, she was trying to keep herself as open as possible to help her tap into her feelings. That last bit about Cade though, wasn't something she expected Collett to find.

Collett fluttered her eyes open and looking to Cynda, her lips turn up happily. Her smile was full and excited. "I did it!" she blurted out.

Cynda, just as excited, conceded cheerfully, "Yes you did."

"I can't believe it. I really did it. I get the feeling you helped me out some," Collett said.

Cynda looked at her, "I did just a little. When you focused on my worry, I thought about things that worry me to make it easier. I am very confident though, that with practice, you'll get the hang of it in no time."

Collett leaned forward over her knees and gave Cynda a quick, excited hug, "I don't care if you helped me. Right now, I'll take any small victory I can get. Thank you, Cynda."

It was a small victory for her, and Cynda enjoyed seeing the happiness on her face. However, her worry didn't completely fade away with the success. She hoped Collett could perfect the skill in time. With that train of thought popping into her head, her concern changed. Now that they knew she could do this, would they figure out how to use it to their advantage?

She gave Collett a serious look, "We'll have to practice this a lot more, but I think we have just taken a huge leap."

Collett reached forward again and put her hand on Cynda's, "Don't keep worrying. It worked. I'll practice as much as it takes, but now, thanks to you, I know more about who I am. I understand something I didn't before. Let go of your worry now."

Cynda felt reassurance run through her. It was a warm, tingling sensation that spread through her body quickly removing the doubt; distributing confidence and comfort in its wake.

For a moment, she completely forgot what bothered her only a minute before. Only after she basked in the warm feeling was she able to snap back. Cynda's thoughts rushed back to another memory.

She looked quickly down at their connected hands, unsure of how to feel. Then with shock in her eyes, she looked back to Collett and asked, "How did you do that?"

Collett gazed at her with a perplexed expression and asked simply, "Do what?"

Cynda didn't need an answer though, her memory was clear now. She remembered keenly another time she had experienced that same warm tingle. It had been a time she heard Collett's voice in that dark, cold place. She jumped from her position on the floor, as if an electric shock ran through her. She stood there for a moment rethinking it over in her mind.

Collett followed filled with concern, "What is it Cynda? Did I do something wrong?"

Cynda shook her head, "No, you did nothing wrong. I am just a little stunned is all."

"What is it then? What did I do?" her voice rang with insecurity.

"You took away my worry. I think," Cynda said.

Collett narrowed her eyes and gave her a look that silently asked, 'Are you crazy?' Though, the only word to escape her mouth was, "What?"

She just ignored it and continued, "I remember now. I was so cold and tired. I just wanted to go to sleep. I didn't want to wake up, was sure, I was not going to wake up."

"What are you talking about?" Collett asked forcefully.

"The river, that day at the river; I heard you. I was there in the dark, and I heard you telling me I needed to come back. I didn't really want to, though. Then I saw Rederrick in my mind, and Tracy, James, and Ashley. Suddenly, I wanted to fight. I wanted to wake up."

"Cynda, I'm still not sure what you're talking about. Yes, I was there, and yes, I spoke to you. Cade was there too. He warmed you up remember? That's why you woke up. It wasn't me. All I did was talk to you."

Cynda glared at her, "I know what I'm talking about. I remember Cade too, but you don't really get it. Until I heard your voice, I had given up. No…it was more than just your voice.

"I remember hearing you that day, but it's strange; I'd forgotten the wonderful warm sensations my body felt when I heard you. I felt tingling all over. Then I remember listening to your soft, almost musical voice, reminding me people loved me and needed me. 'It wasn't my time,' you said.

"And a moment ago I was worried about you. Then you touched my hands and spoke to me with reassuring words. I felt it again. It wasn't as strong as before, but it was there; that warm tingling, a feeling of comfort. Then poof! I didn't feel worried anymore. I almost forgot what I was thinking about."

Tentatively Collett tried to understand, "I'm not sure what you're saying here, and even more certain you're just really confused."

"Alright, if you don't believe me, how about a little experiment?"

"What kind of experiment?" she asked carefully.

"Tomorrow, let's try this empathic thing on Cade and Rederrick, and then see what happens. To make it fair, I won't tell them my theory. You, in turn, have to agree to give it your best shot. We'll just let the chips fall where they may."

Remaining unsure, but willing to consider it, Collett asked, "Why tomorrow?"

"I want your mind clear and focused when you do this. Plus, I noticed it was sort of draining on you."

"It might have been, but it wasn't too bad," Collett supplied quickly.

Cynda scrutinized her carefully. Her cheeks held a pink tint, and her face was alight with excitement. She didn't want to push Collett too hard, but time was short so she relented, "Okay, we'll try it tonight, but if it is too much you have to tell me right away."

Uncertain of this plan, but seeing there was no other way to convince Cynda, Collett considered it. She also wanted to try out her new found skill of sensing emotions some more. So, she nodded her agreement, "What if you're wrong?"

Cynda grinned deviously, "There is something you should learn about me. I may not always be right, but I'm never wrong," she said teasingly.

Collett couldn't help but smile at her confidence, "Okay, what if you are right?"

Her teasing smile fell, an unsure expression replaced it, "I'm not certain, but I have a sneaking suspicion that whatever it means, it must be important."

Unsure how to feel about this possibility, Collett didn't worry too much. To her, it all seemed very unlikely, but it was thrilling and nerve-wracking at the same time. She knew they needed to find out for sure. "Well then, who do we try it on first?"

Enjoying the game, Cynda gave her a sideways glance saying sarcastically, "We'll give them a chance to volunteer first, but if no one steps up to bat-we'll convince my loving, devoted, willing to do anything I say husband, of course."

Collett couldn't help the smile from spreading across her face once again as she replied, "Of course."

CHAPTER 19

As promised, Cynda told no one about how she suspected that Collett had eased away her burden of worry. However, during dinner that night, Cynda did tell them all about Collett reading her feelings and thoughts so easily.

She explained that Collett wanted to try out her new skills and see if she could read any of their emotions. Collett kept her gaze averted from Cade, hoping he would not be the first to volunteer. Oddly, the thought of delving into his feelings made her nervous.

Surprisingly, the first person who volunteered was not Rederrick or Cade. It was Jenny. "I'll do it," she said simply.

Everyone's heads turned and their stunned gazes locked on her. "I think I'd be much easier to read than Mr. Werren or Mr. Williams. With all the, trainin' and experience they've had they could resist better. Besides, I may be old now, but I still have a bit of an adventurous spirit left in these creaky bones."

Cade couldn't hold back his smile as Jenny said his name so formally. Jenny had known him for almost twenty-five years now, and she still stubbornly refused to call him by his first name. He had been an associate of her husband's. He brought a devastated Jenny here, to Cynda and Rederrick, twenty-four years ago to help her start over.

The Faction brutally killed Jenny's husband for helping Cade find and rescue someone they were holding at one of their secure facilities. He knew Jenny would need a safe place for a while, so he brought her to the safest place he could think of. Jenny had been here ever since.

Jenny and Cynda had taken to each other right away. Cynda's mother had passed recently, and Jenny never had children, so they bonded together, lifting each other up, making a strong family.

"All right. You can go first Jenny," agreed Cynda. "We'll go ahead and try this in the parlor after dinner."

"I'll just go now and take dinner to the young Nate in the security room," she said, then she left to make a plate for Nate.

Everyone sat in silence for a time, finishing up their ham and baked potatoes. The only sound in the room was the scrape of flatware against the plates. Cynda gave Rederrick a pointed look, letting him know she expected him to be the next volunteer. Lucky for him, Cade noticed how oblivious he was. "I'll do it, too."

Looking up from her plate, Collett met his eyes. She felt relieved when Jenny spoke first, and had hoped she'd dodged reading him.

She felt her nerves jitter. Most of the time, she couldn't sense a single emotion from him. *What will I sense now?* she thought. Those few times she had sensed emotion from him, the feelings were very strong and intense, almost uncontrolled. Then they had winked out, just as quickly as they had come.

He stared right back at her with a challenge in his warm eyes, "I mean, if that's alright with you, Collett."

"Ye-" she cleared her throat, annoyed that her voice croaked. "Sure, that's fine," she said with false confidence.

He inclined his head and grinned. He didn't have to be an empath to see how nervous the thought of reading him made her.

Truth be told, he wasn't so certain about it himself. He wasn't even sure what compelled him to volunteer. Other than saving Rederrick from Cynda's wrath, there was no good reason for it. The possibility of her sensing his growing feelings for her worried him. She was just getting comfortable around him. She almost welcomed his small light touches now, and his closeness didn't put her on edge anymore. *What would happen,* he wondered, *if she knew the whole truth?*

A part of him wanted Collett to know how he felt, but only when the time was right. Simply, he was afraid that she didn't feel the same. The thought of her pulling back, pulling away from him, was enough to make him regret so easily volunteering. He realized that if she rejected him completely, it might be too much for him to bear. But, curiosity didn't just kill cats; it had a way of trapping all kinds of animals- including wolves.

After dinner was finished and the plates cleared away, they all adjourned to the parlor. Rederrick lit a fire as everyone settled in. Upon Cynda's direction, Cade moved the two wingback chairs to face each other, putting them close together.

Just as he finished, Jenny bustled into the room. Collett invited her to sit in one of the two chairs then sat in the one opposite, putting her back to the fire. Cynda stepped forward, and her green eyes sparkled with unspoken excitement. She opened her hand, revealing the same three crystals they had used earlier that morning.

Collett closed her eyes briefly, then scooped up the stones and laid them in her lap. *I can do this,* she reminded herself. *I have done this before.* "Are you ready?" she asked. Jenny nodded and took a deep steadying breath.

Collett explained, "This morning, it took me a moment to center myself and my emotions. That way, my own feelings won't interfere and get confused with yours. After that I'll try to read some of your emotions, and if we're lucky, maybe some of your thoughts."

"You just take all the time you need, sweetie," Jenny replied. "Do you need to hold my hand or something?"

"No, not right now. If I can't get something after a while, we'll try a physical connection to help, but I would like to try to do this without it first."

"Okay then, do whatever you need to," Jenny replied, clasping her hands together and laying them in her lap.

Closing her eyes, Collett took in several deep breaths, letting them out slowly on a count of ten. She let go of her own thoughts and nervous emotions with each calming breath. She was looking once again for that peaceful white space in her mind. After a few minutes, she felt relaxed enough to start reaching out to Jenny.

She found the process much harder this time, mostly because there were so many different emotions in the room around her. It was something they hadn't accounted for. It was hard to push through until she could feel only Jenny. It was sort of like listening to a radio station with too much static. Collett was unwilling to give up though.

Straining harder, she reached out for the strong nurturing feelings that surrounded Jenny the first time they met. When she finally found it, Collett found it much easier to single Jenny out from the rest of the people in the room and to focus on her emotions.

Searching for a particularly strong emotion, Collett ultimately found a warm, soft emotion that drew her in. She decided to focus on it further. Her brow pinched in concentration, "Love. I can feel love..." she voiced quietly.

So quietly in fact, Rederrick didn't hear. "What did she say?" he whispered to no one specific.

With arms folded tight, in order to keep himself from touching Collett, Cade answered solemnly, "Love."

The voices almost broke her concentration. She pinched her eyes closed tighter, trying harder to shut out the other people in the room. Keeping her focus on Jenny, she started again, "You still love him."

Jenny's chocolate brown eyes watered as she answered the proclamation, "Yes dear, I still do. I love him very much."

"Sometimes, just the strength of that love sees you through each day. You see him-in your dreams. You think of him often. Oh Jenny, you miss him terribly. I can feel it." Collett didn't realize it, but as she spoke, her hand fisted tightly at her breastbone. She felt the loneliness sharply in her heart. It was as if the pain was as much hers as it was Jenny's.

With the feelings so vivid in her heart and the memories so clear in her mind, Jenny's voice cracked, "That I do, dear." A single tear escaped, running down her soft, wrinkled cheek.

Cade moved across the room, not to comfort Collett this time, but to offer his support to Jenny. He reached down and grabbed her hand, and Jenny gripped it tight, welcoming his support.

A fresh wave of raw emotion rushed through Collett. She rode the wave as it pulled her in deeper than ever before. She could feel the same raw, sad loneliness that had broken Jenny's heart so long ago. She startled slightly, as images invaded her thoughts. The crystals in her lap clattered to the floor. She saw vague flashes of a younger man with sandy hair and a dimpled smile. Then, there was blood, and a quick, small, painful memory of a funeral. It was so swift Collett was unsure whether the picture was real or imagined.

She felt the fatigue as well. Her head spun and the images quickly disappeared. Tears leaked from her closed eyes. She eased her eyes open once again; looking past the teary blur, she stared directly into Jenny's sad, love-filled eyes.

"You're so proud of him; his sacrifice and his courage. You never once blamed him. You believed in his choice; believed it was right," Collett observed with awe and wonder in her voice.

This time Jenny only nodded. The words were stuck in her pained chest.

Collett wiped at her unchecked tears and her heart broke for this woman. She stood and put her left hand on Jenny's shoulder as she crouched to meet her gaze, the unshed tears still making her eyes glisten in the firelight. She remembered Cynda's words when they discussed love only days ago.

"Jenny," she began with a soothing voice, "Someone once told me when you love somebody, as strongly and as powerfully as you loved Sam, it never fades, and it never dies. That kind of love follows us into the next life. It is everlasting. You have been truly blessed to have found it and will be blessed again when you meet up with him once more."

Jenny smiled through her tears. She looked up to Cade with glistening brown eyes, squeezing his hand to let Cade know she was alright now and was grateful for his support.

Jenny felt a peaceful calm enter her heart, leaving the strong love she held for Sam and erasing some of her sad loneliness left over by the loss of her husband. Jenny never could have imagined Collett pulling at her old wounds and finding Sam's special place in her heart. And then, somehow, the pain Jenny carried for so many years ebbed, and she felt content.

Cynda carefully watched the entire event unfold; keeping close to Collett in case she needed support or grounding. She tried to examine each change that occurred in both women thoroughly. She waited patiently for this very moment. When she saw it, she lost her focus on Collett and focused intensely on Jenny. She watched the amazing way Jenny's drawn expression shifted into a calm, serene smile, full of love and hope. She couldn't help but smile to herself. Collett had done it again, and Cynda knew it.

Then she directed her smile to Collett giving her an, *I told you so,* smirk. Her smile fell when she saw her. Her cheeks were flushed, but the rest of her was paler than she should be. Beads of moisture dotted her brow, and her crystal blue eyes had dark shadows within them, hinting at the toll this exercise must have taken on her.

Concerned, Cynda approached with weary eyes. "Are you alright?" she asked under her breath, trying not to draw attention.

"Yes, I'm fine. I just have a small headache. It was harder than it was with you." Truthfully, it was more than a little headache. It was more like an icepick jamming at her skull. Collett felt the intense throbbing behind her temples and couldn't help rubbing one side with her free hand.

"Why don't you sit back down for a minute? I'll get you some water," Cynda said and quickly left the room, sending Rederrick a pointed, worried look on her way out.

Of course, Cade's sensitive hearing picked up their whispered conversation, and he focused his attention on her as well. Like Cynda, he noticed the profound change. He patted Jenny's hand and let go, so he could move toward Collett. He brushed a stray hair away from her face and tucked it behind her ear. "Why don't you relax and catch your breath; do something to put some color in those cheeks." He had tried for a calm tone but failed.

"I really am fine, just a small headache. I promise," she explained quietly.

He wasn't buying it. His protective feelings for her came out, and he lost sight of everyone else in the room. Putting his hands on her shoulders, he looked into her now darkened eyes, carefully scrutinizing them for the lie.

She looked back into his warm eyes, and without even trying, Collett felt his strong concern rush through her. Once again, the physical contact somehow amplified the effect. He was concerned for her. She could feel his worry over her pale skin and pained expression. It was looking into a mirror through him. She sensed his fear made him nervous. He wasn't sure what he should do, and he clearly disliked being unsure of his next action. It created a frustrated anger in him, and those emotions poured into her.

Her eyes fluttered, and she felt the dizziness creep in. Reading Cade accidentally was too much. She heard someone say her name. Jenny maybe, but it sounded distant and tinny.

She put a hand to her head to quell the spinning, and her world suddenly tipped on its side. Cade had scooped her up into his arms as if she weighed no more than a small child. He looked into her surprised eyes, with concern all over his face.

"I think that's enough for one day, don't you? I'm taking you to bed."

As he started from the room, she heard Rederrick, "I'll take your turn on watch. You take care of her."

Everything was happening so fast; she couldn't think. Out of nowhere Cynda appeared in the hallway with a glass of water. "Oh, my, what happened?"

"She almost fainted. In fact, I'm sure if I hadn't steadied her, she would have," Cade answered gruffly before she could even form the words. "I'm taking her to her room to lie down."

Steadied her? Collett thought, *Did that happen?*

Cynda nodded, "That's a good idea. I'll make her some revitalizing tea and bring it up shortly."

Collett looked back and forth between them. "You're doing it again; acting as if I'm not in the room. I'm fine really, I promise. Cade, you can put me down now. I can walk," but her voice was weak even to her own ears.

"Not on your life. You just relax now and enjoy the ride. I won't have you falling down the stairs out of sheer stubbornness." She glared at him as he moved past Cynda, making his way to the stairs.

"Really, I'm fine. You can put me down now. I just have a slight headache."

"You don't look so fine to me. You look terribly sick."

"Well thank you very much," she replied in a snippy tone, her voice gaining more strength.

He stopped walking, his eyes filled with heat, his expression turned intense. When he spoke, his voice was deep, throaty, and just as intense as the look in his eyes, "You know very well that's not what I meant. You're also not blind, or dumb. You know exactly how I think you look, even with pale cheeks."

Looking into the depth of his eyes, she had nothing more to say, so she just ducked her head, averting his gaze and laid it against his chest. Surely the color was back in her cheeks now.

He carefully sat her on the bench at the end of the bed, and pulled back the plush comforter and sheets. He then quickly scooped her up again and gently laid her on the bed.

As he pulled the covers up over her, he said, "Now, you just rest a minute. I'll go check on your tea."

She watched as he straightened the comforter over her, effectively tucking her in. She felt uncertain. On one hand, she was somewhat embarrassed. After all, this was the second time Cade brought her to her room because of a slight headache. Admittedly, the first time wasn't this dramatic. Her other thought was centered on how wonderful it was to have somebody care for her so much.

He stood up then and carefully looked at her. "I'll be right back," he said softly, turning to leave.

Before she could even think about what she was saying, she blurted out, "Stay."

His hand on the door, Cade stopped, turned around slowly, and looked into her pleading blue eyes for one heartbeat. This was the first time she willingly requested his presence.

Not risking the chance of her changing her mind, he quickly slipped off his shoes and rounded the bed. He sat on top of the covers, crossing his sock-clad feet at the ankles. Then, leaning his back against the headboard, he wrapped an arm around Collett, pulling her over to him.

She easily nestled into him, laying her head against his chest. Neither one of them spoke for a long while. They simply sat in the silent room, absorbing each other. Collett closed her eyes and enjoyed his crisp, manly scent and steady breathing. Regardless of the fact that she remained unsure what prompted her to ask him to stay, lying here with him felt right.

Cade absently tangled his fingers in her hair, silently thanking heaven for small favors. Or maybe he should thank someone else, because perfect golden hair such as hers should be sinful. It made a man think of all kinds of things.

A knock at the door had her trying to sit up away from him. He negated her efforts and tightened his hold, keeping her there. "Come in, Cynda."

Cynda opened the door and came in with a small tray. She didn't even blink twice at the sight of them cuddled together.

She set the tray down on the bedside table saying, "I brought up some toast too, in case you needed something to restore your strength. I'm sorry it drained you so much Collett."

Looking at Cynda's concerned features made Collett feel guilty, especially since she was beginning to feel better. She simply hadn't counted on feeling Jenny's emotions so deeply herself. It was not so intense with Cynda, nor had images flickered in her mind.

"We'll have to be more careful until you get the hang of it," Cynda told her.

Collett smiled, "It was a powerful experience. I'm glad I got to see something of Jenny. Please reassure her I am fine. I know she was worried. I promise it was worth it, for me anyway."

Cynda still didn't look so sure, but she nodded, "Alright, but before you go looking for more people to test this out on, maybe we should practice some more."

Collett nodded her agreement, "Still, I'm grateful to Jenny. Will you tell her for me?"

"I'm sure she will be glad to hear that."

Cynda turned to leave, and as her hand touched the doorknob she remembered something else she wanted to tell Collett. Her lips twitched into a smile. Cynda craned her neck and shot out, "By the way... I was right, you know."

It took her a moment to understand Cynda's meaning. When she did, she asked cryptically, "You're sure?"

A smug smile spread across Cynda's mouth, "I told you Collett; I'm not always right, but I am never wrong. Get some sleep. We'll talk about it tomorrow. Goodnight Cade. Rederrick says don't worry about coming down at all tonight. He'll take care of it." Cynda walked out the door and closed it quietly behind her.

"What was she right about?" Cade questioned with curiosity.

Collett shrugged her shoulders, "She thinks I can offer people comfort and warm feelings."

"Really?"

"That's what she says."

He thought for a minute reflecting on her tone. "You don't believe her?" he asked distractedly with his fingers still combing through her hair.

Sighing, she sat up, "I'm just not sure. It sounds pretty incredible and unlikely to me."

He laughed at her. His laugh was rich and full. It rumbled and vibrated in his chest. The sound of it warmed her.

Collett smiled, "What's so funny?"

"You had no problem believing that I'm nearing three-hundred years old. No problem believing Selena could read your life story with a touch, and you have seen Cynda use all kinds of incredible magic. Yet you can't believe that you, a person who can feel and read other people's emotions, could possibly make them feel better when you do," as he finished, he laughed some more. "You are a phenomenon, Collett."

She couldn't help her smile from spreading wider, "Well, when you say it like that, it does sound pretty ridiculous."

"Only a little," he said lightly.

She folded her arms, pretending annoyance, "When I originally thought it through in my mind, it didn't sound so possible."

Cade thought about it for a second then replied seriously, "I suppose that is the nature of people isn't it? It's easy to believe in strange things and unnatural possibilities, or have faith in the unseen; until you're the one doing it. Then you automatically question everything, trying to rationalize what happened, doubting what is before your very eyes."

After reflecting on Cade's words, and thinking about how he said it with experience in his voice, Collett changed the subject and asked, "Cade, what's it like to live so long?"

Her question took him aback. Forgetting all about her previous revelation, Cade thought about it for a minute. "Well, it isn't always as easy as they make it seem in the movies or fictional books. It's like any other life in some ways. You have to learn and grow as time goes by. Even after all these years, I continue to learn new things," he answered solemnly.

Laying her head on his chest again, she yawned, "Tell me, Cade, I want to understand you." Cade closed his eyes, enjoying the feel of her snuggling in so close to him. He thought back, trying to decide where to start.

"I guess the first thing I would say about immortality is, adaptability is absolutely necessary. The world has changed a lot since my birth, and continues to do so. Things never stay the same, and yet, some things never change."

"Like what?" she murmured against his chest.

"The nature of mankind I suppose. That never changes. Human-kind is always moving toward the better way or looking for the easier road to the better life. Some are willing to break their backs in order to earn it. I have seen men fight for freedom with nothing but faith and hope to see them through. I watched as a nation was born and grew to take its first small steps. Then watched again as that country made giant leaps, shaping a way of life others coveted.

"It's an awesome thing to watch the conviction of humankind striving for what is good and right. Faith, hope, and idealism are powerful weapons against any foe. In fact, to me, those are more powerful than any sword or gun, more powerful than any magic that can be wielded.

"At the same time, power, greed and betrayal can sway even the strongest of men; causing so much pain and turmoil in its wake."

His mind flashed back to a time when those very things had corrupted someone important to him.

"I can't be like you, Cade. I do not want to help these people! I am not willing to sacrifice myself for their causes. I do what I think is best and damn them! These people you want to save are the very same people that would gladly watch you burn, throwing kindling on the fire, if they ever found out about you. Think about it, if they ever knew your secret. . ."

"You can't do this! It is not right, and you know it," Cade pleaded, *"Have you no conscience? You do not have to be like them. You are better than they are. Come with me. We can leave this place. We don't have to be a part of it."*

"You're right. I am better. We are better than every one of them! Don't you see that? This is not our fight! I will not subjugate myself to any ruler, not even this one and his ideals. Eventually, this war will end like it always does. I intend to profit from it in the meantime. Their laws don't have to apply to us. Why is it you cannot see the possibilities?"

With a broken heart, Cade replied somberly, "Because I cannot be like you, either." With conviction in his voice he continued, "I believe in laws and justice. I believe in mankind! I believe in their capacity for good. I believe in this war. I believe in hope for a better way. I believe in being accountable to a higher authority, and not just doing what brings in a profit."

"Well then, I guess this is where we part, because I can't believe in anyone. Not even God"

"So be it," Cade uttered as he dejectedly turned his back and walked away, knowing things would never be the same between them.

"Cade?" the sound of his name on Collett's lips brought him out of the painful flash of memory.

He cleared his vision, trying to push back the images in his mind. "I'm still here; just thinking."

"Whatever you were remembering was hurtful. I can feel some of your pain. Who hurt you?"

He pulled her in closer, "Someone I thought was important. It doesn't matter anymore. It was a long time ago."

She rubbed her hand over his chest offering him comfort. The light touches distracted him well enough. In fact, they just about drove him crazy.

Clearing his throat, Cade continued, "There is one thing I know that continues throughout the ages. No matter how much time passes, I have seen the wonder and pure power of Love."

Collett's hand stopped moving at his words.

Despite her stilled fingers, he went on in a light, soothing tone, "I've seen many people like Rederrick and Cynda. People like Jenny and Sam. You were right when you told her that kind of love is everlasting."

"Cynda is the one who told me that," she replied, almost whispering.

Cade smiled, and in a natural gesture, kissed the top of her head, "That's because Cynda knows it to be true."

Yawning again Collett asked, "Cynda said Rederrick almost died once to save her. Did you know about that?"

He thought back thirty years ago when his longtime friend had fallen in love with a troubled, green-eyed witch and almost gotten himself killed trying to help her. He would have been killed had it not been for Cade's interference. "Yeah I know all about that," he answered.

"I had a feeling," she mumbled.

Cade grinned at the lost, sleepiness in her tone. "Get some sleep, Collett," he ordered kindly.

"Mm-hm," she barely uttered, her eyelids already closed.

Her breathing began to even out, and her body relaxed against him. As she drifted to sleep in his arms, Cade sat there in the dimly lit room, inhaling her sweet aroma and appreciating the feel of her snuggled tightly against him.

He closed his eyes just for a moment, and he drifted off to sleep along with her. His arms remained tightly wrapped around the woman he was falling in love with.

CHAPTER 20

The next morning, Collett woke to the sunlight streaming in through the blinds in her room. It took her a moment to realize something was different. When her foggy mind finally cleared, she understood it was the heavy arm draped across her waistline and the warm body pressed against her back.

Even without lasts night's memories, she would have known whose body occupied most of her bed right away. Cade laid on a slight slant covering almost the entire bed. She was tucked tightly underneath his arm, curled up in the little space he left for her.

She tried to carefully shift her body from underneath him. To her dismay, the weight of his body on top of the comforter and his arm wrapped around her stomach, kept her firmly in place. The only way she could see out of this predicament would be waking him.

Frankly, she was a little surprised he'd stayed all night. She was even more amazed that his bed-hogging tendencies hadn't caused her to stir once in the night. To her knowledge, she'd slept soundly and deeply with Cade there snuggled against her.

She liked knowing he stayed with her long after she closed her heavy lids and drifted to sleep. Her feelings for him were growing stronger each day, and each day she tried to rationalize why a relationship between them could never work. She was fast running out of reasons, and today that didn't bother her at all.

She didn't care anymore. She wanted her little piece of happiness while she could have it. Even if their time together was short, she was going to make an effort to get to know this man. No matter what happens in her future, Collett decided then and there, she was going to enjoy this part of her present. Starting today.

With a little effort, she pulled her right arm free and moved to reach around to wake Cade. To her surprise, he was already awake. He quickly grabbed her arm, pinned it back down, and pulled her tighter against him. He mumbled something she didn't catch about early risers.

She giggled, "You're going to have to let me up sometime."

Keeping his eyes closed against her back, Cade smiled and mumbled against the pillow, "Yeah? Why is that? I'm fine just like this, very comfortable."

"Because, sooner or later, I'm going to have to pee, and it's looking more and more like sooner the longer I lay here."

He opened his eyes and propped himself up on his elbow. Tugging, he rolled her over onto her back and gazed at her intently. "All right, I will let you go on one condition…"

It was then that she realized that sometime in the night he had removed his shirt, leaving his spectacular chest open for viewing. She had a heck of a time pulling her attention from the amazing sight of him. When she did, she narrowed her eyes playfully, "That is?"

He leaned in closer, "You agree to spend the day with me."

"Don't we do that every day?" she responded teasingly.

He spoke using a deep, sensual voice, "Not the way I have planned, we haven't."

"Oh?"

"Today there will be no training, no magic, and no security. It will be you and me getting to know one another. Since all has been quiet around here, and we haven't seen a single sign of the enemy, whoever they may be, I even have plans to take you out today."

She returned his intense stare, hypnotized by the beauty of his eyes and the deep throaty sound of his voice. Nodding and finding her voice she agreed, "I think I can manage that. Although, my self-defense teacher might not like the idea of me playing hooky. He seems to think I still have a long way to go, or so he tells me regularly."

"As it so happens, I know your teacher personally. I'm sure he'll excuse your absence, just this once, mind you."

"Okay, you let me up to pee, and I agree to spend the day with you. Sounds somewhat fair," she said agreeably.

"I think so."

"Since we are bargaining and all, I would just like to add something to this little arrangement."

"I'm open to suggestions, occasionally," Cade responded lightly.

Collett boldly laid her hand against his bare and muscled chest. He looked down to where her soft hand rested, and then looked back with desire filling his eyes. Her stomach jittered, and her nerves almost had her changing her mind, but the wanting gave her strength. Locking her gaze with his once more, she cleared her throat. "Kiss me," she said quietly.

Somewhat taken aback at her feathery touch and her simple request, Cade found himself the one surprised this time. Never in a million years could he have predicted that would be her addition to their playful bargain. Wariness crept in. He didn't get time to think about it though. She reached up, put her other hand behind his neck and gently, but firmly, pulled him to her until their lips met.

From there, pure instinct took over. All basic thought fled his mind as his senses were overloaded by Collett. The sweet, intoxicating smell of her, the enticing flavor of her lips moving against his, and the feel of her warm body pressed so close to his stirred him. He felt a tingle on his skin as her fingers trailed up his chest to his head and tangled in his hair. A low growl escaped his throat.

He could barely stand it. If he didn't stop her soon, he would lose control, and he might lose his mind as well. No woman ever stirred him up so completely. Her soft slender hand moved back down to his chest, trailing down his sensitized skin in a blazing wake.

Then, just as quickly as the amazingly powerful kiss started, it suddenly ended. She pushed him back and whispered, "I didn't imagine it then," and licked her lips tauntingly. Then more firmly she said, "Well, a deal's a deal, let me up."

Still trying to regain his senses, Cade easily rolled onto his back, unpinning her. He was still having a difficult time thinking. Hell, he was having difficult time breathing. She threw the covers back, covering him, and eased her way out of the bed. On her way to the bathroom, he managed to regain a small fraction of his ability to think.

"Imagine what?" He was astonished to find that his words came out in a croaked voice.

She smiled at him over her shoulder, "The way you make me feel." With that, she stepped over the threshold between the rooms and shut the bathroom door with a soft click.

Sitting there with his back against the hand-carved wooden headboard, unable to process what had just happened, he tried to think. He couldn't help wondering what caused this startling change in her from last night to this morning. He pulled his fingers through his midnight black hair and decided it didn't matter. He would just have to thank whomever was responsible for it when he found out who they were.

Hearing the shower turn on, Cade decided that was his cue to leave. There was no sense torturing himself further by picturing her in the shower with only a flimsy wooden door to separate them. He swung from the bed and picked up his shirt on his way out. As he left her room and crossed the hall to go shower, all he could think about was Rederrick's words about Fate. It sure looked like it would be smiling upon him today.

After a refreshing shower, Collett all but skipped down the stairs into the kitchen. When she breezed into the room and saw Rederrick, Cynda, and Nate sitting silently at the table, she suddenly felt a quick moment of embarrassment. Her cheeks heated slightly as she thought about them all knowing that Cade had spent the night with her. Though, nothing happened, well… if you didn't count this morning's kiss, she couldn't help feeling slightly self-conscious.

She tried to ignore the fact that her cheeks were now probably red and moved to sit in the unoccupied chair between Cynda and Nate. Nate gave her his customary silent nod and continued eating. Cynda didn't look up from the book she was reading too intently, but Collett was sure she was smiling and using her shiny auburn hair as a curtain to hide it. Rederrick didn't hide his smile or his eyes. He looked right at her with those teasing gray orbs, "Get enough sleep?"

She wasn't sure why she blushed so frantically. It wasn't like that, and she knew he was just teasing her. "Yes, thank you," she said primly.

She saw movement out of the corner of her eye and twisted her head to look at Nate. It was the first time Collett saw him smile. Even though he was tipping his head away from her, she knew the rat was definitely smiling. No, she corrected, he was actually laughing- though he was doing his best to cover it.

Jenny momentarily distracted her attention from him, saving him from a sharp elbow to his ribs, when she bustled over to place a glass of orange juice in front of her. "What would you like on your omelet, dear?" she asked.

Collett gave Nate one final glare and tipped her head up to Jenny, looking for any signs of pain or sadness from last night. "Um... whatever, I'm not picky," she replied as she scrutinized.

Jenny's need to nurture had her doing the very same thing as Collett. She was carefully looking for any sign Collett was still weakened. As she did this, Jenny saw the worry on Collett's face, worry for her. She didn't need empathic powers when you had years of wisdom. She gave Collett a stern look, "I'm fine. Don't you go on worryin' about me. Actually, I feel great. You should worry about yourself instead. Though, you are lookin' much better this mornin'; got some color in your cheeks anyway."

Collett heard a snort come from Nate's direction and glared at him, her cheeks brightening even more.

"I'll get you that omelet now," Jenny said, then she moved over to the counter to get started.

Relieved to see Jenny doing so well, Collett smiled. She turned her attention to her juice, refusing to look up. By this time, Nate had regained his composure and was digging into his food as if nothing happened.

"Collett, what time would you like to come upstairs today?" Cynda asked, breaking the short silence.

"Actually, I think Cade has something in mind for today. I'm not exactly sure what he has planned or how long it will take."

"Oh, okay. I'll just do some more research or something," Cynda replied happily.

"No, Cynda. We're all taking a day off," Cade explained coming into the kitchen. He lithely moved across the floor without making a sound. When he reached Collett, he casually placed a kiss atop her head, "Feel better?"

What had been a fading pink color in her cheeks turned bright red once again. *Good grief!* she thought.

He tilted his head and considered. He thought her embarrassment curious. His brow tilted up and he smiled, "That's a good color on you, I like it." He easily ignored her embarrassment and turned to Rederrick, "When did Cody get here?"

"Oh, I think it was around one. He slept for a couple hours then said he was ready to go. He may be new, but he is eager. I put him on watch and got some sleep myself. I tell you, it will be nice to have an extra man on duty."

Cade nodded, "Agreed. In fact, because we have an extra man here, I'm taking Collett out today. I think we could all use a break. Therefore, I will take the evening watch if you and Nate can split the rest. Then we can all manage a little time to ourselves."

Collett looked to Rederrick, "You don't have to go into the office today?"

"Nope, I have no court dates scheduled, and things are running smoothly. I'm off through Thanksgiving," he replied.

"Oh. If you're sure. I mean, I hope it is not my fault," she hedged.

A fatherly expression of patience covered his features, and his eyes sparkled. "Haven't we already been over this? Besides, it is my firm, and there are a few perks that come with being your own boss."

Reminded of her previous reassurance from Cade and Rederrick the day before, plus her new outlook this morning, she accepted his words for truth. She nodded her understanding and accepted that it wasn't always her fault.

"What will you two be doing today?" Cynda asked sweetly.

"Oh, nothing special. I think I'll just take her up the mountain," Cade replied. "We'll get some fresh air, but we're going stay close."

Collett looked to him curiously, "A hike? Do you know how cold it is out there? I don't even have any boots."

Cynda stood to clear her plate, "You can just use mine," she offered, "We're about the same size. I also have any winter gear you could possibly need. It's supposed to be pretty sunny today, you'll be fine."

Cade smiled, "Are you trying to get out of our little deal?"

"No. I just didn't expect this, that's all," Collett replied honestly.

He smiled, "Don't worry so much. It won't be all bad. I'll meet you outside in about an hour. I have to check in with Cody and gas up the snowmobile." He bent down, kissed Collett fully on the mouth, and left as soundlessly as he came in. She watched him leave the room, spun around, and looked straight at Rederrick's smiling eyes and smug grin.

Nate stood quickly, then in an out-of-character move, bent down to Collett's ear. "Don't worry," he told her, "He'll get most of the teasing. I'll personally make sure to give him hell. It was just fun to make you blush. He's right, it looks good on you." As if in response, her cheeks turned pink. "You two kids have fun now." Then he walked over to the sink, added his plate to the dishes, thanked Jenny with a peck on her wrinkled cheek, and sauntered from the room following Cade's path.

Rederrick scooped up a mouthful of food as Jenny came over with her omelet. Jenny patted her back and Collett thought she might have said, "Enjoy." She was too focused on the size of her omelet to be certain. It took up most of the large dinner plate in front of her. She'd be lucky if she could finish half of it, no, make that one fourth of it.

She sighed and picked up her fork to dig in. She was starting to wonder if it wasn't Jenny's personal goal to make her gain twenty pounds. She turned to say as much, and then noticed the woman in question had left as well.

Cynda redirected her attention when she spoke from over by the sink as she put her empty juice glass in with the other dishes, "When you're done, Collett, come and find me upstairs. I'll round up some winter gear for you."

She could only nod due to the fact that her mouth was now full. As Cynda parted the room, Collett felt a slight pinch in her gut. She was somewhat reluctant to be left with a grinning Rederrick. She sensed he waited on purpose though, wanting to talk to her.

He cleared his throat and tried for a casual tone, "How are you feeling today?"

"Oh, I'm fine. I just wasn't fully prepared for last night I think. I'll get better," she replied.

"Of that, I have no doubt," he added confidently.

The room fell silent for a moment as she took another bite of Jenny's wonderful omelet that had a marvelous spicy, Santa Fe flavor. She took another bite, savoring the multiple flavors tickling her tongue.

Rederrick finally put down his fork and wiped his mouth with his linen napkin. His next words could have just as well been a punch to her stomach. It would've had the same effect. "He's in love with you."

She about choked on her omelet. Coughing and sputtering, she tried to clear her throat without embarrassing herself. Rederrick moved over a chair, taking the chair Nate occupied only moments ago. He lightly slapped her back, helping her choke it all down.

Then, when she had regained control, he explained, "I only tell you because it is important for you to understand. I have known Cade my whole life. He's almost always been a part of our family. It goes all the way back to my great, great Aunt Delia. After he helped her once, she made him a promise; a promise that he would always be a part of her family. My family has taken that vow very seriously. We have all happily been a part of that bargain, and each one of us has been blessed for it in some way. I thank God every day for that."

She simply listened, and in keeping silent, she heard his heartfelt words, understanding the feelings behind them. His tone was reverent when he spoke of Cade, and she could tell he honestly needed to share this with her. Without even trying to use her abilities, she could sense and feel the strong love and respect Rederrick had for him.

"He's important to me," Rederrick explained, "to my whole family, he always will be. More than that though, Cade is important to the world. You have to understand, people like him don't really exist anymore. Some of us try our best to mimic him, but his level of compassion and his idealistic nature isn't easily attained. Who knows how long it has taken him to achieve it. Maybe we just don't live long enough to see things the way he does. I don't really know. I just don't want to see him lose that, to lose himself."

She thought hard about what he was trying to say. While Rederrick was happy for Cade, he was afraid of what a relationship with her would mean. Her eyes narrowed. She felt the truth behind his words, yet they still hurt her. She would never intentionally hurt Cade.

Rederrick watched her features change and knew Collett understood some of what he was telling her, but she did not understand the whole. He quickly continued before she jumped to the wrong conclusions.

"I want to be clear on something, Collett. No matter what happens, Cade is better off knowing you, better off loving somebody in his long, lonely life. I'm not sure Cade has ever fallen so fully in love, and the two of you together fit so well. You give him a type of happiness I have never before seen.

"I just don't want either one of you to lose here, is all. Please see that I only want you both to be careful. I could never have picked a better woman for him. There are times when I feel like you could be one of my own children, and I even see Cade as a brother, as hard as that is to believe…."

He broke eye contact with her and looked down at his hands. Rederrick thought carefully about each word as he finished, "I know I have only known you for a few months, but in that time, I have come to care for you and your well-being. You must know that."

Even though he wasn't looking at her, Collett nodded slightly.

"If you're both lucky enough to find a little happiness in all this mess, even if only for a moment, I will be happy for you. Just try to understand the power you have over him. That's all I'm saying. You are the only person I have ever known that has the power to break his spirit."

As he finished, he raised his head again looking into her now sad eyes. In his heart, he felt a heavy guilt for putting that look there when she had been so happy earlier, but he knew she needed to know.

Collett sighed deeply and returned Rederrick's stare. She could feel the guilt now coming at her in waves. This time she was trying to feel for it, trying to take his words into her heart in their full context.

In a natural gesture and without even realizing it, she put her hand on his knee. "Please don't feel guilty," she said softly. "I know you are worried for both of us. You were right in telling me. I'm not sure whether Cade does love me or not. I'm not even sure what's happening between us. I do promise you though, no matter what happens, I would never hurt him on purpose.

"I can't guarantee that it will never happen; that Cade will never hurt because of me. I don't have any idea what our future holds. I know in the end though, whatever does or doesn't happen, he will have you, and he will have your family. You would never allow him to stumble down a dark, lonely path. I may have the power to hurt his spirit as you said, but you, Rederrick—you have the power to pull him though."

Stunned by the wisdom of her words and how much better he felt, it took him a moment to reply. He was unaware of Collett's ability still, so he didn't think too deeply on how melodic her voice sounded or the warm feeling of comfort running through him. He easily accepted them and looked at her with his sharp old eyes. "I'm glad we talked. Thank you for understanding."

She nodded. "Now then, on a lighter topic," she said with a conspirator's smile, "I have to go get some winter things from Cynda. Will you please take the rest of my breakfast to Cade? I would hate to see it wasted, and I notice he hasn't eaten yet."

Rederrick narrowed his eyes, "You've hardly touched it."

"I know, and it is wonderful, but I'm really not hungry right now."

He gave her a contemplative look, "If you're sure. I'll take it to him then." Rederrick stood.

She smiled at him, "Don't worry, I'm fine; just not hungry. You did the right thing. Thank you for coming to me with your concerns."

"All right." With one last look, he picked up her plate and left the kitchen.

No matter what she had told him, in truth, she was not fine.

After his footsteps faded down the hallway and she was alone, she felt the heavy weight in her chest settle more fully. The false smile she'd given Rederrick fell. She leaned against the back of the chair staring out the window at the sparkling snow covered ground, wondering what to do now.

She heard a soft shuffle behind her and realized she wasn't as alone as she thought. She straightened her spine again and looked around. Jenny was standing there with a curious expression. She shook her head slightly, and then moved around to the sink to start the dishes. Collett stood and moved toward the kitchen stairway to head upstairs.

When she reached the first step, Jenny stopped her, "He's not completely wrong, you know."

Collett backtracked a few steps to look at her more fully. She was just rinsing off the plates with her plump elderly hands and putting them in the dishwasher, not even giving Collett a second glace.

Jenny wore black knit slacks and a soft, purple button-up shirt. She donned an old apron to do her chores. The apron had multicolored children's handprints all over it. The handprints were now faded from many washes and years of use.

Collett didn't say anything. She understood Jenny would say more when she was ready. After she loaded two more plates she began again, "I heard him. I waited until he was done to come in. I didn't want to interrupt. Clever thing you did then, makin' him feel happy, so he wouldn't worry so much."

Ignoring her last comment, Collett responded, "You said he wasn't completely wrong?"

"No… not completely. You do have power over Cade. That, in all likelihood, is somethin' no one else has ever been blessed with. We all see it; see the changes in him since you came."

She blinked, confused because Jenny referred to Cade by his first name for the first time since they met. "So, which part was wrong?" she questioned.

Jenny looked up from her dishes and softened her features, "The part where he forgot to mention the power Cade has over you and your spirit."

She was stunned by Jenny's insight. "I'm not sure what you're trying to tell me, Jenny," she barely mumbled.

Jenny went back to the dishes while saying, "Yes you are, dear. You know exactly what I'm sayin'." She loaded her mixing bowl next. Closing the dishwasher, she looked up smiling as if she hadn't just thrown Collett a major curveball with no bat to hit it, "You best get up to Mrs. Williams now and get ready for your day out."

Collett couldn't move. She simply stood there and stared at Jenny as she went about her chores. After a few minutes, she concluded Jenny would say nothing more. Her simple words were now etched in Collett's brain.

Finally, she turned and walked back to the stairs. She gave one last glance to Jenny, hearing her words again as she did. *I am not in love with him,* she told herself.

She looked up the stairway and reminded herself, *One step at a time.* She slowly walked up the stairs to get ready for her trip, trying to set aside her conflicting feelings as she went.

CHAPTER 21

Deep within the shadows of the thick tree line, a safe distance away from the house, The Hunter watched, evaluated, and learned. A man he immediately recognized as the werewolf pulled a sleek, black Polaris snowmobile from an extra garage built a stone's throw away from the massive home. When the slender woman joined him, The Hunter wondered if maybe it was a ploy to draw him out.

It was difficult to resist the urge to kill her now. This assignment was one he did not relish. He wanted so badly to be done with it, but people didn't call him, The Hunter because of his impatience. They didn't fear him because he was sloppy. No, he could wait. The time wasn't right. Soon enough, it would all be over.

As he watched the woman and the werewolf, he noticed something else, something he believed he'd dealt with. It looked like his buddy Jeffery was going to need another reminder to stay away. The happy couple mounted their vehicle and started off. He moved quickly, running at his full speed right on the edge of the perimeter, where the cameras couldn't see, over to where he had detected his quarry. He plowed right into the scrawny little mage and didn't even bother to check his speed as he did.

He heard the audible, "Oomph," and a couple of curses as Jeffery hit the ground a good distance away. To Jeffery it felt like a soccer ball being kicked hard enough to make it into the goal halfway across the field. Not giving him a chance to get up, The Hunter grabbed him and slammed him against the nearest object, which in this case was a thick pine tree.

Jeffery found himself frustrated and horribly confused. He had surrounded himself with a powerful shield, knowing he might cross paths with the dark man from the other night. He hoped to not even be seen at all. He shouldn't have been. This was the second time this stranger saw through his magic.

He had prepared so carefully over the last week. How did this stranger get past his magic? He had no more time to ponder it. He felt a painful crack as he was slammed into something behind him. If not for his shield, he would likely have had a few broken ribs.

Jeffery spun around, his head snapping back and forth, looking for his attacker. To his surprise, through his daze and the sun glaring off the snow, he couldn't spot him. Not anywhere. From behind again, he heard the deep gravelly voice, "Am I going to have to kill you, too?"

His problem was getting more desperate every day. "No... no don't kill me. Hear me out," he begged.

"You don't seem to comprehend the situation. Didn't I tell you to leave? What part of the words, 'My kill,' don't you understand? "

Jeffery tried hard to figure out where the gravelly voice was coming from. Now it sounded like it was to his left, but he hadn't heard the man move. He didn't even hear the slightest ruffle on the ground. His head was killing him from being slammed into the tree.

He reached back and probed to see if he was bleeding as he complained, "What do you want from me, man? You don't understand, I have to do this!"

The Hunter cut him off, "I want you gone! Disappear! I don't care about what you need. I don't care about your motives or why you came. I don't care about you. You're becoming a problem for me. Do you know what I do with problems that get in my way?"

The hand probing his head froze. He heard the deep voice from behind the tree. Before he could look around though, Jeffery felt his left arm wrenched around violently, and quickly he found his face shoved down into the cold, wet ground with the frozen snow scraping against his skin. A crippling pain shot up his arm, running through his whole body, and he heard a slight popping as his shoulder dislocated. He cried out as burning pain erupted through his shoulder down through his fingers, but the cry was muffled by the freezing snow that now stung and pricked his skin. Then the voice spoke again, closer this time.

"I Want You Gone," the stranger said with his deep baritone voice, carefully enunciating each word.

He couldn't move. Couldn't speak. He could only listen.

"I wonder,–is it true? Do you need your hands to cast a spell?" the man said strangely curious.

Jeffery felt the pressure on his hand suddenly increase. It felt like his hand would snap at any moment. Unable to answer verbally, he could only nod his head vigorously, scraping it against the ice and snow even more.

The Hunter contemplated his options for a moment, not saying a single word. He could hear Jeffery pant from the pain he was inflicting. He could feel his anger rise because of Jeffery's idiotic choice to return. The Hunter knew he could break the hand easily. He knew it would be a simple fix to this problem. He also knew if he did, Jeffery would need a new way out of there. He knew could just eliminate Jeffery, right here, right now, solving any further problem from arising.

Finally, The Hunter decided. He leaned down next to Jeffery's ear and snarled cruelly, "Have you learned your lesson yet? Or will I have to eliminate you?"

Jeffery just bobbed his head up and down again and felt the sting digging into his cheeks, but it mattered little. His face had gone numb anyway. He knew if he opened his mouth again, or even tried to, he would cry out from the pain. He also knew it would do him no good, so he bit down on his lip to keep quiet. This man felt no pity. It was over.

"I wonder, had you known who I am, would you have still come back for more?" The Hunter asked.

Jeffery started, "They have my mo..." but it just came out as a muffled sob, as his face was shoved deeper into the snow. He let out a whimper as his hand was bent further.

"You're just not listening here! I don't care. You will not come back!" The Hunter grated out as he increased the painful pressure.

"I got it, I got-" Jeffery mumbled indecipherably through the snow.

"I'm not surprised Finnawick saw fit not to tell you. He knew you wouldn't have bothered if you'd known. So, to ensure this is the last time I'll lay eyes on you, let me enlighten you myself. I am The Hunter."

Jeffery's blood turned to ice. He'd heard of this man, but thought it only a story told by Finnawick the imp to keep people in line. He shivered, and not as a result of the cold.

"I'm flattered. You have heard of me," he said cruelly.

Jeffery didn't even nod this time. He could not think past his fear. This man, the man now holding all control over his life, was the same man Finnawick sent to terminate anyone and everyone who got power hungry or stepped out of line. He was a legend among The Faction. No one even knew who he really was. Jeffery could have met him before, and he would never have known, though he seriously doubted that. The only men that might have seen The Hunter long enough to realize who he was had not lived long enough to tell anyone. It was the first time he felt grateful that he could not identify this man.

The Hunter spoke once again, "Now then, I'll pretend you were never here, and you agree to never come back. How's that sound to you?"

Biting his lip to keep from yelling out again, Jeffery bobbed his head up and down once more.

"Now that we understand each other clearly, I'll let go and you; you will leave. I know all of your little tricks, so don't try anything. Have we come to a suitable agreement? "

Jeffery moved his head again, agreeing.

Suddenly, he felt the pressure on his hand release. Blood rushed back into his hand and fingers. He let it drop to the side, letting the cold ease the burn in his arm. He flexed his fingers back and forth to make sure he could still use them. Though it was painful, he would still be able to cast the spell to leave. He rolled to his side, cradling his injured arm for a moment. Huffing out a defeated breath, he started to cast his transport spell.

The Hunter interrupted him once again, his voice now sounding somewhere off to his right, and "You know the problem with young idiots like you casting your lot in with demons like Finnawick?" Jeffery was unsure if he should answer, so he opted not to. "They will always find a way to control you. By using men like me or what you care for, either way, they own you," The Hunter finished.

A deep sadness crept over Jeffery. He knew all too well the truth of that profound statement. Now his mother would pay for his poor choices. He moved his hands again and cast his transport spell, leaving this place and any hope to save his mother.

Collett leaned into Cade, wrapping her arms tightly around his middle as he sped off across the frozen, snow-covered ground. The engine revved as they climbed the mountain. He didn't seem to be using any known trail. He simply cut through the powdery snow weaving the Polaris skillfully through the trees.

C.B. Haight

She didn't bother to ask if he knew where he was going. It didn't really matter to her. Cynda had equipped her well. The cold snow didn't bite at her too much. As Cade made a sharp left turn, the snow blew out from underneath the machine, brushing across the already covered ground. Her tinted goggles attached to the helmet were covered in water droplets where the powdery flakes landed and then melted away.

They made their way swiftly across the rough terrain. Collett enjoyed every minute of the trip. She was sure this was something she'd never experienced before. When they made a short leap over an embankment, her stomach dropped then resettled. It was exhilarating.

They passed a thick tree line where she saw three deer leap away in the distance. Even though it was a small thing to most people, she felt giddy at the sight of them.

"Look!" she shouted above the engine's roar and pointed them out to Cade.

"I see them," he shouted back over his shoulder.

The truth was, he'd smelled them before she sighted the doe and her two fawns. He felt somewhat smug and satisfied by her enthusiasm. It easily rubbed off on him, making him feel like this was his first adventure in the woods.

He steered the vehicle toward a drop-off where the view was spectacular. He had been there many times himself and knew it was an excellent place to think and figure out those difficult dilemmas life threw at you.

She was much more reserved earlier when they met outside. He'd given her a kiss, and she had pulled back quickly. He didn't know what she was thinking so hard about, but he could give her a beautiful place to do it. He zipped through another cluster of trees and pulled the Polaris to a halt.

He removed his helmet and twisted his head back in her direction, "From here we hike a bit. There's not much room for the snowmobile up there."

"How far are we going?" she asked after pulling off her own helmet.

"Just about a mile. Don't worry, it's not too bad."

She swung her leg around lithely and jumped off the new machine. "Okay, where are we going?"

Cade moved his eyes over her slender body, all snug in the dark-pink snowsuit that Cynda loaned her. He would have to thank Cynda later. The sight of her in the form-fitting gear was so incredible he forgot what she had asked him.

"Where are we going?" she repeated a little louder.

"Oh, just up to a drop-off into a valley I know about. You'll love it," he answered.

"Lead the way."

He easily moved from the snowmobile and grabbed her gloved hand. "Come on then," he said, pulling her along beside him.

Almost 30 minutes later, she was huffing and puffing alongside Cade, who breathed easily. She narrowed her eyes at him and snipped sarcastically, "Oh don't worry, it's not too bad. Ha! What a load of crap. This hill is straight up and down, or haven't you noticed?" Her breath was huffing in and out through each of her words.

He thought about it for a minute, and answered sheepishly, "I guess not. It has always been easy for me. Do you need a break?"

She narrowed her eyes, "How much farther?"

"Not too far, just past that group of boulders up there," he answered, pointing out the rocks several yards away.

"I'll just rest when we get there. Let's go," she groused.

He tipped his head to the side, "Do you want me to…"

Understanding what he was going to say from the look in his eyes, she stopped him short, "No. I'll do it myself. You're not going to carry me. I'm fine. Anyway I knew you would figure out a way to work in some physical training today."

He grinned devilishly, "You're sure then? I don't mind."

"I'm sure. Let's go."

They started moving again; Collett stomping through snow still huffing and puffing. Cade was breaking the trail with smooth, fluid strides, barely making a sound at all. His breathing remained even and easy. When they finally reached the cluster of boulders poking out from the deep snow, she leaned against them, bending forward slightly to catch her breath.

He put a hand on her back, "Alright?"

She nodded and took two more deep breaths, "Fine, but I'll never believe your version of, 'Not too bad,' again."

He smiled, "I promise it will be worth it. Now come on, we're here." Cade hooked his hand around her elbow and nudged her forward.

She could suddenly feel his boyish excitement. She stepped forward a few more paces and her breath caught in her throat with an audible gasp. The view was literally breathtaking.

This place, this land, was something you only heard of in fairytales with great white dragons or enchanting white witches. They stood atop a sloping peak looking into a majestic winter valley.

There was a small, placid lake that looked to be made of glass within the center of the valley. Massive snow-covered mountain peaks jutted up from the earth, kissing the soft white clouds. The crystalline lake was lightly frozen all around the edges, leaving the middle a glossy black mirror, as if Jack Frost himself knew that freezing the center of the lake would have robbed the valley of its beauty. The vast and powerful mountain range was mirrored within the lake as a perfect reflection.

Trees of all types and sizes speared up from the white, blanketed earth, reaching toward the sun's warming rays. A few soft, white clouds drifted slowly across the sky. They were pushed by a slight, soothing breeze that tickled your skin and whispered of nature's secrets.

This place was one of the few places left untouched and unspoiled by man. This perfect valley could have touched even the heaviest of souls. The serene landscape was one of the creator's many gifts to mankind.

Neither she nor Cade spoke. They simply stood there in the perfect stillness. Collett closed her eyes, taking it all in through every one of her senses. She breathed in the crisp winter air, absorbing the smell of the fresh pine scent. It was as refreshing to her soul as a clean, cold drink of water would have been to a man dying of thirst. It filled her.

She could hear the slight breeze move in and around the trees. She opened her eyes again and looked at the sparkling earth. She could almost imagine the musical tinkling of the crystals in her mind as the tranquil breeze floated across the frozen snow.

Most of all, she could feel the peace and serenity that surrounded this picturesque valley. Time seemed to fade away as if it had no meaning in this place. Minutes felt like seconds, and hours could pass for minutes.

She looked to Cade with her crystal-blue eyes, and in that perfect moment, she knew Jenny was right. He did have a power over her. She had fallen in love with him. She knew that now. It seemed impossible to have happened in such a short time, but she loved this man.

She was not ready to tell him yet, and she wasn't sure she would ever be able to. A long relationship with Cade would be impossible. Unlike him, she could not live forever. If she voiced her love to him, knowing she would need to leave eventually, it would hurt him too deeply. She could see that now. She could see what Rederrick meant by the power to break his spirit. It would certainly break hers when the time came to walk away.

So, for now, she would just cherish every moment, every second she had with him. Imprint every minute they shared together into her memory, making it a part of her. Then when the time came, she would have these special moments to sustain her.

She understood she could never allow Cade to tie himself to a mortal woman and watch her life fade away in a few short years, leaving him to live on alone. If she never told him of her love, then maybe it wouldn't hurt him so much when she left. He could move on and find someone like him, someone to share eternity with.

He felt her gaze on him as he looked out into the valley. He turned to her, smiled, and saw the glistening of unshed tears in her eyes, "What is it?"

When she spoke, Collett used hushed tones, not wanting to disturb the reverent nature of this beautiful place, or this perfect moment, "Thank you. This is incredibly wonderful." She stood on tiptoes and kissed his lips ever so softly, then withdrew, keeping her eyes locked with his as she did.

He cupped her cheek with his bare hand and wiped at the rogue tear that escaped her hold with the pad of his thumb. Despite the cold temperature, his hand was warm. She leaned into his touch, her ivory cheek against his warm skin and closed her eyes, just to feel his tenderness.

When the time came, she understood, leaving him might very well do what her mystery stalkers hadn't been able to do. It might kill her.

He moved his hand away from her face and put his arms around her, pulling her close to him. She laid her head against his chest, listening to the beat of his heart, as it fell into rhythm with her own. In that moment, there was nothing else. There were no dark evils, no hard decisions. The rest of the real world simply didn't exist in this wonderful place. They stayed like that for so long, silently looking out into the landscape. She shivered from the cold.

"We should go," he said reluctantly.

She nodded, feeling just as reluctant. They'd stayed so long the afternoon sun had moved across the sky, tinting the clouds a soft pink.

They turned together to start their descent down the steep slope, and they both froze. Collett's eyes went frantic at the sight before her.

CHAPTER 22

Beyond the tree line, stood a beautiful, majestic silver wolf with deep, brown eyes staring right at them. "Cade?" she asked hesitantly.

He let go of his hold on her, stepped forward slowly, and answered her unspoken question, "No, she's not like me."

"She?" Collett asked nervously.

"She," he stated as he carefully moved toward the large female grey. He knew this wolf, and knew that she was a little skittish around strangers.

"What are you doing?" Collett whispered.

"I'm reassuring her," he answered using a calm tone.

"Why?"

"Because she doesn't trust you," he said simply.

"What?" she asked a little confused.

"Jiya doesn't like strangers, especially since her pups are nearby."

She was a little surprised. Not only did Cade know this wolf, but he had named her Jiya.

He waited for Jiya to feel comfortable enough to creep forward. He could tell she wanted to come and see him, but was hesitant to do so with her so close. After a couple of minutes, Jiya crept forward using her front paws while keeping her body low to the ground. As soon as she reached him, Jiya angled her head and licked at his chin.

He grinned happily and ruffled her ears, wrestling with her a little, just to let her know he missed her.

Collett carefully watched the scene play out before her. He had a strong bond with this female wolf, and it was an amazing thing to see.

"You can come over here now," Cade said after a minute of playing. "Just do it carefully, and don't make any threatening moves."

"Exactly what would be threatening?" she said dryly.

He found himself amused at her reluctance, "Come on. It'll be fine. Just move slowly."

She inched her way to Cade and Jiya. She kept her hands down and took each step carefully.

Not sure of her cautious moves, Jiya never once took her deep brown eyes away from her.

When she was only a couple steps away, Cade instructed softly, "Now get down to her level like me. It will make her more comfortable."

"Oh sure...let's make her comfortable," Collett replied with a glare. His grin only widened more, and it made her feel a little safer.

"Come on, you're doing fine," he assured her. "Besides, you didn't let fear stop you from facing me down when we were at the river, and I'm much bigger."

She couldn't rationalize that, so she ignored it, inching down to her knees and met Jiya's gaze. Only a couple of feet separated her from Jiya now.

Jiya moved cautiously toward her, covering the remaining distance. Instead of creeping as she had done with Cade, she stood tall and straight. Only one word could describe her stance: Proud.

The wolf before her was incredible. Jiya had thick, off-white fur covering her broad chest. That color continued down her front and rear legs. Her head and back were a perfect blend of black, silver-grey and white fur. There was even a slight tint of brownish-red mixed in. The very tips of her ears were outlined in black, which matched the very tip of her tail. She was a magnificent animal.

Jiya paced around Collett twice, assessing her carefully. She even looked to Cade, as if needing his reassurance. Finally, she decided on indifference, and moving back to Cade's side, she plopped down and leaned against him.

In a natural gesture he stroked her soft fur as if she was a longtime pet, "She likes you. She just doesn't want you to know it, yet."

"How can you tell?"

He grinned, "Because if she didn't she would have snapped at you, to let you know she's the one in charge here, thus putting you in your place so to speak."

She narrowed her eyes, giving him the, '*You're in big trouble,*' look and said, "That's nice to know."

"I knew she'd like you. Otherwise, I would have never introduced you."

"How? I mean, how did you know?"

"It's simple, really. I knew she would like you, because I like you, and you're important to me," he finished softly.

Collett's expression changed so many times, and so quickly he wasn't sure what to think. She went from smiling, to concern, then to sadness, then back to a soft, wistful smile.

"Cade? I'm not sure what's happing here," she said carefully.

Pretending not to understand her meaning he turned his gaze back to the wolf, "You're meeting my friend Jiya, and now, we're going to go meet her pups."

He stood quickly, pulled her to her feet, and nodded at Jiya. Understanding, Jiya bounded off through the trees.

"Come on, you're going to love this," he promised pulling her arm.

They jogged off after the female grey, he seemed to know exactly where he was going. Cade pulled her along at a stiff pace that made it hard to keep her balance. Once, she stumbled over a fallen tree, and he easily caught her, setting her right.

After what felt like forever to her tired legs, they stopped suddenly. Cade moved behind her so she could see.

In a small outcropping of trees and rocks was the third most amazing sight she had seen today. It was as if nature had decided to gift her with its best-kept secrets, all in one day.

There, in that small, protected place, were several little wolf puppies rolling and tumbling over each other. They nipped at each other, pulled on ears, and yipped and barked in their playful antics.

Having beaten them to the clearing, Jiya was now lying beneath a small natural stone ledge, while another large adult wolf sat on his haunches upon it.

This wolf was much darker than Jiya. His sleek coat was made up of a smoky-grey, with more black mixed in. His eyes were almost the same tawny gold as Cade's. He sat there strong and proud, like a sentinel prepared to keep any danger at bay.

His head tipped their direction when Cade put his hand on the small of her back and urged her forward. The male let out a short yip. She started at the sound.

"Cade? I don't think this is a good idea," she said quietly, as she pushed back against his hand, resisting.

"Nonsense, he's just welcoming me in."

"Yeah, well what about me?"

"He thinks you're my potential mate, so for right now you're welcome too," he answered simply.

Her head whipped around quickly, "He thinks I'm what?"

He grinned deviously, "My mate." Then he walked right past her to scoop up two scrapping pups, separating them from their snarling play.

She stood still right where he had left her, and she watched as the two little puppies wriggled and squirmed in his hands, licking and nipping at his chin. He laid one near his neck and let it snuggle into him.

If she hadn't already decided she was in love with him, this tender side of him would have probably done her in for sure. He stepped over three more pups at his feet yipping and whining for his attention and came toward her.

He held out the fluffy, brownish-red pup in his left hand and said, "This is Ahote, it means restless one. She can never keep still." At that very moment, the puppy was wriggling vigorously in his hands, rolling her head around to nip at his arm with her young needle-like teeth.

When she didn't take the energetic puppy right away, Cade simply plopped Ahote right into her arms. She looked up instinctively to the parents of the little fluff-ball, hoping they wouldn't tear out her throat for touching one of the puppies. They both looked calm and relaxed. The large male watched carefully from a distance.

He laughed at her hesitant reaction, "I told you it's okay. I'm what you would call an honorary member of the pack, like a distant cousin who comes to visit occasionally."

She gave him a puzzled look, took off one glove to stroke the wiggly puppy, "I didn't think there were any more wolves here, there was an article about their reintroduction recently in the paper."

"People don't always know everything, and sometimes it's for the best. If they knew about this pack, they would come up here and tag them, track them. They would pester them until they were forced to leave, or worse," he explained.

She understood his double meaning. It was better when normal people were kept blind to things they didn't understand.

The little puppy in her arms had buried its head into the inside of her elbow, effectively covering her eyes and now lay still. Ahote breathed the deep, even breaths of sleep. Collett looked down at the still pup and smiled. "Restless one?" she questioned lightly.

"Usually," he replied with a shrug. She arched up her brows not quite believing him.

"Who's that snuggled into your neck?"

Cade stroked his large hand over the small puppy's back, "This one is Catori. It means spirit."

Catori favored her mother. She was the same light, silvery-grey with a black tipped tail. Cade set her down gently and picked up two more. He brought them in close to his chest and let them lick at his chin playfully. One nipped lightly at Cade's ear lobe, while the other nipped at its sibling. These two looked almost identical. They both had their father's darker looks, more black and brown than grey, but each had received their mother's darker eyes.

He laughed again as the one on the right put a little paw to his mouth, "These girls I call Nashota and Nova. They look almost identical except Nova has the black tipped tail."

Curious Collett asked, "What do their names mean?"

"Well... Nova means chases butterfly, and Nashota means twin."

She looked down to the last, lone puppy whimpering at his feet. She gently set down the sleeping Ahote and boldly scooped it up. This one was almost all white. It had the same gold eyes as the father. Just his ears were tipped black like his mother's. Collett also realized this was the only male among the five puppies.

She nuzzled him, brushing her cheek against his soft coat. "Who is this little guy?"

"That's Dave," he said simply.

"Dave. That's it? Just Dave?"

"Just Dave," he replied.

She broke into a little giggle at his name choice for the only male pup. The best part was, she truly liked the simple name. It suited the lovable white pup perfectly.

He watched as she snuggled the little puppy, letting him crawl up by her neck and lick her ear, his soft claws scrabbling for purchase. Dave had taken right to her, lapping up any affection she would give. He repeatedly sniffed at her neck. He knew exactly how the little guy felt. The woman had a great scent.

"Where did their names come from?" she asked as Dave licked and nibbled at her hands when she stroked him.

Cade got down on his knees in the snow and engaged the other three pups. They nipped and pawed at his large hands as he pushed and tugged at them in return. Eventually, the sleeping Ahote roused and joined in as well. Finally Cade replied, "Native American; mostly Hopi. I spent a few years with them a very long time ago."

"Oh. It must have been a special time for you."

"I've done a lot of things in my life. Why would you think that?" he questioned as he continued his play with the pups.

"From the wistful tone in your voice, and the way you named this pack using an almost lost language. I'll even bet the name Dave means something to you. You have a strong loyalty to people you love and care for. It is a part of who you are," she rubbed Dave's wet black nose with her cold pink one as she finished.

He stopped playing and sprung up to a crouch. He furrowed his brow, "Are you reading me with your abilities?"

She shook her head and pulled Dave to her chest, stroking his downy fur, "No. You're too guarded for me to read most of the time, and I don't like to intrude. I am just beginning to understand you is all."

He looked into her blue eyes. He felt a little off balance by her on-the-mark assessment of him. He was curious how she could have so easily known, just from a few simple names.

With his sharp ears, he heard the approach of another curious male. Alo, the alpha male and father of this small pack, approached them. When Collett looked past him and noticed this large male was so close, her eyes widened.

Alo did not stop by Cade and greet him as usual. He walked right by to stand directly in front of Collett. He tipped his head much like Cade did when considering something curious and stared at her. He was tall. His large head reached just above her waistline.

She looked frantically to Cade for help, and he could hear the pounding beat of her heart.

"It's alright. Alo is just curious. He sees how comfortable his pups are with you and wants to understand."

"Alo?" she questioned.

Cade nodded.

"What should I do?" she barely whispered.

"Get down like you did with Jiya, then wait."

She carefully and slowly eased down to her knees, putting herself face-to-face with this deadly and curious alpha male. Alo didn't pace as Jiya had, and he didn't look to Cade for reassurance. He didn't growl or bark. He simply stared at her for a long while, as if he was trying to figure her out. Eventually, he sat back on his hind legs right in front of her.

She looked up to Cade, unsure.

"Put out your hand for him," Cade coaxed.

"What!" she asked stunned.

"Trust me. I wouldn't do anything to hurt you."

She did as he instructed and reached out with an unsteady hand. Although she was afraid Alo could take her hand off, Collett was also enticed by Cade's, 'Trust me,' and the power of this unbelievable experience.

He sniffed casually at her hand for a time and then leaned into it. She stroked his head softly with her shaky hand. His fur was much thicker than the little ones. Gaining confidence, she dug into his hair and rubbed him just behind the ear.

After a few minutes of her affection, Alo stood and walked back to Jiya. Settling in next to the she wolf, he laid his muzzle on her back and closed his eyes, trusting in Cade and Collett to watch the pups.

She stood up, still a little jittery from the intimidating experience, "What was that all about?"

Cade looked back to Alo, somewhat surprised himself. He understood what had truly happened here. Alo's easy acceptance of Collett as a part of his family was staggering. Their chance encounter with Jiya had taken a surprising turn.

"Alo has accepted you not only as my mate, but as a part of his pack," he explained, making sure to hide his astonishment.

"Really, are you sure? That seems pretty improbable. I'm not like you. I mean, you know, the distant relation thing."

He smiled at her nervous correction. She had no idea how rare it really was to accept a human as part of the pack. Occasionally, a pack would tolerate a human hanging around now and again, that is, after months of building trust. Even then, the humans were still considered outsiders.

Cade had never seen a pack leader so readily accept one as part of the family. There had been no posturing, no growling. Both adult wolves just acted as if Collett had always been there. It only reaffirmed how mysterious and special this woman truly was.

"Well it's getting late. We should probably start back. I don't want to be exposed in the dark too long," he said absently.

She nodded her head, agreeing with him. She didn't want to worry anybody back at the house. They had already stayed out too long. With one more longing look back at little Dave, she turned and started back.

He made sure Alo and Jiya knew they were leaving by moving loudly. When Alo looked up and stared into his eyes with his knowing animal insight, Cade understood that the alpha male saw something in Collett that, even with his own animal instincts, Cade couldn't see.

When he turned to leave, Cade couldn't help himself from wondering what it meant. He easily caught up to Collett and came up behind her. Once again, he grabbed her glove-covered hand as they headed back to the snowmobile.

As they walked silently, hand-in-hand through the woods, each wondered to themselves what other surprises would come from their unlikely meeting, a little more than two weeks ago.

For Collett, today had been full of wonder, discovery, and self-realization. This day would be burned into her memory for all time. She would forever cherish what he had given her. When she had to let him go, the memory of this perfect day would see her through.

For Cade, this day was a complete moment of pleasure in a world of chaos. He would always remember the way a little pup named Dave changed everything for him by bringing a curious Alo to Collett. Alo had agreed with his choice for a mate and had easily taken her into the pack. What Collett didn't know, that Cade and Alo did, was a wolf mated for life, and Cade was now sure that this is exactly what Collett was. She was his mate.

She had come to mean everything to him. He would willingly give up all that he had, all that he was, just to have a single human lifetime with her. Now all he had to do was convince her of that, without scaring her away. In the meantime, he still needed to stop whomever wanted her dead from cutting their time even shorter.

He was beginning to feel like fate was no longer just smiling on him. No, Fate was now roaring with laughter. The strangest thing was, he didn't mind at all.

After dispatching Jeffery, The Hunter followed the couple throughout their trip. He just needed a little more time in order to put his plan in place. He had watched carefully this last week, and today's trip had been very insightful. *Not much longer now,* he thought to himself. He only needed the perfect opportunity, and he knew if he was patient he would find it.

Timing was everything, and her time was almost up.

CHAPTER 23

During the next few days, Collett continued her training. They fell back into a smooth pattern. Cynda continued to help her learn to channel her energy properly. At night, she read and studied about empathic abilities. She was consumed by the need to master her new-found skills. Each time she tried, she got just a little better, a little more resistant to the drain on her physical body.

She mostly practiced on Cynda. Rederrick volunteered once, and Jenny was glad to help as well. She felt it was too presumptuous to ask anyone up front if she could delve into their personal feelings. So for now, she settled for volunteers.

She reached into Cynda so many times now Collett could identify her thoughts almost immediately. She could even sense Cynda from a distance. The same was true for Jenny too. Though, she hadn't experienced any images or memories again as she had with Jenny that first night. She began to assume it was the intense sadness and pain she experienced with Jenny that made her imagine them. They'd been so vague at the time, so she put it out of her mind.

She could almost pick Rederrick out at a distance as well. One or two more times with him, and she would be able find him anywhere in the house simply by reaching for him. It was strange. It was as if she could identify a person from the nature of their feelings, almost as if it was a kind of fingerprint.

Nate, Cade, and Cody had yet to volunteer. In fact, she still hadn't met Cody. He took the latest watch each night and slept during the day. Their schedules conflicted constantly, and she was too busy to think about it.

It was four-thirty, and she was waiting for Cade in the workout room upstairs. They kept things on a schedule to make it simpler for everybody. She found she liked the routine. Currently, she sat in her traditional meditation pose trying to focus her mind and clear her stray thoughts. Each day she came up here about an hour before her training with Cade to meditate. She was still hoping for some clue to her past, though she still had yet to be successful.

However, right now, she thought about her upcoming session with Cade. The tone of her self-defense training had begun changing since their outing into the woods. If Collett was honest with herself, she would admit things began changing long before that.

His touches over time became more familiar, and she welcomed each one. She used to loathe their workouts together, but now she found herself eagerly looking forward to them each day. She was like a schoolgirl waiting for the bell to ring so she could meet her boyfriend after class. Her legs started to bounce in anticipation, and she forced herself to stop before it really got started.

With her eyes closed, she heard him enter the room. Smiling, she opened her eyes and looked into his intense gaze. He smiled right back. He looked just as eager to see her.

"You're late," she scolded lightly.

He extended his hand down to help her up, "Couldn't be helped. I had to get Rederrick to free Nate. He is going to come up here in a minute and help us out."

She couldn't keep the disappointment from her eyes, "With what?"

He grinned as he also heard the disappointment in her voice. There was a satisfaction in knowing she wanted time alone with him. "You need to learn how to work in tangent with someone," he told her.

Her brows furrowed.

"While you're getting better with your self-defense, it's likely you'll have one of us with you. You need to learn each of our strengths. That way, in a bad situation we can work as a team. Today you get to team up with Nate."

"Against you? Two against one hardly seems fair."

"Don't you worry about me," he replied with confidence.

"When do we get to team up?" she quipped.

"I think you know my strengths by now," he kissed her forehead tenderly then finished, "and my weakness." He moved to her lips, brushing his against hers sweetly.

She loved and hated hearing that at the same time. She didn't want to be his downfall. Another thought suddenly occurred to her. What other weaknesses did Cade have?

"Cade, are the legends true about you?"

He stepped back and his brows pinched in confusion, "What do you mean?"

"You know about silver and regeneration, and other stuff like that. The stuff you hear about in fiction."

Out of reflex, he lifted a hand to the scar on his chin, "Yeah, some of it's true. I can heal fast, regenerate as you said, but not from wounds inflicted by silver weapons. It's kinda like a poison. A bad enough wound can become infected.

"As far as the whole vampire slave thing," he shrugged, "I don't really know. They exist, but not in the ways people think. Really they are just another form of demon. They can't turn people into beings like them, but they do live on blood. Most of us call them leech demons. I do know that when I smell one, their putrid odor sets my temper off right away. My skin tingles and my hair rises. I have never met one I didn't want to tear into pieces on the most basic level.

"Really though, any demon gets my adrenaline pumping for battle, and there is no shortage on them. So maybe it is inherited, or maybe it's just because of their evil bloodsucking nature. Who really knows?"

She considered it, "What about the full moon? In the movies werewolves lose control. Can you control what you are even then?"

His mind flashed back to a time long ago when he couldn't, a time long ago when he had to fight to control his urges and instincts. "Some of what you hear is myth, and before you ask, we can't infect people by biting them, or at least I have never been able to. So don't worry, you're safe," he teased with a grin. Cade thought for a moment, then answered as best he could, "The full moon stuff is partly true, partly myth. It's complicated, but I can control myself now." He rubbed at his scarred chin again.

Just when Collett was going to ask him what he meant, Nate strode into the room, saving Cade from having to explain, for now anyway.

"Nate asked me once," Cade accused as he came in.

"Asked what?" she questioned.

"For me to bite him. He wanted to be like me."

"In my defense, I was thirteen and being a lycan sounded like a good idea. Besides, back then I thought you were cool. Now I realize, not so much," Nate teased then challenged, "You ready for a piece of me, Cade?"

Collett considered Nate more fully. He was full of energy and excitement. He stepped onto the mat and jumped on the balls of his feet a couple of times, much like a coiled spring. She was slightly stunned by his appearance. He wore loose, black jogging pants with white stripes down the legs, and his feet were bare. But what shocked Collett the most was not his pants, nor his bare feet. It was his upper body.

He wore no shirt today to cover his trim and sculpted torso. Collett knew he was fit and that he had been in the military, but she honestly would have never guessed Nate would look like this. Each and every muscle on his body was shaped and defined. Toned and puckered abs stretched tightly across his middle. Sharp, distinct muscles defined his chest, and round, bulging biceps were cut into his arms. There wasn't a single unused muscle on this man.

His usual long-sleeved, button-up shirts and jeans were amazingly deceiving. Underneath his clothing was an entirely different person.

"You can quit staring now," Cade teased.

She looked back to him with wide eyes, "How exactly am I supposed to help him?"

He couldn't help but chuckle, "He's not so tough. First you're going to warm up with us, then we'll take it one step at a time. Trust me, we need to do this. You need to understand his techniques."

She turned to her partner and watched as Nate bounced twice more, then easily back-flipped, landing smoothly on his feet. She shook her head in wonderment at his perfect balance.

He stood still for a moment, "Ready?"

Collett almost said no, but Cade answered for them both, "Yeah we're ready. You?"

"Born ready," he responded eagerly.

Cade tilted his head at the challenge, "We'll try a basic hostage first. Remember Nate, she doesn't have much experience."

He smiled playfully, "So what do you think? I play the hostage. I'll let you save me."

"I don't think so. She's the one The Faction is after, and she'll play my hostage."

"I see. I didn't realize you were into that kind of thing," Nate quipped, grinning at Collett and raising his eyebrow suggestively.

She blushed at his teasing nature. She had no idea he was so full of it. The one time he'd shown her how to properly load a 9mm handgun, among a few others, he had been all business. Of course, he had laughed at her expense the other morning at the breakfast table, but still, he was cheerfully full of himself at the moment. Intrigued, she decided she was looking forward to getting to know him better.

Cade put his hand on her back, and they moved onto the mat together. After warming up and stretching out, he said, "I'm going to pin you against me with my arm around your neck and the other one around your waist. You need to learn how to anticipate and silently communicate with Nate or anyone else."

After he had carefully wrapped his arm around her, they proceeded to instruct her on all sorts of signals and moves to get away from an attacker. Sometimes their opinions conflicted. Other times they agreed.

After more than thirty minutes into her instruction, she began to feel the slight change between them. She sensed the pure energy and frustration in Nate. He was edgy and alert, as if he wanted to get past the instruction and onto the fighting.

Once again, Cade wrapped her up in his arms tightly, effectively immobilizing her head. Just like they had instructed her, Collett gripped his thumb and forefinger and pretended to yank back. As quick as a rattlesnake, Nate used her choreographed distraction to attack Cade. Only this time, his fists connected in a fast double punch to the back of Cade's ribs.

Cade let go of Collett as practiced, and let go of an oath, too. "What was that?" he snapped unbelieving.

"Just keeping it realistic." Then in an almost childlike plea Nate begged, "Come on, Cade, let's go one round. It's been a really long time, and I think I can actually take you this time."

"We'll go one round later. Right now, I think teaching Collett is far more important," he answered like a patient father.

She could feel Nate's urgent need to expel his energy, and she sympathized with it. She tried offering assistance, "You know, it might be a good idea. If I watch, I can get a feel for Nate's style, right?"

Cade smiled. Truthfully, he was just as eager to mess around as Nate. He bowed his head slightly, "Point taken." He looked to his eager opponent, "But after I kick your butt, you agree to help me some more with her training."

"Yeah, yeah c'mon. Let's go, old man." He bounced up and down again punching the air with his fists.

"Don't go too far, Collett. This won't take very long." Cade quipped,

She smiled, and she moved back away from the mat out of range.

They moved around each other, both men sizing up his opponent, carefully assessing each other. Then, in a flash of flesh, they both rushed at each other. It was so quick that Collett was afraid if she blinked she would miss something. They both threw fists and arms up. Some were offensive punches, others defensive blocks. Cade hit Nate in the stomach, and Nate arched his back slightly, letting the movement absorb some of the blow, but he still grunted from the impact. In retaliation, Nate then promptly swung his body around and kicked Cade in the back. He stumbled forward a step and spun around.

"You've gotten quicker," he said impressed. He rushed forward with unnatural speed, and somehow Nate ended up on the floor. Cade laughed, "Still not quick enough, though."

Nate bucked his hips and swung his legs, flipping his prone body upright, "Again," he said forcefully.

They traded fists and kicks once again in a speeding blur of motion. Obviously, Nate had extensive training in martial arts. His movements were quick and fluid, one move leading into the next. This time, their combat went on for several minutes. Nate fought like a demon, forcefully trading blows with Cade.

She noticed Cade easily moved into the same routine that had dropped Nate to the mat the first time. This time however, Nate had learned his lesson. He ducked low, avoiding the quick grab. Then he swung gracefully around, kicking out at the back of Cade's knees so hard Collett started at the sound of the sickening impact.

Cade's knees buckled and hit the mat, though he seemed uninjured. He sprang up quickly and adjusted his neck back and forth with a loud popping. Then turning around, he faced Nate's smug look. "Not bad. Two out of three, then?" he asked, lifting one eyebrow inquisitively.

Just like that, it started again. However, this time, the intensity increased. Nate's skill and speed were impressive. It was obvious to Collett he was a rarity among men. She knew firsthand how quickly Cade could move, and Nate's skill and tenacity were still keeping him on his toes. He was clever and learned quickly. It was obvious Cade was superior. Nate would make a very close second though.

Finally, Cade flipped Nate up and slammed him down to the mat.

Both men grinned. The room was charged with testosterone. Nate was breathing harder now. His sandy blond hair was wet from his sweat. "Almost," he muttered.

"Not even close," Cade shot back. "Come see me when you're older." He extended his hand to Nate, "Done?"

Nate nodded, "For now." He let Cade pull him up from the floor.

"Now that you feel better, can we get back to helping Collett?" he asked lightly.

"You're the boss."

Collett stepped forward asking, "How did you learn to do that? It was absolutely remarkable."

Nate smiled and pointed to Cade, "Mostly I learned from him, and then I picked up a few other things here and there. One of these days I'll get him down."

Cade's lips tilted, "Not likely, pup."

She looked at Nate, still impressed with his skill. "Well, if this comes down to a fight, I'll be very grateful to have you on our side," she stated earnestly.

Nate's smile was sincere when he boasted, "If it comes down to a fight, there is no better team in the world to keep you safe. We won't let you down. Now then, shall we?" he invited, leading her onto the mat.

And just that easily, Collett had found one more friend, one more person who cared about her, and one more person who was willing to fight for her.

Collett's training with the two men left her stiff and sore later that night. Cade had insisted on going over several possible scenarios, several times. After dinner she had come up to her room for a long, hot bath to soak her aching body. Though she to healed quickly, Collett found she wasn't immune to the annoyance of minor, temporary pain.

After the water had gone from scalding to tepid, she eased out of the tub and wrapped herself in a large body towel. She took her time and rubbed lotion over her arms and legs. She opened the door to get dressed, and a little squeak of surprise escaped her lips at the sight of Cade sitting on her bed with a smug smile.

"We have to quit meeting like this," he teased, referring to their first awkward meeting in the hallway. Truthfully though, that was their second meeting, if you counted him saving her in the woods.

She went to the dresser and roughly pulled out her clothes. "What are you doing here, Cade? What if I had come out of that bathroom naked?" she snipped at him.

He shrugged, "Lucky me?" he replied innocently. "Besides, you're too shy to stride around here naked. Not that I'd mind if you did."

She felt the heat in her face as her cheeks turned pink. "Next time let me know you're here, just in case I lose my inhibitions."

"How exactly, is that comment supposed to motivate me to announce my arrival?" he teased.

She rolled her head around to loosen her stiff neck, "Just think about how mad I'll be if you don't."

He pretended to think about it, and then shook his head, "Still not helping. In fact, I think that might have hurt your case."

Collett glared at him sharply, and she raised her hand to knead the tightness in her shoulder.

Cade recognized her movements. "Stiff neck?" he asked, concerned.

"A little. My trainer is unforgiving," she proclaimed with a sweet smile.

"Come here," he said and swung his legs down and patted the bed in front of him.

Collett narrowed her eyes suspiciously. "I don't think so. I need to get dressed."

He put his hands up in surrender, "No funny business. I swear. Just let me help you loosen some of those knots in your neck before you get dressed."

She continued to gaze at him suspiciously, considering his offer. Then she relented and made sure he understood her terms, "No funny business," she said in a mock scold.

"Nope, Scout's honor!"

She glared at him skeptically and chastened, "You probably weren't even a Boy Scout."

"Honey, I'm old enough to be the original Boy Scout," his eyes glinted.

Smirking, she moved closer and tucked her towel tighter. She sat in front of him on the edge of the bed. He kneeled behind her and put his hands on her shoulders. His warm touch gave her butterflies in the pit of her stomach. He carefully and gently kneaded her muscles, knowing exactly where to focus. She closed her eyes and relaxed into the soothing motions.

"Better?" he asked.

"Yes, much better. I'll give you another hour to stop."

He chuckled and continued to rub her neck and shoulders for a little longer. Then he surprised her by asking, "You said the other day you have a hard time reading me. Why is that?"

She opened her eyes and thought about it, "I don't really know. Why?"

He sat back on his heels and shrugged, "I've been thinking about it."

She said nothing for a moment then offered him her theory, "Maybe you can guard your feelings. I have felt things from you before, just slight impressions really."

His hands stopped the gentle massage. "Like what?" he asked genuinely curious.

"When we first met, you were so angry at the man holding me captive," she explained. "I was terribly afraid of you then."

Even the memory of it ignited the fires of his temper. "He wasn't a man," Cade ground out fiercely.

She tipped her head back, "I can feel you now; feel your anger."

"Is that all you've felt from me, anger?"

"No. I've felt your worry once before. And the other night when your mind drifted off, when you went where I couldn't follow, I felt a deep ache in you; a heavy sadness."

"Oh," he muttered.

"It seems to me, I only get impressions from you when you let your guard down." It was silent for a moment, and then Cade began rubbing her shoulders again. "It bothers you that I can't," she stated more than asked.

"Can you sense that?"

"No, but I can see it on your face."

"It doesn't really bother me so much as it makes me wonder."

She smiled, knowing it bothered him. "It's not just you. I have a harder time with Nate too," she reassured.

"Huh," he replied, still thinking about it.

"Do you want me to try?" she offered.

"Try what?"

She just looked back at him pointedly.

He stammered, "Oh. Well, no… It's okay. I mean, only if you want to."

"I can try," she assured. It was odd to see Cade so nervous. He always acted so sure of himself. He was strong and confident, yet now he stammered. He was vulnerable, unsure of what he wanted. "Let me get dressed, and then we'll give it a try," she gripped her towel tightly and stood.

"You don't have to if you're tired. We can do this another time," he said quietly to her back.

"I'll be right out," she softly reassured. Then she went into the bathroom to change.

She came out shortly, wearing a soft white t-shirt and navy blue cotton pants that fit her like a second skin. Cade held back his groan at the sight of her, but he felt it within himself.

There was nothing special or alluring about her nightclothes. There were no pretenses, no fancy negligée, and no dangling earrings. Her perfect ivory skin was left unpainted by makeup. Her soft, golden hair was pulled smoothly back then twisted up and held by a clip of some kind. For Cade, her simplistic attire and the natural beauty of her was even more alluring than any slinky black gown. To him, she was real, perfect, exquisite.

He met her gaze. Her eyes were like the most flawless blue crystals, plucked from the deepest mines.

"You're beautiful," he confessed reverently.

"I'm sorry?" she asked, as she hadn't heard him correctly.

He stood and approached her. He put the palm of his hand to her cheek and said it again, this time with strong heartfelt sincerity, "You are absolutely beautiful." He held her captive in his gaze and continued, "I'm in love with you."

"Cade…"

"No, don't. I want you to know that. I want to you to feel that. When you reach into me, to understand my emotions, look for that.

Then you'll know and feel what I know and feel. It is important to me that you know. With the whole of my heart, I love you, Collett."

He moved both of his hands down and grabbed her left hand. Cade brought her hand to his chest, pressing it against his heart. She could feel the quick, steady beats of his heart beneath her palm. She looked at her hand, covered by his, and then back to his face, with the makings of tears in her vivid blue eyes.

He spoke softly again, "Look for that, please… I have lived a very long time. In that time, I have seen people come and go. I watched as people let their fear stop them from telling that one person they cared for the most how they truly felt until it was too late. I won't do that. I need you to know."

She closed her eyes, took a deep, shuddering breath and reached into him.

The warmth of his feelings poured into her. It was an avalanche of emotions that she felt in him. She sensed the strength behind his words; could feel the heartfelt sincerity of his love for her. She felt his nervous fear. He had been afraid to tell her, afraid of how she would feel for him. Most of all, he was afraid to lose her. She felt the pain and frustration of her not knowing recede, turning into relief now that he had told her. A heavy weight lifted from his chest.

Collett opened her eyes and realized he still had not released her from his hypnotic gaze. He just gripped her hand tighter, afraid she would pull back. He was afraid she would hate him like Mary had.

And then, just as suddenly as the impressions came to her, they were shut off like a faucet. Someone turned the knob, and they were gone.

"Cade, I don't-" she tried.

He shook his head, stopping her, "You don't have to say anything. I needed you to know, and I know you felt it. I could feel you with me the whole time. It was truly amazing."

"You stopped me," she whispered.

"You let me," he whispered back, keeping her hand on his heart. He leaned in and kissed her tenderly. Lying his lips softly upon hers, lingering for a single, perfect moment. He pulled back, reluctantly, or so it seemed to her. "Goodnight Collett," he whispered. He gently put her hand down and left the room, softly closing the door behind him.

Collett was frozen still. She couldn't get her feet to move. She couldn't get her foggy brain to process anything. *So much love,* she thought. She looked down at the hand he had held in his grasp. It was still warm from his touch. It felt as if she could still feel the beat of his heart against her palm, even though she no longer touched him.

Finally, after a time, she walked over and shut off the lamp, then eased herself into bed. She was no longer tired. Her thoughts raced. *What now?* she wondered. The man she was in love with had not only professed his own love, but he had shared the unbridled power of his love with her, despite the fact that he was afraid she would hate him for it. She thought again of the name Mary. Who was Mary? And how could she possibly hate Cade?

As she lay in bed under a warm, soft comforter, she thought about how she had earlier resolved not to tell him her true feelings. Now her only thought was, *What am I going to do now?*

CHAPTER 24

The next day, Cade sat in the hidden security room with Nate going over a list of possible threats in the area. Suddenly, Cynda came bursting into the room with a sharp, mean glare that could have cut through glass, and it was aimed directly at him.

"What did you do?" she snapped furiously.

He wasn't entirely sure what she was upset about, so he opted not to answer her; taking the fifth. Instead, he simply waited, knowing Cynda would eventually tell him.

She narrowed her angry, green eyes at him, "What did you do to Collett?"

Her words grabbed his attention. "What's wrong?" he asked, clearly worried.

She scrutinized his quick reaction, and wondered if she hadn't jumped the gun. Then reasoned once again it had to be something he did. "You tell me," she answered him, this time trying to use a softer tone. She failed. Instead, it sounded snide.

He still looked confused, so she elaborated further, "Yesterday Collett was happy and smiling. I even caught her humming to

C.B. Haight

herself. Then suddenly today she acts like she's been run over by a bulldozer. She's walking around here like a robot on autopilot. She hasn't eaten a thing, and it looks like she didn't sleep at all last night. I know you went to her room last night."

Nate couldn't help it, "Trouble in paradise, already?" he asked, waggling his eyebrows suggestively.

Cade and Cynda both shot fierce and angry glares at him. "Shut up, Nate!" they said at the same time.

Nate defensively put his hands up and rolled his chair over to the computers, out of the line of fire. He feigned being busy at the computers, but he couldn't help listening.

Cade looked back to Cynda, "How did you know that I was in her room?"

She met his gaze with fire in her eyes, "It may be a big house Cade, but it's not so big that I don't know what goes on under my own roof."

"How come you automatically assume it's something I did?" he replied defensively.

Now it was her turn to remain silent. Instead, she rolled her eyes at him.

He conceded, "Okay, fine. It might have been me. What do you want me to say, Cynda?"

"I want you to fix it!"

Frustrated, Cade let out a weighted breath. His voice quieted, "I don't think I can."

Cynda brought her hands up to her hips and asked sharply, "What did you do? What did you say that upset her so badly?"

Rederrick came into the room and asked politely, "Hey, does anyone know what's wrong with Collett? I saw her in the kitchen, and she looks like a walking zombie." Of course he had no idea he just rubbed salt into a festering wound.

A frustrated Cade pinched the bridge of his nose with his thumb and forefinger and huffed out another heavy breath. Cynda sharpened her cutting glare even more and lifted her hand to gesture in Rederrick's direction as if he proved her point precisely.

Rederrick looked from Cynda's furious expression and back to Cade. "Did I miss something here?" he questioned cautiously.

"No you haven't missed anything! We're still waiting on Cade to enlighten us. Go ahead Cade, enlighten us," she snapped.

He stared back at her now, but he knew she wouldn't back down. When it came to people she cared about, Cynda could give a hungry dog, clutching its only bone, a run for its money. No, he knew she would hang on to this particular bone, chewing and biting until he cracked under the pressure.

"I told her I love her! Satisfied?" he admitted, "That's what I did. I told Collet I love her."

Nate and Cynda just stared at him with open mouths, and shocked expressions. Even though they had all begun to suspect as much, to have Cade actually say the words was so out of character for him. Rederrick smiled.

Cade threw up his hands in exasperation, "So you see, Cynda, I can't fix it. You can't either. She'll either come to terms with it, or she won't. But I can't, no- I won't take it back!

"Now if you'll excuse me, I think I'll go for a run. Nate, take my place training Collett this afternoon, obviously she needs a little space from me right now." then he stormed right past Cynda and Rederrick, leaving the room.

Nate looked right at Rederrick, "I guess that answers that."

"I guess so. No question about it now," Rederrick muttered. Both men could no longer contain their grins as they considered what had happened.

Cynda noticed their smug, satisfied looks, and because she was now worried about Cade as well as Collett, she snapped, "Oh, what do you two idiots know?" She spun on her heel and followed Cade's lead, by storming from the room as well.

After she left, Rederrick took a step forward and held out his hand, rubbing his fingers together. Nate stood and with slight disappointment, removed a hundred-dollar bill from his wallet, handing it over to Rederrick.

With a smug and satisfied smile still on his face, Rederrick tucked the bill carefully into his money-clip. Nate watched as Rederrick put the clip away, then his smile returned. Arching one brow he asked, "Double or nothing?"

Rederrick's grin spread wider, revealing his laugh lines and dimples, as he replied mockingly, "You know, Nate, gambling is a bad habit. I feel it is my duty, as your friend and mentor, to break you of this terrible habit by helping you lose as much of your money as I can. Purely in the interest of teaching you a lesson, of course." Then he asked deviously, "So tell me, what exactly do you have in mind?"

When Cade finally arrived back at the house, he had gone from mildly irritated to steaming mad. He had tried to run off his frustration, tried to push his body to its ultimate endurance, but it was no use. He couldn't reach his physical limits when he had to stay so close to the house. Besides, it wouldn't help, and deep down he knew it. In his heart, he wanted Collett to accept him right away.

This really made him mad at himself more than anybody. Mad that he had confessed his feelings to her so readily and subconsciously expected her to reciprocate. He hadn't meant to tell her yet, but seeing her standing there before him looking so perfect and real... he simply hadn't been able to hold back any longer.

He'd meant it when he told her about the many people he'd known missing their chance. He wanted to wait, but he wasn't willing to take that risk. So now, he would just have to live with the consequences of his choice.

He bounded up the stairs and went to his room to shower and change, but when he opened the door, surprise rippled through him. Stunned, he stood in the entrance a moment. Collett sat on the edge of his bed with her back straight and her hands neatly folded in her lap. Her legs were tucked back and crossed at the ankles, and her blue eyes gave him a cool, controlled look. And damn if it didn't make her look pretty, sitting there all prim and proper. He was beginning to wonder if she would ever look anything less than perfect to him.

She cleared her throat and softly greeted, "Hello."

He stepped forward and shut the door. His anger was still close to the surface and he asked sharply, "What are you doing in here?"

"We need to talk, and since you're avoiding me, I thought I would pin you down."

"So talk."

Refusing to let his bad mood goad her, she stood and pulled down on the hem of her cream sweater, straightening it out. "I can see this is a bad time," she said coolly. "You can come find me when you're ready." She tried to pass him to get to the door, but Cade stepped into her path.

"No. You came here to talk, so talk."

"Cade it's obvious you're not in the mood. I'll come back later," she replied with a condescending bite to her voice.

"Fine. Have it your way," he stepped out of her path to let her leave, but feelings of rejection were evident in his tone.

Taking a step toward the door, she stopped, straightened her shoulders, and turned around sharply. Her temper snapped. She laid it out for him, "You know, you really have no right to be mad at me. If you want to be angry, fine! Be angry, but don't be angry with me!"

If only she could see into my mind now, he thought. Hadn't he already decided that he was just mad at himself? Unfortunately, all that came out of his mouth was a clipped, "Is that what you came to tell me?"

"As a matter a fact, it's not. How dare you expect me to act normal! How dare you think I should act like nothing happened, when only last night you drop the emotional equivalent of a bomb right in my lap, then you walked away before it went off. What exactly do you want from me, Cade? Did you think I would be able to act like it didn't happen? Did you want me to fall into your arms and confess how much you mean to me? Telling you how much I love you won't change a thing! It won't suddenly make everything better, so we can live happily ever after," her last words trailed off quietly, and her shoulders slumped.

He blinked and stepped closer to her. With astonishment in his eyes, "Say that again?"

Knowing what he wanted, and not ready to repeat it with his intent gaze on her, she evaded, "Say what, that it won't change anything?"

He shook his head, "No. Not that."

She averted her eyes from the intensity of his gaze by looking off to the side at the painting on the wall. "I can't," she whispered desperately.

Cade prayed for patience and tried very hard to put it to good use, "Why? Why can't you say it?"

"Because then it's real; then it will only hurt more," she responded.

"If you don't say it, it won't make it any less real. I've fallen in love with you, Collett. I can't change that. I don't want to change it. Please tell me I'm not a fool for doing so. Please! Say it again," he begged.

Collett lifted her face back up to meet his eyes, "You're a fool Cade!" she insisted wholeheartedly. "You fell in love with a woman with no memory of her past. You fell in love with a woman who, for some unknown reason, several people seem to want dead. Most of all,-you fell in love with a mortal woman who loves you so much it hurts. It hurts me right here," she put her hand on her chest, and her voice cracked.

Quickly, before she could take it back, for Cade saw the doubt in her iridescent eyes, he gathered her tightly to him. He could hardly believe this was really happening.

"I may be a fool, but I would rather be a fool than have another minute without you."

She pulled away from him and pleaded, "Don't you see that's the problem? This won't work. I do love you Cade. I love you enough to know that this can't be. The longer I'm with you the more I want. Cade, I want a lot, but I won't live forever like you. What happens when I grow old only to wither away and die? I don't want that for you."

He could see what she was trying to tell him, and a familiar bitterness came to him. His body stiffened. "So, you don't love me enough to be with me because I'll live longer than you will, because I won't be able to grow old, because, you want a normal life? Is that it?" He heaved a heavy breath to pull back his anger. "Never mind, it hardly matters," he finished dejectedly.

"NO! That's not-"

"I understand.-You love me; just not enough. It's fine. Now if you'll excuse me, I need a shower."

Suddenly, Collett understood the name Mary from last night. Mary must have not understood Cade or accepted him for what he was. She couldn't let him walk away believing this about her. How could he think her so shallow?

"Cade stop!"

He did, but he didn't turn around to look at her. The muscles in his back were bunched, whether out of frustration or anger, she couldn't tell for sure.

He couldn't turn to look at her. He felt like he was on the edge of a very steep precipice and at any moment he would lose his balance.

"Cade, please, you don't understand. You didn't hear me right. I love you too much. I'm not worried about you not growing old, and I don't really care about having a normal life. Who decides what's normal anyway? My life is certainly not normal. It's nothing like that."

"Then what is it that bothers you?" he asked.

"Hurting you. I don't want to hurt you," she spoke so softly that, even with his sensitive hearing, he barely heard her.

Now he did turn, his confusion apparent in his expression, "I don't understand."

She sighed, "Cade when I die... if we stay together. Tell me, where does that leave you?" He opened his mouth but didn't get a chance to answer before she continued, "Alone! That's where it leaves you. It leaves you hollow and alone. Do you really believe you'll be satisfied with my short life span? I could feel the strength of your love for me last night. I know the strength of my own feelings. One lifetime, a few short years, is all I can give you. I can't do that to you. Please don't ask me to hurt you like that."

"What makes you think walking away from me now won't leave me just as hollow and alone?" he asked sincerely.

"Cade, time will only make your feelings stronger. It will just make it that much harder."

He smirked, "You're right about that, it will make our feelings stronger. I'm counting on that. Collett, you have this way of being wrong about things. I would rather have those few short years with you than none at all. Sure it will be hard, but it is better than nothing. "

"Cade-"

"No, you had your turn. Let me finish."

She sighed again and conceded with a nod.

"I have loved many people in my lifespan." At her jealous glare, he felt a slight satisfaction. He held up his hand to stop her response and continued, "And of all those people I have loved, not one passed on without me feeling grief and loss. It's just a part of who I am; what I am.

"But I would have never traded the joy of those few, short years, as you called it, to avoid that grief. Each person I knew gave me precious memories. Without them, my life would be a hollow shell. Because of them, I am the man who stands before you. If you love me, trust me."

Collett just stared at him with her soft, saddened eyes. She wasn't sure what to do now. When she came up here this afternoon, she intended to tell him this had to stop. Now she longed to be with him. She badly wanted to trust him.

Cade approached her once again, gently he moved her face, forcing her to meet his gaze, "Of all those people, not one of them has meant as much to me as you do now. Never in all my years have I loved anyone the way I love you. Maybe you can believe me now when I tell you; I will take whatever time you are willing to give me. And I will cherish every minute of that time."

"Even if it is only a few days; a few months? I can't give you any promises, Cade. Not only do I not remember my past, I don't know what's in my future."

He smiled at her and kissed her on the forehead. His kiss was so tender. For some reason, she felt that sweet, tender kiss was more intimate than that first startling, passion-filled kiss they shared in the gym.

He moved down, kissing both her cheeks. He moved over her lips and gave her a soft melting kiss there, too. He pulled back, "One day at a time. We'll just take it one day at a time."

She nodded. "One day at a time," she whispered.

Folding her into his warm embrace, he pulled her close to him. She closed her eyes to savor the moment fully. He kissed her neck and she felt the scrape of his teeth.

"Are you sure you can't change me with a bite?" she asked quietly, almost wishing it could be that simple.

He chuckled, "Well, I could nibble on you a bit and see what happens."

She huffed out a breath and begged softly, "Tell me again."

He laughed a little from relief, hugged her tighter, and gave her the words she sought, "I love you, Collett."

"I love you, too."

He pulled back and, putting his hands on her shoulders, replied, "Now, you need to go downstairs, and I need to take a shower."

"Oh, well before you shower; I didn't train with Nate earlier. I was angry with you. Do you want to go over a few things today in physical training?"

Sudden images came to him, "No, I don't think we'll worry about today."

"Are you sure? I could be ready in a couple minutes."

He gave her a heated look, one full of promises and innuendo. "Collett, I'm trying to be honorable here. I want a lot too, just not until we're both ready. Right this minute, I don't think I could hold back if I were upstairs- touching you," his eyes raked roguishly over her. "To tell you the truth, I wouldn't mind just staying right here, but I've lived long enough to learn that good things come to those who wait. I'm willing to wait until the time is right, until you're ready."

She blushed at the implications of his words, "Okay. I'll...um...just go downstairs, and I'll uh...see you at dinner then." She backed up toward the door.

As her hand reached the doorknob, Cade let go of a low growl. Her shocked innocence pulled at him. In two strides he reached her, pinned her against the door, and kissed her passionately. His hands ran over her in sharp, quick motions. She reached up, twining her fingers through his thick, glossy hair. She pulled him closer, urging him on, needing more. He obliged. Leaning in, he savored the flavor of her. As the intensity of their kissing increased, his fists tightened at her hips knowing he had to stop. He forced himself to pull back with the tiny fraction of self-discipline he had left.

She unconsciously let out a little moan of protest as he did.

With panting breaths, Cade declared, "I really think you should go now."

She nodded and twisted the knob behind her. When Cade heard the click from the door latch, he backed up a step, letting her pull the door open slightly. She started out the door then turned back to look at him with her lust-glazed eyes.

"You're killing me here...Go!" he begged.

She quickly escaped through the thin opening into the safety of the hallway, closing the door behind her. While Collett leaned her head against the door with a grin spreading across her face, Cade stared at the wooden barrier wondering if he was out of his mind. What kind of idiot would have sent her away? Frustrated, he stalked to his bathroom and turned on the cold water. He punished himself by standing under the frigid spray for a very long time.

Just before dinner time, Cynda came downstairs to the kitchen and found Collett sitting at the table, staring outside. She approached and sat down in front of her.

To her surprise, Collett turned her head and gave Cynda a full, radiant smile. The beauty of her expression extended over her entirely. Her blue eyes sparkled, and her soft, white cheeks were tinged a rosy pink.

Cynda couldn't help her surprise from showing on her own face. "You don't have to worry. I'm fine," Collett offered.

"You weren't an hour ago," Cynda accused.

"No, I wasn't," she replied kindly.

"What changed?"

"An understanding." Seeing her perplexed expression, Collett explained, "Cade and I have come to an understanding."

"Which is?"

"He loves me, and I love him," she replied simply. "Whatever else happens, at least we know that. The rest I suppose will have to come as it will."

Relief flooded Cynda. With an elated smile on her face she added, "Well, since you're in such a good mood, how about you help me with dinner. Jenny is not feeling well tonight. Can you cook?"

Collett smiled, "As a matter of fact, that's something I can remember, and I am an excellent cook."

"That's good, because I can't," Cynda replied with a laugh. "That's why Jenny took over my kitchen so many years ago. I can brew potions and make healing salves, but when it needs to be tasty, don't count on me."

Collett laughed, "Can you chop vegetables?"

"Why yes I can," Cynda replied lightly.

"Then let's get to work."

CHAPTER 25

The next couple days passed in a blur for everyone. Since there had been no recent attacks, they all agreed that they could lighten up a bit and prepare for the upcoming holiday. They still kept a vigilant eye on security. Collett still stayed inside mostly, keeping up with her continuing training in self-defense with Cade. She even had the opportunity to spar with Cynda once; all under Cade's careful direction. Nate also instructed her some more about the use of several handguns. She really was a quick learner, or so they kept telling her. Her aptitude with hand-to-hand combat was, in fact, surprising by Cade's reckoning.

Cynda now allowed Collett to explore her empathic abilities on her own, while she moved on to train Collett in some basic evocation magic. Collett seemed to grasp the concept of magic pretty well for a novice, which gave her another boost in her self-esteem.

Now that Cody was here to lighten the load on watches, Rederrick returned to his law office during the day. Collett still hadn't met Cody, because he continued to take the latest watch and these days her evenings were mostly spent with Cade. She found it slightly odd that, even being under the same roof, they had not run into each other once, but she was too happy to dwell on it. In fact, she didn't think about her problems much at all. She simply continued with her routines and enjoyed the friendships around her.

Jenny was ill for several more days, so Collett happily assumed the role of cook too. Despite the puzzle that was her life, chores had to be done. The necessities of life waited for no one. She reveled in the chance to help out and take on her share of duties. More than that though, Collett hadn't realized how much she had missed cooking. The basic task kept her hands busy and her mind at ease. The simplicity of everyday life was a relief to her.

Everyone was looking forward to the levity of Thanksgiving, making the mood around the house light. Collett could feel the excitement from Cynda. She was looking forward to having all three of her children under one roof, even if it was just for a few days. It would be a full house this week.

Cynda had cleaned and prepared all three of their rooms with careful and loving hands. And though Rederrick didn't show his excitement outright as Cynda did, Collett felt it in him as well.

Time passed quickly now, and it was the Monday before Thanksgiving. Collett was in the process of peeling red potatoes for the roasted potatoes she intended to prepare to complement the chicken breasts for dinner, when the back kitchen door swung open.

James strode into the room with a confident gait in his stride, wearing his army greens. He feigned surprise, "She's perfect. Not only is she attractive, but she can cook too. I've been waiting my whole life for you. Run away with me."

She giggled a little, "Why, if that's all you've been looking for, you should have been married by now."

He shrugged, "If you've ever had my mom's cooking you'd understand."

Just then, Cynda stepped into the room from the hallway entrance. "I heard that, young man," she scolded.

Assuming a sheepish expression, James corrected, "What I meant was, no one can cook like my mom. And I really mean that."

Cynda narrowed her eyes slightly, but her lips twitched in a smile, "Quit digging a hole to jump in, and get over here and give me a hug."

He dropped his green duffle on the tile floor to approach his mother, and with his arms now free, he wrapped them tightly around her. He gave her a smacking kiss on the cheek and then pulled back, "When will my bratty sisters get here?" he asked with affectionate mirth.

"Ashley will be here on Wednesday, and Tracy flies in tomorrow. You can even go pick her up for me," she offered.

Turning his head James met Collett's eyes, "It's not too late. We can still run away together. We'll elope in Vegas, and then I'll take you to Hawaii."

Collett enjoyed bantering with him, but before she could reply, Cade came down the stairs. "Go beg some other woman. She's already spoken for," he teased gruffly as he walked over to Collett and draped his arm possessively over her shoulders. "Besides, she has way too much class for you."

James let out an over-exaggerated sigh and pretended melancholy, "The story of my life. All the good ones are spoken for." Then he looked to Collett and waggled his eyebrows, "Still, if you ever get tired of him and want some younger blood, you know where to find me."

Collett chuckled under her breath, then tried to straighten her face as she replied with feigned seriousness, "Thank you, James. I'll keep that in mind."

James bent and picked up his duffle bag, throwing it over his shoulder, "Chicks dig the uniform."

Cade inclined his head in mock agreement, "Yeah, I can see that."

He looked back to his mother, "Where's the old man?"

"He's watching security with Nate," she told him.

James bent down, gave his mother a quick peck on the cheek, and turned his head, smiling. "See you at dinner, Collett," he said with ridiculous husky tones in his voice, and winked at her as he left the room.

Cade shook his head, "Kid's got a smart mouth."

Collett couldn't help but agree, "Yeah, but I like him."

It wasn't only James that she liked either. Over the next two days, Collett easily found that she enjoyed Tracy and Ashley's company just as much.

At twenty-six, Tracy was the eldest in the family. Her hair was cut short in a playful style that flipped out at the ends. The color was a shiny auburn, much like her mother's. It held more red than brown. Her eyes were green too, but instead of the deep shade of green that Cynda and James had, Tracy's eyes were a softer, muted green that sparkled with intelligence. Her facial features favored Rederrick, with more angles than curves. The whole combination was incredibly flattering.

From what bits of conversation she could piece together, she learned Tracy was an art-history major. She worked at one of the most prestigious antiquities auction houses in the country, Located in New York thus making it necessary for her to live far from home. It was something Rederrick was not willing to let her forget.

Late Tuesday, Collett overheard one such conversation. She'd been coming down the stairs when she sensed a frustrated turmoil in Rederrick. She approached to see if she could help, then she realized he wasn't alone.

"You know there are closer auction houses. I could put a word in for you." Rederrick stated with a concerned fatherly tone.

"Dad, we talked about this before. I like New York. I like my job, and despite what you may believe, it's called the Big Apple; not the Big Bad Center of All That is Evil."

He grunted his reply, letting Tracy know he didn't agree with that assessment.

She let go of an exasperated sigh, then she wrapped her arms around him and laid her head on his shoulder, saying, "I love you too, Dad."

Just like that, Collett felt his irritation melt away. He folded his arms around her and kissed the top of her head. "You're careful, right? You watch yourself?"

"Yes Dad, I'm careful. No one knows I'm a witch. No one really cares about little ol' me in that big city full of weird people." Then she quickly maneuvered him to change the subject, "So, why don't you tell me about this woman who has Uncle Cade all out of sorts?"

Thinking it best to leave them alone and not wanting to hear anything more, she stepped away from the door.

Later, when Collett was formerly introduced to the eldest Williams daughter, she sensed a strong independence within Tracy. She was confident and at peace with who, and what, she was. Collett felt a slight twinge of envy. She longed for that kind of self-confidence. It was the kind of surety that made it impossible to doubt your decisions.

Tracy was open and forward. Her honesty and easy nature made it impossible for Collett not to like her.

On Wednesday afternoon, James arrived back from the airport with another radiant, young woman. Rederrick and Cynda sure made pretty kids, she thought.

James introduced the young woman to Collett as Ashley. Even though she figured it out due to the family resemblance.

Ashley had shiny brown hair that reached just past her shoulders. It was layered and full, cut in a style that drew attention to her face. Her features were softer, more round than Tracy's and

James', but that didn't diminish the effect of her beauty. She was the only one of the three children who had inherited Rederrick's steel-gray eyes. To Collett, Ashley's twinkling eyes looked to be full of compassion and kindness. There was something in them that spoke to her.

She was slim, but curvy, and was shorter than Collett's five-five height by a good couple of inches. At twenty-four, Ashley was the middle child in this family, and unlike her siblings, she exhibited a calmer, quieter nature. She was more timid.

She wasn't prone to quick sarcastic quips like James and didn't emanate Tracy's self-confidence. She carefully assessed conversations around her before including her opinions. Collett felt a profound kinship with the woman. It was a connection she didn't completely understand, but she did understand that simple need for solace and peace more than anybody.

Through conversations, she later learned that Ashley was currently studying to be a veterinarian at Michigan State University. Collett wondered if having Cade in her life had influenced Ashley's career choice.

Oddly enough, despite their similarities, and the odd kinship she felt, when James had introduced them, Collett immediately sensed a small flash of jealousy, as if Ashley had feelings for Cade. Cade of course, was oblivious.

On Thursday morning, Collett was in the kitchen helping a recovered Jenny with the Thanksgiving preparations, when Ashley and Tracy wandered in. Tracy still wore her cotton pajamas. Ashley, on the other hand was fully dressed, with hair and makeup done.

Ashley sauntered over to Jenny and kissed the older woman on her wrinkled cheek. "I heard you've been sick. Are you okay?"

"Pish, posh. Just a cold is all," Jenny answered.

"Well, Mom said we should come and help you, so how can we help?" Tracy stated.

"You can start by washin' and choppin' those veggies for me. While you're at it, tell me about this boy you've been seein'.

Ashley, why don't you get the fruit salad made for me? And when I'm finished hearin' about Tracy, you can tell me all about school."

With that, both girls got down to business. Collett remained quiet while she prepared stuffing for the turkey. She watched the way both women chattered and confided in Jenny as they all moved from one task to the next. It was all so very normal to her.

Suddenly, the conversation took a quick and unexpected turn. "So Collett, tell me, are you in love with Uncle Cade?" Tracy asked abruptly.

Collett's eyes widened, "Um…" was all she could get out.

Ashley used her soft voice to reprimand Tracy, "That isn't any of your business."

"Yes it is. He's our Uncle, and we care about him. If they intend to be together it affects us, in a roundabout way," she insisted with a shrug.

Annoyed, Ashley shook her head, and Jenny gave Collett a sympathetic glance, but otherwise kept quiet.

"So, do you love him?" She asked again.

Collett took a breath, then answered bravely, "Yes, Tracy. I do. I love him very much."

Tracy smiled, "Good! I am glad to hear it. From what I gather, he loves you. I just wanted to verify it wasn't one sided."

Collett nodded, bringing the two women to an easy understanding. She felt a small sadness in the room and suspected it came from Ashley. Though, because it was so slight, she had a difficult time filtering and confirming that.

Jenny smoothly moved the conversation along to a different topic and that was that. From there they all talked of inconsequential things. The rest of the morning slipped by in easy conversation and welcomed companionship.

Several times, different people slipped in and out of the room to check on the dinner progress. James would come in so he could tease and joke with them occasionally. He would also try to sneak the food, only to be quickly reprimanded by Jenny. She would slap his hand and scold him. He would plead starvation, and she always relented by giving him a small taste of this or that.

James pretended to hit on Collett, and when he was politely rebuffed, he promptly promised Jenny marriage, something Collett realized he did often. The mood was happy and light.

When Cynda wandered in and joined them, she was under several watchful eyes. She was not allowed to mess with anything. They reminisced of past dinners when Cynda contributed, and they laughed about the botched, inedible foods.

"Do you remember the time Mom tried to make homemade bread?" Tracy snickered.

"Yeah, I remember," Ashley replied, giggling.

Collett wanted to know what had them both laughing so hard, The memory made Cynda glare daggers at the two women, and half-heartedly scold them, "Alright now, that's enough."

Realizing she didn't understand the joke, Tracy obliged with choking giggles, "She forgot the yeast. She couldn't figure out why it wouldn't rise. The recipe said, 'let rise until doubled,' and it wouldn't rise. Ooh! Mom got so frustrated."

Ashley offered, in a poor imitation of Jenny's southern voice, "Well dear, how much yeast did you put in?"

"Then Mom answered," Tracy explained, even more poorly imitating Cynda, "Yeast... I didn't use yeast. The recipe doesn't call for yeast."

"So I took her in the kitchen and showed her the little white recipe card," Jenny chimed in, "Sure enough, it didn't call for yeast; on the front of the card anyway. There it was, plainly written the on back of the card: Two tablespoons yeast. Put in warm water to soften." Then Jenny indulged in a little chortle herself.

They were all laughing, including Collett and even an embarrassed Cynda, when Rederrick, Cade and Nate sauntered in.

"What's so funny?" Nate asked.

"We're just remembering Mom's attempt at homemade bread," Ashley answered.

Rederrick and Cade grinned, each of them also easily understanding the reference to the fond memory. Then Rederrick lightly jested, "That's nothing. None of you remember what it was like before Jenny came along."

Cade smiled and teased, "You better be careful, or you won't have a bed to sleep in tonight."

"Nah. She wouldn't do that. She loves me too much," Rederrick replied. He topped off his bold proclamation with a wink to Cynda, who smiled in return.

"We'll see, won't we?" she quipped.

Cade moved around the other two men and went to Collett, who now sat in one of the four wrought-iron stools, cutting apples for a pie. He dipped down, kissed her cheek, and said easily, "At least I know now that you can cook."

She smiled up at him, "Would it have mattered if I couldn't?"

"Not a bit. We'd simply have to eat here for the rest of our lives," Cade teased.

Everyone's eyes were now focused intently on the two of them, and Collett felt slightly embarrassed.

He stole an apple slice from Collett's pile and bit into it. "When do we get to eat? I'm hungry."

"The sooner you boys leave us be, the sooner we'll eat." Jenny huffed.

"You heard her, get out of here. Shoo!" Tracy agreed moving to push them out.

Cade grinned, "Alright we're leaving." He pulled Collett's chin up and kissed her smoothly on the mouth, melting her insides with the brief kiss. When he was finished and had pulled away, her cheeks bloomed, the reddish color of embarrassment that often accompanied such public displays of affection. She knew everyone was watching them. He smiled unabashedly and rubbed the pad of his thumb over her warmed cheeks.

"Now, I think the boy over there has a good idea. There are many different kinds of sustenance in the world," Rederrick proclaimed as he grabbed Cynda's arm and pulled her to him, planting a firm kiss on her lips and dipping her down dramatically low as he did. When he swung the now laughing Cynda back up, he said, "Now, we'll leave you ladies to it."

"Now just hold on a minute," declared Nate, "I'll be damned if I'm going to be the only man in this room, to walk out of this room without a kiss." He promptly stepped up and wrapped Ashley into his arms, kissing her soundly right in front of everyone.

Ashley was too stunned to put up any sort of a fight. Not that she would have, and Rederrick and Cynda were too flabbergasted to offer any protest. Neither one of them said a word as Nate plopped Ashley back on unsteady legs and tipped his head saying, "Ladies," before he waltzed out of the room, whistling lightly as he went.

As Rederrick and Cade followed fast on his heels, four out of five women stared at each other with bemused or surprised expressions plastered across their faces. The fifth woman, Collett, decided then, she wouldn't have to worry so much about Ashley's feelings for Cade.

He may have made it look like a joke, but she felt Nate's sudden, unguarded and unexpected feelings for the younger Williams daughter, as if he'd been waiting years to do that. And though Ashley was stunned, Collett felt the excitement from her as well. She smiled to herself. As she continued to slice apples for her pie, she understood that feeling little snippets of emotion wasn't so bad after all.

Thanksgiving dinner was a chaotic and lively event. They all gathered in the formal dining room together. Cynda had taken extreme efforts to set an elegant table. She pulled out her very fragile China to eat on. The gold-rimmed China was adorned with dainty, hand-painted pink flowers. It was all set on an exquisite lace tablecloth.

Waterford Crystal goblets and gold cutlery accented the beauty of the place settings on the long, formal table. Soft, cream-colored, linen napkins were expertly folded and placed in the center of each plate. The crystal chandelier that hung from the ceiling sparkled almost magically, and the glow coming from it set the perfect mood in the room.

It was a warm and inviting setting, one Collett felt honored to be a part of. Cade pulled out one of the high-backed chairs for her and she gracefully slid into it. He constantly made old-fashioned gestures such as this, and she was woman enough to love all of them.

He sat down next to her. Unlike most days, today he wore a suit coat to match his slacks. He looked very distinguished, sitting there in a fancy, candlelit dining room, in his handsome clothes that she suspected he secretly hated.

Everyone else, including her, was similarly dressed. They all wore nice dress clothes, nothing too flashy or too formal, just simply nice. She had chosen a dressy skirt that reached her ankles. The skirt had slits on both sides that ran back up to her knees. She had picked a red, button-up blouse for her top.

Cade leaned over to her, "You look better than any Red Riding Hood I could have dreamed up," he teased.

"Hmm, maybe I'll sneak off to see the big bad wolf later," she boldly replied, despite the rising color in her cheeks again.

Eventually, everyone else found their seats. As they did, she reflected on all that happened to her these past weeks. She, more than anyone here, had so much to be thankful for.

After everyone was seated, a young man with soft brown hair and angular features came into the room. Collett smiled to him assuming he must be Cody. When he seated himself directly across from her, she scrutinized him.

He was tall and slim, with sharp blue eyes, framed by dark brown brows. His brown hair was cut in a shaggy modern style, and his long stride had eaten up the distance from the door to the table in a few easy steps. His thin, angular features didn't make him less handsome. He was young, maybe twenty at the most. But something about him bothered her right away, though she couldn't figure out why. He didn't smile when he came in. Instead he kept his head down. He was holding something in, and she tried to reach it, but he avoided looking directly at her. Plus there were so many other emotions in the room she feared opening up to them.

When he settled in his seat, Collett introduced herself. "Hi, I'm Collett."

Cody looked up, realizing she was talking to him.

"I forgot you two haven't met yet. Cody, meet Collett, Collett…Cody," injected Cade.

"Hi," replied Cody with a quick, awkward wave from across the table.

"I'm glad to meet you," Collett politely responded.

"Yeah," he replied.

Collett was slightly confused by his disinterested reaction, but then Rederrick stood distracting her, "Alright now, let's say grace. After that we can dig into this delicious meal. Before we do though, I would like to thank everyone one here for all their hard work. These past weeks have been taxing on all of us, so let's enjoy tonight. Let's be thankful we have each other. Because good friends and a loving family are all a man really needs to survive."

"Here, here," everyone agreed.

She noticed Cody didn't say a word. Instead he averted his eyes to the floor once more. She tried to sense his emotions again, and found a small inkling of guilt. As she looked across the table, trying to understand what bothered him, he lifted his gaze. When their eyes met she shivered.

She wondered what it was about him that bothered her, he seemed conflicted, she didn't have any further time to think on it. After Rederrick said grace, expressing thanks for his many blessings, the room immediately erupted into a cacophony of separate conversations and rattling dishes. Everyone seemed to be talking at once, and yet to Collett, they all acted like they understood each other perfectly.

The confusing chaos warmed her. She was surprised to find that she was good at keeping up with the multiple conversations. Overall, she mostly kept to herself, just observing the goings on, learning and understanding the family dynamic.

She saw that Nate placed himself next to Ashley, and it made her smile inside. As before in the kitchen it was more than obvious to her that Nate had his sights set on Ashley; probably had for a long time. He kept her engaged in conversation, asking how school was, and did she like Michigan. It was a simple conversation. Cody sat on Ashley's other side. He added his input once in a while, but mostly kept to himself throughout the meal.

She listened when Tracy teased James. James, in turn, playfully took jabs at Cade's expense. She watched the way they all understood references to long-past memories, and even older jokes. She enjoyed observing the lighthearted antics and listening to the fun, boisterous, laughter that erupted between them.

She was witness to the way Rederrick kept touching Cynda. A pat on her shoulder, a rub on her back, holding her hand, they were easy familiar touches for him. Cynda was so used to them, Collett doubted she noticed anymore. Much like Rederrick didn't notice the long sparkly looks Cynda gave him. It was just a natural part of their relationship, as natural as breathing.

To them, this was simply another Thanksgiving dinner; something they'd done time and time again in years past. It was all so easy and basic, and yet it wasn't. She realized then; this was her family now. These people here at this table accepted her, protected her, and sacrificed for her. All the things a family does for each other, they did for her; despite the fact that some of them barely even knew her.

Collett suspected it had always been that way. She wondered what life tragedies had originally brought Nate and Cody into the fold of this loving family. Because it was plain to see that they were as much a part of this family as Tracy, James and Ashley. They were just as important as Cade or Jenny. And now Collett was like them. *I am part of a family*, she thought, *this family*. Knowing that gave her an odd kind of comfort.

She opened herself to the warmth and love and soaked it all into her soul. Collett decided her future no longer mattered this, right here, was all that mattered to her now.

CHAPTER 26

The fun and levity went on well into the evening. After dinner, the men cleared the dishes and saw to cleaning them; a rule Cynda put in place years ago. She explained to Collett it was only fair, seeing how the ladies slaved all day with the cooking and preparations.

Cody avoided his fate with a scrub brush by claiming he would check on security. Nate, James, Cade, and Rederrick all did the task with little complaint, due to years of training, or so Cynda claimed.

The women went into the parlor to relax. They were enjoying each other's company when Cynda asked Tracy casually, "Tell me, is it serious with this boy you've been seeing?"

"Not yet. We're still getting to know each other."

"What's his name again?" Ashley questioned.

"Derek," said Tracy.

"Well get on it, will ya?" Cynda chirped. "I keep hoping eventually one of you children will get married and give me grandchildren I can dote on."

Tracy gave her mother a sideways glance, "Give me a break. I'm not even thinking of a brood of kids right now. My life is too complicated."

Collett smiled as vivid images of three pretty girls running around this very room came into her mind. "Such pretty girls," she said wistfully without realizing she said it aloud.

Everyone turned to her, puzzled by her out of context statement. "What?" she asked.

"You said, 'Such pretty girls,' with a dewy sigh, right out of the blue," Cynda explained.

"What were you talking about?" Ashley asked more than a little curious.

"I said it out loud?"

They all answered her question with varying confirmations.

She sheepishly apologized, "I'm sorry, I didn't realize. I didn't mean to."

"Don't apologize. Did you remember something?" Cynda asked comfortingly.

"Not exactly," she replied hesitantly, feeling foolish, "It was more like I…um…"

"You can tell us," Ashley prodded.

"Well I pictured something. At least, I think I did anyway. Maybe I imagined it."

Everybody's expressions shifted from polite curiosity, to avid interest.

Tentatively, she explained. "You mentioned Tracy having children. I saw three children here in this room. They were running around. They were little girls with long dark hair, green eyes, and soft, bell-like giggles bubbled from them as they chased each other."

All the women looked back and forth to each other, with astonished, yet knowing expressions.

"When did you see this?" Tracy asked firmly.

"Um…well, a second ago, when Cynda was prodding you to get married."

"You said she was an empath," Tracy accused Cynda.

"She is," her mother insisted. Then she narrowed her eyes as she thought about it more carefully, "But she can do something else. Something I've never seen an ordinary empath do."

"What are you talking about, Mom?" Ashley questioned.

"No I can't explain it. You have to experience it yourself. You probably wouldn't believe me in any case, and she would have to show you regardless. Collett, show Ashley."

Collett was taken aback. She didn't understand the whole of this conversation. "What do you want me to show her?" she questioned with a calm she didn't feel. In fact, her stomach had twisted into a tight knot at this point, making her regret the second helping of sweet potatoes.

"Just read her emotions, she'll understand," Cynda explained.

"Oh," Collett replied. She turned to Ashley, "Can I have your permission to read your emotions, Ashley?"

"Okay…" came her reluctant response.

Collett walked closer to her to make it a bit simpler to reach into her. She closed her eyes, filtered through the emotions in the room, and reaching for Ashley's feelings, she easily brushed aside Cynda and Jenny because she was so familiar with them now. She passed Tracy and her feelings quicker than she would have expected, whether it was because of long hours of practice, or because she immediately recognized the woman's self-confidence hardly mattered. Right now, Collett concentrated on Ashley.

When she could focus on Ashley, the first thing Collett felt was the small, sad pang of a lost childhood crush. A crush Ashley clung to as a safety net. She understood more clearly now. Ashley had a crush on Cade, as she suspected, but it was more fantasy than reality. Really, she was more saddened by the loss of her fantasy than she was by the loss of him.

She probed a little further and felt Ashley's fear of finding someone to love her like her father loved her mother. In her timid and logical mind, love like theirs was rare and almost unheard of.

Collett became aware of other feelings as well, such as the love she had for her family, worries she had over school, and a slight trace of guilt for kept secrets.

Knowing enough to help her now, she quickly withdrew, not wanting to intrude further than necessary on Ashley's thoughts. She looked Ashley in the eyes and stated with surety, "Ashley, love isn't as rare as you believe, and it is worth waiting for."

Ashley knew right away what she referred to. Collett brought forth the buried emotions to the surface when she reached for them, making them clear and vivid. She felt Ashley's embarrassment as a result.

Instinctively, Collett felt the need to ease this burden on Ashley, much like when she'd read Jenny the first time. So once again she laid her hand on Ashley's shoulder and whispered, "Feel. It is real."

Feeling the strong urge to share the power of true love at its fullest with Ashley, she compiled her new-found feelings for Cade, Jenny's tender feelings for her lost Sam, and Cynda's undying feelings for Rederrick. They were all emotions Collett somehow retained upon experiencing them.

According to her current memories, they were three of the most powerful feelings she had ever felt, and she poured only a fraction of each one into Ashley.

Ashley gasped as the force of them rushed through her. Though Collett held back most of it, it was still enough to drain her and have Ashley staggering backward in awe and wonder when it was over.

Collett closed her eyes in order to calm her now spinning head. She felt someone ease her down into a chair and recognized Cade's steady, firm grip. "How long have you been in the room?" she asked quietly.

"Long enough," he answered, "Are you okay?"

"Yes, I'll be fine. Is Ashley all right?"

Kneeling in front of her, he chuckled, "Still worrying about everyone else I see." He looked back to a surprised Ashley, "She's okay."

With her eyes still closed, Collett said, "I think I overwhelmed her."

Ashley spoke up on her own behalf, "I'm fine Collett, but that... that was absolutely incredible. Never would I have expected that. I've never known any empath who could do that. You can't be any ordinary empath, and I should know, I'm empathic too."

Collett opened her eyes carefully, "You are?"

"Well yes, but I'm better with animals. That's why I want to be a vet."

Collett looked back to Cynda, "Why didn't you tell me?"

"Because she knows I don't like people to know," Ashley answered for her.

"It's not my secret to tell," Cynda added.

"You could help me then?" Collett asked Ashley.

Ashley drew her brows with disappointment, "No. I can't. You are far more powerful than I am. For that matter, like I said before, I've never heard of anyone capable of doing what you just did. I mean, I've heard of it in theory, but I've never met someone who could actually do it."

"And if you add in her little premonition, it makes for a pretty big combination," Tracy supplied.

Tracy's words distracted Cade from Ashley's statement; He twisted his head to Tracy and questioned, "Premonition?"

"Yeah," Tracy answered.

He swung his head back to Collett, waiting for her to explain. She sighed and told him of her vision of the three little girls. Then she tried to put it aside, "I don't know what it was, but it did feel real to me."

Cynda eased her way back into the conversation, "I know how we can find out."

"How?" Cade asked.

"We test it," she answered. "Let her try to specifically focus on someone's future."

He shook his head, "She's too drained to try something like that right now."

Collett narrowed her eyes and glared at him. "You're speaking for me again. I can do this." However, her words held no weight. She was tired.

He stood and pleaded, "Collett, I don't fully understand what you did there with Ashley, but I'm not blind to the effect it had on you. And now you're ready to plow on to something you don't truly understand. We have no idea the effect it could have on you. You can wait one more day. Rest first."

"Wait," Ashley said with confusion in her voice. "You don't understand? Are you telling me she hasn't projected to you before?"

"Projected? She's been projecting?" Cade fired back.

"I told you Cynda thought I could share warmth and comfort with people and make them feel better," Collett told him.

Cade snapped his gaze to Cynda, "You didn't tell me she was projecting."

Cynda repeated her earlier statement, "Not my secret to tell. Besides, it sounds like Collett told you herself. I didn't know what to call it. I've never seen it before."

"I have only heard the theory of it being a skill with powerful empaths," Ashley added.

"No, what she told me was different." *Wasn't it*, he wondered. "I didn't think she could project." He silently cursed, realizing he should have put it together, and knew why he hadn't. He was too distracted by his feelings for her. He was the most experienced. He should have figured it out sooner.

Cynda shrugged, "I didn't tell Rederrick either. Besides I didn't think it was a big deal, until now. I suppose I should have known it was important, especially after I remembered that day at the river, when Collett brought me back from darkness. We've been too close to her. It took Tracy and Ashley to see it for both of us."

"Let's see if I can put this into perspective for everybody. Collett is not only empathic, she can also read thoughts linked to emotions, project emotional feelings to people," he looked to Ashley for agreement and receiving her nod continued, "And now you all believe she could possibly have the power of premonition."

This time Cade directed his attention to Tracy and witnessed her soft nod confirming all he listed. He roughly ran his hand through his hair, as he was prone to do when upset. "That's a pretty odd and powerful list."

"It's not so odd," Cynda added. "If you think about it, each ability is linked to the other in some way, and all are linked to her empathy. I also think it's best if we include everything here. So don't forget that Collett has easily picked up on my basic teaching in evocation with elements. She heals fast, and she's pretty darn good in a sparring match."

Cade looked back at Collett, locking his golden eyes with her crystal blue orbs and couldn't help wondering, who *is this woman I'm in love with?*

He glanced to Nate and Rederrick looking for some sort of insight. They had both entered the parlor with him, but had stayed quiet during the entire exchange. Even though he knew the answer, Cade began to ask a stoic Rederrick, "Have you ever…?"

"No, never."

Nate shook his head negatively as well.

"Neither have I," he uttered in a low tone, "And for my lifetime that's saying something."

Collett stood, "Never, what? Just what's going on?" she said with confusion and nervousness infusing her words.

"Collett," Cynda hedged carefully, "No one in this room has ever heard of someone having that many powers of influence. And despite what you may think, you wield them fairly easily. We didn't put it together before now, but the prospects of this many abilities have very promising possibilities."

"Or scary ones, depending on how you look at it," Tracy scoffed.

Cade gave her a quick and sharp glare, warning her to shut up.

She ignored it and with a shrug, explaining unabashedly, "She needs to know."

"What do I need to know? What do you mean by, *powers of influence?*"

Rederrick agreed with Tracy, "Tell her, Cade. Help her understand."

Cade moved his attention back to her and tried to infuse his voice with a patience he didn't feel, "While your discovery of these *abilities* is amazing, Rederrick and Tracy are concerned the combination of them could be…"

"Disastrous," Tracy finished for him tersely.

Collett lifted her gaze to meet Tracy's, horrified by her one word statement.

"Disastrous?" she muttered, as her mind flashed back to the day she woke on the beach in Texas.

"Tracy, enough!" Rederrick snapped as only a father could.

She held up her hands in a gesture of surrender, though her green eyes showed her impatience.

Rederrick jumped in, helping a frustrated Cade explain better, "Collett, each of your abilities are what we would call influential. With just one of them mastered, you could have the ability to easily affect a person's fate or change their direction. Un-mastered, you could still possibly change a person's future course.

"These are powers of influence. So far, you have four of them: empathy, the ability to feel emotions; precognition, the ability to see the future; telepathy, the ability to read thoughts; and the last one projection, the ability of projecting or even controlling emotions. I should tell you that projection is very rare.

"So to help you understand, let's consider for a moment, that you could project feelings to anybody, affecting their decisions by their emotions, a world leader perhaps? Or, maybe, you could help a general predict the outcome of a battle with a quick flash of the future. Therefore, you could affect the outcome of an important event in a war, or the war in its entirety.

"What if you could sense someone's greatest weakness simply by reading that person's thoughts, and then pass it to their enemies?

"These abilities are like points on a compass. Individually, they can alter a person's future course or affect the paths in life they choose to take. Together, the possibilities are almost limitless, and each one of these abilities would be great and powerful weapons if used properly or held in the right hands."

"But put in the wrong hands…" Collett mumbled, knowing where Rederrick's suggestions were now leading. They led her down an extremely daunting path. A path she had been afraid of from the very beginning. She worried maybe at some point she was on the wrong side before the abrupt memory loss. She sank back into her chair, with a horrible foreboding settling heavily in her chest.

"And you not only have one of these sentient gifts," Cynda offered kindly, "You have all four. There have been the rare occasions when witches have been gifted with two, but never all four. That, in and of itself is likely the reason we didn't piece it all together sooner. I would've never expected this, so I missed it. We all did."

The heavy weight on her chest felt even heavier. It settled in pressing down, and each breath she took ached. "What am I?" she mumbled.

The room fell silent. No one moved or shuffled. No one spoke a single word for what felt like a long time, though it was merely a minute or two. The tension and worry over this new insight hung in the air like a thick heavy cloud. Cade and Rederrick, looked at each other with concern in their eyes. The women in the room looked to Collett, who in turn closed her eyes and buried her face in her hands.

Unexpectedly, it was Nate who spoke first, "All of you aren't seeing the bright side of this." Unlike everyone who spoke before him, Nate's tone was unconcerned, as was his posture. He leaned against the wall easily, unbothered by the conversation taking place.

"What's that?" Tracy asked skeptically.

Nate shrugged, "You can be sure that now we know why The Faction is after her. And you can also be dead certain it is The Faction. Who else would risk trying to control all of that?" he gestured to her with a wave of his hand. "Plus, we know more about where she stands. Because in general, Faction policy is, if you won't join them, the only alternative is death." He shrugged, "It's simple, they want her dead, so it stands to reason Collett wasn't willing to sign on the dotted line."

Ashley agreed. She looked back to her pessimistic sister, "I'm with Nate. Collett isn't on the daunting or disastrous side of this. She doesn't have that kind of greedy malice in her. I would have felt it. She's not power hungry either. Moreover, they wouldn't want Collett dead if she had already agreed to join them. For that matter, given her talents, they would have at least tried to manipulate her to their cause in some way if they could have."

With Ashley's statement, a cold, tingling feeling trickled its way down Cade's spine. So much became clear, and he understood why there had been no move against them in recent days. That's why after Jeffery's attack at the river all had remained quiet.

They were trying to capture Collett before. Hadn't the demon said something about killing her and to hell with the bounty? Then there was Jeffery. He hadn't hurt Collett. In fact, with little regard, Jeffery had hurt Cynda, he almost killed her, but not Collett. It was as if he'd been pushing them into the river to weaken her for capture, and then he would have left Cynda for dead. Things clicked into place for him, one by one, like cogs on a slow clock.

Cade berated himself. *How could I have been so stupid?* The waiting, it was just a way to re-strategize. Decisions like this took time, and recruiting took time. They were coming up with a new game plan, and now, the game would be even deadlier.

By helping Collett and making it known that The Brotherhood, a sworn enemy of The Faction, and a serious thorn in their side, was protecting her, they had unwittingly changed the strike order from capture, to kill!

Heaven knew that The Faction definitely couldn't afford to have someone like her working against them. Cade looked away from her, not wanting her to see the regret in his eyes and swept his eyes swiftly across everyone in the room. There were too many possible casualties now. "Tracy, Ashley, pack your bags. Your trip has just been cut short. Get on the next flight out of Colorado," he ordered harshly.

"Just what the hell are you doing?" Rederrick protested.

"Think, Rederrick!" he snapped, "They didn't intend to kill her before like we thought. Ashley said it. They wanted to manipulate her, capture her, or torture her, until she complied with what they wanted." Cade ground out the last of it, the mere thought of such actions knotted his insides, sickening him. He pushed it back and finished with more calm than he felt, "Rederrick, they would never risk Collett's mixed abilities being of use to us. Think how bad that would be for them. They wanted her for themselves! They intended to use her!"

Nate put it together for everyone, "So now that we have her, they'll send in the real hit squad. Jeffery was just the warm up. She's better lost to them, than possibly helpful to us."

"Exactly," confirmed Cade, "And if they sent a demon and Jeffery for the first task imagine the possibilities of who they'll hire for the second job. They won't take any risks on her living. They're coming, and you can bet they're coming soon!"

"Well, you heard the man. Pack your bags, girls. You're outta here. Jenny, you too, you can go stay with Tracy for a while. Cynda you're with Ashley," Rederrick thundered. "They won't be sending in the second-string players this time."

"Ha!" Cynda boasted, "All the more reason for me to stay."

Rederrick's brows drew together, and his eyes turned flinty. He looked to his wife of twenty-nine years and prepared to order her to go.

Before he could get out a single syllable however, Cynda snapped with an authority that only an Irish blooded witch could manage, "Don't you dare think you can order me out of my own house. I don't care one whit about your self-righteous need to play the role of the hero. We have been over this before, Rederrick James Williams! I am *not* the little woman. I am *not* helpless, and I will not wait idly by some phone for you to call and tell me when it's all clear! You need me, and I'll hear nothing more on the subject. As for our children and Jenny, I agree, they can all be on the next plane ride away from here. Get on the phone and get their tickets changed," she ordered, storming out of the room; stomping right past a now contrite Rederrick.

Tracy stepped past her father and moved to follow Cynda.

Nate pushed himself off the wall he'd been leaning on. "I'll help with the travel arrangements," he said, then he left to sit at a computer and work on finding tickets out of Colorado.

Rederrick mumbled something about going to the den and talking to Cody and James, about security or something like it. Cade wasn't paying attention to Rederrick, so he barely noticed as he slipped out of the room as well.

Cade just stood there, staring out the window, clenching his jaw so tightly you could see the jaw muscles tic. He stared at nothing, as one by one they all left. He was furious with himself and angry at the circumstances. His temper was barely contained at the moment. He desperately wanted to punch or destroy something right then.

Ashley stepped into his view, unaffected by his flinty, rage-filled gaze. She knew he was berating himself for his inability to see this sooner. He was forever taking the responsibility for everyone's safety onto his shoulders. She could feel his emotions, but she could feel turmoil too.

Without a word, she tipped her head in the direction directly behind him. When he saw what she was motioning at, Cade slowly closed his eyes and searched for calm. With one tilt of her head, she reminded him of Collett's presence, giving him slight control again. Collett still sat stunned and confused, and she was much too quiet since the startling revelation of her multiple abilities.

Knowing she did what was needed, Ashley left as well, her soft footfalls sounding against the wood floors as she exited. Cade opened his eyes. He turned around to Collett, trying to smile reassuringly, not that it would have mattered if he had managed the false smile. She wouldn't have noticed. She was far too lost in her own personal thoughts. So he dropped the facade. For the first time in his long memory, Cade was scared, bone-deep scared.

He wanted to reassure her; wanted to whisk her away, and find a way to make it all disappear, but he couldn't. He knew it wouldn't end so easily, knew The Faction would track them down. More than likely, they sat outside this very night, plotting their next move.

He moved over and knelt before her. She gave him a halfhearted smile. He looked for any sign of the telltale tears. He waited for a while, expecting an emotional outburst. He wanted her to lash out because of the unfairness; wanted her to cry and yell because of the frustration. But nothing came.

Her eyes were void of a single tear, and she didn't say a word about the injustice of it all. She just stared off at nothing over his shoulder. Her glazed eyes focused toward the windows that were darkened now by the onset of night.

"Collett?" he questioned softly.

"When?" she whispered.

Without any other words, he knew what she was asking, "Soon," he replied honestly. "It has been almost a month. They must have hired someone new by now. Maybe more than one, as they did when—"

She nodded accepting and cutting off the rest of his statement. He felt as though her cold, quiet acceptance was worse than any other reaction she could have had. He didn't like the way she was behaving now. It was wrong somehow.

"Collett, no matter what happens, no matter who comes, I'll keep you safe. They'll have to go through me to get to you," he promised.

She turned her sad, blue gaze to him and whispered, "I know," and in her head she thought, *that's what I'm afraid of. I've endangered them all.*

She knew it would be better if she left this place. She knew she should be the one catching those flights out of Colorado but a new selfish part of her could not leave Cade. Not now. Not so soon. She wasn't ready to let go.

She would have to leave eventually; she knew that. "I'm sorry," she said softly, apologizing for that upcoming reality.

Misunderstanding, as Collett knew he would, Cade gathered her to his chest. "Don't be sorry, don't ever be sorry. It's not your fault," he consoled. He stroked her hair, more out of an effort to comfort himself by keeping his unsteady hands busy, than to simply soothe her.

It did help. His smooth and easy touch, gave her comfort. It made it easier to bear this burden placed upon her. Just knowing he would go the ends of the earth and beyond to help her, made it all a little easier. She reminded herself she wasn't alone anymore. She knew Cade would fight even the darkest of demons for her no matter the cost.

As she thought about it, she startled, as a sudden image came to her then: Cade screaming out as crippling grief consumed him. He couldn't save her. Falling to his knees he yelled and pleaded for her. Then, the horrible picture vanished as quickly as it had appeared.

At her slight jump, he pulled her in tighter, not understanding the cause and thinking it was just her fear coming through.

She clung to him tighter. It was fear, but not fear of the unknown. It was a fear of what she might know. She closed her eyes to the painful heart-wrenching image, trying to erase it from her mind. *Why do I have to see the future now?* She thought.

Collett knew her already complicated life was about to get terribly more complicated.

CHAPTER 27

A flurry of motion took place throughout that night and into the next day. Bags were packed, arrangements made. Car services were called. Tracy was the first one able to get a flight out and she took a reluctant and protesting Jenny with her.

They'd been able to convince Jenny to go when Collett intervened, and though it sickened her slightly, she used her projection to sway someone for the first time. She had projected her own worry and fear into Jenny, "Please, Jenny. I would never forgive myself if something happened to you." The words were bitter in her mouth because she knew she was manipulating the older woman, but her own fear demanded she ensure Jenny's safety, even if it meant being sneaky.

Cynda had added conspiratorially, "Plus you can meet Tracy's boyfriend and report back to us. I can't wait to get some details. Heaven knows, Tracy hasn't been forthcoming."

With a heavy dose of guilt and the idea of a little conspiracy in her head, Jenny finally conceded, leaving the house with Tracy at five-thirty that morning. They would catch a flight to New York, and there they would stay until they received the all clear.

Unfortunately, Ashley was unable to acquire a flight out until that evening, which had Rederrick pacing all about the house in frustration and worry. His home's security rivaled that of even the government, but the prospect of his children being right in the line of fire, in a potentially deadly situation, made him as nervous as a frightened jackrabbit with a fox clawing and digging at its hole.

It all came down to a waiting game, a game as old as time itself. It came down to strategy and patience. Who would move first, and how; pawn or queen, rook or bishop? Check or check-mate?

They had all faced dangerous scenarios before. It was part of the job. This time was different somehow. They all sensed it. They all knew it. Somehow Collett's presence changed things. Rederrick always knew there was something special about her, and now they all understood a little better why that was true.

As he paced about the room, his son James continued to test and check every system they had. Currently, he was running analysis to make sure there was no tampering with the system. If someone had tampered with it, James would find it. He had a way with computers. It was one of the reasons the government had recruited him. Officially and on paper James worked for the Army, unofficially he was part of the secret Brotherhood branch that operated within the military.

Cade, Cody, and Nate were checking the grounds themselves, at regular intervals, in irregular patterns. No one was willing to leave it all to electronics, including Rederrick. Like a well-oiled machine, they all easily fell into their roles.

As James sarcastically put it, "It's time for Homeland Security. Hit the button boy's, and take us from defcon-4 to defcon-1." He wasn't far off the mark. Their Defensive Condition was now at a stage of maximum readiness. Though no one truly felt ready. It was like being strapped to a bomb that had no timer. You knew it would go off, but you didn't know when.

As a result they were all on edge, especially Cade. When he wasn't attached to Collett at the hip, he was taking his turn prowling the grounds looking for someone he could tear into pieces. Rederrick knew Cade needed someone to hold accountable, and he worried that if they didn't find someone soon, he would go looking.

Something was coming for her. Their instincts had been spot on. Now that they understood better the why, they wanted to get their hands on the who. For the first time, Rederrick wondered if this might be their chance.

For years now they had sought out the leader of the supernatural Faction. The Faction preyed on new talents, often convincing them to use their abilities against those without powers or those who wouldn't join with them. The problem was that no matter what they did, The Brotherhood had not been able to find or pin down the leader of their group.

James pulled Rederrick away from his thoughts. "Nothing," he stated confidently.

Rederrick stopped his forward movement and turned toward his son, "You're sure?"

"I'm telling you, Dad, no one has been in your system. You're still secure. Just to be safe I've changed all the codes, encrypted everything, and rerouted your networks. They won't get in by hacking their way through. You can be sure of that. Now you'll just have to prepare for a direct assault."

Rederrick arched a brow, "And the other?"

"Done. If anyone tries to get in this way we'll be able to follow the trail. I also set the exit codes to wipe everything if they do."

Rederrick grinned with pride. "Good," he said. "Now, get on your way. Nate's waiting for you." With a firmer voice he said, "And you better stay on that base where there are plenty of witnesses and even more security."

"Dad, you know I can help. And I really don't need an escort in any case."

C.B. Haight

"I know you can, and you have. I promise I'll call if we need you. As for the last, you know I believe in safety in numbers."

Knowing it was an undefeatable argument, James matched his father's gaze with a similar look of his own. His feelings were for the man he was lucky enough to have as a father. "Be careful old man, don't be a hero, and watch Cade. He's not himself. He's in too deep this time."

Rederrick pulled his boy in for a hug, "Don't you worry about us. We'll be fine. Now get going," he ordered gently and released him. He moved to the door and exited to find his mom and tell her goodbye, while Rederrick stood in the empty room scanning the bank of monitors that flashed images randomly across the screens.

He sat in his favorite chair and watched, using his sharp eyes to detect anything out of the ordinary. Every now and then, he would make the computer focus on certain areas which held the best advantage for a skilled assassin.

As he did, Rederrick couldn't help but wonder a little if he was getting too old for this game of cat and mouse. He knew one thing; he would sure love to find the nasty Tom Cat responsible and sic a Big Bad Wolf on him.

They needed a break, something that would give them an offensive advantage. He was getting tired of being on defense all the time.

Cade opened the door, advancing across the room with a scowl on his face. He swung a chair around close to Rederrick and sat down on it backwards. Leaning forward, he folded his arms across the back of the chair. His posture was tense, his features stern, and Rederrick didn't need to be empathic to sense the roiling anger in him.

Cade said nothing. He simply stared at the bank of screens with him. Several minutes passed before either of them broke the silence.

Finally, Rederrick spoke, "Nate went with James. He'll be back late tonight."

"Yep."

"Tracy and Jenny are safely on their way to New York."

"Yep."

"Cynda and I will take Ashley to the airport later," Rederrick told him.

"Fine."

"You'll be on your own with Cody. He's not too experienced. You think you'll be all right?"

Cade didn't speak this time, only nodded. The clipped conversation lapsed. For several more minutes the only noise in the room came from the hum of monitors and equipment.

Rederrick tried again, "Collett sleeping finally?"

"Yep."

He let go of a deep breath, "We'll stop them, Cade. We'll figure this out."

He could see the further narrowing of Cade's brows and a tic in his clenched jaw.

"You know, a long time ago when I was ready to go take on a small cell of The Faction by myself, I clearly remember someone reminding me the cost would be too great to the one person I was trying to save." Rederrick let the comment sit for a moment, then continued, "I feel it is my turn to do the same for you. Cade, we don't even know who to go after yet, and you must think of the cost to Collett if you get yourself killed."

"What makes you think I'm going after them?" he countered.

Pointedly glancing at him, Rederrick answered, "I've known you for a long time now. I know how you think. Right now, you're contemplating a direct move, something to draw them away from her."

Cade grunted.

"Once again, I'll remind you, you don't even know who to go after. Tell me, what's your plan?"

"I don't have one yet. When I do come up with one, I'll make sure to get your approval," he replied snidely.

"What about Collett? Will you tell her?"

"I don't need this from you! I've been fighting The Faction longer than you've been alive!" Cade pushed out of his chair so hard he sent it forward on a gliding spin. It smacked into the tabletop underneath the monitors. A loud clank reverberated through the room.

"You're right," Rederrick said calmly, "You've been doing this much longer than me. So you go ahead, run out there, charge your unknown battlefield. Pound on and question every known member of The Faction. You'll just get more frustrated and angrier. We both know the odds of getting anything. Hell, we've both tried that already." He didn't turn, but Rederrick knew he was listening. "We founded the Brotherhood so we could do this with a team. It's not just you anymore. You're not alone in this, and now, neither is she.

"You should consider one thing this matters more. We both know regardless of how many times you've fought The Faction and won, no matter how many times you've gone to rescue someone and saved lives, it didn't matter as much then. It never mattered as much as it does now. Because *she* matters. You love her. You know that makes you dangerous, not only to them, but to yourself."

His on-the-mark accusation caused Cade's stomach to twist. If it was possible, his jaw clenched even tighter. His expression stern, he turned back to his long-time friend with fear in his eyes.

"Think man!" Rederrick scolded, "Just think for a second. Running out there after a ghost won't save her. It won't help. In fact, it might even make things worse. Be patient. We'll figure it out. We can beat them this time. I feel it, but we have to do it right."

Exasperated and frustrated, Cade lifted his gaze to the ceiling. "I'm all out of patience," he admitted, trying hard to reign in his temper.

Nodding, Rederrick responded, "I know what it's like to be in your position, Cade. I also know, without you, I wouldn't have all that I have today. I'd be dust and bones, six feet under. Cynda probably would be too. Patience is hard to come by when those you love need you, but it's the most vital time to have it."

With his frustration calming slightly, Cade looked back down, "I can't lose her, Rederrick."

"I know."

"We need to do something. I'm tired of waiting."

"Do you know what makes us different from them?"

Cade met his gaze but said nothing.

"Endurance," Rederrick stated simply.

"Endurance?" Cade repeated skeptically.

"We keep going. We endure. They want to stop our happiness, destroy our hope, but we keep going. Even during the worst tragedies in history, you'll find humanity. We continue to have Thanksgiving dinners and other holiday parties. We celebrate weddings and births. We dance and sing. When the worst happens and we're faced with loss, we cherish the lives of our loved ones by remembering how they lived. We make sacrifices to help others, but most of all, we love, Cade.

"Life, no matter how long or short that is, will never be a sprint. It is a long distance race that requires endurance. Take that away, and we become like them, always running along as fast as we can, without a purpose or happiness.

"That's what we fight for. That's what we live for. You think back through your long lifetime and the history of this world, and you'll know it's true. We go on, Cade. No matter how bad things get, those of us with the strength to endure hold faith that things will eventually change, and we pull together until it does. In the meantime, we find all the happiness we can, gathering our strength from it, so that when the time comes, we can and will prevail."

Cade stood still for a moment looking at Rederrick. After a minute, he quietly walked over and pulled his chair around. Once again he sat down next to him. Both men turned their attention back to the flashing screens. The room was silent for what felt like a long time, but at least now the angry tension was gone. They both sat there thinking. Finally, Cade asked, "How'd you get so smart, Old Man?"

Rederrick smiled, "I have good friends."

Cade turned his head and looked to him quizzically.

"I partly stole the speech from someone I know."

"Yeah, who was that?"

"You. You spouted off something similar when you stopped me from going after Cynda half-cocked."

"I don't remember that," Cade said his brow pinched in thought.

"Well, the way I said it certainly had more finesse. You shouted and growled something about it at me when you had me pinned on the ground," Rederrick said lightly.

"Huh, maybe I'm smarter than I thought." Cade said lightly.

"Don't bet on it, boy," Rederrick teased.

They sat there companionably for a time. After a while though, Rederrick noticed Cade's leg bounce up and down and saw the way his eyes kept going back to the video feeds of Collett's bedroom window.

"Go, be with her, and gather your strength. You don't need to be here," he ordered.

"Yes I do. You'll need to get going to the airport soon," He replied.

"And I'll get Cody to take over for me, or I can set the perimeter alarms. James says they are running fine. Go, Cade."

He studied his friend for a long minute before standing, "Set the alarms for now, I'll have Cody keep checking the grounds and the house. A live person can spot things electronics can miss. I'll bring her in here with me later."

"Fine. On your way up, remind Cynda and Ashley we need to be ready within the hour."

He nodded to Rederrick and made his way upstairs. When he got to Ashley's room, he knocked softly. "Come in," he heard from the other side of the door.

Entering the room, Cade found her carefully folding and tucking her clothing into her black suitcase. She looked up at him and offered a small smile. "Cade," She acknowledged.

"The old man says you've got about an hour."

"I know," she replied softly.

Ashley was always soft-spoken and quiet. To his knowledge, she never raised her voice once in the whole of her twenty-four years. She was also the most tender-hearted person he knew. Part of that came from being empathic, but most of it was just who she was. She was kind and considerate, loving and affectionate. She was a very special person.

"I'm sorry you have to go. I know you love your trips home."

She returned to her folding, "Don't worry about me. I'll come back for Christmas or maybe sooner if I can manage a weekend away from my studying."

"All the same, I'm sorry this happened."

"Cade, you and Dad have been battling this evil all my life. I know the drill. I'm not sorry for it either. I know how important this is. I know what it means to people like me." She did too. She learned recently, on a personal level, how truly evil The Faction was. Ashley felt a pang of guilt for keeping that secret from him, but knew he wasn't ready to hear about it right now. "So go, do your thing. Help Collett, and don't worry so much about my feelings. I can come home anytime. She needs your help now."

He leaned against the door jam. "Aren't you going to give me a hug goodbye?"

Her hands fumbled, and a familiar awkwardness came to her. Then she quickly recomposed herself. Ashley reminded herself of the strength of Collett's feelings for Cade, and now she knew without a doubt, that what she felt for him was a small crush in comparison. She would never again have to wonder, *What if?* Or feel awkward around him. There was freedom in that, and it felt good.

She grinned and her eyes twinkled. "You know what, I think I will." She approached him and wrapped her arms enthusiastically around him, much like a sister would for a brother, and it felt right.

He returned the embrace with a tight squeeze and murmured, "Be careful out there in Michigan, Ashley."

She pulled back to say, "I'm happy for you, Cade. She loves you very much. I like her too, which is a bonus."

He looked at her quizzically, "How do you know?"

"She showed me, and let me feel it. That's what she projected to me last night. She loves you more than her very life. Her love for you is almost like a fairytale, it's timeless." She shrugged, "I thought you should know."

"Thanks." He muttered, then he asked slightly disconcerted, "You felt it?"

"Yes Cade, I did."

"Oh. Well I'll, just ah…I'll let you get finished up here," he backed up to the door.

She could sense Cade's slight embarrassment, and laughed. It was a little funny to her.

Because she was close to him, and because he had always been a part of her life, or perhaps because of his animal side, she could usually sense his emotions. She considered that maybe that's why she invariably wondered about them. Maybe it was simply a result of her close emotional connection to him.

She teased him, "Don't worry so much. It's not as if I would tell James. I wouldn't want to give him any more ammo to tell bad jokes."

Cade's lips tilted up in a smile, "Thanks for that."

She covered her mouth muffling a small giggle, "Now go on. Get out of here. I have clothes to pack."

He moved to leave the room, then stopped suddenly in the hall. He back-tracked a step and poked his head in the room, "See ya later, alligator."

Ashley was touched that he used their little routine from when she was a little girl and he had to go away. She always protested vehemently when he would leave them, knowing that sometimes it would be months before his return. Even back then, she could sense his worry. No matter how they sugar-coated it, even as a little girl, she understood what Cade did was dangerous.

After they discovered her empathy and understood her protests, he promised her he would never say goodbye again, because he would always come back. That's when Ashley had told him those very same words, thus starting their tradition.

She felt emotion choke her as she whispered back, "After a while crocodile." With concerned tears glistening in her eyes; she conveyed her worry for him without saying a word.

"We'll be careful, Ashley."

"I know. Take care of her, Cade," she replied.

Then with one last shared glance between them, he left Ashley to finish her packing. Making his way down the hall to the last room near the stairs, he carefully opened the door. He didn't want to wake Collett. So he eased into the room and sat on the bench at the end of the bed, and contented himself with watching her sleep.

She hadn't slept at all last night because of her concerns for everybody else. She had jumped right in by helping Jenny and Tracy pack, and making sure Nate made proper travel arrangements. She even attempted to talk Cynda into leaving as Rederrick suggested, but quickly learned about the wrath of Cynda Williams.

When it was all done, everyone went off to bed and the house was quiet. He had found her in the kitchen alone, staring out the window at something only she could see.

He begged her to get some sleep, but she insisted she couldn't close her eyes. With no more than a thought, he stayed up with her and kept her company all night. Collett hadn't really been much company. She remained withdrawn and pulled into herself. Much like she had been when they first met. Cody came into the kitchen twice while they were in there, and Collett barely noticed.

She stayed that same way throughout most of the day, and his worry over her fueled his frustration even more. Finally, that afternoon, Cynda had seen enough. She insisted Collett get some rest. Cynda took her from Cade's care and ushered her up here, tucking her into bed like a child. He was sure she likely used a bit of magic to get the job done.

Now, as he watched, Collett lay there underneath the plush comforter, curled into a tight protective ball. The room darkened as the sun dipped below the mountains, leaving a cloud-covered, night sky in its wake.

Almost as if it was an omen, the weather began to change. Dark gloomy clouds moved in with a cold, biting wind pushing them along. A nasty winter storm was on its way with an oppressive darkness coming right behind it.

Cade noticed, even in sleep, she was tense. Her lips were pressed into a tight, hard line and her brow was furrowed in concentration. Her soft, blonde hair fanned across the pillow, standing out in contrast to the white linen pillowcase.

Her breathing was the steady even breath of sleep, but her body was tense and rigid. Even her jaw was clenched tightly. He swore he could hear her grind her teeth against each other. He found himself wondering what she was dreaming about.

He moved closer to her and brushed his fingers lightly across her brow, pushing her hair away from her face. Her brow relaxed slightly at his warm touch. Tired and wanting to offer her comfort, as well as just be close to her, he moved around the bed and cautiously eased in next to her. He laid his arm over her and closed his eyes. *Just for a minute*, he told himself.

The next thing he knew, she jerked and whimpered. He opened his heavy eyelids and realized he had fallen asleep. Suddenly, he was jolted fully awake when he heard a painful scream coming from next to him. Instinctively, he tightened his grip around Collett, trying to pull her to him.

Still sleeping, she clawed at his arm, leaving angry red scratches across his skin, and kicked out with her blanket-tangled legs. She whined, "No, please no!"

Holding tight, he tried to wake her, "Collett, it's just a dream, wake up."

She started sobbing, "No." she cried again.

"Come on honey, come back to me. Wake up, it's okay...I'm here," he coaxed.

Eventually, her eyes fluttered open. She peered through the darkness, and looking at Cade's shadowed features as he leaned over her. She bolted up like a coiled spring; so quickly in fact, she almost smacked his head with hers.

Reaching over, she clicked on the lamp sitting on the bedside table. Her sad, confused eyes stared at him for a moment. Then, she threw herself into his arms.

Collett clung to him, holding him as tightly as she could. Her dream seemed so real. For a brief terrifying moment, she believed it was real, believed he had died. *It was a dream,* she thought. She closed her eyes trying to shut out the image, but it was still clear and real. She saw him crying out in horrible agony. She felt the burning pain rushing through him as he was held aloft in the sky by some strange force. Then he fell to the ground, and she couldn't get to him.

She held him fiercely for a long time, letting the silent tears leak from her tired eyes. He held her just as fiercely, whispering reassurance. Finally, she sniffled and pulled away.

He wiped a tear from her cheek, "Better?"

She shook her head negatively.

"What happened?" he questioned gently.

She looked back to the bedroom door, "I have to leave."

"You want to go downstairs?"

She shook her head again, "No. I have to leave this house. I can't stay here."

His expression changed. He narrowed his eyes, "I thought we were past this."

She jumped from the bed and bending down grabbed the suitcase from underneath. She plopped it right on top of the now tangled sheets and moved to the closet.

Cade leaped from the bed, quickly intercepting her to stand in her path. "What's going on?"

She tried to sidestep him, but he just altered his stance. "Cade, I have to leave. Please don't make this any harder," she insisted, but it was a weak reply.

"If you think I'm going to just stand by while you waltz out of the safety of this house, you're going to find yourself surprised and severely disappointed."

She turned her back to him and took a deep breath. If what she had seen last night and if her dream were possibilities, if she really could tell the future, she knew she had to go. It was either him or her. Her life or his; one of them would not live through this. Her decision was simple.

She tried a different tactic, "Cade, I can't do this. It was a nice dream, but you and I will never work. Your immortality does bother me, more than I care to admit. So let's just call it what it is. No harm, no foul." With her back to him, she closed her eyes and finished the lie, "I'm not even sure I did love you. I think I just got caught up in the moment. It's been a long time since I had a connection with someone. I took it too far is all." Her heart broke as she uttered each word.

Cade said nothing. He just stood there quietly.

She turned, and to her surprise, she saw he was completely unbothered by her statement.

"You'll have to do better than that load of crap," he said simply.

"What do you mean?" she asked.

He moved up right in front of her, "I know you love me. You can't lie worth a damn. Keep that in mind for the future, in case you ever try to play poker."

She tilted her head up and met his gaze, "I have to leave! I can't stay here," she pleaded quietly.

"Why?"

"I just have to."

"Fine, we'll go together. Tell me where, and we'll go. We'll leave tonight."

"Please Cade. Let me go."

"No, Collett. Tell me what's wrong. Can't you trust me to help you?"

"You can't help. You're the problem!" The tears began to slip free of her hold over them.

He tipped his head puzzled by her curious statement. "Say again?"

"If I stay, you'll die! I won't let you die. Please, Cade. Let me go!"

CHAPTER 28

The house was practically empty. He watched them leave one by one. He almost reconsidered his whole plan. The Hunter still wondered if it would be so simple. Truthfully, he wanted to try the direct approach and see what would happen. He itched for a good fight.

Almost right away, he noticed the bustle of activity that went on, the change in the atmosphere. He saw the men patrolling the grounds in regular patterns. They were tense and alert. Keeping his distance, he watched throughout that night, the next day, and still continued his vigilant scrutiny.

Something had changed. He didn't really care what it was, but he knew he could take advantage of it.

When night fell once again and the old man and his wife left with their younger daughter, he knew there would be no better opportunity. He swiftly went to his hidden supplies and got to work. He took caution when he spotted the young, lanky boy leaning against the tree not far away. He heard the kid on his phone and pricked his ears, picking up the muffled conversation. The Hunter couldn't help but be surprised at what he heard. *Idiots were born every day*, he thought. Not that it would matter in a few minutes anyway.

 He had laid the trap, learned all he needed to learn, and it was time to act.

He moved quickly, and after taking care of the minor hiccup, he hastily doused the dried winter brush with the gasoline then struck a match. He watched the tiny, blue-yellow flame spark to life. The small flame danced back and forth in the winter breeze. It was amazing to him that something so small could spread so fast; that it could cause so much havoc and pain.

His mind flashed back to another time when fire irrevocably changed his life. The recurring nightmarish image invaded his mind against his will. He could still smell the acrid scent of burning flesh to this day.

Roughly shaking off the horrifying childhood memory, and berating himself for even allowing it into his thoughts, he dropped the match, putting his long-awaited plan into motion. He sped away from the location of the now burning fire to take up his planned position. Now all he needed to do was wait and let the rabbits come out of their hole.

Stunned shock covered Cade's features, "What are you talking about?"

"I saw it in my dream. You died," she said desperately with emotion still fresh in her voice.

"It was only a dream. It's just your nerves."

"No! It was more than that. I saw him kill you!" She insisted.

His eyes sharpened, "Who?" he demanded.

Her brow pinched as she tried to explain, "That's just it. I know, but I don't know. I can't see him. His voice is so real, so familiar. I know his voice."

Locking gazes with her Cade lowered his voice, "Have you dreamed of his voice before?"

"Yes, a few times. Different dreams, but I've heard his voice before. 'You can't save them,' that's what he says." She waved it away with her hand. "It doesn't change the fact that I still have to get as far away from you as possible," she said stubbornly.

"Not going to happen." Cade responded, shaking his head, with confidence.

"And I'm not going to let you get yourself killed protecting me."

"I can handle myself just fine. So I guess that settles it, you'll continue to stay here and I'll agree not to do anything stupid."

"I don't think that settles anything," she protested.

"That's fine, you'll—" Cade abruptly stopped mid-sentence and sniffed the air. His eyes darkened, turning hard. He reached up to his ear and pressing the com, "Cody?"

After a moment, his brows drew together, "Cody!" he repeated with more force.

His warm, honey-golden eyes turned cold and flinty. Grabbing her hand, he pulled her to the door.

"Cade, what is it?" she asked concerned.

Instead of answering her, she heard him angrily mutter under his breath, "If you're not hurt or bleeding, you're going to be."

Chills crawled down Collett's spine. It was happening. Something was terribly wrong. She knew their time had run out.

He pulled her along with him downstairs, practically dragging her along behind him. His worry for Cody mounted. Several possible scenarios raced through his mind. Cody should have answered his call. He should have been patrolling the grounds. Where could he be? What happened to him?

He depressed the button on his com link again and shouted this time, "Cody!" He was hoping Cody fell asleep.

Nothing.

"Cody, you better answer me, boy!"

Still nothing.

When they finally entered the security room, he frantically searched each screen looking for any sign of Cody. After running through several different angles and views, Cade saw what he was looking for. The leaping flames jumped and danced across the screen. He knew he smelled smoke and now understood why. Out near the small creek, a fire raged and sparks flew. Even though the screens didn't give him audio, he could imagine the crackle and snapping sounds that would be coming from the wood and brush that currently lit up the night.

Behind him, seeing the image, Collett gasped. She brought up her hand, covering her lips in shock. The bright, orange-yellow flames stood out in direct contrast with the black of the night surrounding them.

Cade noticed the fire was right on the border of where the perimeter alarms had been set. Whoever lit the fire must have known that, which meant that person likely knew even more.

Dammit Cody, you better be okay, Cade thought to himself. Still even more troubling to him was the fact that the fire would eventually burn itself out. It wasn't a direct threat to them here. He understood this was a calling card.

His worry for Cody shifted into fear. Something was wrong. He couldn't leave Cody out there to die if someone captured him, but he didn't want to leave Collett here alone. There was no one else to stay with her and keep her safe.

Knowing he had no alternative, Cade made the only choice left to him. He would have to help Cody. He could not leave him to The Faction's killers. Turning quickly, he ordered, "Stay here, in this room, where it's safe, and call Rederrick! Tell him to get a move on!" Then he ran from the room.

Collett rushed to the phone as he hurried from the room leaving the vaulted door open in his hurry. She picked up the cordless phone and dialed the emergency number for Rederrick that had been drilled into her mind.

After two rings, she heard his voice on the other end of the line, "What is it?" his tone fully alert.

"There's a fire near the stream. Cade already left. You need to get here now. I think it's a trap," she answered.

"We're on our way. Find a safe place to hide. Go to the security room and lock the door. There is a gun in my desk drawer in the den. It's loaded already, so be careful. We will be there in... thirty seven minutes."

She felt her worry for Cade and the missing Cody increase. That was too much time. "I've got to go help him," she said, voicing her thoughts aloud.

"NO! Collett, listen to me. You need to stay where it's safe. Cade can handle himself. Cody should be on the grounds, he must have seen the fire—"

"Cody's missing! You need to hurry!" She cried.

Rederrick let out a curse, "Just get to a safe place. I'll have Cynda come and get you as soon as we arrive. Now GO!"

She didn't even answer. She'd hung up the phone already. Prying the drawer open, she quickly grabbed the gun Rederrick told her about, and with a nervous grip, she rushed from the room. She entered the foyer and hesitated.

She looked over her shoulder, back toward the den and the hidden security room she had come from, and then looked to the front door. It only took her a split second to decide. She would not leave Cade to face her demons and die. She would not let her fear cost her all that she found here. She would not let fear cost her the man she loved.

She rushed to the door and practically flew through the opening into the darkened night. She ran out intending to find Cade and help him, until she noticed he was running at full speed back in her direction, waving her back to the house. Relief flooded her.

When he approached her, he gripped her arm forcefully and dragged her back into the house. Powerful waves of anger rolled off of him, and a dark, flinty look glinted in his eyes. "What the hell do you think you're doing charging out there?" he snapped.

She stepped back away from him to distance herself from his anger. She felt how strong it was, and oddly, she could feel hate coming from him too. She had never felt his feelings so strongly. Not even when they first met in the woods.

It was hard for her to answer him, as his emotions clawed at her, confused her, but she finally managed to say, "I was coming to help you."

He looked down at the .22 she held in her hands and scoffed, "With that little thing?"

Why was he being so harsh? She wondered. She just wanted to help. "Where's Cody?" She questioned. He squinted at her slightly confused. "Cody, did you find Cody?"

Finally understanding it she spoke of the boy he just shook his head negatively.

Collett gasped. She prayed silently. No! Please let him be okay.

"Come on we have to go. It's not safe here." He gripped her arm again intending to pull her to the garage.

"No wait," she yelled. "What about Cynda and Rederrick? They are on the way here. We have to warn them!"

"Fine, get some keys, and meet me in the garage. I'll call them," he ordered.

She stared at him wondering what made him so angry. Knowing now was not the right time to ask, she nodded her head and went to do as directed.

She ran down to the door that led to the garage and yanked it open. Then, going over to the wall safe, she punched in the code Rederrick had given her. When it clicked, she reached in and grabbed the keys to the bullet-grey Hummer. By the time she had them in her hand, he had made his way out to her.

She passed the '68 Camaro and jumped into the passenger side of the Hummer next to it. He bent down and inspected the undercarriage. She heard a slight clunk. He climbed into the SUV. Collett handed the keys to him and asked forlornly, "Now what?"

He turned the keys and said with a cold voice, "Now we get to play a little game."

She felt chills run through her body. This was a side of him she'd never seen. She wasn't sure she liked it. Trying again, she asked, "I meant, where are we going?"

"I know of a little place in the mountains. We'll go there for a while. After that, who knows what will happen."

She looked across the console between them still wondering what could have happened to put so much anger in him. Whatever it was, Collett wasn't sure she wanted to know.

They drove for a long time. So long, in fact, she drifted in and out of sleep. She was too exhausted from the previous night's lack of sleep to keep her heavy lids open in the warm comfort of the Hummer. When they arrived at a rutted dirt road, the vehicle's jarring back and forth woke her up. She looked to him, "Where are we?"

He looked to her and smiled coldly. "We're headed to a small cabin in the mountains that I know about."

"Whose place is it?" she inquired.

He gave her a glare, "Just someone I know. Does it matter?"

Collett was baffled at his strange disconnection from her and the anger she still felt.

She was feeling pretty angry herself. His emotions were affecting her in a way she never felt before. His attitude was so out of character. Collett snapped back dryly, "No, I guess it really doesn't. Will we be safe there?"

He said nothing, didn't even look at her, and she assumed he wasn't sure.

Neither one of them spoke for the rest of the drive down the bumpy, snow covered road. When they finally arrived at a log cabin at the end of the path, he pulled the SUV to a stop and turned off the engine.

"Get out," he said shortly.

Collett watched as he opened his door, got out and slammed it shut. The hard slam of his door made her jump in her seat. He walked through the snow and bounded up the two stairs, landing on the covered porch. Then he looked back pointedly to her still sitting inside the Hummer.

Huffing out a breath, she decided she would find a way to figure out whatever it was. Maybe he knew something. Maybe he figured out who she was, and it wasn't a good thing. With another deep breath she resolved that whatever it was, she would have to deal with it.

Her decision made, she exited the SUV and crunched her way through the snow to the front door where he now stood waiting. When she finally reached the threshold she looked carefully at him, trying to understand what bothered him.

His eyes that were usually warm and comforting, now looked cold and callous. Gazing into his fierce gold orbs, she felt afraid. Fear was something she had only felt once around him. *What is happening here,* Collett thought to herself.

He spat out, "Anytime now."

His voice was so harsh. She stood there staring at him, shocked by his tone. He just grabbed her arm forcefully and pushed her inside. She almost stumbled and fell because of the aggressive maneuvering.

She whipped around and faced him. Enough was enough, "Just what is your problem? You have been rude and mean since you came back from the fire," she snapped.

He inclined his head in the way she usually found endearing. Right now though, it was intimidating. "My problem, honey, is you. For the moment anyway."

The way the words rolled off his tongue and the deep tone of his voice made her nervous enough to take a cautious step away from him. It wasn't just his eyes that were different, his voice was odd too. It was darker, deeper. She pleaded, "Cade, tell me what's wrong with you. What made you so angry? Let me help you!"

He took a step closer to her, "You really want to help me?"

She nervously stepped back again. Her reply came out barely above a whisper, "Yes."

Another step forward, "Are you sure?" he asked while raking her body with his intense gaze.

She couldn't even get the word out this time. She could only nod under his scrutiny. She once again tried to take a couple steps back. She ran out of room. The back of her heel bumped up against the wall.

He braced his hands against the wall on either side of her, effectively blocking her in.

There was nowhere to go, no room for escape. She thought. She tried to hold his gaze, but couldn't stand the cold rage in them.

For a brief moment, she thought his face looked different somehow, but she pushed the errant thought away. The fury in his eyes, was making him different, she reasoned. When she tipped her head down to escape the intense power of those eyes, he put a hand under her chin and forced her to face him; forced her to really look. When she did, Collett gasped as it dawned on her.

Then grinning, he roughly crushed his lips to hers.

The kiss was fierce and unfeeling. He plundered and took. Collett pushed hard at his chest, trying to pull away. He just ignored her efforts and continued to move his lips forcefully against hers. His hands gripped her hips painfully as he pushed her violently into the wall with his hard body.

She felt panic setting in. She increased her efforts to get away from this man. She pushed again forcefully and began hitting at him. He only tightened his grip, as his solid frame simply absorbed her meager blows.

Something flashed in her mind, but was buried in his anger and her own panic.

With desperation clawing through her, she collected her wits and did the next thing that came to her mind. As his lips moved forcefully against hers, she parted her lips, as if in invitation, then when he shifted his bruising assault, she bit down hard on his bottom lip.

She tasted the salty tang of his blood and heard his low, throaty growl. She released his lip and looked up into his now crimson, glowing eyes.

He cursed foully and pulled away from her, pressing the back of his hand to his bleeding mouth. The brief respite was all she required to duck under his arm and around him. She didn't run, though. She could only stand there and look at the stranger's back.

A stranger, who wore Cade's face.

CHAPTER 29

When Cade came back to consciousness, he was lying in the cold, wet snow. He found it difficult to focus. His vision blurred and wavered. He moved a hand to where he felt like the throbbing originated and felt the wet stickiness of blood on his scalp. The sweet copper aroma confirmed what he already knew. He had smelled it before, many times. He tried to think about what happened.

Then, as a slight clarity came to his foggy brain, the blood in his veins turned cold. *Collett!* He had to get to Collett!

He wondered to himself how long he'd been unconscious. Rolling over, he tried to get up. His stomach pitched and his head swam from the effort. He pushed past it and stood. He fell back to his knees immediately. His head spun, but he didn't care. All that mattered to him was Collett. He had to get to her! He stumbled and staggered like a career drunk, picking his way back to the house. It took him three times as long as it should have.

As he made his way across the grounds, several scents assaulted him. The smell of burning brush and pine, much like that of a campfire. He could also smell the sickly-sweet aroma of his own blood. Lastly, Cade could still smell his assailant, even though he was no longer close by. His animal instincts would never forget that familiar scent.

When he finally reached the door, he leaned against it, taking a moment for balance. Opening the door, he staggered inside and fell to his knees.

"Collett!" he croaked as loudly as he could. Pain lanced through his throbbing head as he bellowed her name.

She didn't come running into the room as he'd hoped, but Cynda did. The shock on her face told him he must look pretty bad. She ran over to help him asking, "Cade, what happened? Rederrick!" she called.

Her piercing shout almost made his head explode. He looked up at her eyes, "Collett. Where is Collett?"

Cynda's expression told Cade all he needed to know, "Cade, she was with you. You left a note,"

Cade felt the nauseating blackness creeping in again, but he fought it back. "I didn't leave a note. She was here, in the house, waiting for me."

He must have lost consciousness for a minute because when he came to again Rederrick was there, bending down over him. He helped him back to his feet. Rederrick threw his arm over his shoulders and gripped him around the waist. "Come on Cade, stay with me," he encouraged.

"Where is Collett?" he asked with panic tearing through him, even as he leaned heavily against his friend.

Rederrick answered gruffly, "Don't you worry. We'll find her, Cade. Right now, let's take care of you."

"No! There's no time! We have to find her. He'll kill her! We have to stop him."

Rederrick sat him on the couch in the parlor, and inspected his head wound. It stopped bleeding, but the wound was vicious.

"Whatever hit you must have cracked your skull. This is pretty bad. Did you see who attacked you?"

He closed his eyes, both to stop his head from spinning and to fight for control over his growing terror. Then he spat with venom in his voice, "Jarrett. It was Jarrett."

Cynda came into the room with some water and healing ointment for him. When she heard his words, the glass of water fell from her hand in shock. Her expression filled with worry, "Are you sure? He wouldn't do that. You have to be mistaken! I know you two don't see eye to eye, but he wouldn't kill her. Would he?"

He started to shake his head, but the pain made him rethink the movement. "I don't know what he will or won't do, but I am not willing to leave her life in Jarrett's hands. I'll kill him if he hurts her." As he spoke, his eyes burned blood-red, leaving no room for doubt that he would carry out the promise.

This was Cade's demon; the shadow from his past. He remembered meeting Jarrett for the first time in 1862, but that was not when their relationship began. As unconsciousness clawed at him again, so did the age-old memory.

"A blood-thirsty werewolf I tell ya."

Several soldiers hooted and laughed at the outrageous proclamation.

Cade heard these words from a distance. He didn't laugh. He decided he better investigate. If people were starting to guess his nature, it was time for him to leave. As he cautiously approached the campfire, he heard, "You're nuts John, ain't no such thing."

"Believe what ya want. I saw it with my own eyes." John snapped. "Appeared out of nowhere, it did. He tore the man to shreds. Was the worst thing I ever seen."

The other man hooted, saying sarcastically, *"Why is it you're still here, then? If it was a werewolf you should be all torn up lying with them. You're big enough to make a good meal, I'd wager."*

John answered emphatically, *"I'm telling ya what I seen. Ain't nobody gonna tell me different! It looked at me with its gold eyes and took off. Just like that, gone, and heaven knows I wasn't gonna question why. I was just happy to still be breathing."*

Cade stepped into the light of the fire, *"Where?"*

All the men around the fire looked up at him, surprised by his presence. No one had heard him coming. They all started to stand until he waved them back, *"As you were."*

Cade knew the man telling the story was John Furwood. He looked up at Cade, grateful someone would listen to him. *"I saw him down by the river when we ran into those Johnny Rebs."*

"What did it look like, corporal?" he demanded. It wasn't so much the idea of another werewolf around that bothered him. It was the open way it handled itself that worried him. Werewolves needed to be very careful to avoid exposure. He had seen what panicked mobs could do. A person was smart; people were stupid. He needed to find out this werewolf's intentions.

"Well, I didn't see too much," John explained, *"But I could tell it was all black and stood on two legs. Had the strangest gold eyes, reminded me of something."* He screwed up his face thinking about it, *"When it looked at me, I swore I was a dead man standin'."*

He was never more grateful for the dim light. He knew it would be hard for them to see his eyes at this angle. All the same though, he didn't want to chance it. *"Well I'll check into it, but I am sure you were mistaken. Sometimes the terror of battle has us imagining things,"* he said with authority, and walked away.

The other men at the campfire covered their snickering laughs. There was only one man there that night that believed John's every word. That man was Cade.

He spent weeks looking for the other werewolf, seeking any clue he could find. He finally found it one day when his regimen came to *a clearing with broken, torn bodies lying on the wet earth. It had rained the night before. The bodies of the Confederate soldiers were torn and shredded. The wounds came from no sword. Men blamed the carnage on some sort of great bear or a pack of rabid wolves.*

He knew what had caused their deaths. He had seen these sweeping marks before, had caused similar wounds himself. It hadn't been a pack of wolves, just one. He knew he was out of time. He knew he must find the werewolf behind this and soon.

That night, he snuck away from camp and went looking for him. He tracked him from the site where they had seen the dead rebels. It took almost the whole night to find him. He finally found him sitting on a large rock all by himself, without a fire. Not that creatures like them needed one.

The man on the rock kept his back turned to him, but Cade could smell the scent of the wild beast within him. It was a scent he would never forget. Even though the other werewolf was in the form of a man, He knew this was the werewolf he was seeking.

The man spoke with a deep voice, "I knew you would come eventually."

Surprised Cade asked, "You did?"

"Yes, I have been waiting a long time to meet you," he replied.

He was not sure what to say so he kept silent.

The man on the rock stood. With his keen eyesight, he could see the man was about his same height, same build. Though he looked a slightly leaner, his muscles were toned. His hair was long and dark. Even with his back turned to him, he knew if this came to blows, it would not be an easy fight to win. Then the man turned to face Cade, "Yes. I have been waiting a long time to meet you, brother."

Cade would never forget that stunned feeling, when he saw his own face staring back at him. That was the day he learned he was not alone. He had always known that others like him existed. He'd even met two of them, but this…this was entirely different. This was his brother, a brother of his blood, his twin.

Collett stood her ground as worry for Cade consumed her. Where was he? Was he hurt? Had Rederrick and Cynda found him yet? As these thoughts raced frantically through her mind, his doppelganger turned around.

His expression was cruel and calculating. The anger she felt earlier was now unbearable. It invaded her on a personal level. She wondered how it was possible he survive with such a powerful force of rage coursing through him? Now that she knew he wasn't Cade, she took a closer look at the man before her.

His body was slightly leaner than Cade's, and he didn't have the small scar on his jaw as Cade did. How could she have possibly missed these differences? Even now, as she reflected on it, she realized this man's voice was deeper, darker.

He pulled his hand away from his bleeding lip and examined the blood. When he spoke, she startled slightly from the sound of his gruff, angry voice, "Nice trick. Did Cade teach you that?"

She just glared at him unwilling to give this man anything, "Who are you?" She demanded.

"Me? Well, I'm not really sure that matters considering you'll be dead soon enough."

She looked at him carefully, feeling his emotions as she did. She couldn't feel the evil, or malice. She couldn't feel a trace of the cruelty he displayed in his eyes. His anger dominated him. She concentrated and reached out looking deeper, as she had been practicing. Then she felt it. Buried underneath his anger and hate was apprehension.

She tried again, "I need to know; Who are you?"

He chose not to answer her question and instead asked one of his own, "I wonder, since you're banging Cade, let's you and me go a round? It's not as if you'd have to imagine him. I know I could do much better."

His crude remark put her on edge even more, until she noticed the mean, angry smile and the conflicting sad, lost look in his eyes. He was trying to get a rise out of her, trying to provoke her. She could sense it now. He wanted her to attack him, or accept his offer, either would help. He wanted, no, he needed her to make this easier on him. He needed a reason.

She knew then she might be able to find a way out of this. Deep down, even though he was deadly to be sure, he did not want to kill her. That was the apprehension she could feel. She had little doubt now. It was the only reason she wasn't already dead.

Praying she was right, Collett bravely decided to call his bluff, "I won't give you what you want."

He grinned mockingly. She understood, this man had not given anyone a sincere smile in years, his anger went far too deep. "And just what exactly is it I want, Sweetheart?" he asked amused.

Defiantly, she straightened her body trying to gain height, and courage. Reminding herself of Cynda's words, she whispered, "There is no courage without fear." She needed to hold on to the little bit of courage she had.

"Ha!" he laughed cruelly, his keen ears hearing her every word. Narrowing his eyes, he said with venom lacing every word. "Did my brother teach you that too? Honey, there is no such thing as courage. There's only power and desperation."

She was shocked. One word echoed throughout her mind. Brother! He wasn't just posing with magic. He was actually Cade's brother. She had suspected maybe, but hearing the word was still a lot. This man was Cade's brother. So many things tumbled into place at once, clicking and connecting the bigger picture. The man standing before her, this man who was so full of dark anger, was Cade's demon, his fear; his twin.

On top of that, she quickly realized, this man had his own demons. She was not referring to the wolf that must reside in him either. The anger in him was a clawing, vicious monster all by itself.

"Why are you doing this?" she pleaded tentatively.

He gazed at her and tilted his head. It was odd, she had seen Cade do the very same thing so many times before, "This honey, is what I do." His words she thought, she'd heard Cade use those words.

He moved toward her deliberately. She refused to back away. All too soon, he stood before her again, no more than an inch between them. She gazed up, looking into his cold eyes, knowing it was now or never. Hoping she was reading him correctly, she ordered obstinately, "Then do it."

He stopped, "What?"

"You heard me. If you intend to kill me, do it. Get it over with. It is after all, *what you do*," she said with conviction she didn't feel.

He stared at her for a moment then asked, "That's it then? You're ready to die, just like that."

"Just like that," she said indignantly. "Whoever sent you here, paid you I assume. There has been talk of a bounty and all. You best get on with it. Time is money, or so I hear." She trembled inside, but still holding her courage she asked simply, "I am curious though, how much does a soul go for these days?"

His eyes flared again that same ominous, eerie red she had seen on Cade before. He grabbed ahold of her tightly with both hands, lifting her from her feet and bringing her to his eye level. Losing her newfound courage, Collett paled, wondering if she had pushed too hard too soon. She wondered if she had given him motive to kill her after all.

He growled deep and low as if on the verge of change, then snarled in a raspy, demon-like voice, "You know nothing about me, or my soul! You could never understand what drives me. You're right though, I am here to do a job. I'm just not doing it for the reasons that you think."

As he spoke, she felt it. A tiny feeling in him, buried so deep he didn't even know it was there. His anger was too strong and too consuming. She realized the rage within him stemmed from emotional pain. He was hurting and wasn't even aware of it anymore. He let his anger cover it up like a shield protecting him from the pain. His physical contact with her amplified his emotions and made it easier to find.

She closed her eyes, and quickly, desperately reached for the part of him still holding on to the pain, pulling it forward. She searched for the cause.

Suddenly, images she was unprepared for quickly raced through her mind. It was like a speeding slideshow clicking before her eyes. They swept in, assaulting her, letting her see and feel so much, letting her understand.

There were so many though, and she lost control of it. It was hard to grab onto any of it for very long. The overwhelming bombardment continued for several minutes, but the final images replayed in slow motion, and were so unexpected and astonishing. Collett lost the last of her strength and concentration. She was harshly jolted back to reality.

Cade's twin dropped her so suddenly she fell hard to her knees, painfully bruising them. Her legs would not have supported her anyway. She was unprepared to deal with the side effects of pulling the memories and the emotions attached to them free. Her body's strength ebbed. Collett's mind was weakened. Her eyes felt so heavy.

She tried sorting through the painful things she saw, looking for the last one again to make sense of it. When she recalled it, a shocking realization struck her.

With wide, astonished eyes, she looked up meeting his gaze. She knew his name. *Jarrett.* She watched as he stepped back away from her, putting a good three feet of distance between them. His horrified expression was full of pain from the memories she invoked. His anger was now mixed with sorrow, and all of it pulled tightly against her chest.

"What did you do? You have no right!" Jarrett spat venomously at her, putting a hand to his head. She had brought forth memories he fought furiously to forget, and she forced him to see the painful history that was his life. She forced him to remember the events that made him a monster.

She didn't answer him. She couldn't. She was so drained and weak from the effort and the concentration it had taken to reach into him. She didn't even mean to do it to that extent, and was sure if he hadn't pulled away, she wouldn't have been able to stop the torrent of memories. It was too much and she had no control over what happened. She was as shocked and surprised as he was.

"You stupid witch!" he seethed, "You think bringing up the past will help you? You just succeeded in making my job much easier!" He bent down and pulled her up roughly by her arm, jerking her to her feet.

"It wasn't your fault, Jarrett," she croaked weakly.

He glared at her and asked, "What do you know?"

With a weak quiet voice, she answered his loaded question even though she understood it may cost her life to do so, "I know she made a very difficult choice, a choice that affected you for the rest of your life. I know you're still angry with her. After such a long time; you're still so angry with her. You still want to see her dead, want her to suffer, even though so much time has passed, you still hate her," she finished carefully.

He shook her. "She could have saved her! Should have saved her and left me. Rowena burned instead of me! She saved me when it was my fault. Why didn't she save her? If you think you know so much, then answer that! Tell me why! Why HER?" his pain turned to rage as he yelled. His face was right there, a breath away from hers.

He punched out with his closed fist right by her head, hitting the solid wood door behind her with a loud thump. Collett flinched at the quick violent movement. His knuckles split open and bled. His powerful strength caused the door to slam open, hit the outside wall, and then come back again. Only the door didn't close. The screws in the top hinge ripped free of the door frame, causing the door to lean open at an odd angle. The cold wind blew in, chilling her, and she shivered.

She looked at him with her weak, glazed over, tear-filled eyes, and confessed weakly, "I am so sorry... I couldn't. I wanted to—" As Collett made the startling confession the tears slipped down her colorless cheeks.

She was weak, but somehow she projected the weight of the overwhelming remorse she felt for the little boy and the mother he lost.

She couldn't remember why she had been there, why she couldn't save Rowena, but she could feel the pressing guilt and sadness from that day. It was horrifying to realize that she was the source of his hate. With the last of her wavering strength, she projected her regret and sorrow into him. The effort caused a buzzing in her head, and dots formed in her vision.

For the third time that night, Jarrett released his grip on Collett. This time he did so carefully and slowly. She was lucky enough to find her feet. She leaned against the doorframe for support. Her body felt heavy, drugged. Her legs felt like jelly. Through sheer strength of will she kept her eyes locked with his.

Stunned shock covered his handsome features. Pain lanced sharply through his heart and recognition was in his tawny eyes.

Years ago he swore he would know this woman if he ever saw her again. Jarrett swore he would never forget the mystery woman who saved him when he was a boy. Then, when he never found her, he figured her long dead. He had been unable to enact his revenge. Now somehow, here she was, standing there before him. She was the same woman who had saved his life as a boy, the same woman who had allowed Rowena to die. She looked at him now with sad, blue eyes, filled with tears. They were tears for him and the boy he had been.

He stammered out the words while pacing, "It was you! How can that be? No. It isn't possible. I would have known; would have remembered." He turned to her and his eyes pinched as he looked at her more carefully. "*It was you.*"

She tried hard to remain focused on him. She wanted to help him through the shocking revelation they were both suffering from. She wanted so badly to remember more, remember why, explain herself, but her vision was darkening. Instead, all she could do was mumble, "Forgive me," as the blackness closed in around her. She could no longer keep herself upright. Her eyes rolled back, fluttering closed, and her legs gave out as she ultimately lost the battle for consciousness.

Pure reflexes had Jarrett rushing to catch her before she crumpled to the ground. As she lay there cold, weak and helpless before him, he thought of all the times he had cursed the woman who had saved his life when he had been a twelve-year-old boy. He thought of all the times he swore he would kill her if he ever laid eyes on her again.

Here she is, he thought. Trying to shake away the horrible feelings of guilt and sadness she somehow put in him, he gazed at her soft, pale beauty and tried to hate her as he had long ago.

He couldn't erase it though, and he couldn't forget the sad, painful regret that entered her pretty, crystal eyes as she apologized, confessing who she was in the process. Now here he sat knowing this was his chance to fulfill every promise he ever made. The only problem was, now he found he wanted answers more.

Cade woke with a start. He jolted up quickly, causing the room to spin a little. Trying to orient himself, he put the heel of his hand to his aching forehead.

"Careful there, that's some hit you took. I wouldn't be surprised if it cracked through your thick skull," Nate cautioned.

Cade lifted his head and glared at him, "Stuff it, Nate. Where's Rederrick?"

"Upstairs with Cynda. She's scrying for Collett. Jarrett took the Hummer and made sure we couldn't track it."

Cade opened his eyes again and looked at him, "Cody?"

Nate shook his head solemnly, "No sign of him."

"What are you doing here then? Go find him!" He growled.

"I was put in charge of babysitting you. You know, to keep you from doing anything stupid." Nate retorted.

Cade stood, "Let me know how that goes for you. I'm going to get her back before Jarrett kills her."

"We both know how he operates. If he was going to kill her, he would have already. Something doesn't fit here. If you could just look past your anger for one second you'd see. . ."

"Why you—" despite his throbbing head, he rushed Nate, grabbed his shirt and slammed him against the wall. "I won't take that chance with her life," he growled. "I will not give him that chance. Do you hear me? I will not lose her!"

Unbothered by Cade's emotional response, Nate arched a single brow, "Let's say you find her without help. Then what? Are you going to kill him, your own brother?"

"He stopped being my brother a long time ago," he said with a cold bite in his voice.

"That's funny coming from you. Aren't you the same man who stopped me from taking him out three years ago? As I recall I had a clean shot with a silver bullet. You won't do it, Cade and we both know it," he replied calmly.

His eyes glowed red as the beast rose within him, clawing for release. Every nerve in him tensed for battle, for blood. "If he's hurt Collett in any way, I will have no problem tearing him to pieces," he snarled.

"And if he hasn't? What then?" he questioned.

Tempering the monster inside, he let go of Nate and stepped back. He didn't have the answer to that question. The truth was he didn't know. He roughly pulled his fingers through his black hair.

Cynda burst into the den pointing at her map, both men swung their gazes her direction.

"I found her! She's not too far from here. About three hours away. It looks like he's at your cabin."

Seeing the look in Cade's eyes, as the crimson color returned, Nate knew they were about to find out the answer to his question. Could Cade kill his brother?

A curse made its way past Cade's clenched teeth. The dark werewolf of children's nightmares burst forth with a sudden ferocity, right there in front of everyone. Clothes tore free. Bones cracked and hair covered his body. Because of his fear for Collett he let his rage fully consume him for the first time in over a century. He burst from the room and ran out of the house, tearing the front door from its hinges as he did. Anyone who was within miles heard the loud, mournful howl that echoed eerily through the darkness.

Rederrick grabbed Cynda's arm, pulling her down the hall and said, "Let's go. We better pray we get there first or there will be a lot of blood spilled tonight."

CHAPTER 30

He ran the entire distance at full speed, pushing his supernatural speed and stamina to the absolute limit. He cut through the mountains on a straight path, arriving long before Rederrick, Cynda, and Nate. He prayed the whole time that he would get there before it was too late. As he ran through the darkness the storm that had been brewing, let loose. The snow didn't drift down lazily. It angrily cut through the sky on a biting windy slant. The fierce storm matched his raging mood.

When he finally arrived at his secluded cabin home, still in his strong and powerful hybrid form, he burst through the leaning doorway, not even bothering to note the previously damaged hinges.

He stood in the entrance looking like a monster with his ribs moving in and out as his hot breaths puffed a small cloud from his mouth. The storm behind him continued to rage, while the storm within him grew even more furious. Raking his keen eyes across the dim room, and seeing no sign of Collett, he crashed down the unlit hallway, her perfect scent leading the way to the back bedroom.

He had no care to be stealthy or quiet. The red haze of his fury would not allow it of him. With every passing second his anger became more intense, his fear more pressing.

When he blasted his way through the flimsy bedroom door, he saw Collett's still form laying on the bed. Her face was as pale as porcelain. His heart stopped in his chest. Horrible pain lanced through him. Suddenly, he could barely draw breath. He was too late! He let out another long, chilling howl, this one full of pain and anguish.

In cruel response, a dark unfeeling voice came from the corner near the tall window.

"You're a little slow these days."

Cade whipped his fierce, wolf-like head around. Seeing the very cause of all his rage, all his pain, standing right there, his animal lips vibrated with a low warning growl.

A warning they both knew Jarrett would not heed. He stood there with his arms folded across his chest, his stance wide, poised, ready. Cade's eyes lit up like smoldering metal, his fury mounted. All rational thought fled. He let loose a feral and chilling snarl and then charged.

Cade snarled, Jarrett forced his body to change into one that would equal his in battle. His clothing ripped away from his skin as midnight black fur replaced them. The monster he hated burst free of its human prison. The only thing left on Jarrett's dark and imposing form was a gold and green amulet. It hung on a long, gold chain around his massive neck. He met Cade's charge head on by planting his large paws firmly and leaning directly into it.

Their bodies slammed into one another with an audible and sickening impact. Cade's extra momentum and hazy rage temporarily gave him the advantage. They smashed into the window behind Jarrett. Wood splintered and cracked. The window shattered from the force, and the glass showered them both, making superficial nicks and cuts. They tumbled through the impromptu opening, crashing to the hard and frozen ground with rattling force.

Jarrett lay beneath Cade, a threatening growl rumbling past his canine lips. Jarrett's long, sharp, teeth were poised to tear into flesh.

Cade didn't give him a chance. Gathering his clawed fist, he rammed it into Jarrett's face, letting his fury lend him strength. He heard bone crunch, both in his hand and from Jarrett's muzzle. Skin and fur tore, blood spilled, staining the snow-covered ground with crimson rivulets. He pulled back his fist for another satisfying blow when Jarrett slammed one home into Cade's ribcage with breath-stealing impact. His ribs cracked from the force.

Cade grunted through the pain, landing two more ferocious, heavy punches of his own, while the sky punished them both with its wet, stinging assault.

They grappled. Jarrett rolled his body, keeping a firm grip on Cade as he did so, reversing their positions. "Do you really want to do this with me?" he growled out inhumanly.

In reply, Cade dug his sharp claws deep into Jarrett's thick muscled arms. He pulled Jarrett closer, in a direct challenge, snarling and baring his fearsome teeth.

With an uncaring shrug, Jarrett then moved to bury his fist into Cade's face. Cade's quick thinking helped him avoid the damaging blow. He bucked his hips and flipped Jarrett up and over him with his lower body. He continued the flow of the move to jump to his feet.

Jarrett easily rolled with his own momentum and sprang gracefully upright, with the quick reflexes of his deadly heritage. For a moment neither moved. While they stared each other down, Cade growled out, "I loved her."

"Your mistake," Jarrett rasped cruelly. He didn't even bother to correct Cade's reference to the past tense regarding Collett.

Cade charged again, his red, hazy rage coming back in full. He threw the whole force of his body into Jarrett's midsection, grabbing his arm and flinging Jarrett's heavy body into the base of a medium-sized pine tree. A loud popping crack echoed throughout the woods.

Jarrett felt the horrific pain radiate up and down his spine. Something was definitely broken. Cade's brutality surprised him. He quickly gained his feet, ignoring the pain and took a step forward. Just as he did, a splitting crack rent the air as the pine tree snapped jaggedly and fell to the ground, barely missing Jarrett.

He looked back at Cade, impressed by his brother's viciousness. Jarrett wiped at the blood dripping from his maw and smiled as only a monster could. He bared his sharp teeth and growled with satisfaction. He'd been waiting a very long time for this fight; more than a hundred years.

Jarrett rolled his shoulders and let his anger come back in full force. It infused his body, pouring over him like a warm blanket. Anger remained his only companion all these years. Why let go of it now?

His natural instincts flooded back. His thoughts went into the dark place in his mind that had become The Hunter so long ago.

Normally, Jarrett was a fiercer fighter, a fact he had proven twice before. Though, it looked like Cade learned something new since the last time they fought.

Pleased, Jarrett advanced. He reveled in the challenge before him.

Not willing to give Cade the satisfaction of knowing the pain he had inflicted, Jarrett sneered, "If that's all you've got, she didn't stand a chance."

Cade tipped his head smugly, he knew from experience a slam like that hurt. "You want some more then? Your mistake." he taunted, repeating Jarrett's callous words from before. Then he rushed forward furiously, intending to finish this here, now!

He had to pay, Cade thought, but somewhere in the back of his mind, he heard a soft, ghostly voice that sounded familiar. He lost the concentration on his fury for a split second.

That second was all his experienced opponent needed. Jarrett jumped up high and slammed his black, fur-covered head into Cade's with staggering force. The sound of the skulls cracking echoed in the night. Cade stumbled back, struggling to keep his balance.

He refused to go down, refused to let Jarrett walk away this time. He would never again give Jarrett the chance to keep killing. A flash of Collett's lifeless body lying on the bed inside the cabin renewed his wrath, clearing his head of its fog. Cade snapped his angry gold eyes back to the matching ones across from him. Jarrett glared back with a cold emptiness.

Cade and Jarrett growled at each other, baring fang and claw alike. They were now ruled by the law of the jungle in its most primitive form; kill or be killed!

Cade thought he heard Collett's singsong voice in his mind once more. It was so quiet and ghostly sounding when mixed with the ringing in his ears. The combination of two hard blows to his head in one day was making him crazy. He channeled the sound of her perfect voice back into anger. He let it feed his fury.

Jarrett rasped out through his blood-covered muzzle, "You're still weak, Cade."

"I'm strong enough to kill you," Cade growled back.

Jarrett let go of a bitter, gravelly laugh, "You wouldn't be the first to try. By all means give it your best shot," he beckoned.

They rushed at each other once again, tearing and biting. Skin was ripped open and blood spilled. Wounds began to seal themselves, only to be torn open again. The heavy grappling melee moved them deeper into the woods, tearing up the ground as they went. For a time it seemed the combatants were evenly matched.

Then the tempo of this deadly dance began to increase. The vicious and draining battle slowly began to favor Jarrett. Cade had never tried to match his cruel methods and savage skill. Jarrett built his life on those skills. It was all he had; all he was.

Finally, Jarrett effectively gained the upper hand. He whipped Cade around, smashing him against a boulder with crushing impact. The sound of the bones cracking pierced Jarrett's conscience. He watched as Cade bent forward, hacking up blood through his canine jaw. Guilt assaulted Jarrett, a rare and foreign feeling to him. This is not what he wanted. This was not why he came.

He quickly pushed it all back, refusing to feel. Feelings only made you weak. It gave your opponent the advantage. The cold seeped in, reminding Jarrett it was better to be cold and in control, than weak. Cade's weakness for this woman clouded his mind with fury. He hadn't even bothered to notice that Collett still breathed.

Disgusted with his own weakness and thinking he'd bested Cade once again, Jarrett turned his back on his brother one more time.

Only this time, he didn't count on the intensity of Cade's feelings. He didn't count on the painful fury tearing through his brother's heart with an unrelenting hate filling the void. In this battle, Cade refused to be the weaker man. His wrath was a living, breathing thing, aiding him in his need for revenge.

Cade pushed away from the boulder and leaped forward. He was not finished! Not by a long shot.

He knocked Jarrett to the ground with the full weight of his body and an elbow to the back of his head. They rolled. Pain sliced through Cade from the effort. The copper tang of blood filled his mouth and his breath was a rattling gasp, indicating one of his broken ribs had pushed through his lung. The regenerative powers of his body were trying to knit the wound together as quickly as it could, which was often just as painful as the injury.

It didn't matter though. Nothing but revenge mattered. Not the sharp pain, not the small voice in his head that said this was wrong. Nothing! Right then, the will of the beast was stronger than the man.

Cade tightly wrapped his long, animal-like hands around Jarrett's throat, squeezing with all the strength he possessed. Jarrett gripped one hand and wrenched it back slightly, but Cade obstinately refused to lose. He stiffened his arm, using his unnatural strength. His muscles bulged as he overpowered Jarrett and redirected his grip. Cade numbed his body to the pain as Jarrett kicked and clawed savagely at him. He would not relent!

Jarrett's vision began to blur. His lungs burned for oxygen. He stared into Cade's hate-filled eyes, knowing now, how horrific he must have looked to all the bounties he had killed in the past.

It didn't matter though. His only true regrets in life had been not saving Rowena, and now putting this cold, empty look into Cade's eyes. Even though it was too late, Jarrett realized that it bothered him to see real and genuine hate in Cade. For so many years, he tried to convince Cade to be more like him, and now after more than a century Jarrett was finally getting what he wanted.

Blackness began to creep in around Jarrett. He no longer fought back. He no longer wanted to fight back. He accepted this fate, almost welcomed it.

The storm had stopped at some point. He wasn't even sure when it happened. As the soft light of the new morning crept over the shadows of the white-capped Rocky Mountains, Jarrett suddenly realized something. In that moment, he knew he had always counted on Cade to be the better man between them. He counted on Cade to have the stronger will and act with honor. It was the only constant in his long, miserable life.

Jarrett's body began to feel light as unconsciousness started taking over. Somehow he had always known it would come to this. It would take someone as strong as Cade to end that misery.

The only thing that saved Jarrett as he lay there on the cold, blood-covered ground, was a slender, gentle hand laid down on Cade's arm.

"Cade. Stop."

Cade heard Collett's firm tone and looked up surprised. He felt warmth pour into him. His deadly grip eased slightly, but he didn't let go. Wouldn't let go! He couldn't believe she was real. Jarrett gasped deeply beneath him, using the reprieve to pull in the much needed oxygen.

"He killed you," Cade croaked.

Sensing his emotions, Collett gently replied, "No, he didn't, I'm here. I'm real."

He shook his head, tightening his grip determinedly once again, "I can't let him live. He'll come back. He'll kill you."

A sad expression dominated Collett's features. She shook her head gently, "Not for me, Cade. Please, don't kill him for me. This is not you. This is not the man I love."

Looking into her pleading blue eyes, Cade couldn't hold onto his fury. He let go, staggering to his feet. He stared at her, still wondering if she was real, almost afraid to touch the illusion, for fear it would disappear. She was certainly pale enough to be a ghost, and she seemed different to him, more radiant, angelic. He twisted his large monster-like head back to the house where Collett once laid. Confused, he snapped his head back to where she stood between Jarrett's prone form and himself.

Jarrett coughed and wheezed through his crushed larynx as oxygen came back to him. Each breath squeezed painfully into his deprived lungs. His vision began to clear, and he began to ease his way up. Collett bent down and tried to help him.

Cade jumped forward and yanked her away from him.

To his own surprise, Jarrett, leaped up ready to defend her, effectively putting Collett between two growling and towering titans. Eyes glowed. Teeth were bared, and canine lips vibrated with audible snarls. It was like two rabid dogs fighting for a bone.

Collett threw her arms up, a hand on each of their chests to stop their advance. "Enough!" Her echoing shout lanced through her throbbing head with sharp efficiency. She was still very weak from accidentally tapping into Jarrett's memories earlier. The episode drained her thoroughly, and she had very little time to recover. She tried again, more quietly, "That's enough."

Cade narrowed his golden, hate-filled eyes. Even though seeing Collett alive was giving way to reason, he was still filled with hostility and the need for vengeance.

"Give me one reason, one excuse not to kill him. Why would you want to help him? He intends to kill you, don't you see that?"

He was desperately clinging to his anger to avoid thinking about how close he had come to finishing what he started.

"He won't. He didn't," she insisted. "He had his chance, and he didn't take it. Let him go, Cade. Let it all go."

He looked back to Jarrett and stared into eyes just like his. He wanted so badly to hate him. He heard noise coming from the distance. He shook he head, snarling, "No! He would have killed you for money! He makes a living killing people!"

Trying to keep this from escalating all over again, Collett moved into his view and looking into his eyes and insisted, "No, Cade. Think. Can't you see? He was going to kill me to save you, but he couldn't do it."

Both werewolves turned their curious golden eyes to her, stunned by her accusation.

Jarrett growled, the vibrations hurting his bruised throat. "She's wrong. I was going to kill her," his in-human voice insisted.

Collett snapped her head around and glared at him with her cool, blue eyes, letting Jarrett know in that moment, she wasn't afraid of him; would never again be afraid of him, not in the way he wanted anyway. She had seen too much of his soul; seen why he came to Colorado. She would not allow him to lie, not only to Cade, but to himself, "No, he wouldn't have gone through with it."

They all heard the metallic click of a rifle being cocked. Not one of them turned to look.

"You want me to take the shot this time?" Nate asked, announcing his presence. He already knew the answer to his question though. He heard the last part of the conversation and understood what Collett was saying, even if Cade didn't.

Cade replayed what happened through his clearing mind; Collett lying on the bed, Jarrett, standing in the back corner, not even near her. Jarrett could have killed her at any time in the long hours since he took her. Nate had been right all along. Something didn't add up.

"Cody?" Cade asked Jarrett.

He shrugged. "Alive when I left him out cold in the snow," He answered, knowing Collett had seen that image in his memory.

"Cade?" Nate asked again.

"No, Nate. There will be no shots taken today," Rederrick answered. In the stillness, the three of them once again heard the sound of metal slipping against metal, as Nate un-chambered the silver round.

Jarrett looked back to his brother standing across from him. Their matching gazes met; Cade's full of questions, Jarrett's full of secrets.

Cade's focus shifted, as well as his body. He let his body change into a man once more, letting go of the animal inside. Releasing his rage, finally Cade let go of more than a century of resentment. He wanted to hold Collett, needed to hold Collett.

He grabbed her, desperately pulling her into his arms. His need to touch her, to confirm she was real was as vital as his need to breathe. Now that his anger receded, relief flooded him. She was alive and safe.

He closed his eyes as she wrapped her arms tightly around him, her hands clinging to his naked and bruised back. She returned his desperate embrace fully, despite his healing broken ribs.

"I love you," Collett whispered.

Her soft, sincere words washed over his aching body. He drew in a deep breath of her sweet sultry scent. He wrapped his fingers in her long, golden hair absorbing the silky feel as Collett buried her head into his neck.

"I'll never let you go, Collett," he choked out, "I don't care what you think anymore. I love you too much to let go. I need you too much."

"You won't have to, Cade. You won't ever have to let me go again," she assured him.

They held each other that way for a long time. Nothing else in the world mattered; not the wounds or the blood, not the cold, the pain, or even the people watching. Collett was alive, and compared to that, the rest of the world seemed small.

"Put some clothes on, man," Nate teased, breaking the silence. "I didn't trudge all the way out here in the dead of winter to see your naked rear end." The sound of his heavy boots crunching in the snow indicated his departure.

"Um, we'll give you a minute," Cynda hedged and pulled a reluctant Rederrick along with her.

Cade smiled and opened his eyes, only to find himself looking directly into Jarrett's animal eyes across from him. He had almost forgotten Jarrett was still there. With his head tilted, curiosity and pain, filled Jarrett's gaze as he stared back at them. It was something he never saw in his brother before now. That first day they met he had seen hope. After that, Cade had only seen anger and hate. It was the reason they never connected strongly.

Feeling the sudden awkward tension between the brothers, Collett untangled herself from Cade. She turned around and stood in front of Cade. He put his hand protectively on her shoulder, still craving the physical contact.

Collett mouthed the words, I'm sorry, to Jarrett, not wanting to give away his pain and secrets.

Jarrett tipped his wolfish head in a slight bow to her. Collett knew that today changed things for Jarrett. These events made him wonder, for the first time, if clinging to his vengeful hate for so long had been worth it. He had looked into the mirror image of hate and found he didn't like what he saw. He would have to rediscover himself, rethink who he was; face his guilt.

She knew that, for him, the path was not certain. The direction he took would have to be up to him. Even though she played a part in his past, she still wasn't sure what it all meant for the future. What she remembered in that tragic moment in both their lives, came from his mind. Her memory was still lost to her.

Not uttering a single word, Jarrett contorted into a large wolf on four legs. He gave Cade one last, faraway look that seemed to say, *If only things were different*. Then he bounded off into the woods.

Collett felt the urge in Cade, that instinct that wanted to follow Jarrett. She laid her hand on his and quietly said, "No. It's not time."

Cade questioned, "What?"

"It's not time," she repeated.

Seeing Cade standing there stark naked with a puzzled expression on his face made Collett smile. She knew he wouldn't truly understand. She barely understood herself. Collett turned to him and laid her hands on his chest. She tipped her head up so she could look into his eyes, "Cade?"

He tilted his head and mimicking her soft tone asked, "What?"

"Let's go."

Cade agreed, putting his arm around her waist and together they walked back down the path that Cade and Jarrett's battle had created, making their way toward his cabin.

EPILOGUE

Six days later-

The phone rang once, twice, a click. He heard a hissing, "What?"

"It's done." came the deep reply from the other end.

"Ooooh, do you have the body?" Finnawick hissed excitedly. His pleasure over this success oozed out in his tone. This would please his master.

Jarrett ground his teeth at the imp's gleeful tone. "I have it."

"I knew you could do it," he responded.

You know nothing! he thought, but continued the game, "If you want it, my price has changed."

"WHAT? We agreed. I won't pay more than a million," Finnawick snapped.

"Don't worry. It's not more money I want. In fact, you can keep the money. I have something else in mind."

Apprehensively, Finnawick asked, "What is it you want then?"

"I want to teach a certain black-haired, pain in the ass mage a lesson. I want whoever you are keeping for his—what was it you called it? Ah yes, his motivation," Jarrett replied darkly.

Finnawick could barely contain his excitement. This was the perfect ending for him. He told Jeffery the first person to kill the girl gets the prize. If he failed, well, there we consequences. He knew the kind of pain The Hunter could inflict, had seen the battered bodies in the past. Only one thing could possibly make it better, "Can I stay and watch?" he asked inquisitively.

"No, this is between him and me. Just meet me in Lyons, Colorado at my hotel. Bring my payment, and I'll give you what you've been waiting for. Agreed?"

Disappointed, Finnawick groused, "Agreed."

"Oh and, Finnawick? Bring it to me whole and healthy, or the deal's off," he growled. Then flipped his phone closed. Jarrett went to the safe and pulled a long, serrated dagger from it. He stared at the shiny silver blade, remembering the past; remembering a time when he almost killed Cade with this very blade, leaving a jagged scar on his jawline. He supposed they were even now.

Shaking off his deep ponderings, Jarrett tucked the blade into his shirtsleeve, concealing it from sight. He moved to the back of the room, putting his back to the corner, effectively protecting his flank.

Finnawick popped into the room soon after with a short, plump, grey-haired woman in tow. Her big, brown eyes were wide with fear and they darted all around the room with panic. When she saw Jarrett, her eyes widened even more. She gasped and back-peddled a step right into the smelly Finnawick.

Jarrett recognized that she was smart enough to know death when she looked it in the face.

The imp's eyes darted around the room too, though his search was not frantic. It was eager. He was looking for something specific, a body. "Where is it?" he snapped.

Jarrett gave him a cold smile and indicated the answer with a tilt of his head toward the bathroom.

Finnawick didn't even think it through, something Jarrett had counted on. Idiots were so predictable. Finnawick pushed the plump woman out of his way. She fell to her knees heavily. Jarrett twisted his neck to the side, an audible pop sounded from his spine realigning itself. He let The Hunter come to the surface, let the anger wash over him.

As soon as Finnawick carelessly passed him, Jarrett sprang into action. He wrapped one thick powerful arm around Finnawick's neck, squeezing with painful and unforgiving strength. With lightning speed, he whipped his left hand around and plunged the silver dagger deep into sniveling imp's black heart.

Finnawick's body jerked hard once. Jarrett twisted the blade viciously and Finnawick could only gasp desperately for air as Jarrett held him firm and whispered cruelly in his ear. "I told you I'd kill you. It was only a matter of time. Now go back to hell where you came from."

Thick, almost black blood pumped out of the fatal wound as the imp's heart slowed to a stop. When Jarrett was sure the imp had taken his very last breath, he viciously ripped the blade free and let the body fall. It crumpled lifelessly to the ground before his feet with surprisingly little noise. Finnawick was half-man and still possessed a soul. As a result, he would not turn to dust as other demons did when sent from this plane. Instead, he died like men did.

He turned to the woman on her knees. She had closed her eyes to the horrific and gruesome scene before her. Tears streaked down her dirty face.

"Now, let's deal with you," Jarrett stated flatly.

The old woman opened her frightened eyes and stared, horrified by the sight of him standing there covered in her tormentor's blood. The sight was too much for her. The woman's eyes rolled back into her head and she fainted, falling to the floor.

Jarrett shook his head at the weak will of humans. Very few weren't afraid of him. It is better that way, he reminded himself.

He bent down, easily scooped up her limp body and left the bloody scene at the hotel. There was one more thing to do before he left town.

"Hello Jeffery."

Jeffery didn't even bother to look at the man sitting on the barstool next to him. He knew whose voice it was. He would never be able to forget the voice of the man who forced him away from the only chance he had to save his mother.

He came here drunk to drink more. Sitting at the bar with a whiskey bottle within reach and the smell of cigarette smoke all around him, Jeffery knew that no amount of alcohol would erase the sound of his mother pleading for him to help her. He would never forget the sound of Finnawick's raspy promise of pain and torture.

The man spoke again, "I am here to present you with an opportunity; the opportunity to save your mother's life."

Jeffery did look up then. What he saw caused him to fall right out of his chair. "Holy shit!" he slurred as he fell to the ground.

Everyone in the bar looked over to them, curious about what was going on. When they saw it was nothing more than a patron who was just a little too drunk, they turned their attention back to their own business.

Jeffery tried to get back to his feet, but couldn't seem to feel his wobbly legs. Finally, The Hunter got annoyed, pulled him up by his jacket with ease, and plopped him back into the chair with a little more force than necessary.

Feeling his head spin, he slurred, "I can't believe, it was you," The words catching on his thick tongue as he forced them out.

The Hunter answered simply, "That's because it wasn't."

"Huh?" he asked, while putting a hand to his head in order to try to quell the spinning.

"I'm not who you think I am," The Hunter said vehemently.

"Yeah, I'll say. You was helpin that chick, but then you took my job. I don't get you man." Jeffery was starting to think this through as best as his drunken mind could allow. Carefully he asked, "Hey, wait, how'd you know bout my mom?"

Speaking fiercely The Hunter lost all patience, "Look you scrawny little piss ant, I don't have time for this. Do you want the information I have or not?"

Still slurring slightly, but beginning to think more clearly, he asked, "W-What's the cost?"

The Hunter knew what was coming for him, so he answered with resignation, "You have to pass on a message."

"To who?" Jeffery asked.

"To Cade Werren," The Hunter then slipped out a small envelope and handed it to Jeffery.

"I must be really drunk. You just want me to give this to him?" he slurred.

"Something like that," Jarrett answered with irritation. "Tomorrow; give it to him tomorrow."

Jarrett stood from the stool casually. "What 'bout my mom, man?" he asked desperately.

"She is already at your motel waiting for you."

Jeffery could only stare after the dark, confusing man, as he walked out of the dimly lit bar into the cold winter night. He looked down at the sealed white envelope that had the word, "Cade," scrawled across the center, standing out with black ink.

Jeffery stumbled from his seat and walked out the door to follow. When he got outside into the freezing cold air, The Hunter was already long gone.

After seeing his mother, Jeffery was eager to deliver the message to repay the debt. He blinked himself right into the heart of the enemy, so to speak. He knew he was supposed to wait until tomorrow to deliver his message, but he just couldn't wait for some reason.

When he popped into view of the house, Jeffery immediately knew his timing sucked. Twinkling white lights decorated the trees, and an extravagant floral garlands adorned the entrance of the home everywhere he looked. Several cars were parked outside, indicating several guests must be inside.

After careful thought, he decided that maybe it would be best to wait until tomorrow as instructed. He stepped back once more and started waving his hand, when suddenly, something knocked his legs right out from underneath him.

He hit the cold, ice-covered ground with a painful thud, releasing a curse as he smacked his head against the pavement.

"Lookey here, James. Look what I found."

Jeffery groaned and rolled over. A man with sandy blond hair and blue eyes now stood threateningly over him. He was wearing a tuxedo, but that didn't make Jeffery feel any better, fancy suit or not, this man was tense and ready to fight.

"Man oh man, I would sure hate to be in his shoes right now. He didn't even come dressed for the occasion. Doesn't anyone have manners anymore?" another man voiced sarcastically.

"I don't know about manners," replied the blond man next to him. "But him showing up here tonight might save me two-hundred bucks. I have a bet with your old man." He said with a wink, and then he bent down and roughly scooped Jeffery up by his shirt collar, lifting him easily.

The man he assumed to be James painfully wrenched his arms behind him, holding fast to keep him from casting any spells, while the man in front of him patted him down, taking the envelope from his pocket. Jeffery started to protest when the man said, "Ah, ah, let's go see what Cade thinks, shall we?"

Jeffery let go of a shaky breath. Feeling defeated he reminded himself, this is what he came for. He tried again to convince himself, *you're doing the right thing.*

Though, he couldn't help but be afraid. He and Cade didn't exactly have a great relationship. In fact, he was almost positive Cade would kill him slowly and painfully on sight.

As they walked him inside, he noticed the lights and floral décor extended throughout the expansive house as well. The fresh perfume of hundreds of roses and soft white orchids hung heavy in the air. White tapered candle groupings with lush greenery wrapped around them, were lit and sat on either side of a wide entrance to another room down just a little further.

Jeffery bowed his head low thinking, *Yep, my timing seriously sucks.*

Shortly after entering the house, they took him into what looked to be a lavish office or den of some kind. James pushed him forward forcefully. He stumbled a step. Then losing the battle for balance, tripped over his feet and fell to the ground.

No one bothered to help him up. He knew no one here probably cared. He had given them good reason not to. As he hit his knees, Jeffery's gaze fell on two very shiny, very large, men's dress shoes no more than two feet away. His stomach flipped. He let his gaze travel up to the owner of those shoes.

There he was. Cade Werren stood tall and imposing before him. His hand was frozen on the cuff of his sleek black tuxedo, as if only a moment ago he had been adjusting it and had forgotten what he'd been doing upon seeing Jeffery thrown at his feet. His shiny black hair was perfectly groomed. A small, white rose adorned the lapel of his jacket, completing the entire look.

The expensive attire only made Cade look that much darker, that much more dangerous. Jeffery knew personally, underneath it all was a fierce and frightening monster. His feral and angry expression gave Jeffery a little hope. At least a margin of little hope that his death would be quick, instead of painfully slow.

Cade growled low in his throat. His rage at the sight of Jeffery here, on this day, would allow no words to come forward.

To Jeffery's surprise, James placed a hand on Cade's chest to stop his forward movement. "The suit man, think of the suit. Do you really want to explain to Collett why you're striding around here naked, especially today? "

Cade glared at James with a mean cold look. James even thought he might have seen Cade's eyes smolder red, just for a split second. "Okay then," James backed up a step, "He's all yours."

"I think he has a point. You should at least take the suit off before you kill him," Nate added unconcerned.

A soft feminine voice came from the entrance, "Cade, it's time to decide. Cross the bridge or burn it?"

Cade's gaze snapped up, looking directly into Selena's soft knowing eyes. The other three men were very confused by her cryptic words.

Understanding something important was happening now, Nate took a step forward. In the awkwardly silent room, the scrape of his dress shoe against the polished wooden floor echoed loudly around them all.

Cade still could not tear his golden eyes from Selena's as Nate said to him, "This is all he had on him."

Cade blinked and turned to Nate, who held out a small white envelope. He tore it from Nate's easy grip, then looked down at his name, written in a sharp, manly script. As Cade broke the seal on the envelope and read the letter, he wondered, what he should do next. When it came to his brother Jarrett, could there be any hope?

Turn the page for a sneak peek at book two in
The Powers of Influence:

THE PRICE OF KNOWING

"Jarrett!" the soft and urging female whisper that kept haunting his dreams of late called for him to wake.

The dark images of the dream turned off as quickly as if someone had flipped a switch. Jarrett's eyes snapped open. His heart rapped hard against his chest. The memories of the past were raw and fresh in his mind. They pressed down on him heavily, but he knew that wasn't what woke him.

Acting on instinct, and using his lighting fast reflexes, Jarrett rolled to the left, spun off the bed and landing easily on his feet, crouching to face his attacker. He barely missed being skewered through the heart by a long wicked dagger. The sleek shiny blade glinted in the dim moonlight, as its wielder lifted it from the mattress where he had lain a second before.

His preternatural gaze penetrated the shadows of his room, and he looked down the length of the blade to see who his assassin was. Standing on the opposite side of his bed stood a tall thin woman. A thick floral odor permeated his senses the moment she had entered his room. Her sickly sweet odor and the soft dreamy whisper in his memories became his saving grace. He drew in the scent of her again and smelled a hint of something else.

Demon. The woman was definitely part demon.

Demons carried a specific scent that was unmistakable, even if it was diluted. Half-demons were common enough in his world, and often easily dealt with. In fact, most humans dealt with them every day without realizing it. More often than not, they looked completely normal.

Then again, so did he. But death could often look normal until it came knocking on your door.

In less than a minute his sensitive eyes assessed his would-be assassin. The woman's spiked, blonde hair looked white in the dim light and matched her pale, almost translucent skin perfectly. Her ears boasted several small hoops and studs, beginning at her lobes and climbing their way up to the elfin like tips. She wore a long, shiny, white pleather jacket over a tight, low-cut, green dress that left little to the imagination. The picture wasn't a good one. Years of tapping into the dark side of magic drained her body of its beauty long ago. He had seen the look before, enough times to understand its cause.

Jarrett rolled his eyes at his circumstance. He knew she was one of The Factions mindless lackeys. She was the first in what would likely be a long line of them. He'd run out of time.

She stood there looking into his animal eyes with her cold, grayish orbs, holding the wicked blade she had almost killed him with. He'd heard of her before, but he couldn't recall her name. Not that it really mattered, the name was unimportant to him, just as she was.

Her thin angular eyebrows lifted in mock surprise, "You are good. I guess I'll have to earn my money tonight." Her voice was low and throaty from too many cigarettes over the years, "You're not bad looking either, too bad."

"How'd you get lucky enough to draw the short straw?" he questioned, his tone almost amused.

She tipped back her head and laughed, "Draw?" she chortled. "There was no need to draw. We've all been called out for you. Such is the consequence of failure. Although I'm glad I got here first."

Jarrett shrugged, her words didn't tell him anything that he didn't already know. Using The Faction's commonly used mantra, "first come, first serve," Jarrett replied, "First to come, first to die. The order of who dies hardly matters to me."

Her brows drew together angrily and her mouth pinched into a tight slit. She spun the intricate dagger she held around with proficient ease, as she considered his words with less care than she probably should have.

"Tell me," she said with a curious tone. "In the interest of self-preservation, I'm curious, what did you do to have him calling us all out to take you down? You were after all, his favorite."

He tilted his head to the side and answered, "Don't worry, you won't live long enough to be able to make the same mistake." Moving quickly he leaped forward right over the large bed that separated them only to meet empty space.

Jarrett didn't bother to scan the darkened room with his superior sight. He identified where she stood almost right away. Not only could he smell her pungent perfume, but his hunter's instincts were with him. He could feel it, sense it.

She now stood in the back corner of his sparsely furnished room. He immediately knew she was using magic to enhance her speed, otherwise she would already be dead in his grasp. Her cold grey eyes stared back at him with a lifelessness he'd seen often. It happened to any who lived like her, on the hard edge of a life with The Faction.

He didn't rush her though. Jarrett knew how to play this game. In fact, he was an expert. He learned over the many years of his life, patience was the key. In life or in battle, Jarrett never made any move unless it brought purpose to his own designs.

He also knew, whether through stupidity, confidence, or greed, the people whom The Faction recruited always made mistakes. They were mistakes that he, The Hunter, capitalized on, costing many their very lives. He held his position right there in the middle of his room and waited patiently for the witch to do that very thing. He adjusted his neck around to display his annoyance.

"If you leave now, I might let you live," he said with a low, raspy voice that promised death.

She shrank back slightly. His deadly gaze penetrated the darkness with an eerie and unsettling glow. She could only make out his imposing silhouette in the darkened room. The moonlight clung to the bare skin of his muscled chest, and glinted off a green gem that hung from his neck. The site of him there was so disarming. It gave the illusion that the night welcomed him within its dark embrace, and that moonlight falling around his form, existed solely for him.

Shaking off the peculiar thoughts, she reminded herself that she dealt with killers and fighters her whole life. Her skills as yet were unsurpassed, evident in the fact she was still alive today. Straightening her shoulders, she sauntered forward a couple of steps in her spiked, high-heeled boots. The sound of her heels, clicking on the polished wooden floor beneath her, echoed ominously through the silence.

She gave Jarrett what he assumed was meant to be a coy look, and then spoke low, trying to make her words sound sultry.

"Sweetie, I've played with many of your kind before and lived to tell the tale. You'll be no different."

As Jarrett predicted she would, the witch made her first mistake. She assumed him to be like any other bounty. He arched one of his dark brows, "Well then, did you come to kill me or did you come here to talk me to death?"

Something about the way Jarrett stood there, completely relaxed, looking at her with his precise and controlled gaze, made the tiny hairs on the back of her neck stand on end. Suddenly, she realized that he would be different. This man wouldn't be like any of her past assignments. His corded muscles were not even the slightest bit tense. He didn't look ready for battle. His easy tone, and his relaxed demeanor, hinted at his comfort level with the current situation, as if the event was an everyday occurrence.

"Who are you?" she uttered, before she even realized she said the words out loud. She took a step back, this time cautiously squinting in slight confusion.

Jarrett grinned devilishly. She was no longer so glad she got here first. Mistake two, hesitation. Jarrett understood, knowing your opponent was really the first rule of hunting. Rule two, make your play and complete your kill quickly. Hesitation was a death sentence.

His excited eyes flickered red. It was all he needed. Really one mistake was enough, two of course was better.

Using the witch's hesitation and her new-found fear against her, Jarrett made his move. His body flew forward. He moved so quickly, he held the half-demon witch in his grasp before she could even blink her eyes. Barely any sound was made as he whipped her around with unnatural strength, forcing her against his body, pressing her back against his front.

He underestimated her though, something Jarrett rarely did. She was not without a trick or two of her own. She was after all half-demon. With practiced skill she aimed her dagger behind her, and plunged the shining blade deep into his low right side. But the odd angle of her attack caused her to lose her grip on the dagger.

Her effort impressed him. He admitted to himself that the woman was skilled with the blade. It was something he would have normally appreciated, except the blade in question was now embedded deep in his side.

While Jarrett stood still, growling from the sharp burning pain running down the entire right side of his body, she stomped the heel of her boot down as hard as she could into his left foot.

Though caught off guard, and now in pain, Jarrett didn't release his grip on the scrawny woman. If anything, he tightened it. He sensed her surprise.

The burn he felt around the weapon and in the wound told him that the blade buried deep in his flesh must be silver. *So, she did know a little bit about him*, he thought grimly. The intense burning sensation coursing through his blood, caused by the cursed metal for any of his kind, was a distinctive and unforgettable pain that would quickly get worse. The silver would infect his blood, hindering his natural ability to heal quickly.

The witch ground her spiked heel in harder and made an unsuccessful attempt to grab the protruding dagger. He dodged her attempt. Despite her fierce struggling to gain freedom from his bruising grip, he held her firm, which only seemed to make her struggle harder. He wrapped his left hand around her fragile neck and held her arms down firmly with his free arm while trying to decide what he wanted to do, kill her or leave her unconscious.

She suddenly went still. Jarrett heard her quiet chanting. Knowing her intent and also knowing the unpredictability of magic all too well, his decision was made for him. He knew if he let her go she would come back. They always came back. *End it now*, he told himself.

A strange sort of disappointment coursed through him. He felt none of his usual satisfaction. There was no excitement from the justice in this. She'd killed many before, and deserved to die, but he was sick of it all, tired of the game. He grew tired of it years ago, but it always seemed to follow him no matter what he did. *How many will I have to kill to buy my freedom?* He wondered.

He knew she would be still until the spell was cast. Keeping a firm grip on her neck, he released her captive arms. Jarrett didn't even bother to flinch as he reached down and viciously yanked the offending blade free from his body. The ease in which he did the gruesome act would lead someone watching to believe that he just removed a thorn from his finger instead of a dagger from his bleeding side. Crimson blood flowed freely from the fresh wound. Jarrett gritted his teeth against the pain and lifted the blood covered blade before his eyes.

He ignored her quiet chanting and focused his attention on the finely crafted silver blade for just a moment. It was only mere seconds, but to him, it seemed to play out in long slow minutes. Shaking off his strange attitude, Jarrett waited patiently for her to finish every delicate syllable. When she did, he felt the slight distortion in the air around him as the spell tried to take effect. He tightened his grip on her neck, cutting of her precious air flow, and heard her breath wheeze in response.

True fear made its way through her cold and evil veins. He could smell it, feel it. Her panic rose. Her spell didn't work on him of course, and he was sure the demon-witch must have never seen such a thing before. People can often fight effects of paralyzing magic, but it takes them several moments to do so. He, on the other hand, was immune to it.

She shivered. He knew she understood. He wasn't affected in the slightest way by her spell. Because of her error, she would die.

He tilted his head toward the ceiling, closed his eyes, and he let the hated demon within him rise. Though his body made no change, his senses heightened. He took in a deep draw of the rich, fear-scented air in the room. "Tell me," he said mimicking her earlier words, his voice a growling whisper in her ear, "What did you plan to do if this went badly?"

She couldn't answer of course, due to his painful grip on her throat. She began to struggle once more. Rule three, always plan a contingency.

Almost with an easy and casual movement, Jarrett flipped the blade, caught it, and buried it with deadly precision deep into her breastbone. He spun her around to face him, looked right into her wide, shocked eyes, and said, "Because it just did."

Jarrett let the body fall and inspected his side. Pressing his hand to the injury, he winced slightly from the sensitive wound, and cursed himself for being so slow. Ever since his encounter with Cade, Jarrett seemed to have lost his edge. This happened to be the second time someone almost got the drop on him, and the first time in many years he found himself wounded so severely

His memories of the past plagued him regularly now. That was something he never allowed of himself, at least not since he'd been no more than a boy, with little control. He forced those painful images down deep long ago, burying them under his fury, and that's where he wanted to keep them. Unless he could find a way to push them back, the nightmare of his past would continue distracting him.

Jarrett could only figure his recent encounter with the woman named Collett was the cause of his unwanted recollection of the long-forgotten images. It was a cruel irony that the woman in question, was currently shacked up with his estranged brother Cade, and she was the same woman who forced him from his burning home as a boy centuries ago.

No. Jarrett thought to himself. Not forgotten, but repressed. In truth, he knew he could never forget anything about Rowena. Even if the curse of his life would be to live for 1000 years, he would never forget.

Sweat dotted his forehead and he cursed again. The infection from the silver began spreading already. He grabbed a hand-towel from the bathroom, pressed it firmly to the stab wound and tied it there with one of his belts. He winced at the applied pressure. Then he dressed quickly, threw a few belongings into a black duffle, and left without looking back. It wasn't the first time Jarrett left everything to start over.

Where he would end up remained unknown even to him, he didn't have a clue how to get out of his latest predicament. It wasn't like anyone he knew could, or even would, help him. His contingency had always been in place. He had hired strong people to watch over his substantial assets, like his club among other things, to offer him time to figure it out.

And if he didn't, well, Jarrett mused glumly, *maybe the world would be better off without The Hunter.*

OTHER POWERS OF INFLUENCE NOVELS

THE PRICE OF KNOWING
THE TRUTH OF VICTORY

www.ingramcontent.com/pod-product-compliance
Lightning Source LLC
Chambersburg PA
CBHW070620260626
47161CB00007B/2510